THE LEGEND OF TRYSTAN AND YSEULT

THE LEGEND OF TRYSTAN AND YSEULT

KATE HAWKS

AVON BOOKS NEW YORK

This is a work of fiction. Names, characters, places, and incidents either are the product of the author's imagination or are used fictitiously. Any resemblance to actual events, locales, organizations, or persons, living or dead, is entirely coincidental and beyond the intent of either the author or the publisher.

AVON BOOKS, INC.
1350 Avenue of the Americas
New York, New York 10019

The Death of Tristam, 1902 (oil on canvas) by Marianne Stokes/Whitford & Hughes, London, U.K./The Bridgeman Art Library International Ltd., London, New York
Interior design by Kellan Peck
Published by arrangement with the author
ISBN: 0-380-72676-9
www.avonbooks.com

Library of Congress Cataloging in Publication Data:

Hawks, Kate.
The lovers : the legend of Trystan and Yseult / Kate Hawks.
p. cm.
1. Tristan (Legendary character) Fiction. 2. Yseult (Legendary character) Fiction. 3. Arthurian romances Adaptations. I. Title.
PS3557.0316L66 1999 99-20840
813'.54—dc21 CIP

First Avon Books Trade Paperback Printing: July 1999

Printed in the U.S.A.

QPM 10 9 8 7 6 5 4 3 2 1

To Morgan Llywelyn without whom—period. And deep thanks to Parke Godwin for allowing me to write variations on characters and relationships created by him/ KH

Glossary of Irish Names and Terms

Brannin (Bran-yin)
buaileingh (boo-lee-ing)—moving cattle seasonally from one pasture to another
Cerball (Kah-rul)
clochan (claw-kan)—peasant dwelling
Deigh (Day)
Deireadh Fomhair (Day-ra Fo-var)—late October, Celtic New Year
Ehne (Oin-ya)
eachra (awk-ra)—herd of horses
eachra-man—a horse handler such as Deigh mac Diarmuid
Etain (Eh-tan)
fear cogaidh (feer coe-gah)—men at arms
Garbhan (Gor-van)
ghillie (gilly)—a war companion of the cattle lord
rade—as in *raid* but simply a nomadic band of Faerie on the move
rath—as in *wrath,* the large circular dwelling of a cattle lord
Rhian (Ree-yon)—Welsh feminine name, literally "maiden"

CANONICAL HOURS

Most people in early Christian and medieval times measured the hours by the ringing of the canonical offices: matins (midnight), prime (daybreak), terce (about eight A.M.), nones (early afternoon), vespers (six P.M., earlier in winter), and compline (middle of the evening, last religious office of the normal day).

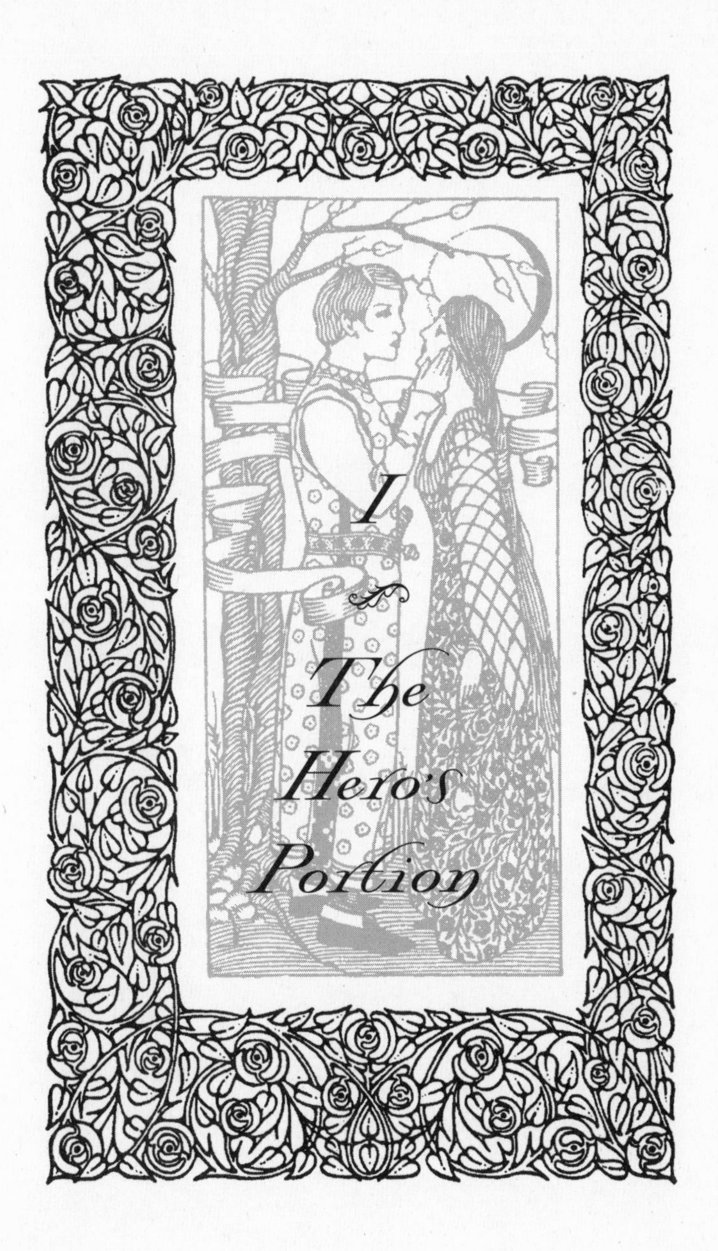

I

The Hero's Portion

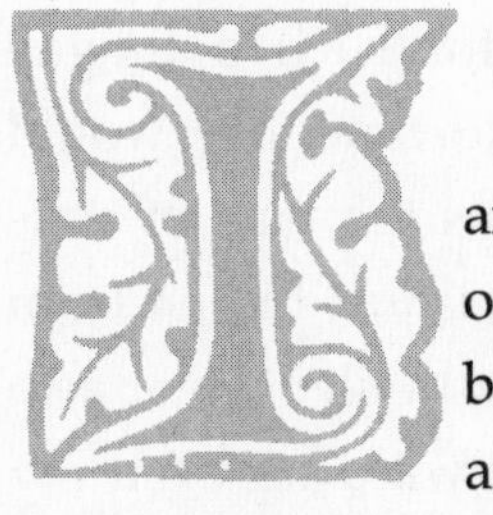

am Gareth mac Diarmuid, once lord-milite of King Arthur's *Combrogi,* the cavalry that broke the Saxons on Mount Badon, and after his death the same to Queen Guenevere, she that's exiled. God's blessing on the old lady wherever she bides.

Many joys and sorrows past, in an Eire Rhian and I have all but forgotten, we were Ehne and Deigh, peasants who served the cattle lord Feargus in the mountains above Lough Tay. Our *bo aire* was a good man and did what he must for his people. I've never blamed him for banishing us oversea to Britain. We found a new life there under different names: Lord Gareth and Lady Rhian, no less of an honor. When I became a centurion of horse in the *alae* of the Sixth Legion, I painted a golden sunburst on my blue shield, never dreaming that sun would blazon the bursting of my own heart or that contentment and happiness would ever be separate houses, one open to me, the other forever closed.

You would think a man come to mature years, friend to a king in a life sure as seasons, would know himself through and through. Yet in a day, a moment, a glance, he can be a lost boy again, sure of nothing in a world where his own heart is a stranger. Wiser is not always happier. That soft spring morning at home began my troubles, and her name was Etain, daughter to Lord Feargus.

Etain ni Feargus was as spoiled and willful a child as ever plagued a father's rath. Fifteen and starting to fill out to beauty, with kissable lips but an adder's tongue between them, Etain would have *her* way and no other. If she grudged you three words, two were sharp. Ehne reckoned the girl might never find a husband, for such a tongue would drive any man away. To our misfortune, one would not go away, the wrong one, and this was the way of it.

When I woke that spring day, night was just fading from black to grey beyond our *clochan.* Ehne still slept, one arm flung over me as always, as if she would ward off even my bad dreams. Not to wake her, I slipped off the ledge into my shoes and moved mouse-quiet up the incline that led outside. After finishing at the latrine trench, I walked along the hilltop to breathe in the fine day coming up over our home. Far below down the steep hillside, Lough Tay lay peaceful as my wife, scarce a ripple on the waters. There, hard by the lough: the lord's low pasture, and up the near hillside, the cattle and horse pens and the high pasture beyond where we'd driven up Feargus's cattle weeks before at *buaileingh* time. On the near heights the Nob, a steep and rounded hill crowned by bank and ditch and high stone walls about the great round rath of Feargus himself. At the base of the Nob our own *clochan,* reed-thatched and rounded by our own wall I'd sweated to raise stone by stone.

I loved this time of morning before God woke the world: soft as Ehne's face in sleep before she rose to fire the bake oven and peck at me over breakfast. Not that Ehne was a scold, mind, just lacking my easier ways. As Lord Feargus said, "No better manager of horses than Deigh and no better manager of Deigh than Ehne ni Donal."

We were young and content, my wife and I. In the Leinster mountains we called the Knuckles of God, the country of clan ui Byrne of the tribe Culain, the land was green and generous. We never knew cold or want, our horses fleet, our pigs and cattle fat. Ui Byrne throve so well that other clans like the ui Chellaig often raided to steal our cattle wealth.

In the grey morning light I was startled by a hint of movement near the horse pen and thought at first it might be a scout from such a war band. Far above on the rath walls, a guard paced slowly, spear resting on his shoulder, but he was moving toward me and saw nothing. Movement again, fast and furtive, crouching along the pen fence: a small figure stealing away, cloak flying in the morning wind to reveal a dark blue kirtle and flash of gold piping at the hem. The girl scurried toward the brow of the hill over the low pasture and disappeared into the trees there.

Etain it was; I knew the kirtle and cloak. Why I did not cry out to the sentinel I will never know. I should have, but like any servant wanting to avoid too much close attention from his master, I thought it best to mind my own business; the matter would sort itself out without me.

Better light now. As the girl broke out onto the low pasture, running furiously, I saw the horseman trot out from the trees on the other side. My first fear was nothing beside the next. They were far below me, but my eyes were and are still my best part. The horse was one of those small, half-wild beasts ridden by the Sidhe, those dangerous folk called Faerie in Britain. We called them, with careful respect, the Good People. When the rider leaped down to crush the girl in his arms, I saw trouble coming far worse than any ui Chellaig. I watched as he lifted Etain onto the horse and mounted behind, turning the shaggy little horse away toward the high mountain beyond Tay. I knew where he was going. That year the Sidhe had pastured their scraggly sheep somewhere on those heights and in the valley beyond. None of us on Feargus's *tuath* wanted them that close, but a wise man does not deny the Good People anything. They have been in the land from the beginning of time. They are more than human, their first king and queen the gods Dagda and Dana. We of the ui Byrne are mostly Christian since the coming of Padraic, but something much older in our souls bars the door with rowan and iron on Samhain night and knows the Sidhe have the magic for good or ill. They are powerful and unforgiving, willful as Etain. No jokes are made at their expense, and warriors who'd spit in the eye of Goliath walk wide of them.

When I returned to our *clochan,* Ehne was up and warming yesterday's bread in the oven, the cheese laid by and buttermilk poured. I sat down by the firepit and began to eat, too frightened to taste anything.

Ehne knew me too well even then. "What is wrong?"

"Good cheese this is."

Her brow creased in a frown. "Did I ask of cheese? Did you whistle or smile when you came in or greet me at all? It is a sour man who sits with me."

"A troubled man. See if the bread is warm enough."

Ehne rose to bend her tall height over the clay oven. Much joking at my expense came from the fact that my long, slender wife was a mite taller than myself. Later in life her strong, square face took on a dour cast under thick brows, but in the time I speak of she was barely twenty, never beautiful but glowing with youth and health. She set the bread between us and tore off a chunk for me. "What trouble, Deigh?"

I told her what I'd had the misfortune to see. At mention of the Good People, Ehne sucked in her lower lip. A bad business, the girl not stolen but run off willingly to her own and her father's shame. The wrong born this morning would be Feargus's deep disgrace by nightfall unless something was done quickly.

"Against the Good People?" Unthinkable to Ehne, who would not pluck a whitethorn blossom without a whispered charm that begged pardon of the Sidhe for taking one of their favored blooms. "What *can* be done?"

"As if I would know."

"*Fich!* That girl's needed a good hiding since womanhood came on her. But . . . perhaps?" Her eyes held mine and pleaded for reassurance. "Perhaps she'll return before long, and you'll not have to speak what you know."

If heaven were kind or Etain that wise. The first held a fair chance, the second none.

Ehne said, "Thank God her mother did not live to see this day."

"Amen."

"Eat the bread before it cools."

Then we spoke no more of the evil lest it fall on us.

Soon enough we knew the morning custom of the rath was awry. Breakfast smoke rose up, then ceased. Feargus's *ghillies,* his war companions, hurried out, dressing as they went, to saddle and ride, most of them northeast toward the land of the ui Chellaig. Riders and several charioteers raced off to the west.

"All for that little vixen," Ehne muttered, never having

much use for Etain. Now, as we saw Feargus appear at his gate high above, I agreed with her thought. Our lord was not one to hover long between need and act, but now in the stance of the man I read helpless fear. No direction he could reach to pluck her from danger, couldn't hold her close for all the careless times he did not.

"And he does not know she ran to it like a bitch in heat," Ehne mourned coldly for the lonely figure above. "I am more sorry for you, Deigh. Who else can tell him?"

"Do not remind me." Why on this morning of all did *I* have to notice the girl? Where was Feargus's real strength if he couldn't restrain one spoiled child? Now he was between two fires. He must act when he learned, yet whatever he did could bring worse than ruin from the vengeful Sidhe.

"You must go to him now," Ehne said.

Not moving: "I must."

"Now, Deigh."

"I *know*. Leave off, woman."

With a frozen heart I climbed the hill toward the *bo aire*'s rath.

Old Murtagh who kept the gate that day had been of the *fear coghaidh* in younger days, the foot troops who form the greater part of a lord's fighting force. He'd suffered a shattered hip in some long ago battle and ever after bent to one side like a sawed tree about to fall. He denied me entrance at first.

"The lord is troubled today. His *eachra*-man is the last sight he wishes now. What do you want?"

Nothing more than to go back down the hill and forget all. Impatient at my reluctant silence, Murtagh barked: "Well, what, horse handler?"

"It is that I know the cause of his troubles, where come from and where gone."

"Wait." He scurried into the rath and very quickly returned to wave me in. Feargus sat cross-legged by the pit where the morning fire was all but dead, sharpening his sword on a whetstone. A big man just going to fat about the middle and hating it, for he still wore his trousers and tunic tight to show what remained of manly pride. The shaggy head with its great crest of fading copper hair bent over the weapon, hand moving along the blade in long, deliberate strokes, *zang-zang.*

I hailed him from the doorway with more cheer in my mouth than my heart. "God bless you in the morning, Lord."

"And you." Feargus looked up at me. "You saw who stole my child?"

"I did."

"When? How?"

"At first light, Lord."

The look bent on me turned dangerous. I quaked under it. "So long? Why did you wait? Why did you not call the guard? Speak!"

I wondered would he use the sword on me when he heard all. "*Bo Aire,* I—I was afraid."

Zang! Zang! The strokes came quicker and angrier. "Ui Chellaig this is, must be. It has the stink of them. Just how they got past the guards—but it could only be them."

"No, my lord." I took a deep breath and prayed it not be my last. "A man of the Sidhe."

The whetstone paused mid-zang. Feargus raised his face to me: such a small face in that large head, the expression seldom mild, dangerous now, fear in one eye, denial in the other. "Impossible."

"I wish that were so, but—"

"Impossible! Sidhe have the magic, and would need all

of it to get across the ditch and over the wall past the watch and out again. And not a shadow seen or a sound heard? Impossible."

"Sir, he . . . he never came so close. There was no need."

Who would stop the daughter of the house padding out at dawn to the latrine trench, perhaps passing a word with the sleepy sentry before putting the cattle and horse pens between her and the rath? "That was the way of it, Lord. She went to meet him."

I could see his pain as Feargus struggled to deny truth. "You are sure? You would not lie?"

"I would not, sir. I do not." I felt miserable and afraid for all of us, and the shame Feargus had to swallow then I could taste as he lowered his head over the sword.

"I must think on this."

"Aye, Lord. Not a matter to decide in haste."

"Do I need my horse-breaker to tell me that?" he spat. Then quieter: "It is good you tell me alone but ill you did not come earlier. Go, mac Diarmuid. Get out."

Considering his mood, I heeded the advice.

By twos and threes the riders and charioteers returned, the *fear coghaidh* trudged in with nothing to report but failure. Night came and another morning and noon, but no Etain. Warriors sat to meat in the rath as usual but without music or their raucous boasting. So it went as one day followed another. In the midst of fine May weather, a cloud of fear hung over all of Fergus's *tuath.* At any time I expected horsemen and chariots to go forth again in strength, but none did.

"He's not one to jump before he looks," I reasoned to Ehne. "He will think this through."

And through and through while the war companions of Feargus's rath showed no haste to confront the Good People, as what sane man would? Proven as they were against human enemies, no sound of heroes came from the rath those fearful days.

Another truth: The Sidhe having as much brains as magic, they might well have moved to new pasture by now. Like candle tallow, each passing day melted away our chances of finding the girl, the good or ill of that leaning on your regard for Etain, for the rath was much quieter without her.

Another morning came with no sign of Etain or comfort for her father's grief. I was replacing stones in the earth of the horse pens when old Murtagh hobbled out to say I was asked for by the lord. Not summoned, mind, but invited to enter his rath through the gate of welcomes, which is a great difference. Feargus had been awed by his one visit to Tara, which had many entrances, each for a different purpose. His own rath having only the one, Feargus built another for visitors of honor. But Deigh? I was impressed beyond words.

"Does he mean to honor you?" Ehne wondered, fetching my cloak and inlaid shoes. I fastened the *brat* about me with the one piece of gold I owned, a round brooch.

"Would he invite me so to do me ill? We will see." I pecked her goodbye on the cheek and set out to climb the Nob.

When I stood in the gate of welcomes waiting for the lord to recognize me, some of the *ghillies* were still in their stalls, others stumbling about, hawking and spitting with last night's drink sour in their mouths. But Feargus himself sat on his bench in a bright red *leine* that only half covered his hairy legs, lifting a golden goblet to me in greeting far warmer than his last.

"God bless you in the morning, Deigh!"

"And my lord in the afternoon as well."

"Thank you. Sit, sit, Deigh. Have you eaten?"

"I have."

Feargus held up a pitcher. "Will you take a drop, then?"

"I will and thank you."

More impressed with each moment, I received from his hand another golden goblet. These were his most prized possessions after Etain, a gift of Aillil of Connaught when the ui Byrne submitted to him as high king. Now Feargus poured whisky for me, which he never offered to any but the most honored guests. *Walk wary,* the mouse in my stomach warned. *Smile and sip and listen. This is a long mile from natural.*

Feargus beamed at me with such affection I thought he might spring from the bench to embrace me. More than that, the *ghillies* lounging about, men who hardly looked at me before, now favored me with expressions I could only read as pity and compassion. Feargus ordered them outside and gave me his full attention with a smile broad and warm enough to bloom flowers in winter.

"And how is good Ehne today?"

"At her loom, Lord."

"She is a good wife. I forget your degree of marriage."

"The second. I had a mite more property than she."

"Och, what matter, man? Who is not rich among the Knuckles of God with summer coming in? Who knows want among my *tuatha*? Ah, but," he sighed, "if only a man could lift a heavy head to warm his face by that sun." Feargus saluted me with his drink. "*Slainte.*"

Quick as I finished the whisky, there was Feargus offering more. "Heavy with care, but I will not speak of troubles.

You are a master with horses, Deigh. My *ghillies* say you speak their tongue."

"With patience horses are easily understood." Nor half so devious as men. My mouse remained alert. All this flattery for his mere *eachra*-man? What price on that, now?

"Very true," Feargus sighed again. "If only other matters could be mended with patience alone."

"My lord would best know the truth of that." As the strong liquor warmed me, it seemed to whet an edge in Feargus. He ceased to smile, scowling about him morosely. Once more he grunted *"Slainte."* Once more I drank and was refilled, taking the liberty of a generous slop of water in the fiery cup.

"Deigh, I am a man stretched thin between need and shame. The need is to bring my daughter home. The shame—" Feargus glanced about at the curtained stalls and lowered his voice. "The shame, as well you know, is the girl's own part in this. I hope you have not spoken of that."

"Not a whisper, sir." None beyond Ehne, whose silence, like my own, was locked by plain fear.

"That she could leave her father's house for what is no better than a soldier's marriage, and with such a creature as that." He made a furtive warding sign. "Beyond their evil they are filthy as their own sheep, are they not?"

"Lord, I have never come so close to the Good People that I could tell, but I would stay upwind."

"So would I. Now, my warriors would face death for me. So they have and will again. The black ui Chellaig are raiding anew for cattle. To face death for one's lord is an honorable thing, would you not agree?"

None would deny that, I assured him, certainly not one humble and low as myself.

"Low, my friend? Do not wrong yourself." Feargus leaned forward to me, suddenly intense. "Like the best *ghillie,* you would face death for me if I asked."

Well, deathly sickness at least. Listening to the man, I felt the way of this talk begin to sink me in dangerous bog. "What is it my lord is saying?"

The sound of him went sharp as his sword. "A needful act of courage beyond the reckoning of any bard. Would you face the Sidhe?"

"Jesus!" Stunned beyond manners I dropped the cup, spilling whisky over Feargus's fine shoes, and scrambled clumsily to pick it up. "My lord will please pardon me, I—"

"It is nothing, man, nothing. Do not trouble yourself."

"Just that—"

"It is my fault, for I put the question badly."

"With the deepest respect, Lord, how can such be put well?"

"Not face them," Feargus amended, "but in a manner of speaking come at them sidewise."

"Side or straight on, sir, I am no fit man to do such a thing."

But Feargus was not to be put off. "Sidewise, Deigh. Any warrior can make a roaring charge afoot or in a chariot. So they must and will soon again against ui Chellaig. But you? What man has a wiser hand or subtler mind with horses? Who has night-borrowed for me more fine mounts than can be seen in any other *eachra* among the Knuckles of God? Who is a better tracker? No, a *ghillie* would charge in where tiptoe might get a man farther."

Once more he raised his cup to me and drank. "There will be no shame on my house, Deigh mac Diarmuid. None!

This will be seen by all as abduction by magic and against the will of my unsoiled daughter."

Miserable: "As my lord wills."

"You will have the best weapons and horses of your own choosing. You will carry my own sword to rescue my grateful child."

Jesus and Mary, why me? However grateful Etain, my doom was sure. Frightened, I was about to lay this fact before Feargus when he hammered a tight bung into any argument. "You will profit. There will be gold, I promise you. You will be the richest *eachra*-man among the ui Byrne. Then again . . ."

Feargus inspected the sword's edge. The point dipped toward me. "I do not ask what you do not owe. Some of my shame falls on you, Deigh. You saw the child and did not stop her. You did not come when you should have."

Feargus stood up, towering over me. I hasted onto my own feet as his big hand came down heavily on my shoulder, part kindly, part lowering storm. "But as my admiration for you will be boundless, so will my disappointment if you fail me."

As if I'd live that long for a start.

Feargus asked: "Do you know the art of the sword?"

"I—I have watched the *fear coghaidh* practice and played at it some. But what need if I'm to rescue the dear child by stealth?"

"That is the other half of the matter." Feargus wove a bit with the whisky in him, but nothing unsteady about that eye on me. "He that took her, his head will rot on a pole outside my rath, taken by my sword in your hand. Do you have my meaning?"

And wished I did not.

"Go make you ready."

* * *

I found Ehne behind the *clochan* scattering grain for our half dozen chickens clucking and pecking about her feet.

"What did the lord have to say worth wearing your good *brat* and new shoes?"

"Chosen," I said heavily. "Chosen sure as Moses on the mount. It's a task he's set me." And I told her what.

Ehne let out a stricken cry that sent hens flying in all directions. Unbelieving at first, then her fear rebounded in anger. "Why you? You are a brave man but no warrior. It is mad entire."

"He promised gold to our profit."

"Gold?" she seethed. "That I may wear it keening over a dead husband?" She whirled about to hurl her fury at the rath high above. "Curse that man. Curse him and the spawn out of his loins. If harm comes to you, may she burn in hell with her Sidhe man, for fire and pleasure are all the little slut knows of loving."

Ehne dashed the rest of the grain to the ground, wilting. "What's to befall us?"

I held her close and stroked her trembling back. "I will be well armed on a fine horse."

"What use against *them?* Oh, he's a sly manny, Feargus is, and well knows what he's about. Cannot spare a *ghillie* or chariot but sees the thrift in sending you against the black Sidhe to return blighted or not at all. What will you do, Deigh?"

That was beyond me at the moment, but for sure I would not put my hand in a wolf's mouth before removing his fangs. As I walked along the base of the Nob toward the horse pens, old Murtagh hailed me from the gate above, lifting his spear in salute.

"Dia dhuit, Deigh. And good fortune to a brave man!"

I thanked him with all of a heavy heart; no man needed luck more. Damn that girl. I hoped the Sidhe had raded clear to Connaught by now and Etain with them, never to plague us again. No—I repented the thought, for that would break her father's heart. Ah, repentance be damned. The man made mightily free with my life, did he not? And for a selfish little snip not worth a spit in the wind.

Fire and pleasure are all she knows of love.

The thought halted me at the pen gate. The fire: that was a mystery to me who'd never known it. My eye went over the animals milling about the pen while thoughts trod a stranger path. Three years married to a fine strong girl who cleaved to me like a second skin. We were content, we had sharing and trust and as much loving as either of us needed, though we'd not yet been blessed with the children we wanted. We "got on" as the Britons say, in bright day or soft haven of night, but never had I been seared by that flame harpers sing of, the demon piper shrilling the mad to dance, the forge fire heating iron white to twist it into shapes it never dreamed lying cold in the earth.

The next thought stranger still: What if such a fire caught in me? What pain or pleasure would it be to burn so and, when molten, what new shape to me that Ehne might not recognize?

Ah, foolish. I brought my mind back to common sense and good horses. In the mountains of Leinster there are often only two directions, up and down. I needed a surefooted animal to manage a steep climb and descent without stumbling or breaking a leg. For this reason I'd floored the pens with round stones the size of my fist to strengthen their pasterns and tendons. One horse would serve better than two. Two might be hard to manage when I snatched Etain away. Even a steady horse may panic or bolt in a strange place among smells it can't recognize, and I'd have my hands full enough with Sidhe and a girl furious as a sackful of cats. I chose Cloud, black as my humor the day I named her after a thundering fight with Ehne, black as my humor now but with a steady nature and firm mouth that took the bit without forcing. Carefully I inspected her shoes and scraped out the hooves.

At sunset, as if knowing the weight of the task laid on me, Feargus came to my house himself, Murtagh scuttling after, and a woman bearing food and mead. Feargus himself carried the gold-worked sword in its baldric, and three charioteer's javelins, Murtagh the round alderwood shield. Ehne and I stood aside respectfully and offered them supper. Feargus declined, his mind bent to purpose.

"You will go in the morning?"

"Lord, I will."

"Then God hold you in his hand until we meet again." Feargus waved Murtagh and the woman to leave but paused on the entrance ramp, the manner of him gone from blessing to something between hope and warning. "When I see your face again, I will see that of my child. And the other. I set the sword edge myself."

Feargus lumbered out the door. Ehne muttered after him, "I am glad he would not sit to eat, for I was minded to poison him."

At least he brought softer gifts with the iron. I opened the pot of mead with a well-deserved flourish. "Will you take a drop, mac Diarmuid? I will and thanks. *Slainte mhath.* Oh, that is good. He brought his best."

"Should he not?" From the tightness in her voice and

the vengeful strokes as she cut the cheese, I read my wife's fear. "Deigh . . ."

"Hush now. Hush. See to the supper."

We did not speak much over the meal, put out the rush light and went early to bed. In the soft May night our loving was much fiercer and more desperate than usual, and I felt Ehne's tears against my cheek. Once she cried out, in passion or fear I couldn't tell, but she burst with something that I couldn't share, and I wondered: Am I empty of this or has it merely lain asleep? Afterward we lay a long time close together without a word, but both of us awake.

Before I was full awake in the morning, I felt Ehne slip over me and off the shelf to light the morning fire. When I sat up and reached for my trews, the cooked pork was warming over peat, wrinkling my nose with pleasure and appetite. The weapons were stacked against the entrance ramp, and Ehne sat by the fire combing out her hair with that sweep of the hand and twist of the head that makes any woman graceful.

"Come eat. I've put you some of the pork and cheese to carry with you."

Over the food we spoke of small things, how the hens were laying, our garden plot, everything but where I must go. Only when we were done did Ehne look directly at me. "Husband, pray with me before you go. I have brought out the Samhain ash."

"That is a good thought."

First we crossed ourselves and prayed to God and Jesus as the holy Padraic had taught since he first lit his fire on the hill of Slane. The faith of Christ for us was a simple step from Druids to holy priests. The new religion had the strength of one creed and one heaven for all, just as once there'd been the Land of the Young, if more difficult to reach. Padraic was strong and wise, as all say, but less gifted priests came after with fire in their eyes and souls to swear that Christ and Padraic had driven out all the old gods, the "serpents" that plagued us, but how could that be? How could they know that Dagda and Dana, the ancestor gods of the Sidhe, had dwelt for ages in their palace beneath the earth and dwelt there still? In the very first commandment, when God ruled we should have no other gods before him, did he say there *were* no others? Well then, it was in the spirit of needing all the help I could find that Ehne and I rubbed our eyelids with sacred ash from last year's Samhain fire and begged mercy and understanding of Dagda and Dana for what must be done.

Full light over Lough Tay now. Ehne kissed me hard, then turned her back. "Go quickly, Deigh."

"Wife—"

"Please."

But as I gathered up the weapons heavy as my heart, I heard her move behind me, and then her hand stayed mine. She'd put on her hooded cloak. "That was weak of me and not fitting for the wife of a strong man, which you are whether those beer-braggarts in the rath know or not. I will carry your spears to the pen and watch you out of sight, and I swear if any harm comes to you, I will curse Feargus by every saint, devil, and demon who walks this world. To his fat red face I will."

I looked into her plain face and felt pride well up in me. "It is a wife and a half I have. You needn't fear, love. I'll cut my courage as you do our cheese, only as much as I need and no more."

Ehne laid her hand along my cheek. Strong hands she

had, hard from work and red to the wrist from scrubbing, but warm. Only that; then we set out for the horse pens.

I skirted wide of the low Tayside pasture, making for the far side of the mountain. No point in searching for a cold trail when I knew where the tracks would lead. If Sidhe are children of the gods, they have enough human habits to make them readable in some things. The movement of sheep would be far easier to follow by droppings and grass cropped much shorter than cattle would.

By mid morning there was no need to search out any rath. They'd gone at least two days past, moving slowly south following the fresh grass, not more than ten including small children who trudged after parents from the time they could walk at all. Six unshod horses, one ridden double from the depth of the hoofprints. Sidhe did not gather in clans but small family groups. Often I'd found where one group had split off from a larger in travel and never returned. They moved usually by night or in concealing fog, rarely seen on rade, and bad luck to the poor soul who did. No man in memory has seen them often and never in large numbers. I think now as I did then, that Sidhe were not many in the land.

To Ehne once I dared to speak the unthinkable. "Many children die in their first year, and Sidhe are few to begin with. Perhaps they fade out of Eire."

"Hush." Ehne put her hand over my mouth. "They will take you to task for saying so."

Yet I pondered then and often afterward: Why did they fear iron? Or did they? When I was small many folk told of Sidhe women appearing at their door to ask the use of their pots or looms, and I wondered: If they had such terrible magic, why were they so unable in the simplest things? I quickly crossed myself and made a warding against the disrespect. Still, we fear them and they easily kill those bold or stupid enough to pursue them, because they know the secrets of this land and play on them like a harp. In places where sheep have nibbled the land bare or it has been cleared by men and then abandoned, there are wide stretches of heath. Some are dangerous because Sidhe magic causes them in places to become bog to swallow up unwary men and cattle. They know every bog in Eire and the narrow paths across. That man mad enough to follow them at night across such places by the light of their flickering reed torches—well, if Eire is blanketed green, it is white with bones beneath.

I trailed their rade all day, trusting Cloud's nose. Sidhe horses graze wild and smell different from ours. She would know how close they were long before I did. They moved ever south following the grass, using the mountains to conceal themselves from our kind. Before the long summer twilight darkened, the tracks and droppings told me they were only a few hours ahead. Cloud's head drooped wearily as mine. I chose a spot above a trickle of stream with good grass for the mare, sheltered behind a rocky outcrop, ate some cheese and meat, said my prayers, and rolled up in my *brat* to sleep.

By next noon so close we were that Cloud skittered nervously, ears twitching. I led her on foot toward a high saddle gap that sloped gently down into a green bowl of pasture, and there I saw their flock and the few small horses grazing beyond. I walked Cloud back perhaps thirty paces and spent considerable time soothing her, then tied the rein to a stout bush. Easy, my girl. E-e-asy, Cloud. With the sword and one spear I climbed back up to have a very careful look, for I'm not great Lord Garbhan to go storming into peril with a harper at my side to see and sing my bravery.

Where was the lookout? They always left one with the flock. Slowly, from left to right and back again, I swept my eyes over the near hundred paces, then the next and next across the pasture and both hillsides. There: the watchdog circling the sheep with that steady, tireless trot that showed its wolf blood. The dog, yes, but no one else in sight. Look again. Find their rath. First hundred paces . . . careful, *see* what you look at. Low grey granite hump fifty or so paces below me . . .

Did it move? I thought . . . no, still as stone should be. But the shape of it is a hair changed. Stupid, Deigh, *stupid.* It is no stone but a Sidhe still as death under sewn wolf hides. Freeze still yourself. Wait. Watch. Where are the rest? And where that misbegotten child of Feargus who is taking years from my poor life even as I lie here on the hard earth with a rock digging into my belly?

There: movement on one far slope to my right. Two small figures. Meandering hand in hand they make their way down the hillside. The woman wears a long blue gown. *Must* be Etain. From the faint glimpse of a white leg, the garment has been slit up the side for riding. Now the grey "rock" moves, becomes a woman rising to wave with one graceful sweep of her arm to the strolling couple. She is mostly bare in an open vest of raw sheepskin and a short kilt of mottled brown wool fringes. No wonder they are so hard to see when their garments have the colors of earth itself, and they can be still as a hunted bird gone to ground.

As Etain and the boy drifted nearer, he drew her close, she with her head drooped on his shoulder, and any fool could see from the way she pressed her thigh against his that this was a road they'd traveled before. *I can save your girl, Lord, but not what she is no longer.* What kind of marriage could her father be making for her now? Whatever of her went to a husband, there'd be as well the shadow of this unless he married her far away where the shame was not known.

A wee manny this Sidhe boy, hardly taller than Etain but with broad shoulders and skin like dirty copper, skinny ribs showing plain as if he'd never eaten a full meal in his life. He led Etain to the waiting older woman and pointed up the slope just toward me. I froze, praying I'd not been seen, but then he laughed, took the wolf hide from the woman and came on, Etain clinging to him close as wish to temptation. The other woman moved down toward the pasture, whistling to the herd dog.

As they came on up the hill their movements took on an urgency. The boy stopped and kissed Etain, his hands roving over and back and down and around where he'd been before for sure. Nearer still they came, slowly, mouths locked together as they walked, their hands wandering feverish-wild over each other, until the boy threw down the hide blanket in the midst of some scrub bush and pulled Etain down beside him. I couldn't see much of them save the torn blue kirtle tossed one way and a vest the other, and no hard thinking needed to keep me informed. I lowered my head against the granite outcrop that hid me. Some would say to leap on them now would be plain indelicate, but what better time? If the boy fled, as I dearly hoped he would, I might whisk the girl away, and if I managed to stay alive that long, Feargus might forget about heads on poles.

A distant rumble, thunderheads building in the sky, and

the wind pushing them my way. We'd have rain, perhaps a proper drench, enough to put out any fire those two might kindle, and send them scampering for dry cover. Whatever came about came now or not at all. I rose and crept forward, crouching low, spear ready, sword in the off hand, sick inside. I'd never killed a man before, such was not my place in the world, and everything in me cried out against it now. The red-angry face of Feargus rose up before me: *Do not think, just do what you must.*

Silent I moved. It was the west wind betrayed me, carrying the smell of Sidhe horses too in a strong, sudden rush to Cloud, who snorted—not loud but the Sidhe boy heard and rose up suddenly. I saw only surprise in his dark face, no time for fear before my spear flew. Etain screamed, scrambling to her feet, knowing me—

"Deigh, no!"

—trying to reach for her gown and the boy all at once as he went down with the spear clean through him, God forgive me. Etain screamed on and on and tried to run. I bounded after her, caught her by the hair, but the woman below had heard. She wheeled her arm at the dog. The animal loped toward us, bounding long-legged over the pasture and up the hill. So little time, sword in one hand, wailing Etain struggling to be free of me, and a great hound coming fast to do me no good. Deigh was finished.

Mere breaths now before the dog was on me, Etain shrieking, the boy lying there, his own death accusing me out of smoky grey eyes. I raised the sword over him—

—and let it drop. I could not do it, Feargus, could only mumble pathetically, "Sorry . . . I am sorry."

No more. I dragged Etain away up the slope. The huge dog was so close I could hear it growling as it ate the hill in great strides. I rounded on it, flailing with the sword, felt it land on the brute's shoulder. The dog yelped and lurched aside, whimpering. Once more I brought the blade down and felt it hit and sever bone. Killed or not I didn't wait to discover, just hauled Etain along with me. In the pasture below, Sidhe were shouting, running for their horses, some sprinting on foot toward us. Grim-comical: we reached the high saddle, Etain trying to get her gown on and tug free of me at the same time. I threw her astride Cloud, leaped up behind her just as the rain started. Oh, fine. Splendid. If we weren't overtaken on the spot, they could track us easily. The luck of the world was with me and all of it bad.

Etain squirmed, spitting her fury at me. "You little pig, mac Diarmuid, let me *go*."

I only held her tighter. "Don't talk, not now. I do not feel charitable or understanding. Cloud, go. Up!"

I pushed Cloud through the pelting rain, trotting wherever possible, always keeping to the hardest ground, though Sidhe can trail a whisper through a noisy world. Once, far back on a ridge, I caught moving shadows sliding below the skyline. Straddled in front of me, soaked and miserable, Etain had long gone silent. The saddle must be chafing her something cruel, but no matter. All through the day we rode, and when she begged to get down to relieve herself, I was trusting enough to let her. She went behind a granite boulder, and the next I spied of Etain, she's sprinting away, skirts up and legs churning. I caught up with her on Cloud, grabbed her by the hair and jumped down.

"In all respect to the *bo aire*, you are the daughter from hell."

She was hard to hold, all wiry young strength and fury. "When he hears how you've mauled me—"

"Shut it and get on the horse. Who do you think sent me?"

"You smell like the horse."

"And what blossom would your Sidhe boy remind me of?"

"You dirty little peasant. His name was Declan, and he did not have to steal me."

"Your father knows that. It is a knife in his heart."

Etain looked me up and down with all the contempt I'll ever need. "He might at least have sent a man."

God, the girl would be a thorn in any man's bed. Cloud snorted. The wind had shifted, blowing from the north now, carrying the scent of us to Sidhe horses. I tied one end of hide thong to Etain's wrist. "You know nothing, child. Because of you I've blood on my hands. Don't threaten me with your father who wanted much more. I was to bring him the boy's head."

"His . . . ?" The sudden horror was naked in her face. Perhaps for the first time the full meaning of what she'd caused came home to Etain. "My father wanted that?"

"No less than that and on a pole, but I had not the time or the cold heart left to do it, sick as I was already. And do not insult this good horse who has more sense than you. Girl, what did you suffer at home that you must run from? What had that boy that you must run to and shame your father?"

She turned away. "Such as you could not understand."

That did it. The spoiled, sulking sound of her set me off, touched the sick knot in me and boiled it over. "Would I not?"

I bent the little bitch over my knee and lustily did what Fergus should have long since and often, beating the lesson into her rump. "Not under*stand,* is it?"

"Ai! Stop!"

"Do you understand now what you've done?"

"You are hurting me!"

"I am glad you can feel something somewhere. And *there.*" I released her. Etain backed to the length of the prisoning thong, holding her smarting rear. "Up in the saddle and no more trouble, mind, or you'll get worse."

I mounted behind her with an anxious scanning of the country behind. We'd lost time; they'd be closer.

"You are a brute beast, mac Diarmuid."

"I am a man who dearly wants to see his wife again. Now, child of misery, for the love of sweet Jesus, please shut up."

"You hurt me."

"Set your mind to endure. We cannot stop tonight."

Etain twisted about. "We have ridden all day," she protested. "I am tired and in pain."

And I, but night would not halt the Sidhe. I had no notion of how many they were or how near in the time we lost, but Feargus would sooner forgive the loss of the boy's head than his daughter. "When Cloud needs rest, we walk, but we cannot stop."

Hour after hour, on and on. I cursed the long light of summer, praying for dark. Luck was with me. Night brought only a pale sliver of moon behind scudding clouds. I led Cloud with Etain up, but when the mare stumbled and almost fell, I pulled the girl down to walk, knowing the hard ground punished her blistered, bleeding feet but more afraid to miss landmarks to guide us and sick with fear.

Cloud pulled at her bridle, wanting to stop, but I pushed her on, staying below the high ridges where sudden moonlight might reveal us to the Sidhe.

The light comes early as the year grows to midsummer. Well before the fourth hour of the morning, myself fighting to put one foot before the other, the last great knuckle before Lough Tay loomed over us. We stumbled along the base toward the shallow cut above Feargus's low pasture. Thirsty, Cloud smelled the lough water and wanted to pull that way. She was limping badly now. I pulled Etain down.

"She can bare carry herself now. Walk."

Pushed for a full day and night, the girl was too spent to show mean spirit, lurching along silent beside me. As we came up from the cut beyond the deserted horse pens, I could see the guard walking the rath wall: home. Glory be, I'd done it all, brought the child back and lived to tell Ehne—but in the midst of relief, something turned me back toward the great mountain across Tay. There, tiny against the skyline, the four figures sat their horses and watched us.

"They almost got you," Etain said with bitter pleasure.

I only pushed her on toward the Nob.

"They will know who killed my husband."

"Ah, put a bung in it. Come on."

"I promise you, *eachra*-man. They will know who you are."

At the base of the Nob, Etain stumbled and cried out, hopping on one foot. "A rock cut me. I can't climb the hill."

She showed me the raw soles of her feet with broken blisters and dirt-smeared blood. Worn to the bone myself, I hoisted her back into the saddle. "You can thank this good woman horse for the last of her strength."

I led suffering Cloud up the path toward the stone walls

where the night guard raised his spear in salute. Breccan mac Brion it was, one of the youngest of our *ghillies.* "God bless you, Deigh. You may kick me if ever I make jokes on you again."

"Where are the horses and chariots? Have the men gone out against ui Chellaig again?"

"They have." Breccan hurried down from the wall to open the heavy timber gate. "I will tell Lord Feargus you bring him joy."

The young warrior returned quickly, still regarding me with respect and wonder, as if what he'd long chided for a squirrel had changed into a bull. "Enter through the gate of welcomes, mac Diarmuid."

The rath was already smoky with the morning fire where two women stirred oats into boiling water for porridge. No others were about. As we limped to the firepit, Feargus lunged out of his stall clad only in ungartered trews, wrestling a linen shirt over his head.

"Deigh mac Diarmuid, you have my thanks." The glare he daggered at Etain was as clear: *and you my shame.*

The women busied themselves with the porridge but missed none of this. No doubt they knew. It is a mystery what women can guess from nothing said. How their tongues must have wagged in the stalls or over the wool carding.

"He made me walk day and night, cruel far." Etain winced, lifting one foot. "See? And he struck me more than once."

"Lord, she tried to run. The Sidhe were close after us. I spanked her."

One of the listening women ducked her head over the pot to hide a satisfied smirk.

"Well enough," Feargus judged. "You save me the labor. Girl, you are filthy. That gown is indecent. Wash and go to bed."

Etain stabbed an angry finger at me. "He is a murderer."

"He did what he was given to do," her father said heavily. "Deigh, where is the other matter we spoke of?"

"That was too difficult. What with holding on to the girl and the Sidhe up like a swarm of angry bees and a great dog coming at me, there was no time."

"He *did,*" Etain screeched. "He would have. He put a spear in my Declan and then took the sword to him."

"Where then is the head I would have on a pole?"

I was shamed for the lack of that which would have washed his shame away. "I could not do it, *Bo Aire,* though I tried."

"You bring but half of what I commanded. Were you not told—"

"The boy was dying already, halfway to Dagda's hall. Does my lord not know what I say? I *could* not. I looked into his eyes and watched the life go out of them, himself bare older than the girl here and so thin his ribs showed plain, and I . . . could not. A *ghillie*—aye, a warrior would have done all better, but your child is safe home."

I laid Feargus's sword, baldric, and shield by the firepit. "May I now see to the pitiful ailing horse that helped me?"

"Yes. Go with my thanks," Feargus said. "And you to bed, Etain."

The girl straightened with cold pride, glaring at me and then the two women as if to say: *I am a woman as you now.* "As my father bids, but I will mourn a husband there."

She just had to say it, and there too much. Feargus

turned her about savagely and inspired her with the broad back of his hand across her already martyred rump. *"Out!"*

That one blow drained the man of all, his anger, shame, and vast relief. Feargus sagged down on a bench, haggard. "Husband is it? While my men beat the ui Chellaig into the ground, my own flesh fouls their glory with dishonor. Why does not the land swallow me up and the sea the land? What is the world come to?"

I left the rath with Feargus desolate on his bench, Etain sobbing in her stall, and she made the sound of a sorrowing woman grown too fast to that state. Still early morning; after I grained and watered Cloud, curried her and saw the poor woman just collapse on fresh straw, I limped home to my own *clochan* where no smoke rose from the roof hole. Inside, Ehne still lay asleep on the ledge. I kissed her awake. "God bless, *Acushla.*"

". . . Deigh?" She blinked, then woke fast and her arms went tight around me. "Oh, thank God, thank God you're safe. And Dagda too: We were wise to remember the sacred ash. What will you think?" she remembered, starting to rise. "No fire or breakfast yet. Just that with yourself gone for days—"

Women often do not know when to shut up, so I showed her with a long kiss from which she broke away, grimacing. *"Och,* your mouth is sour and you smell of every mile."

"Is that a way to greet a husband? Worse than that little bitch I brought home."

"Let me up, then. I'll have the fire before you know it." But she stayed nestled in my arms with her great, serious eyes glad and shining as I'd never seen them before. "Deigh, you are trembling."

"It is only my fool legs that think they are still walking.

Never mind the breakfast, lass. Move over and let me hold you."

I did tremble but not all from the miles. *God, Dagda, Dana, all you saints, whatever darkness follows, let the curse fall on him who commanded the death, not on me. Not on my Ehne.*

But did it not anyway?

The fighting men came home. Cattle tribute would be demanded of the ui Chellaig, keeping their defeated chieftains poor enough to have little stomach for raiding the ui Byrne. For a year or two, we thought, our clan would be foremost in Leinster. Fresh heads taken in the battle now decorated the poles outside the great rath, and there would be feasting for all. In the excitement I almost forgot those distant figures who'd watched me from the Knuckle. But they had not forgotten. They simply bided their time.

Just after my return, as Ehne came from our well with a bucket of water, I caught her studying me curiously in the bright sunlight. "What is it?"

"No, just . . ." Ehne blinked and shook her head. "It is different, you—you are not the same as before."

"I am the same. What should change?"

Ehne took my face in both hands, scanning me close as a Brehon law. "Different. Older you look."

"I do not. Don't push me toward my grave."

She pointed to the brimming bucket. "Look and see."

The still surface of the water showed my horse-homely face as always. Yet, to look closer, not *quite* the same. "Well then, is this the look of heroes?"

"I need no battles for you to be hero to me," Ehne vowed. "Not Cerball mac Fiach or even Garbhan mac Loinseach would dare as you have. Would they? The lord's need crying out, their chance clear, and they would not go." She took up the bucket, wiping her brow with the back of one wash-reddened forearm. "But we'll have our ears stuffed with their bravery soon enough."

On the day of the feast every man and woman who called Feargus lord trudged up the Nob, poured through the gate and packed themselves into the great rath by mid-day, some having to wait and eat outside. Did I say every-one? The mild and shrinking Etain did not appear, banished to her stall with the hide curtain closed. She could hear the celebration, smell the beer and mead, the heavenly roasting pig rubbed with mustard and wild garlic, chickens and geese turning on spits while she spooned her plain porridge in disgrace. Those few who didn't yet know the full tale were politely informed the lord's daughter was unwell.

Unless, as today, there were special reasons to rejoice, such gatherings of the entire *tuatha* were held only at the great fire festivals, Beltaine and Samhain. The great round rath was full of ui Byrne but not scattered just anywhere. Custom decreed the order of seating.

Lord Feargus sat facing the open gate of welcomes, *ghillies* to his right, charioteers to his left. Before him in the great circles of us, the *fear coghaidh.* Among his lords some commanded foot soldiers, some fought from the saddle or from chariots, but title gave them honored place as lords. In the next circle were the chariot drivers cross-legged on the earthen floor, the outer circles formed by we common folk.

Always in a circle we gather, for the circle is unity, harmony, and eternity. High up above, running clear around the rath and forming a roof for the stalls, was the balcony where women of rank, the wives of lords, sat on benches looking down on the like of Ehne and me to show how exalted and dainty they were. Etain should have had a place among them were the modest child not forbidden this night.

"But her ears must be burning," Ehne guessed with cold satisfaction. "The sight of them up there gossiping away."

"Do you think they know?"

She slid a cool eye at me and back to the women above. "The tightest bucket will leak a drop or two."

The feast made a grand picture: lords in their bright checked or striped *brats,* the roar of fellowship, the smell of beer and mead and the great pig turning on the spit dripping its juices like delicious tears to hone our appetites. Cheese, hot loaves, and boiled eggs munched, the whole of us growing louder as wine went down and cups were refilled. Louder still in greeting when a late arriving lord entered, hailed Feargus and made a great leap of victory over our enemies before jostling into his proper place.

Long before the pig was done, Ehne and I nestled close together, troubles melting under the balm of good wine. Yet when the roast was ready, none could carve the smallest morsel; such right is holy as Mass. In later years Arthur was amused at my telling of the hero's portion. Britons have forgotten. They have seen so many tribes and races come and leave their footprints, it must be like living in a busy doorway. In Eire we dreamed out our destiny undisturbed for a thousand years without change. What wonder we kept the old ways?

Any man whose bravery stood out in battle might claim the hero's portion of meat if he could prove that claim against others of the same mind. Ehne and I, already tipsy and looking forward to our own celebration on our sleeping ledge, would first have to listen and cheer in the right places as warriors enriched their valor with more manure than a good crop needs in a warm spring, loudly injured when doubted, roaring to comrades to witness what they spoke. Brave men all and not for me to deny them, but I've since seen courage as great (and quieter) from soft-walking men like Bedwyr ap Gryffyn or Peredur who was the brother of Guenevere and near to being a saint. Trystan? No . . . no, I won't speak of Tryst until I must, except to wonder sadly why the brightest stars soonest go dark. The man is a pain in my heart.

Forgive me; it's the way of old men to go on so with souls full to bursting with memories sharp as a sword, while they can't find the cane they put down moments ago. I was making a point. In Eire, fighting was now and then. In Britain, Arthur and the rest of us had donkey's years of it, and the shine on glory wore thin.

Born to look up to our betters, Ehne and I got a spiritual crick in the neck from the arrogance of *ghillies*, but nothing for it. We sighed in resignation to see Cerball mac Fiach rise from his place when Feargus bellowed: "Who ran out before his lines first to challenge the black Chellaig?"

"That was myself," Cerball shouted back. "Seen by all but dared by none."

"He did!" his companions vouched.

Cerball peered about the rath in challenge, eyes already red from drink and the cooking smoke. "What man has better claim to the first portion? Let him speak for my knife is ready to carve."

"Put your dull little knife away," Garbhan mac Loinseach scorned. "Can you claim no more than loud insults to our enemies?"

"And two of the heads you saw as you came to this feast."

"Three more I brought myself," Gorbhan cried back. "Lord Feargus knows that for truth. Aidan drove my chariot on the flank straight into their lines. I hurled spears until there were no more, then leaped out onto the chariot tongue and into battle afoot."

"It is so," young Aidan slurred, beery and bleary. "I saw the deeds."

More of this and tedious as lord after lord rose to boast and claim the first portion. Drunk, it was hard to focus my eyes, but I happened to see the small, hooded figure of a woman glide from the cooking pots with a steaming bowl toward Etain's stall and disappear inside.

"We should not drink more," Ehne advised with a thickening tongue. "We'll not be able to taste good meat even when these great warriors end arguing over it, and you'll not be much use in loving later."

My head was heavy as the rath air that reeked of food, sweat, and liquor. My drunken mind floated free over one thought or sight to the next, missing the large, seeing the small, like the slight figure sliding out of Etain's stall, gliding so smoothly toward the firepit she seemed borne on air. Once she turned her head my way, but the folds of the hood hid her face from me.

The gabble of lords became one sea-roar in my ears, but over it rose one musical voice.

"Some . . . someone is singing." No, more of an unearthly humming in my fuddled brain, such notes as never I'd heard before, rising and falling, half sung, half sighed, coming from nowhere but inside my head as Lord Feargus heaved up from the bench, calling for silence. By now our lord had more than a drop in but not so much as to forget the manners of the occasion.

"We have heard of such deeds that I can truly say none deserves the first portion more than another."

"Decide, *Bo Aire,*" someone urged. "The meat is ready. Who is the bravest?"

Feargus turned to the speaker. "I do not know. In the clear light of day, your deeds were seen by many. But who has gone beyond courage in the day and dark of night with no friendly eye but his own to see?"

Ehne whispered, "None but my Deigh."

One deep voice came back from the *ghillies.* "What does the *bo aire* mean by this question?"

"My meaning is no riddle. To fight ui Chellaig is one thing and a brave one, but who has dared the Sidhe by night or day when his lord begged it of him?"

Ehne nudged me with an elbow. "Stand up and answer clear."

My head was going round with what I'd drunk. If I managed to rise, only an even chance I'd stay up. The rath, the people, were so far away and the humming louder in my head. A strange, sad sound, the keening of heartbreak. Then a man's voice rose from the circle of warrior lords—young, strong, and not to be denied. "Such a thing was done by Deigh mac Diarmuid," said Breccan mac Brion. "I was guard on the walls when he returned with our lord's daughter safe."

The question rustled and murmured through the twilit rath: *Who? Who?*

"So he did!" Feargus boomed. "And with my own sword at his side. But for the desperate need to have my daughter returned, I did not expect to greet Deigh mac Diarmuid again."

From a great distance Ehne murmured something and squeezed my arm in pride.

"To go against the Good People needs a word for courage not yet heard even in this home of heroes," Feargus admitted. "Deigh, choose and be served the first portion."

Not a word of dispute from any lord, but a great cheer from the common folk as the small woman held up the shining knife. I was on my feet with no notion how I got there. "Let it be cut from the shoulder!" Another cheer as the small, hooded woman plunged her knife through the crackling skin to do my bidding.

Much of what happened then will never be clear in my head; much I can never forget or escape, for the shape of my life was carved with that portion. The woman made her way toward me bearing the platter of steaming meat, and somehow I was sitting again. I went cold all over as I saw the face within the hood: the coppery skin and eyes of slate grey, and all about her an *otherness* not of this world. I could not tear my sight from her. Nothing in my head but frozen stillness and her voice.

Savor your portion, Irish murderer. Take your shameful victory. The children of Danaan were once many in the land, but now we are so few that in each death each sees our own nearing. It is you who have bought fame with my sorrow. Declan was my last living child-wealth. You killed him for the hollow pride of a stupid old man, and now I have nothing in this world to love.

Neither shall you, then.

The whispered words were horrible music in my spinning head. "*Mo mhallact ar!*"

Deigh mac Diarmuid, I curse the air you breathe and your very name. I curse the meat and grain, the fields that nourish you and all who gather in this rath. Hear me, murderer. As you have taken love from me, so I deny it you forever. You will be loved but never truly love in return. Your heart will break for love that will never be answered, and from the day you truly know this, like to myself you will never draw one more breath in happiness.

I tried to speak, to shake my drunken head clear, but could not move. There was a darkness falling over my eyes that looked on deeper night within hers.

As you killed my Declan, see the spear that will pierce your heart.

I have never forgotten the words that doomed me or what I saw then, bright against swirling shadow. The face of a woman never seen before who bent on me a look of such love and longing that I could not breathe. Yet, as her lips parted to speak, I had known and loved all my life that face and the soul that glowed in it; I was born to be loved by her. Her white hand reached for me as she breathed my name—

—and Ehne shook me as the clamor of the rath around me shattered the dream. "Will you just stare at the meat you've won? What ails you?"

"The woman, the . . . one who was here. Where . . . ?"

Ehne only stared as I lurched up, pushing my way through the press of people, crying. "She is here!"—only to be shoved aside, more mortally afraid than drunk now.

"She is here!"

Feargus and his lords broke off their eating as I stumbled forward to fall on my knees before the *bo aire.* "She is here. The Sidhe are here. I saw—"

"Saw what, man?"

"The mother of him I killed for you. She cursed me, she . . . cursed all of us." Casting about wildly, I could no longer see the woman anywhere, only Etain in the entrance to her stall, alight with pure vengeance.

"She curses all of us."

Two things I heard clearly as the men crowded about me, my wife's cry of terror and cold laughter from Etain.

That summer the most blessed land among the Knuckles of God became the most blighted, and no need to question why. Milk soured too fast or would not make butter no matter how Ehne and other wives sweated and churned. Of our own six hens, three stopped laying. Despite our keen eye for rain before the lord's haying, no sooner was it cut and laid in stooks but the heavens darkened and dropped Noah's own Flood on us, so that we had to do our panting best to save the quarter of it from damp rot. We would have to slaughter and salt all our pigs, even our sow from Ehne's father when we married. On a day that came, I was exercising Cloud in the high pasture when she shied suddenly and bolted away, tearing the lead from my hand, only to stumble and fall badly. With a shattered foreleg she had to be put down.

Then there came the failure of Feargus's stallion, a prime four-year-old that earned our lord a full trading stick in gold weight for every stand and never a poor showing. A mare covered by that fine fellow came away with foal for sure, and, if mares can smile, one of pure contentment. So it was a serious matter when, full of hope and increase, Lord Cerball turned Feargus's pride loose at stand with his best mare, and the great lump could not rise to the occasion in any sense of the word. Jesus, it was shameful. He walked about the mare, sniffed at her, then just stood there with all the passion I'd show for a hen. I do believe Feargus as crushed by this last straw as in the matter of Etain, his own manhood drooping with the stud's.

For the first time in memory a lean winter faced our whole *tuatha.* People muttered and shunned Ehne and I. Graver than all, the *bo aire* sent Lord Garbhan and five of his bravest warriors south through Leinster to seek out the Sidhe mother and plead with her to lift the curse and name her price in gold. The time of Samhain drew near, the ending of the year. Who knew on that night what spirits loosed from the other world to this might wreak on us if the Sidhe would not relent? We waited through *Deireadh Fomhair,* which you call October, for the return of our men. Some whispered fearfully that they would never return, lost forever under the hill.

On a dreary day when rain began before morning and never stopped, guards on the rath wall sighted the six riders plodding slowly up the cut above the low pasture. They straggled up toward the rath and disappeared through the gate.

"They are back," I told Ehne. These days we spoke few words, and those muffled with worry and fear.

"Do you think the Good People were merciful?" she hoped.

Scant hope. I knew what price one woman put on a son, though I dared not speak that to Ehne.

That evening as we sat to a meager meal, Lord Feargus hailed us at our door. Lord Garbhan was with him, both cloaked and hooded against the driving rain. Ehne rose to greet them as they dropped the wet garments aside. "God bless all here," Feargus said.

I bade Ehne get them supper but Feargus declined politely, seeing how little we had before us, barley with a few mushrooms flavored with a bit of hoarded pork fat.

From their manner they bore no good tidings. Lord Garbhan looked fearful. Strapping buck that he was, boasting at the feast of heads taken, now he seemed to shrink where he sat before us. You'd think the curse had fallen on him alone. Seeing the gravity of them, Ehne busied herself kneading the last of her dough by the oven.

Feargus barely looked at me. "Lord Garbhan found them. He will tell you."

Clear to me the *ghillie* would not have spoken by choice and did not come to the heart of his subject before creeping round the edges. They'd had to trail far south into the country of the ui Cennselach. That cost them more of their gold before they could go on, but go they did, Cennselach wanting no more trouble with Sidhe than any sensible folk. Finally the faint, cold sheep trail grew fresher.

"The way of it was their finding us," Garbhan said. A morning came when his men rolled out of their *brats* in a mist so thick a man could stand a spoon in it, and out of it, like spirits, there were the Sidhe standing before them. They looked like the fog, like the earth itself when color fades in autumn. The men carried ready slings. Then the woman came forward but not too near.

"She told me her name, but I cannot remember it. Queer scars cut on both her cheeks and eyes the color of smoke."

"Like storm clouds before a rain," I remembered.

Garbhan stared into the fire. "I've never been so close to the Good People. God keep me from it soon again. I showed the gold to her for lifting the curse. She and the others only laughed. It is a sad sound, their laughter, like long dead ghosts over a long dead joke, and all around us the fog. She said the gold in this land had been theirs from the time of the ice. What ice? I did not understand."

Beside the gold, Feargus offered cattle to the fifth part of tribute exacted from ui Chellaig, though we could scarce afford it. Again the woman refused, saying cattle were a poor bargain, being not near so hardy as their own sheep, and anyway they could relieve Irish of a cow whenever they had a taste for the meat.

"And much needed," the *ghillie* reflected, "from the starved look of them."

"I've thought on that," I told him. "Such fearsome magic when they can barely live in the land."

Feargus shushed me anxiously. "Have more respect, man. The Good People live as they have always lived. Let Lord Garbhan tell the tale. Yet one more offer I made."

Which surely was as much as any lord dared and a dangerous measure. Many of the *ghillies* argued hard against it before the mission set out. Few as the Sidhe were, Feargus reasoned, it might bring more peace than peril. Beside the gold and cattle, he offered her band yearly summer pasturage so she kept her flock to the high ground beyond Tay and away from our cattle.

But all to nothing. Garbhan wagged his head hopelessly. "Never have I see a woman so bitter or so set, sorrow and vengeance together."

Had I not seen that too?

"Deigh," he said simply, "I have known nothing in battle but joy and taken heads, as well you know. But I felt as much fear with that small woman as you must have, yet cannot say why. She refused me for the third time. Then she said: 'Tell the *bo aire* when I was young in the land, I traded with your kind with no fear. Sometimes you were honest. More often you cheated us and drove us away with stones and curses and put foolish spells over your doors to ward us off. You hate us because you fear us. Now Deigh mac Diarmuid has sent my last child under the hill, and I have learned to curse as well.' "

Garbhan's whole heart was in his eyes, and I believed what he spoke then. "I am sorry for you, *eachra*-man."

"Tell the rest and be done," Feargus grumbled.

"She says the curse upon Deigh will touch all he owns and all those of the lord's rath, all of this *tuatha*."

Splat! Ehne's fist came down hard on the bread dough as the curse on me, but she said nothing.

"It is myself put this on you," Feargus admitted, "yet what can we do? There it is and there all."

"All indeed!" Ehne could no longer keep silent but came to the fire, dough-smeared hands fisted on her hips. "Our lord is sorry, and I thank him for the sentiment, but what now? What will he do for his bravest and best?"

"All within my power," Feargus promised.

"You must leave here!" Garbhan blurted, pained with the need to condemn us, for he did no less. "No, more. You must leave Leinster and the land entire. For your own good, Deigh. The curse cannot cross water."

Leave the Knuckles of God, all of the world we knew? While I just stared at them, Feargus assured me quickly, "You will have the gold I promised and Roman coin beside to sustain you in Britain."

I felt Ehne stiffen beside me, stunned as myself. "Britain?" she echoed as if the word were new to her ear. "What . . . what can we do in Britain? Where will we go?"

"That has been thought on," Feargus said. "Our own king, Aughaire of Leinster, is just after marrying his daughter to Mark of Cornwall. But you must leave quickly. Before Samhain nightfall."

"Soon indeed." I looked down at my hands. "Is there no other way?"

"None. The people are desperate afraid." Then in a tone that set the seal hard on our fate: "It has been decided."

"I see." I gazed from one lord to the other, knowing the haste they urged was fear for themselves, not concern for us. *You are both just wee mannys like myself and terrified. So be it, Feargus.* What I spoke then he well deserved. "Then you can cut my name on a stone and let bards tell how I was cast out for doing no more than my lord's command to save his pride."

"Let him do more," Ehne said through her teeth. "Banished from our home, we are like the dead. And all for our own good, is it? After the bard sings, let your daughter keen for our passing, for little Etain has killed us."

Never before had we dared such anger or disgust toward our lord, but he said nothing, knowing it all too true. Nothing more to say. The helpless silence drew out and became one more troubled soul in the house while the dreary rain fell on the roof and our life. Then the two lords wrapped their cloaks about them, and in parting Feargus said only, "You deserve far better. I am sorry. Were it possible for you to stay, you could have a place among the *fear coghaidh.*"

I smiled in parting but couldn't keep the poison from it: "But that is for heroes, my lord."

By next day's noon the word of our going had spread among the people, for this or that man or woman happened by to say farewell before hurrying off.

"Handsome of them," Ehne grumbled, scrubbing out our

peat brazier. "And they without a word to spare us all these months."

"Aye, you'd think they were glad to see us go."

"Well, of *course* they—" Then her face softened, and I saw her first weak smile for many days. "You always joke on me, Deigh. I do not have your quick wit."

"Only my heart, love."

"Oh, be seeing to the poor hens. There might be an egg or two. The pullet goes into the pot tonight. No sense wasting."

The other chickens we traded away for whatever folk could spare and we could use in Britain. Time was short, only days to Samhain. That very afternoon Feargus came with three trading sticks of gold, a heavy bag that jingled, and two bolts of fine woven wool.

"Ehne can make new clothes. My daughter was minded to send it."

Minded with his boot, I hoped.

He dug into the bag and placed a coin in my hand, old and worn but with the faint image of a man's head on the face. "This is British."

"And this one of their gods on it?"

"One of their high kings whom they call *imperator*. Do not ask me why. They have the new faith as we do, but their ways are different since the Romans came."

I studied the object curiously, never having seen such "money" before. It struck me cold with all the familiar, loved things we must leave and the vast, frightening strangeness lying before us.

On the day of our leaving, Lord Feargus provided us a cart and escort of four warriors including Lord Garbhan. Ehne said little when we left the *clochan* but plucked a charred end of wood from our last fire for starting the first in the new land. The *bo aire* came himself to bid us farewell, making honesty blush with words of regret at our parting.

Once settled in the cart Ehne would not spare him a glance or the home we were leaving.

At Baile Atha Cliath, Lord Garbhan paid our passage on the largest ship I'd ever seen: not covered in tarred hide like ours but of timbers and planks, rowed by slaves with many oars that stuck out of holes in the sides like the legs of some great beetle. A Roman trading galley, we were told, plying regularly from the Middle Sea to all the ports of Gaul and Britain. Mark, king of the Cornwall we sailed to, did much trading with them.

Everything was new and strange to us: the huge ship riding at anchor, more people than we'd ever seen in one place before, all shouting in foreign tongues, sailors shouldering us out of their way as they carried aboard casks and bales of Irish wool. Never a timid soul, still Ehne squeezed very close to me by the rail as the sail was hoisted, broader end to end than our little home on Lough Tay.

She might have read my own thought when she whispered in awe: "Did you ever dream the world so terrible big?"

I did not. As Eire sank down the horizon, now a bare smudge over the sea, now gone, we prayed fervently that the Sidhe curse could not follow to find us. As for where we sailed, we had only a letter writ for Feargus by a priest to a lord named Trystan in a place called Bard's Tor.

The miles swallowed the past as if it had never been, leaving us only the little brown gulls for company and the *wash-wash* of oars. We never saw our home again.

II

Harper, What Song?

here could never have been much love lost between King Mark of Cornwall and his nephew Trystan, even less after Mark married Yseult of Leinster. In the way of it, Leinster's warriors struck at Cornwall in a luckless raid that taxed King Aughaire heavily in cattle tribute, or would have had not our king offered Mark an attractive bargain: half the tribute and his own daughter in marriage. The bargain was sealed, and Lord Trystan the very man to escort the bride to his uncle.

Praise travels at a walk while scandal rides the wind. Years it was before Rome recognized the strength and majesty of Arthur, but Trystan and Yseult? Even among the Knuckles of God visiting bards sang of the girl, how her hair glistened black as winter midnight against the new snowfall of her skin, and they told no lie. Lazarus himself, without the aid of miracle, would rise from the tomb to love her. Before the altar candles burned low by which Yseult married Mark, and he much older than herself, gossip flew that Trystan enjoyed the first night before their ship made landfall at Castle Dore. Dangerous talk and not for Ehne or me to spread. We'd already been cruelly burned at fires we did not build, true as the rumors were.

To say Trystan loved her is to say the world's wide and the ocean deep. I saw her young and knew her old, though her spell never touched me. Queer it is how such a plague of beauty will lay one man low and leave another untouched. For good or ill, the woman was the fate and breaking of Trystan when another just as fine should have been. Strange and sad, for at his best he was the breathing image of what our warriors like to think themselves, that and more. Fighter-poet, courageous in battle, though not without human fear, courteous, loyal and generous, inspired by the music his fingers plucked from a harp, yet all at a terrible cost. What is there in perfection cannot live with itself, that turns from its brightness to its own dark shadow? There was a black pit in Trystan no song could lighten nor woman fill.

"Such men are alone all their lives," Guenevere said once. "Any woman could love him, too many have, but none should." That was years later when she and I, like the weeping world, came to wisdom and the right words too late.

There was a terrible, warring beauty in Trystan. Imagine God out of sorts on a black day, squeezing man-clay through his fingers and saying, "I will make this one half perfection and in the other half everything to destroy and see which side tips the balance."

We needed a week to raise Castle Dore, days and nights of misery. The wind is northerly that time of year and the sea a living, angry beast that hung poor Ehne and myself over the rail, unable to think of eating until the sailors out of pity told us to force food down. Our galley made for the nearest British coast, then crawled south and southeast, wind screaming in the taut rigging until the blessed land rose out of the calming sea before us, high, sudden cliffs with the sea white froth at their base.

I asked of a giant sailor, "Castle Dore?"

"*Ja,*" said he without much interest. To him this was just another port of call where cargo would be unloaded and taken on, not knowing that to us it was death and rebirth, passing from one life to the next.

"Then we are in the kingdom of Cornwall."

"*Ja,*" he said again with pitying tolerance: poor Irish savage, never been anywhere. "And will be tomorrow too."

"We are to take service with a great lord here," Ehne informed him, put out by the indifference in his chilly blue eyes. The sailor held up the tool with which he'd been loosening knots in a length of rope. "I wouldn't know a great lord from this marlinspike."

"He is Lord Trystan, nephew to King Mark himself," I flourished grandly. "And where would you be from that you don't know?"

The sailor tucked the tool in his belt and strolled away. "Dover. I'm Saxon. Gather your stowage. We'll be putting in soon."

Ehne touched my shoulder, bidding me kneel with her on the deck, where we gave thanks to God for delivering us from the cursed sea. "And may the Sidhe evil never find us here. Amen."

As the ship drew close in to the stone quay, Ehne gasped. "Look there! The madman, he's about to kill himself."

Down the steep path from the cliff top, the horse and rider might have slipped any moment and plunged to their death, taking with them the tethered mule laboring to keep up. The young man broke out onto the narrow beach, by miracle unscathed, shouting as he came. "Deigh? Deigh mac Diarmuid?"

"I did not think the man born who could sit a horse like you," Ehne admired. "But there he is."

And here he came, clattering along the quay to fling himself off the horse as the sailors slid out the boarding plank. He bounded aboard, a buck no older than myself, crackling with energy as he searched briefly about to find us. "You must be the ones, Deigh and Ehne. Both look a bit green. Rough crossing?"

"Cruel rough, sir."

He flashed Ehne a dazzling smile. "I'm Trystan."

"My lord rides well." She could not resist adding, "Almost as well as my Deigh."

"So the letter said." Our new lord ignored or never noticed the slight, hands on slender hips as he surveyed us, fair brimming over with good spirits. "From one of your priests writing for a cattle lord . . . Feargus? Says you're a very wizard with horses. There's luck, I can use you. Brave, he said, reliable, swore he hated to part with either of you."

"For sure," Ehne commented, tart as green apple. "You'd think his heart fair broke to see the back of us."

I jumped in quickly. "I'm glad there's a mule, sir, though it is little we brought."

And that little quickly unloaded and onto the waiting mule. Trystan had a cart above at the cliff top.

"Why, he's only a young one like us," Ehne judged. "Seems a-boil with good humor though."

There was a blessing. After the clammy fear all round us at home and the miserable voyage, I was glad to see a face that didn't wish us gone. Trystan rode ahead up the cliff path while we trudged after, leading the mule, wrapped tight in our shabby *brats* against the sea wind.

"But that you might be jealous," Ehne confided with a female eye to Trystan. "He is easy on a woman's sight."

"I'm always jealous." I chucked my wife on her firm rump. "And you are shameless."

Trystan turned in the saddle to wave us on. "Almost there. The cart's just at the top."

Castle Dore was the largest rath and palisade I'd ever seen. Trystan told me it was built anew on one of the old hillforts, surrounded by a wide ditch, the stockade timbers enclosing many buildings, men on the ramparts everywhere you looked. As I gaped up at the hugeness of it all, Trystan threw back the hood of his cloak to let the wind play through the tight black curls crowning his head. The man glowed that day with a joy he couldn't conceal, and soon enough we found the source: a slender figure in gold and green high up on the ramparts. As she lifted her hand in farewell, the gesture wrote tenderness in every line. Trystan put a hand to his lips and flung the kiss to her, then led the way along the cart track toward our new life. No matter how often he turned to gaze back, she was still there, arm lifted in farewell.

That the king's own nephew came to greet mere servants was unusual courtesy until the common gossip came to our ears. The woman on the rampart was our young queen Yseult. We'd only been an excuse for him to see her, no matter how briefly. That winter every soul but the king seemed to have wind of the matter, but in the cruel way of such truths, Mark knew soon enough.

Trystan's rath, Bard's Tor, lay a scant mile north of Castle Dore along the coast that looked ever warily over the sea to Eire, Cornwall's old enemy, though we quickly showed ourselves the humblest and least piratical folk ever to leave Leinster. Trystan's home was far grander than that of Feargus, his rath built on high ground with a bank and ditch outside, a palisade enclosing many buildings within. There were a roofed byre and stable, cook house, and a dozen *clochans* for servants like us. The great round rath was shingled mostly, with tiles ringed about the smoke hole and that collared with tin, no less, better protection against fire, the constant bane of plain thatching. Inside, the earthen floor was covered with gravel and the central places of honor floored with planking. Benches and tables were set about for the lord and his guests close to the stone firepit. Other benches farther back served the commons of Trystan's household, so no need for any of us to squat on the ground.

No *clochans* stood empty at the time; we would live in the lord's rath. With a rush of pride Ehne and I felt ourselves coming up in the world by leaps and bounds. Our stall was as large as Feargus's own, closed off not by a hide flap but fine-woven tapestry with flower designs. The covering swung open or closed on bronze rings set on a bar, secured by hooks on both sides. We felt quite grand though we had less room than at home and far less privacy.

"But at least there's not the cooking twice a day," Ehne reasoned. Trystan had some half dozen older widows to do that. Ehne grumbled about the quality of their cooking, disapproving of all not done just her way.

"I thought you liked cooking, love."

"Oh yes. Feeding my da twice a day and then you, and the peeling and scraping and boiling and all the rest? Likely, Deigh. Likely."

"No denying there's more and better to eat here."

"Ah, they use too much salt."

The dear woman's been so all her life. Though we lived better and rose higher than ever we could at home, Ehne would find something ripe for disapproval. She could not take to the new as I did. Never a good word for Queen Yseult—

"A shame on Leinster and Cornwall alike!"

—and in the years that followed, saints protect Guenevere and Lancelot, had my wife's opinion a killing edge. When she attained the rank of lady as I was made lord-comite by Arthur, Ehne remained a peasant at heart, as I did but far less tolerant. What can a man say? High lords have easier morals, but Ehne? Right there was and wrong there was, and Ehne standing square in judgment between the two. Her early life laid callus over a lively mind as long walking will a foot. Yet some things she saw and sensed more clearly than a man. I found in Trystan a cheerful, hail-fellow sort, easygoing as myself and anything but hard on his servants. He'd a kind of offhanded way with him and always a good word for me when I legged him up onto his horse.

Ehne allowed his charm but saw through it. "As he looks through folk sometimes like they are not there." If the charm was Trystan's halo, she reckoned, the same hedged and armored him about to keep men and women at a distance.

"For all his fine harping and songs, you can get no more hold of him than smoke. I tell you, if that woman at Castle Dore weren't such a slut, I could pity her."

As that first autumn turned sharp with sea wind and winter, our lives went much as they had at home. I cared for the horses, forking fodder, shoeing, mucking out the stalls, now and then breaking an animal of bad habits. Ehne milked cows and worked with the loom, chickens, and hogs as she'd done all her life. Trystan was often away at his uncle's court, accompanied by the few fighting men of his holding. If he returned in excellent spirits, that meant he'd seen Yseult and enjoyed whatever they could contrive alone together. The mood throughout Bard's Tor leaned on just how well they'd managed. They played a dangerous game, and only a matter of time before the storm came down. What then of us, his servants?

One day in late winter, Trystan and his troop returned from hunting with King Mark, a boar slung between two panting horses, our lord in roaring good spirits, so all Trystan's hunting must have been good, if you take my meaning. Food went thin and drab in winter, but that night we ate as we hadn't for weeks. Trystan ordered his best Gaulish wine broached for all, and we went to bed gorged and content. All but our lord, who often stayed up long after the rest of us yawned and stumbled our way to the stalls. We would hear the soft melody his fingers enticed from the harp. If Yseult was the heart of him, his soul was in that harp. How the man could play! He'd studied with the Druids to learn the bard's mysteries, the hundred verses memorized, hours of practice till his long, hardened fingernails rode the brass strings like an angel dancing through a grove of stars, each star a note to lull his people to rest of a cold night.

We listened now, wrapped in our blankets, as the soft music filled the night, lagged and slowed, then went silent. We thought he'd gone to bed, leaving no sound but the wind crying in over the sea. This night it sobbed about the shingles and tiles overhead, and Ehne slipped closer to me under the blankets, full of dread. "There are voices on that wind, Deigh."

"There are not."

"Voices. The sea has not stopped the curse."

"It is foolish you are. Go to sleep."

"No. Listen."

I'd drunk enough for imagination to wake, not enough to make it sleep again. The wind howled, hurled from the sea by some giant hand, and I *could* hear tortured voices. I gathered Ehne to me, scared as herself but not wanting to show it. "There is nothing."

"Close as I am to you, I am still cold." Ehne shuddered. "The Sidhe have found us sure."

"Och, be still now." I was angered by my own fear, for there were voices that cried our names on the wind hurrying cold from the sea, battering over the rocks to wail atop the cliffs, searching us out with all the sorrow and fury of those angels cast from heaven to wander forever through night on earth.

Well, if no cure, at least a comfort. "There might be wine left. Just a nip to warm us to sleep."

"Will not the lord mind if he catches us?"

"He will not. Besides, he's gone to bed."

"Wait. I will come with you."

Some wine was left in one of the small skins. As usual, Lord Trystan had taken more than a drop, though his wooden trencher sat barely touched and cold on the table.

"He should eat more," Ehne noted, "and drink far less."

"Quite right."

We jumped at the sound. There was Trystan in the entrance to his stall, a full-bellied new wineskin in his hand. "Eating is a necessary bore," he said, coming forward to the table. He hadn't gone to bed at all, still fully dressed with the heavy cloak over his shoulders. "Wine is more interesting and . . . passes the time."

Almost no light left in the rath, only the glow from the log embers in the firepit throwing our shadows huge about the walls. Ehne and I sat on a bench, fearful as children caught stealing pastries.

"It was cold, my lord. I thought a little wine—"

Trystan only wrinkled his nose at the trifle. He poured wine all around, head cocked slightly to one side at us as if he could not quite take our measure. Snores issued from the stalls, and the wind cried overhead. "Why are the two of you here?" he asked finally. "Why have you come to me?"

"My lord has the letter."

"Yes, yes. That tells me who and whence but not why. When we see Irish they're usually pirates. If Feargus praised you both so highly, why were you packed off so hastily after years of good and faithful service?"

Ehne ducked her head over the wine cup. "It is an unhappy tale, sir."

"I daresay. Well, the fire's still warm and this seems a night for doleful tales." Trystan emptied his cup and refilled it. "What happened?"

One glance told me Ehne did not wish to be the one to speak. "Lord," I began uneasily, "do you have here those folk we call the Sidhe? The Good People?"

"Tylwyth Teg? Faerie?" Trystan laughed with easy amusement. "No. Oh, you hear tales among the trevs, superstition mostly. I've heard there are some north among the Picts, but none seen lately in these parts. What?" He laughed again. "By all benevolent gods, don't tell me you're bewitched."

"Do not!" Ehne blurted. "Do not show disrespect. It is dangerous. The curse laid on us—" She bit her lip and would say no more.

"My wife is frightened, sir. This is very real to us."

Trystan put down his cup, leaning forward to Ehne. "I can see that. Dear woman, take my apology. Lay my foolish laughter to ignorance—or perhaps my education. Do go on."

There was the best of the man for you: gracious, self-slighting, and all in that soft Cornish drawl that cushioned a sharp wit, showing real concern for Ehne's fear. "What has happened?"

"That's for my husband to tell, sir. He it was who did what others would not dare for all their high place."

Trystan looked to me. "Deigh?"

"When I have told my lord, he must promise never to speak of the matter or mention the Good People aloud."

"You have my word." He put an end of tallow candle to the embers to brighten the red-stained glow about us. "Tell me."

In few, cautious words I told of willful Etain and her lover, how the mother found and cursed me for killing him. Much I left silent, such as her words on love and the vision of the woman. I still did not grasp that. Ehne need not.

"Not a soul on the *tuath* didn't want us gone before the evil fell on them. In our country we believe no curse or spell so strong that it can cross water."

"So I've heard," Trystan said, "but never had occasion to test the notion. May the gods protect you both."

"Jesus defend." Ehne and I crossed ourselves. When Trystan did not, she asked, "Are you not of the new faith, Lord?"

"If no great faith, at least great respect for the Church.

To be frank, my children, between the Druidic mysteries and the Church hanging me head down over hell, I'm confused and very neutral."

Trystan tore off a chunk of bread and dipped it in his wine. "Bread and wine, the body and blood, no? I'm told in magic there's nothing stronger than blood. And a lord must give of himself for his people."

He dipped the bread again. "Names too, I've heard, are powerful in magic. Does this woman know your names?"

"She does."

"Then change them. Be new-christened with names the Faerie spell can't know or find. British names. Now—for whatever sins you carry, I take them on myself."

As we stared at him, Trystan swallowed the bread and washed it down with wine.

"You are a brave and noble lord," Ehne whispered, "but may not know what you have done."

Trystan rose to embrace us both. "You will be newborn in a safe place, happy as I am happy. Go to bed and rest you gentle."

Oh, Tryst. How lightly you swallowed my curse, amused and pitying, like wiping the tears from the face of a hurt child. It was no more than that to you. I'm sorry, Tryst. Jesus God, I am so sorry for all of it.

The "church" Trystan provided for his folk was small and drab, with a priest, Father Glyn, to match the seediness. The wattle and daub building had been enlarged from a byre and still smelled like one. I expected a cow to wander in out of habit. The priest hesitated at rechristening Christians. We bent truth a mite, claiming the Church was new in Eire and ourselves never properly baptized or christened, priests being few and mostly distant. This plus a few *solidi* for the poor gently swayed Father Glyn, who took up the holy water and washed us into a new life. I became Gareth—

"Which means 'civilized,' for so you will be," Trystan prophesied. " 'Rhian' means a maiden." He bathed my wife in that carelessly dazzling smile of his. "For you look yet young enough to be one."

"That man has an angel's tongue in his head," she vowed later. "He could talk Virgin Mary into bed, and that of a Sunday."

"Would you be speaking for yourself, then?"

"Do you not know and trust me better?" My wife's brow furrowed with hard experience. "I lost my innocence learning there's lords like Feargus and Trystan, and those like us who sweat for them all our lives. There's the difference, Deigh."

"Gareth," I corrected. "Gareth and Rhian from this day on. We must never speak the old names again."

The Cornish spring is warmer than Eire's. Sometimes the wind carries the scent of flowers from the isles off Land's End. Following that scented warmth, Trystan rode every day to Castle Dore, yet more and more often the man returned clouded in manner, frowning and short with others, very unlike himself.

"Her it is doing this to him." Rhian shook her head. "Bad begun, bad done."

She was the cause sure. The woman was a sickness in Trystan. Night after night through the lengthening spring twilights he sat alone at the table where so lightly he took our curse and sins upon himself, drawing strange sounds from his harp. What had been beauty was gone sharp as fruit on the turn.

One night, Rhian already asleep beside me, from beyond our curtain I heard a sound I didn't believe a harp could make. It pierced through me, brutal as a blade rending the heart of the world. Again and again it came, louder, harsher, as if the man would claw the living soul from brass strings, trying to free some terrible, wounded thing. I couldn't bear it any longer but got up and threw the curtain back—

"Lord?"

Trystan crouched over the harp, ear against the strings, tearing and tearing that one horrible cry from them.

"Lord Trystan."

The hand paused. In the dim light his face was shadowed, but as he raised his head I saw agony deep as the pain drawn from his tortured harp. "You absurd little creature, what do you want? Who are you?"

"Gareth, sir."

"I don't care. If I look on your face one breath more, I'll kill you. Go."

I believed him, no threat but a promise, and dropped the curtain between myself and the face of murder, for I saw no less than that.

News from Castle Dore. Northeast of us in Dyfneint there'd been a sea raid at Neth Dun More by Saxon pirates. And what a tale! Close to a hundred raiders repelled by three horsemen, Prince Geraint of Dyfneint himself and two officers of the legion at Caerleon, Artorius and Bedwyr. The names meant nothing then, but three against a hundred? That would have inspired rare boasting in Feargus's rath and no whisper of dispute over the hero's portion.

Closer to home a messenger had come to Castle Dore from the emperor Ambrosius himself calling for recruits in a far place called Eburacum.

"Where is that?" Rhian asked without much concern.

None of the servants knew. North somewhere, perhaps a war between clans or even whole tribes, but no business of Cornwall's. As servants will, all of us puzzled why Cornish should go so far to fight strangers, but we didn't ken Roman thinking, which draws straight lines and builds square houses and thinks as a "state."

One afternoon already sweet with the smell of summer, I was in the stable measuring out grain for the horses when Trystan walked in leading his mount, and the man's face was a storm. He held up a horseshoe. "Damn you, didn't you reshoe him as I bade?"

"Two days ago, sir."

"Well, he's thrown another." Trystan hurled the shoe heavily against a stall gate. "Work with more care, you fool. If he's a split hoof, I'll take it out of your back."

I could only gape at him, more shocked than frightened. The man had never threatened any servant with a beating; such was not his way. Trystan sagged down wearily on a mounting block, face in his hands. No sound in the stable but the horses whinnying for their feed and two foolish martins awhirl and squabbling in the eaves above.

"Are you ailing, sir?" When he said nothing, I said, "We've heard the news from Castle Dore."

Dully: "News?"

"The troubles in the north. Word gets back even here in the stable."

The anger had left Trystan, but something dark remained

like a shadow. "Oh yes, word always gets back. What need of paid spies when servants can't wait to tell all they know?"

"Lord, with me and Rhian, what comes to our ears dies there. But were the tidings true about the north?"

"There is no war," Trystan said. "Ambrosius wants cavalry on the Wall. My uncle has strongly suggested I join them *pro patria et gloria.*"

"What wall would that be, sir?"

"*The* Wall," he hissed impatiently, "you benighted little man, the one that's spanned our north from sea to sea since Hadrian's time."

"Sea to sea?"

"And very impressive." Trystan grinned sourly. "Lovely place. Dust, dirt, bad food, and Pictish raids to break the monotony. The far end of Britain, the hind end of the civilized world. Why do you ask, Gareth? Want to go for a soldier?"

I had to laugh at that. "Among all those lords? They wouldn't have me."

Trystan rose from the block. "They'll take anyone who can ride. That's Cador's legion, the Sixth. Call themselves Roman when Rome is years gone. They're desperate. See to that shoe and hoof, mind."

Very confusing. We called our king Mark, he called himself Marcus Conomori (and there a Latin mouthful for poor Irish!) while the Roman emperor of Britain, Ambrosius, called Mark merely prince-magistrate, but by any name, Mark's ambitions climbed higher than his abilities. Along with other footling little kings, he schemed to wear the purple after Ambrosius, but he did sit in the right place and time for other good fortune which should have contented him. With much of the east of Britain in Saxon hands, Mark's seaports brought him Gaulish and Middle Sea trade, and riches from the lead and tin their ships carried away. Only natural that he looked to the sea and what was left of Rome rather than matters beyond his back door.

That spring Mark made a progress along the coast to inspect his ports, leaving Queen Yseult at home. In her husband's absence, Trystan spent much time at Castle Dore. I'm bound to say he came home a changed man. The sun shone from his face again, and no great riddle who lighted it there, but bad followed close behind. With the truth we all knew, not difficult to guess the shape of things. Some eavesdropping little lackey dog-eager for a bone, dog-ready to sit up and bark.

So once again another man's misfortune struck at my life and changed it forever for good and ill alike.

I walked toward the stables, the June sun already warm on my back, when the young shepherd came out of the barn, throwing his leather scrip over one shoulder. "Gareth? Rhian wants you."

"Where, then?"

He jerked his head toward the barn behind him. "Rolling fleeces."

In the barn Rhian worked at a table bundling new fleeces. The place reeked of sheep's oil. At a second table another servant woman did the same, laying out and rolling the fleeces with the speed of long practice. Rhian kept working as she spoke urgently in Irish. "You'd think we'd got shut of trouble."

"Why, what now?"

Rhian tied off her bundle and threw it on a pile. "Reach

me another there. The fool's brought it on himself. Early this morning it was. I was up in the loft there to fetch a bit of clean straw for the hen roosts when I heard the clatter of a cart outside, and then the woman comes hurrying in."

A well-dressed woman who could only have come from Castle Dore, pacing up and down near the door as if waiting for someone and not much time to spare. Rhian would have spoken to her, but just then Lord Trystan hurried in to grasp the woman's hands.

"Now I couldn't get out and wouldn't be caught listening, so I got down in the hay and just hoped they'd be gone."

"The young queen?"

"No, her waiting woman, the one she brought from home, if I know the sound of a Leinster tongue."

Only a little of their talk she caught, but that enough. *He knows,* the woman said. *Dare not come again,* and at the end the woman was clear enough. *She begs you to go.*

"And that was all—there, let me tie that one off." Rhian bundled the fleece by the neck and tail pieces and stacked it with the others.

"What's to become of the man?" I worried. "Not a bad lord, just difficult in drink is all."

"Him you say?" Rhian spread another raw fleece before her. "Leave some charity for us, for what happens to him befalls us of his rath."

"You Irish," the old woman scolded from the next table. "Can't go two breaths without jabbering at each other."

I gave Rhian a swift kiss on the cheek. "Just passing the time of day, love. God bless you, Mother."

And God shield us all, because from Trystan's changed manner, Rhian had understood more than enough. For a few days as Midsummer approached, our master spoke little and seemed withdrawn. Gradually, then, the shadow over him turned to a kind of defiant gaiety. A man may ignore a plain warning, but he's mad to laugh in its teeth, and that Trystan did and did and did again all his life.

When I think of Tryst now, I wish he'd had one drop of Bedwyr's cool common sense. Arthur and Guenevere loved the man but could not admire him. Arthur followed a dream, Bedwyr iron loyalty, but Trystan? Sing what you will, make the poor man into a tale to weep over—all his life he was led by a few inches of flesh between his legs, and that's a cruel short leash.

Trystan let caution go begging and, defying his uncle, decreed a feast to mark the summer solstice of the Old Religion and Saint John's Eve alike. All this full knowing his uncle planned the same at Castle Dore, but nothing for it: slaughter the ewe, the spring lamb, pluck the chickens, spit the doves, bake the bread and broach the wine. All were invited for the two days of feasting, doors thrown open to beggars and monks on holy pilgrimage to Ynnis Witrin. Another glove in Mark's face: Trystan invited Morlais, Mark's favorite harper, to attend and compete with him in performance. Eyebrows went up at that. Such was simply not done, as Rhian and I were told by those longer in service. Morlais was skilled in bardic glories as our lord—some said beyond him—and always attended King Mark upon command. This year, however, Trystan offered not only a larger fee but issued a challenge, one bard to another, in language so arrogant and scornful that Morlais's honor could not refuse.

From early morning on the first fine day of the feasting, we were awakened early by men lumbering in with the ox to be roasted, women boiling puddings, and others traipsing in and out for trestles to be set up outside for traveling strangers to whom the gates were thrown open at sunrise. A warm day promised to be warmer. Trystan turned out in red linen tunic and trousers trimmed in green and a fine gold torc about his neck.

"Doesn't he look grand, Rhian?"

"If death looks grand," she observed. "Drinking half the night and again this morning before he touched a bite."

"Hair of the dog."

"Monstrous great dog, then." Rhian passed the apron between her legs and turned about for me to tuck it through the strings behind. "The day scarce begun, and he's swallowed the whole pelt."

As the morning drew on, folk began to climb the hill to Bard's Tor to be greeted by Trystan himself. Father Glyn came early with a stream of Trystan's folk puffing up the steep path in their colorful holiday best. Poor Rhian would be toiling hard this day, milking the cows, fetch-and-carrying buttermilk and cheese, while I was summoned to join Trystan at the gates.

One look at my lord and the mouse in my stomach squeaked its first warning. By now I could read the changes in him as a sailor reads weather. Sober there was not a gentler man or a sweeter tongue in the world. A few drops and still no difference. A few more started the turn—oh, slowly, like a simmering pot, tiny bubbles rising to the top but still a while to full boil. Trystan was not quite there, and I prayed he'd hold off. Gently, man. Pace yourself, for you ride a dangerous horse in drink.

"There he comes." Trystan pointed far down the track

leading from Castle Dore. "That paragon of bards, Morlais. He's an outlander, not Cornish at all."

While the chariot grew larger below us, gold trim flashing in the sun, Trystan educated me in Morlais. No better bard laid hand to harp (saving himself, of course). But Morlais was mired in musical convention, not daring at all. He knew his poetry, aye, and could stir with songs of heroism, but not the dark agonies of the soul.

"Which is to say, Gareth-fach, the man knows only the half of his art."

"My lord called him an outlander."

"Of the Belgae."

"And who would they be?"

Trystan raked fingers through my hair in rough affection. "They are insufferable, you ignorant man."

The Belgae, he said, were the last Gaulish Celts to cross the Narrow Sea and become Britons before Julius Caesar brought Rome and the troubles. These Belgae then bent much of southern Britain to their sway and ever after looked down on other tribes.

"In Gaul their lands were close to the Rhine." Then, like one who'd found maggots in good meat: "They have the German in them. Go down, take his chariot and drive him up."

This was a courtesy afforded all honored guests. From the bottom of the hill to the gates was a steep climb for carts and chariots. Drivers must know just when to goad horses with rein or whip. I trotted down the path, waving both arms for the tall driver to halt the matched pair of blacks.

"For your safety, sir, my master would have me take you up the hill."

Browned by the sun under red-gold hair, his tunic white

and gold as the chariot, more princely than any prince, Morlais peered down at me with keen interest. "Would you mind uttering that astounding locution once more?"

"Was I not clear, sir?"

"After a fashion, but where in the name of all pleasing speech did you learn to bruise it so?"

I'd labored to learn Cornish speech, not that different from my own, but was still enough of a pipe among fiddles to show me foreign. I answered with just enough tart to stay this side of rudeness. "Among the Knuckles of God, sir, and since beauty is in the ear of the listener, you sound a mite unusual to me."

Morlais laughed with such warmth that I knew no offense had been intended, waving me up with a swipe of his bare arm. "So I must. Come, take the reins. Do I see the king's nephew himself waiting above?"

"You do, sir."

"A moment, please."

From the chariot rim he unfolded the longest and strangest garment I'd ever seen this side of a shroud and surely the least practical. When Morlais had draped and wrapped it this way and that about him, he had to hold it in place with his left hand, with only the right to steady him as I drove the horses up the hill. But he did *look* grand.

"That is a toga," Trystan explained to me later after he and Morlais exchanged greeting polite but cool. "He is the complete Roman today, chariot and all."

"That toga thing: is it not confining?"

I could smell the whisky strong on his breath as he turned to me. "It's a message, Gareth. He accepts my challenge but insults hospitality by flaunting his loyalty to Mark and *Romanitas.* He dares to come so. It smacks of Mark."

From the side of the cart track Trystan lifted a fist-sized stone, turning it this way and that. "Observe my uncle's fine head. The sheer weight of intellect, the classic brow, the mouth strong enough to compliment a bust of Caesar, and yet the sensitivity, the nobility of feature unsoiled by any ignoble thought. What a creation." Trystan kissed the stone and tucked it under his arm. "Ours will be an interesting feast."

He smiled. I fancy wolves smile so before dinner.

The feasting began at midday and continued through a fine afternoon, course after course. Rhian and I had never eaten so. Sharing our meal from a thick trencher of rye meal bread, we did not gobble but selected morsel by morsel as a fortunate fisherman picks a pearl from an oyster shell. Pork marrow fritters fried in oil, vegetables simmered in chicken broth, fish and jellied eel, and when our bread trencher grew too sodden, Rhian had only to cut another, and to it we went again. Rhian considered waste the eighth deadly sin. She carefully wrapped several choice cuts of pig and a whole dove for us to nibble later before the hewed remains were thrown to the dogs or sent outside to the beggars munching in the stockade yard.

Morlais and Trystan dined at two separate tables, Morlais still in his toga, which he would not shed until ready to perform.

"Did you ever see the dainty like?" Rhian marveled. "Not a drop or dab does he spill, yet he eats with the right hand alone."

"He has to. If he lets go of that toga thing, it will fall off."

Apart at his own table, Trystan barely touched the food before him but drank steadily. As a woman will, Rhian counted the times he signaled for more. "I hope that is plain mead he's swilling."

"It is not."

"For what good reason does he fondle that great stone?"

"Poor soul, he fancies it's his uncle."

Now and then Trystan's gaze wandered to Morlais as he caressed the uncle-stone.

The long afternoon waned. Soldiers, common folk, and priests alike sat back, unbuckled, and sent up a great sigh of contentment. The tired servers and carvers sat on the gravel floor, able to rest now and gobble like the rest. The people from the stockade yard crowded now into the rath, eager for what promised to be a duel of champions. As a harper, Morlais was revered far beyond Cornwall. Trystan himself all his life was better known as poet than lord. New songs about this day's contest alone would earn lesser bards bed and board at many Midsummers to come.

Now Father Glyn went forward, listing a bit with all the good food and wine he'd taken aboard, and murmured a word in turn to the two bards. Though I first thought him musty as his barn-born church, it seemed the dear man knew so much of poetry that both harpers accepted him without question as judge between them today.

The gabble in the crowded rath quieted as Trystan tuned his instrument. Morlais rose and slipped off the toga, folding it slowly, each movement exact as Father Glyn presenting the Eucharist at Mass. He drew the triangular harp from its sheepskin bag and began to tune, ear close to the strings, eyes far away, as if the man were completely alone. Much more time he took with this than our lord, who called impatiently to him, "The notion was to perform today, Morlais, not next month."

Morlais glanced up lazily. "I am not ready." He went on tuning, *ping, ping.*

But Trystan was well tuned in another way by now. "Nor are you dressed with any respect for your art."

Ping! Ping! "Your king would not say so."

Murmurs swept through the crowded rath. Trystan did not like to be bested in music or wit. There would be a nasty edge to this competition, yet as much as Trystan had drunk, his tongue did not slur at all.

"It is strange that you would affect the style of men who defeated the Belgae. But then Belgae courage was ever more sung than seen."

Jesus, did the man want to sing or fight right there? Morlais only cradled the harp in his left arm and rose. "The Belgae at least learned from Rome, as who could not? Many Britons were dragged there in chains, but the Belgae went in honor. The sway of Rome will come again to the Isle of the Mighty."

"So will Christ as I hear," Trystan shot back, "but not this week."

"Rome is eternal. Beyond city or empire, she is an idea, an ideal."

"Rome is an old whore, Morlais, as well you and my royal uncle know. She cannot keep barbarians from her door, so she makes love to them and calls them her own."

"Enough of Rome," Father Glyn called them to order and manners. "We are Britons and you are bards. Who will be first to grace us?"

Morlais bowed slightly to Trystan. "You are the host, my lord. Will you perform first or last?"

"You are my guest," Trystan acceded. "I give you the final place and last word."

We'd all tensed a little at the barbed exchange, but now we sat back and applauded them both. Trystan took up his harp, waiting for absolute silence. His nails plucked a chord of sweetness from the brass strings.

Strange, years ago it was, and though I can remember much of Morlais's song of Neth Dun More, Trystan's lay returns only in snatches of color, the gist of his sad tale. A pity he hadn't prepared well and that he was drunk now. He missed a note here, slurred a passage there. No great matter for I'd heard the song often and knew its story from a Leinster tale much the same, of a woman washing a shroud by a riverbank. She is really the goddess Badb or the Morrigu, and it is the worst luck a soul can find to come upon her then, as the shroud she washes will wind his own corpse within the year.

Trystan's version was wistful and lovelorn. He asks for whom she prepares the shroud.

For your heart, the woman replied,
For she is gone and that heart died.

Throughout the tale, behind Trystan's words, that insistent three-note figure sounded again and again, two notes rising, pause, the third falling. Most of the words I've forgotten but will never forget the ending chord, a sudden jarring sound like a scar across beauty that made Morlais wince, but I'd heard it before. The harp *shrieked.*

But for that nightmare sound, Trystan's performance was satisfying. The man could tear the heart from you, and our applause was no polite lie. He returned his harp to its leathern bag and sat down again as Morlais came forward. In the silence he plucked no sweeping chord but one pure note like a bell.

The tale of Neth Dun More has been sung badly or well over many years. It is loved by all—or most, since Arthur and Bedwyr dismissed it as exaggeration. Bedwyr deemed it a flat lie. Cerdic's raiders landed in two keels, not four. There were no hundred raiders (more as the years went by) but eighty at most. Arthur allowed the poets ought to do the fighting; they made it worlds more colorful. But for a poor *eachra*-man hearing for the first time, the tale was rousing and so grandly performed by Morlais that even now I can recall the best of it.

Three horsemen with courage three times three,
Gereint ap Caradoc, prince of an ancient line,
Artos ap Uther and Bedwyr ap Gryffyn,
Soldiers of Ambrosius, the power of Rome in Britain still.
When glory was done, when in the heathen horde
Nearly all lay dead and three swords ran red,
The heathen limped away to tell their nighted kin
That giants yet stride the Land of the Fair,
Heroes yet live in the Isle of the Mighty,
And they ride with the eagles before them.

As he'd begun, Morlais ended with the same single note shivering away into silence. Only one rapt moment, then all leaped to their feet, shouting and applauding. No question of the winner. Trystan himself surely knew that but sat unmoving in his place. Father Glyn held up his hand for order.

"There is much difficulty in choosing between such harpers. I must cast among the fine points of the art for a just decision. In Morlais's performance I heard not one mistake, while Lord Trystan made several and stumbled badly over his final chord."

"I did not," Trystan denied thickly. "That was the sound I meant."

Now Morlais saw his chance to pay Trystan out for earlier insults. "Have the grace to admit, my lord, that no such sound belongs in music."

Trystan's reddened eyes smoldered. "Does it not, you say?"

"It was discord," Morlais insisted. "My lord's power of invention dwarfs mine, but he must practice more."

A cruel stroke. No one played better than our lord—when sober, alas, and none could deny he'd drunk too much that day. Amid a roar of approval, Father Glyn declared Morlais the winner. Trystan did not even nod to Morlais but called for his cup to be refilled.

"How many does that make?" I whispered to Rhian.

She confessed she'd lost count. "And not a drop of water to take the curse off."

Though we agreed with Glyn's decision, and who did not, loyalty decreed we should say we thought our lord best. I got up and started forward through the press of people. And there's lucky Gareth for you, always presenting his arse for some god to kick.

Morlais was chatting with Father Glyn, leaning with his right hand on the table. As I neared them Trystan was already up and moving toward the harper. I thought he'd remembered his graces and went to congratulate the man. No—half turned away, Morlais couldn't see him coming, couldn't hear my gasped warning, didn't see Trystan raise the heavy stone and smash it down on the splayed right hand.

All saw, all heard. Morlais screamed with pain, reeling back, the fine harper's hand shattered, his eyes already going dull with shock. While the stunned disbelief whispered like a dark wind through the rath, all I could see was an act of shame beyond words. Wound a bard, one near sacred as Druids, near high as a king? Feargus would have a man's head for less, but there crouched Trystan like a killing animal with the mad light on him I'd seen before, Trystan vanished entire and a demon in his place, raising the stone to strike again. No time to think, I went for him like an arrow from the string in a high tackle, crashing him to the floor.

He struggled and raged, clawing for his dagger. "You filthy little bastard, get off me—"

I got off him properly with a right fist swung from the shoulder that slammed into his jaw and cracked! through the rath, sending my lord out of his misery. Stumbling up then, frightened, stunned at what I'd done. I'd never struck my betters before, but years at Feargus's forge had not gone to waste. Trystan didn't move.

I searched helplessly for Rhian, pleading. "Rhian . . . Father Glyn, I—please forgive me, but—"

Glyn laid the balm of his office over my agony. "God will forgive you, man." He stepped to Trystan, stirring feebly now, and kicked the stone out of reach. "And so will he when his sickness passes."

I could have kissed the sainted man for that absolution. Wounded Morlais slumped on his bench. Before bandages could be fetched, one look at the bleeding, broken fingers, bone protruding green-white from two of them, told me the harp by his foot would be silent forever. As much as I learned to love Tryst later, I hated him that day for what he did, but more for the heedless rape of his own soul. He'd put a sword in Mark's hand, set the point at his own breast, and dear Uncle thrust it home.

Trusting Father Glyn's forgiveness more than Trystan's, for three days I tried to be invisible. Would we be banished again, myself beaten or worse? Rhian held me close in the night with what comfort she could give.

"A mad thing to do, but you were right."

As for Trystan, his own shame showed scarlet. He did not appear for meals and rode out before sunrise those days, not returning before all were abed. As for King Mark, he lost no time. Two days after the wounding of Morlais, a rider galloped up our hill, calling for Trystan.

"A letter from his uncle," Rhian told me aside. "I heard from the cooks."

"And?"

"And what?" Rhian hissed, worried sick as myself. "Do you think the man is sending his love?"

Not likely. Me in trouble up to the waist, but Trystan to his neck. When Rhian and I were summoned to the stable where the lord awaited us seated on the mounting block, we thought we were finished sure. Trystan was freshly bathed and shaven, pale but sober. He held a wax tablet of the Roman kind still used for urgent messages in place of expensive parchment. I bowed my head, Rhian dropped a careful curtsey, and we waited for lordly vengeance to break about our doomed heads. The bruise along Trystan's jaw was still livid, but when he smiled at me, I dared hope for mercy.

"Good day, Gareth."

"God bless you, sir."

Trystan chuckled, touching the bluish bruise. "Not so

well as you blessed me. You nearly sent me to the Land of the Young."

"Sir, believe me—"

"No, no, you were right. You saved me from doing worse. I might have killed Morlais."

Rhian piped up in a quaver: "Not my good lord. Never."

"Oh yes. At the time I loved the notion."

I believed him. The demon slept in him now, but I remembered when it waked and burned.

Trystan opened the wax tablet. "My royal uncle disapproves of my temper. So violently that I shall be making amends for Morlais until Mass is heard in hell. He's submitted my name to Prince Cador of Eburacum and commanded me to take service with the Sixth Legion."

He scanned the letter again. "In my absence, which Mark intends to be permanent, not to say mortal, my home and lands will be 'protected' by Castle Dore. Which is to say I am banished."

And all in your rath know it is not because of Morlais but her.

Trystan might have read my thought. "Sometimes I'm not myself. Sometimes I go too far."

So does a wild boar. Rhian volunteered softly, "It does ill service to a good lord."

"I know." Trystan closed the tablet and stood up. "But the hours drag on, drag out, and . . ." He left the thought to die in silence. "I feel old sometimes, but no matter. To business. Other Cornish will be joining me, but Mark thinks it healthier for me to be swiftly gone. Gareth, choose out five or six of my best horses and a sturdy cart. And you, Rhian"—Trystan gazed on her in that way of his, as she said once, that could turn stone virtue to sand—"strong, sensible woman that you are. How the wiser gods must love you. Pack bolts of wool from our stores."

I stammered, "W-We are to go with you, sir?"

"Unless you'd remain here to serve my uncle who hates Irish and doesn't care if you live or die. How could I abandon two lost waifs on a strange shore? Besides, I like a brave man, and I've seen you on a horse: might have been born there. Come with me for a soldier, Gareth."

Trystan clapped me on the shoulder, winked at Rhian and strode to the stable door. "Rhian, take your warmest clothes. It's the wild, windy end of the world we're off to."

He vanished out the door.

Rhian clung to me, needing my arms about her. "Sent off again through no fault of our own. Will that curse follow us ever? Is there no place we can lay our heads for good and call our own? Will we never find peace?"

As if the letter hadn't commanded enough haste, another courier came from Mark next day to inquire just when Trystan would leave. We set out east the following morning to strike the Roman road, Trystan riding, Rhian and I in the cart, horses strung out behind. Once, at the top of a hill, Trystan turned to gaze back at Bard's Tor, which he well might never see again. Driving the cart horses up the hill, I watched the lonely figure at the top. Trystan's head drooped and for a time he remained so, bent over the reins. Then he appeared to see something. His head came up and he dashed away down the other side of the hill and disappeared.

When we topped the rise, I stopped to breathe the cart horses—and saw the two of them. They embraced there in the middle of a field below, their horses nuzzling at each other and grazing. The dark-haired girl in Trystan's arms clung to him as if for life, and when Yseult broke away it was only to arm's length, not able to let go for the last time. So long they stood so that Rhian and I felt like indecent spies. I went to see if the extra horses were properly tethered. When I returned to the cart, the two below us had not moved.

I felt for them the pity of one who's never been so burned, but once again I wondered at that passion and why it had never seared me. "Look at them, Rhian. Do you love me that much, girl?"

She dug an elbow into my side. "Not with that panting fever for sure. How would I ever get my work done? Or you?"

"Poor man."

Time crawled by. At last the two distant figures broke apart, moving backward to their mounts, but with arms still reaching for each other. Finally Trystan tore himself away, heaved into the saddle and rode back toward us. He did not turn his head, but the girl yearned after him as he rode.

Poor man, yes, but still with all his life before him if he'd only grasp it. We were peasants and tougher than him, I guess. If his life was broken like a bone that wanted setting, hadn't ours? If Rhian and I could survive in a new place, couldn't he learn?

Rhian said it. "The good in that man must get past her."

But never could, and all that followed came from that.

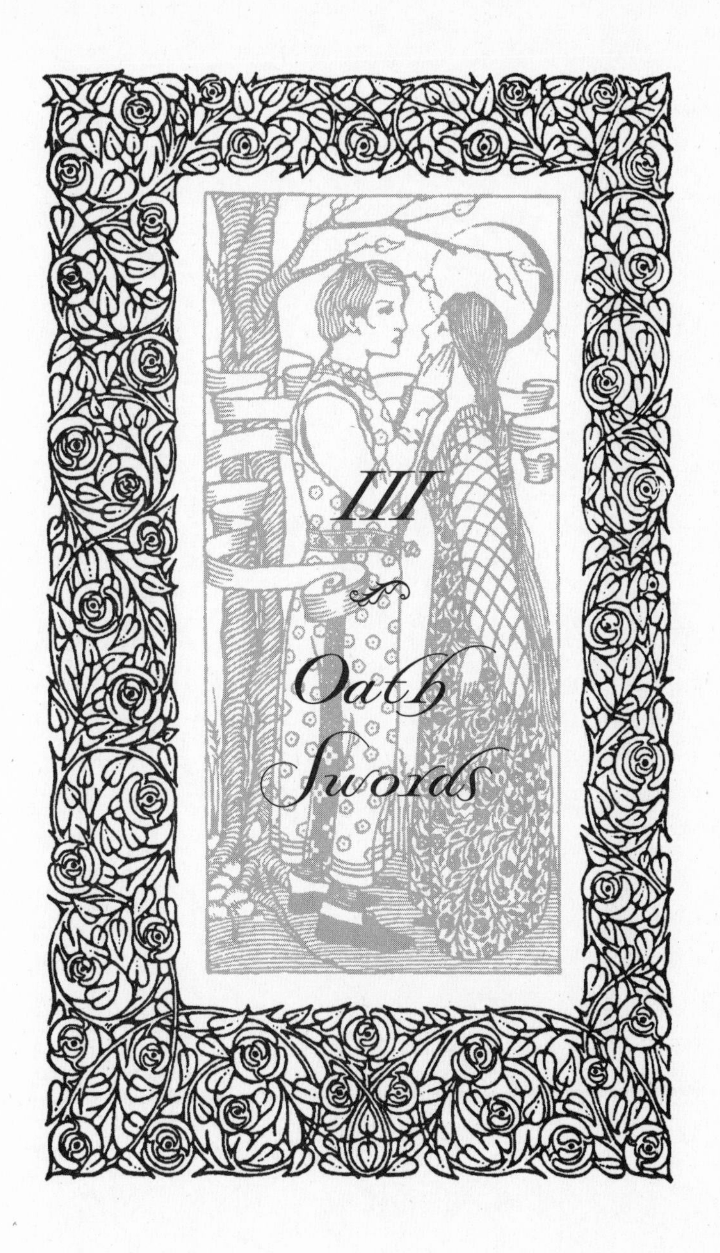

III

Oath Swords

he journey north to Eburacum was a time of wonder and learning for Rhian and me. Eire had no towns or cities, nor any roads beyond cart tracks worn by time. The great road called Foss Way went straight northeast for miles—and such a road! The stamp of Rome was pressed deep into everything: straight lines, square houses, mortared walls, a splendor of building everywhere. If Feargus was awed at the sight of Tara, Eburacum would have struck him dumb, sprawling out on both sides of River Ouse around the old Roman camp, and Prince Cador's fine Roman palace in the midst of it all.

Home and Yseult behind him, Trystan became a newer man with every mile passed, in rising spirits and having a way with words that shortened the miles and might have claimed victory over Morlais without violence. Not a drop passed his lips for weeks.

The Romans, he said, had withdrawn the last of their regular legions over sixty years ago. What passed for such now were no more than local men at arms, loyal to their own lords alone and nigh impossible to move from home.

Britain itself was a patchwork of tribes with no love for each other and little for our emperor Ambrosius, himself only a Brit with a Roman name. A fine soldier, Arthur always said, but fighting and the heavy crown bowed the old man down and killed him at last. All his crowned years he labored like a three-legged sheepdog with a contrary flock, bullying, coaxing, using diplomacy when he could, force when he must. The Saxons were moving west again to take and settle what land they could. Ambrosius could only dash here and there trying to push them back.

"With Cador I hear Ambrosius always uses diplomacy," Trystan said. "As prince he's commander of the Sixth Legion. The Sixth is a joke but all Ambrosius has on the Wall. Across the Wall are the Picts. With none to stop them, they'd raid south half the year, and many do."

Much of this we learned later. Eburacum with its straight lines and crowds of people frightened Rhian, and those markers called milestones. "What sort of men have to measure everything so? You'd think them afeared to lose a hand's span of dirt."

While the cavalry sorted itself out under new commanders, Rhian and I found rooms above a butcher's shop. I was surprised and badly disappointed to learn I was not to join Trystan; he'd recommended me elsewhere.

"But I am *your* servant, my lord."

"Not anymore. Do you have enough money?"

"Yes. No fear while Rhian's managing. If she'd been given a coin at birth, she'd still have it."

"Let me know if you do." Trystan looked about as we stood in the butcher's doorway. "Five squadrons, and the truth is, the lot of us are an unholy bollocks. Motley men, motley gear, officers who are sure only of their noble blood.

I'm hardly a soldier myself, but Prince Peredur lacks even my small talent."

"That would be Prince Cador's son, sir?"

"Who spends more time in church than the saddle." Trystan broke off as three women bustled out of the shop to barge through us, complaining of prices. "To put it plainly, Gareth, Peredur wants to be a priest and should have been. As a cavalry officer he knows not his arse from his elbow. He desperately needs experienced horse handlers. I've submitted your name. Report to his *tesserarius* at the palace. Name of Aulus Silvio."

Trystan just then seemed lost as I felt, but all unknowing he'd pointed me toward the life I was born for. "My lord—"

He stopped me, and I saw the warmth of the man shine through. "Just centurion, Gareth. And between us alone, just Trystan."

"Och, you'll always be a lord."

"Indeed?" He gestured at his gear, mixed as mine: linen tunic, worn breeches, plain oxhide breastplate. "You see where it's got me. No more lording."

I gave him the new salute I'd learned, fist slammed into my shoulder then arm out straight. Trystan returned it. "Very good, *Mulus*."

"What's a *mulus?*"

"Legion slang for a soldier. Go along now."

Damned if I didn't feel like a soldier new made as I set out smartly to find a tesser-somebody at the palace. Feargus would not have dreamed—oh ho, in the way of dreams, when I became centurion of the Third Squadron and later lord-comite, I sometimes imagined the jaw-dropping astonishment on the *bo aire*'s red face if Lord Gareth strode grandly through his gate of welcomes with Lady Rhian on his arm. That vanity faded as the years went by, but dreams? For a cautious man I had not the ghost of a hint what God or Dagda had in store for me.

Peredur's squadron rode north to take up permanent station at Corstopitum. I had to leave Rhian behind.

Our small camp lay on Dere Street, the Roman road running north out of Eburacum. It was also a collection point for all cavalry supplies sent from the city. Peredur was our centurion, Aulus Silvio his second in command. Both were disasters.

When I first laid eye to Peredur I saw a slender, long-haired man of my own age who looked far too delicate for any service. He was—well, Christlike, as if one ear marked you while the other listened to God alone. He spent more time in Eburacum at Mass than he did in camp, leaving command to Aulus and his clerks. Peredur was the living opposite of worldly Trystan but burned with the same love sickness for God and the Church. That fire ate his life away from within, but at least Peredur embraced his love at the end. He took a wound at Eburacum that never properly healed; that and finding the Holy Grail killed him. A different love but the same consuming passion that devoured Trystan. Many years I took to know the heart and meaning of that. The loving, not the loved, the pure strength of passion like strong drink coursing through a man's blood. But I couldn't learn all that at once, an ignorant *eachra*-man bred to stable and saddle and earth, now living among rough soldiers and badly kept horses in a square-walled Roman place of wind and dust so bare and raw I wouldn't have Rhian live there even were it possible.

Food was bad, and pay, like a two-headed sheep, something we heard about but never saw. Supply was a problem from the first, not serious to us at Corstopitum, yet somehow what reached the other squadrons was always less than tallied in the schedule. These supplies were furnished by the families of the squadron commanders, all distant except for Peredur's father, Prince Cador. Trystan's came from Castle Dore (really from Queen Yseult), Arthur's from his half brother Prince Kay of the Dobhunni.

Of all our officers, there was no centurion so squared off and iron-arsed as Arthur Pendragon. In truth, before he disappeared north of the Wall, the man could be hard to swallow as raw thistle. He was of the *regular* legions, by God, nephew to Ambrosius, by God, and if born on the wrong side of his father's blanket and barely a lord, he and his tesser Bedwyr ap Gryffyn were the best cavalrymen in the sorry Sixth *Alae.* I remember the day Arthur galloped into Corstopitum to take large chunks out of Peredur about supplies that never reached him, but Peredur was gone as usual to walk on water with Jesus, so the storm broke over poor, fat little Aulus. Arthur thundered in, brushing past me into headquarters. A shock chilled through me as our eyes briefly met. The same grey eyes as the Sidhe boy and his mother who cursed me—so alike I'd swear they could be related. Arthur was a large, fair-haired Dobhunni, but as it later fell out to the trouble and sorrow of more than one soul, his blood was half Faerie through his mother Ygerna. I've since seen other Faerie in Pictland. Almost all have the same eyes and coloring, the same narrow heads and high cheekbones marked with woad-dyed scars to mark their family group. Rarely marrying "tallfolk," it's hardly strange they'd preserve that look like horses never cross-bred with another strain.

Just outside the tesser's door I heard what Arthur had to say. All of Corstopitum must have heard him, and possibly Castle Dore, heaven-rending as it was. Did I say Etain had a tongue? Arthur's wrath could melt rock.

"What in Christly hell is wrong, Aulus? Do I have to go to Ambrosius to get anything done at all? He's my uncle, you know, and I will if I have to. Kay said he sent all I asked for, but much is missing. Bedwyr was arrow-shot on our last patrol, and my goddamned infirmary didn't even have enough bandage for him. Jesu-Mithras, I wish I were trib over this miserable command for one rutting day, just one. I'd break your *backs!*"

We had no proper tribune then, just a few army clerks sending Cador's orders from Eburacum. When Ambrosius found out, he raised Arthur to tribune. That was the saving of the Sixth and the end of Aulus Silvio. Arthur discovered the tesser had been falsifying reports and selling supplies wherever he could, even across the Wall among the Pict tribes. Our new tribune was good as his threat, dealing with the greedy little man without mercy. The tesser was stripped of his rank and made to stand outside the camp walls for a full day and cold night. Next morning he was flogged through the assembled squadron to the gates which were then forever shut on him.

I became tesser through others' misfortune. Tribune Pendragon went missing in the north. After a month he was presumed dead. Peredur became acting tribune, neglecting the squadron even more, but on a day that came, he suddenly decided to drill us in parade formations. The squadron wheeled right with no difficulty, but in left wheel the same four horses fought the rein and broke formation. For once, saintly Peredur lost his temper, trotting his horse up and down the confused line of us, tearing a proper strip off the four erring riders.

"Why do you have trouble with a drill you did perfectly last week? How could you forget so quickly? Do I command idiots? What is the reason for this?"

No one spoke up, but I had a notion. "The mouth, Tribune."

"What's that? Who spoke?"

I walked my horse out of line to face him. "Mouth and bit, sir. Very common it is. With your permission. You four men look at your horses' mouths on the right side."

As I thought, all four had raw-rubbed bit sores just there and would need attention. Peredur beckoned me to him. "You, *Mulus*. How did you know?"

"As I said, sir, it is common. You see—"

"Louder. Tell the men."

And I did that. A horse with a sore mouth will favor that side against the rein, no matter how well trained or kindly treated. Another mistake was how most men regarded their mounts.

"You mustn't think of your horse as you would a good dog. The dog is much smarter. Your dog likes you. A horse hasn't the brains to like anything but eating, sleeping, and surviving. Always remember you ride a dumb brute, one that can be trained but may well panic and bolt any time he sees or smells or hears something to fright the training out of him. If he trusts anything, it is the herd. Teach him to trust you instead."

Peredur brightened with recognition. "Mac Diarmuid is it? Yes, Lord Trystan told me of you. Glad to have someone out here who knows what he's about. Report to my headquarters."

So I became the hardest working tesser in the entire legion. I had to be everywhere every day, but the routines of feeding and exercise, stalls mucked out and changed, were properly done or I would know why not. We had good horses, mostly the southwestern breed raised and broken for us by Prince Kay. Well gaited, they were fast at the gallop and could hold a steady trot all day on patrol.

Arthur introduced heavier lances and longer swords for fighting from the saddle. One God-sent improvement came to me with Ancellius, a young Gaulish boyo whose name most men couldn't pronounce; they called him simply "Ancelud" or Lancelot. From his service in eastern Gaul against the Huns and with Sarmatian auxiliaries, he'd taken the idea of the stirrup, which braced a rider far better in the saddle than just hugging the horse with his knees. The day of the foot legion was past. With most of them refusing to leave their homes, Ambrosius needed a mounted force able to dash quickly across Britain to anywhere needed. A rumor grew that he would be dispensing with the Roman kind of legion altogether.

"I could have told him that for a start," Trystan said. "Outmoded, dead as Rome herself. It took years to train a legion, and Arthur can't do it with a bag of lordlings and what-all like us."

Nevertheless, there was my own growing confidence, Sidhe-cursed or no, like a foot easing into a perfect shoe, that I'd come to the life I was made for, if one neither I nor Rhian would have dared to dream at home. When I became centurion of the Third, she was dazed at first—

"It is a *ghillie* I am married to!"

—but still a lifetime of thrift would not let her spend one *solidus* more than needed, waste one scrap of cloth or bite of food. I believe she took years off the poor butcher's life haggling the price of mutton. When I bought her a set of fine ivory combs, Rhian would not wear them at first for fear the high lords would snatch my rank away and she would have to return them for the purchase price.

"Peredur won't break me, *Acushla.* He'd have to leave off praying and do it all himself then."

"You never know," said my Rhian, unconvinced as she wrapped the combs and snugged them away in a chest.

Many of the men under me considered themselves high-born and resented taking orders from the "little Irish bastard." Gradually, as time passed, as we shared the dangers of patrol and finally saw action, differences wore away.

Time drags us forward like a man tied behind a running horse. Changes were swooping down on us to turn our lives and all of Britain from an abandoned Roman province into something new. Changes and miracles.

One miracle was Arthur himself, and by another he came back to us, back from wild Pictland, dashing into Corstopitum to warn of Picts and Saxons, a fleet of them, heading for River Humber and Eburacum. No time to say where he'd been for months, just ready the squadrons and ride, ride for the city. With Arthur at our head, we galloped south on Dere Street to raise Eburacum before Cerdic's raiders arrived.

Daring man, Cerdic of the West Saxons. Arthur defeated him at Neth Dun More. Now he tried again with a larger force, thinking the *alae* could never reach Eburacum in time. I said we had years of fighting in Arthur's time and after. Saxons are not ui Chellaig, not for the quick cattle raid, but land. Pushed out of their own homes oversea, they needed new or they and the families brought with them would perish. They kept coming, led by men like Cerdic, but that day at Eburacum luck ran with us because we were swift and Cerdic delayed.

As we swept through Monk Gate, horns and bells announced us to all the city. The citizens poured out to line the narrow streets, looking for sons, lovers, or husbands. I caught the tall sight of Rhian tearing her way through the crowd—

"Gareth, husband!"

—to clutch at my leg and hurry along beside my horse.

"*Dia dhuit,* love. Tired as I am, you are a dear sight."

"What is happening?"

"Glorious and black both. The tribune's back but there's going to be a battle here."

Rhian only held on to me harder. "When can you come home?"

I bent to kiss her hand. "I don't know. God forbid they get here before we've fresh horses. Hot up some soup and a bath for me, there's a love. I'll try to come soon."

We had a day and a night of uneasy rest and hurried preparation. They landed at dawn of the second day. Arthur has spoken of this battle, more bards sung of it than I can count, and all better than I can. Cerdic's raiders tried to burn the city as a diversion, drawing us away from the bank of River Ouse, but we discovered their plan in time and reformed, lances ready as Saxons and Picts poured off their boats.

Arthur led our charge, Bedwyr's squadron and mine first behind him. We hit them hard, gave them no chance to form their shield wall. You forget time in battle. Hours become minutes, minutes hours. Memory is no flowing stream but frozen pictures. Bloodred morning in the eastern sky, redder on the banks and in the river shallows where so many of Cerdic's men never reached the safety of their boats. You remember your lance striking home, a yellow-bearded face dodging under your horse's belly, the animal's high scream as it goes down hamstrung, and yourself struggling to get free of its weight too late, far too late. You know then what death looks and feels like, because you'll never get your leg free before those other running legs are on you.

And then the last vivid sight and sound, a whirlwind of horse and man scattering those legs, milling around and through them, a cursing grand as I ever heard, the pure white rage of a wrathful god. I looked up through sweat and fear to see Trystan's sword rising and falling and Saxons going down before him just as I twisted free.

"Up, Gareth!" he cried. "Stirrup!"

One foot in the stirrup, hanging on to Tryst, I was swept out of the battle to safety, Trystan calling for another horse for me, any damned animal from anywhere, and me shaking, praying and cursing wildly and close to tears as I'd been to death.

We broke them that morning by Ouse bank, but Cerdic would come again. The sun rose higher over men stumbling alone or leading wounded horses along the bank back toward the city gate. A man close in front of me tore off his helmet to scratch at red hair, and I recognized Bedwyr ap Gryffyn.

"Bedwyr, you hurt? Where's your mount?"

His blue Belgae eyes were already closing with exhaustion. "Where d'you think? They rutting love to gut good horses, don't they?"

"They do that, the godless bastards. Where's Tryst?"

"He's down," Bedwyr said.

"Jesus, no. I need to thank the man to his face, not pray over him."

"Saw him being carried. Try the hospital."

We trickled back into Eburacum like slow blood from a wound. The hospital lay along the Via Principalis of the old legion fort, not far from the palace. Built a hundred years past, the place was one square inside another with a corridor between, every bed filled with men, more lying in the walkways waiting to be treated. I found Trystan in the outer ward where the orderlies attended those not seriously hurt. Praise to God because no one wanted to see or hear that inner ward where surgeons were saving only what lives they could. Those past help screamed their lives away over the urgent muttering of priests hurrying through last rites while men could still use them.

Trystan had a cot between two men with leg and shoulder wounds. He lay on his stomach covered to the waist with a blanket, greeting me with a painful grimace he tried to shape to a smile. "Gareth, friend, could I not have been a hero at least once?"

I gripped his arm with vigorous gratitude. "You are that to me from this day on; if you were not, I'd be dead."

"My horse was of another mind. Pray lift the blanket."

There on his rump spread the largest and most colorful bruise in God's world. At its center was stamped the rounded outline of an iron horseshoe. "Oh my, Tryst. That's impressive."

He craned over his shoulder to inspect his prize. "Behold my laurel of valor. Have you ever seen such color, such variety of shading? Red and purple, and that bit there going black."

"And a lovely blue about the edges."

Trystan chuckled sourly. "Perverse, Gareth! In the thick of battle, the very heart of martial drama, the gods cast me in farce. Kicked by my own horse."

"Not funny, damn it! I thought you grievous hurt."

"No, I shall rise and get on with absurdity as soon as the orderly's seen to me. They'll be needing the bed. But days like this I sense my guardian gods are simply not at home."

"Gareth!"

I turned to see Rhian descending on us, fear and relief alike naked in her face. I just had time to throw the blanket over Trystan's shame before she hurled herself into my arms.

"You're not hurt. Tell me you're not. Someone said you were here, and I thought—"

"Not a scratch, girl, and be thanking Lord Trystan for that. He saved my life when I was down and the Saxons all about me. You should have seen him, and he putting the Morrigu to shame for dealing death."

"Oh—*God*!" In a welter of relief, Rhian swooped down on our prostrate friend, hugging, kissing, and thanking him over and over until she remembered he was wounded himself. "Poor dear man, where did you have your hurt?"

"Nothing to speak of," Trystan assured her gallantly. "Really, I'd prefer not to speak of it." He searched our faces with a new wistfulness. "You two. So fortunate. Why could I not have found what you did, Gareth? A good woman like Rhian? A man could starve for simplicity."

"My lord would not find that hard did he put his mind to it," Rhian vowed. "And you must come sup with us soon as you can. You know our rooms above the butcher's."

Some of the old habits and differences yet clung to me. I thought the invitation too bold and out of place, Trystan being our own lord once. But he surprised me then. The old elegant distance vanished, and he was just a friend and a lonely one, glad to have someplace to go, glad not to be alone.

"May I?" He brightened. "I would like that very much."

In later years when Arthur called me a "genius" of cavalry, I had to ask Trystan for the meaning; I thought the king was being critical. No, Arthur was our genius, but between the stiff young tribune "lost" in Pictland and the beautifully human man who returned to lead us against Cerdic lay a vast ocean of difference. He'd found something north of the Wall, perhaps a piece of himself. He also found Morgana, though years before any of us knew the whole, tangled tale. You could well ask: Does hatred wreak more damage on a life than the wrong love at the wrong time? Arthur loved Morgana of the Faerie, and all that got him was a death named Modred.

Trystan looked up to Arthur as an older brother, the only man who could bully, laugh, or shame the whisky thirst out of him for any length of time. One autumn day both he and I came to revere the man who would soon become our next emperor, and Trystan had his first sight of what he'd lightly taken for superstition: one of the Good People.

Picts of the Venicone tribe had slipped south into Cador's territory, looting and burning two villages. At the prince's command, Arthur ordered a show of strength near the Venicone settlement of Camlann. Trystan and I were ordered to join our tribune with sixty riders from each squadron. Whether or not the raiders came from Camlann itself, the village was made an example. We thundered through, torching a few *clochans,* scattering sheep, cattle, and horses, terrifying the Picts. Then we rode two slow circles about the place as the smoke rose up, before turning east toward the Wall crossing and home.

Long before we reached the crossing, a cold rain drenched us without cease. Arthur gave the order to dismount, knowing as I did that men can endure much more than horses. We mucked along on foot for several miles, Arthur, Trystan, and myself in the lead. Two dangerous truths worried at me. Clouds hung low over the hilltops, and Picts were masters at ambush out of nowhere. I volunteered to scout ahead, but Arthur seemed to know this country well.

"That ring of stones up there." He pointed ahead as our strung-out column skirted the base of the hill. "This is *Cnoch-nan-ainneal,* the hill of the fires. There's a Prydn rath and crannog just down the other slope. No Venicone will come near it."

I'd never heard of Picts by that name. "Prydn, sir?"

Arthur clapped me on the back, squelching rain from my cloak. "Faerie, lad."

The old fear twisted my stomach in a sudden cold grip, but Trystan was fascinated. "Honestly now? I thought they didn't exist."

Arthur strode on, eyes fixed on the ring of ancient stones above, their tops blurred by wisps of low cloud. "They exist."

I turned to Trystan. "Did I not tell—" The question froze in my mouth. Far above us part of one of the great stones had become a small human figure. "Tribune, there!"

"I see her," Arthur answered calmly. He stared up at

the figure, signaling the column to halt. "Pwyll, close it up back there! You're straggling." He hardly seemed surprised at the sudden appearance. Indeed, he waved in recognition.

"I'm intrigued," Trystan mused. "Is that one of them?"

I couldn't shake the old fear of those who had cursed me. "Tribune, take care. Such creatures mean us no good ever."

Arthur's gaze remained fixed on that still figure above. They seemed to pass understanding between them with silence alone.

He wheeled about to call his order to our company: Remain in place. He waved Trystan and I to lead our horses up the slope after him—and that I obeyed only under orders, praying in my heart, while Trystan was eager to see this creature at closer hand.

"If she's magical, she certainly doesn't look it."

"Be still," I hissed as we followed behind Arthur. "For once don't be so shaggin' clever."

The rain came down hard, driven by an east wind. When we reached the top, the tiny woman backed warily toward the center of the ring of great stones. Arthur bade us stay where we were. "She trusts me, but she's not sure of you. You're tallfolk."

No fear; I had no desire to go closer—and yet the forlorn sight of her mixed Sidhe-terror with something else I'd felt standing over the dying boy Declan. Young as him this one was, bareheaded and with no cloak against the rain. A torn and shapeless woolen kirtle, oceans too large, clung wetly to her thin body, its frayed hem dragging in the mud at her feet. The garment must have been discarded by or stolen from some Venicone woman. The girl clutched a bundle to her chest, wrapped in raw sheepskin. Only when it moved slightly could I glimpse the top of a dark little head. Her narrow cheeks were marked, as Arthur's, with woad-dyed scars. Lips blue with cold, but pride in her bearing, she stood erect and still as the great stones about her as Arthur approached.

Trystan nudged me. "Gareth, what in hell is he doing?"

I didn't want to know, only to be gone from her presence and that other world I feared, but what Arthur did then spoke with eloquence in a tongue I'd yet to learn. Tribune Arthur Pendragon, snapped-to and squared-off down to his toes, went on his knees in the mud before the Faerie woman and put his palms to her belly. Rising, he undid his heavy cloak and draped it about her. She wrapped the child in it against her breast.

Under the wind and rain, we couldn't hear the few words they passed, but when Arthur returned to us he was deep in a mood heavy as the offered cloak. "Both of you break out half your bread and salt meat. Quick now, hop it."

From his tone, neither Tryst nor I felt inclined to argue, and the food was little enough to ask if it got me shut of her. Arthur collected the rations, bundled them with the same from his own, and took them to the woman. She gave him only a slight nod and glided away to disappear down the other side of the hill. As Arthur walked back to his horse, Trystan began to undo his own cloak. "Here, Tribune. Take mine."

"No." Arthur dropped his head against the horse's withers. "No, Trystan. Thank you."

"But really, you were too generous—"

"Leave *off*, can't you? Just . . . leave off."

"As you wish, sir. So that is one of the Faerie."

"Prydn." Arthur's eyes were far away, perhaps in that different world the woman had somehow brought with her.

"She is *gern-y-fhain,* the leader of her family. They are hungry and her child is ill. If winter is hard, it may not live. She asked only a little food."

"I fail to see the magic," Trystan allowed. "Sorry little beggar."

For a moment I thought Arthur would strike the man. "It's past sorry. They're dying. Picts hate and fear them. They've been driven out everywhere, no land of their own. They move their sheep from one pasture to the next, hoping the grass will be enough for one more year, hoping the Venicone or Taixali or Votadini will leave them in peace. It is long past sorry, man."

Trystan looked past the standing stones where the woman had vanished. "Just that she looked so . . . My old nurse used to spin tales of how they stole babes from cradles, especially little boys who didn't behave."

Arthur shook his head, gathering up the dangling reins. "More often they put their own in tallfolk cradles so they won't starve. Pray you and yours are never that hungry. That desperate. Let's go."

So helpless under his anger, with the new-cut scars on his own cheeks. I would never ask about them; that much of Arthur I understood that day. The man's anguish was like a keening.

As we followed him down the slope I muttered to Trystan, "Do you believe in Faerie now, you godless man? You've seen one."

"I have." He kept his sight on Arthur ahead of us. "I've seen a man as well."

They're dying like the Sidhe in Eire. Perhaps the curse would fade and die with them. Even Trystan felt for the sight and plight of her. Poor little beggar. To this day I must struggle through the ages of fear to the clear question: Were they truly Dagda's children, given magic in the morning of the world? Or just pathetic remnants? Or a bit of both? Arthur said little, but now, in my age, I know it is a sad thing to watch any true part of the world die.

But was it Trystan I called a fool? If the fools of creation coined money, they would stamp on it large not Caesar's face but mine.

When Ambrosius came to Eburacum that winter, we could see the old man had not much web left to spin. He was carried in a litter after being wounded against Saxons in the Midlands. This time Cerdic or someone like him had won because the emperor's cavalry were too few and the Catavellauni troops reached him too late. Refugees from the overrun Midlands were pouring into western provinces. If the Faerie were dying, so was Britain. The rumors of change were true, then, had to be. All we knew was that Arthur and his centurions were summoned to wait on the old emperor.

Ambrosius received us in private. He did not stand; I don't think he could. The rich purple gown he wore had fresh, darker stains on it where the wound in his side would not close, but his voice did not falter as he changed our lives forever.

"My lords, officers, forgive me if I do not return your salute as a soldier should. This last campaign has made it clear we can no longer depend on local troops, if one can call them that. Nor does our imperium any longer have the resources to equip you as regular *alae*."

No shattering news to Brits who never felt Roman at all beyond the names on some of them, and none of us had received the promised pay. Poor as church mice, if there'd been moneylenders among those wee creatures, we'd be begging a loan.

"Yet we cannot think ourselves poor while we have spirit and Artorius Pendragon," Ambrosius went on. "Tribune, you will ready all your cavalry to assemble in the palace hall tomorrow at noon."

He dismissed us all but Arthur, who later called us together again in his palace quarters: myself, Trystan, Bedwyr, the Orkney princes Gawain and Agrivaine. Ambrosius intended to detach us altogether from Cador's legion. He needed a mobile force loyal to its commander and the emperor alone. We were the only large, trained cavalry group in Britain and could no longer be tied to one local prince. Naturally, Cador was to know nothing until the deed was done. Arthur would command; he knew nothing more.

Always a contentious and spiteful little manny, Prince Agrivaine protested. "I will not serve under you, Pendragon. I hold the gold laurel of valor as you and higher blood beside."

"Then keep it well," Arthur advised. "It's my guess that's the last of Rome you'll ever hold."

The last indeed. Next day in the palace hall, Ambrosius tore in half the muster roll of the Sixth *Alae.* He then created Arthur Count of Britain and called each of us to be voluntarily sworn as his men. All but Agrivaine accepted. Each of us of whatever birth or condition swore his fealty by God or his gods and received his sword back from our new count, and with it the title of lord-comite, equal in rank to all his brothers in arms, loyal to a dying emperor and a Britain that somehow must live. As I knelt to Arthur, swore by Holy Church and took my sword from his hands, I wished my father Diarmuid could have lived to warm his heart at such a sight. Bedwyr might have wished the same, the son of a horse handler himself. I will never forget that moment. When Arthur offered my sword, he said, "Rise, Lord Gareth."

Lord Gareth. The sound stunned my hearing, but Rhian fair flamed with the notion of being henceforth addressed as "Lady."

"Now," she flourished grandly, throwing open her chest to retrieve the ivory combs untouched till that hour. "Now you can be placing them in my hair, my lord. But slowly, slowly." She glowed. "As if it were a crown you set on my head, for that is how it feels."

Gently I secured the combs in her hair. "Well, girl?"

Rhian pushed me backward onto our bed and fell on me with gleeful kisses. "Did you *ever,* now? Truly now, at home could we ever— Gareth? What is a lord-comite?"

I had to search our own language for its like. "A sort of *echmilidh,* you might say. A horse lord. With no more than the horse we ride, most of us."

"Need you remind me? We still owe the butcher." Then Rhian smiled again with the dawning of a new prospect. "Can you guess what it is I want more than all else?"

"A child, love?"

"For sure, but as much as that"—with a fierce light to her eye—"I want Feargus, that shameful man, and all his great *ghillies* like Cerball and Garbhan, to see how my husband has risen higher than any in that footling little rath. And that woman of the Sidhe who blighted our lives only to bless them. When can you ask leave of Arthur?"

I couldn't tell. We would be preparing to campaign as soon as weather allowed.

"But I want to go back, Gareth. I want to *show* them."

Did you, Rhian? By then Feargus and Eire were no part of us as time went on ungently shaping our lives.

So the *Combrogi* were born, and the tales spun of us went leagues beyond the wildest sung in Feargus's little rath. The word *combrogus* comes from the bastard Latin which was all of that tongue most Britons could remember. It means "one of us" or "companion." To Britons the word became salvation and a legend. To Saxons carving our stolen Midlands to please themselves, the name became as cursed and feared as Faerie.

The next summer Arthur led us into the Midlands to win back for the Catuvellauni those miles of rich land overrun. We thought we'd been blooded at Eburacum, but that was only a few brutal hours. The horror of the Midlands stretched on for weeks, and ourselves brought it. Some was honest battle; for the rest, we burned their houses and crops, tore the Saxon by his roots out of our land. A dirty task done without pride, but Ambrosius's orders were clear. We killed the men and then their women and children. . . .

I am not a man for drinking deep, but there were times after that summer when Rhian came to know the silence in me and Trystan. On nights when the three of us shared supper, our cheerful talk would falter into long silences. Tryst's fingers would fidget and drum on the board, while I found it impossible to sit still and would whisper to Rhian: "*Uiscebeatha.*"

Without a word she would place the jug of whisky on the board, leave us to it, and I would match Trystan cup for cup until we were numb enough to speak without pain what we must. What haunted us.

"Jesus," I beseeched heaven, "is there an earthly word for what we have done?"

"Latin," Trystan slurred. "The word is genocide."

Saxons came to call that summer the Time of the Smoke. It rose black and stinking in our wake, fouling the air we breathed and the clothes we wore. There were few islands of mercy in that red sea. And all for nothing. The sons of those we scoured out came back and will keep coming. What dreams I sweated through before our servant woman Dilys scrubbed the last grime and stink from my breeches and tunics—well, that is between God and me. The dreams faded. I got past the memories. Trystan never did.

Want to go for a soldier, Gareth?

How lightly he tossed out the question long ago. No man more loving to a friend nor more loyal to Arthur, none more frail. What a gay courage, mind bright as the sun. How the man glowed when his imagination caught fire from something he could learn—or with a darker flame when *she* or the Midlands would not go from his mind. Trystan kept horror at bay with laughter, heartbreak with drink. No matter what joy the man found in the world, drew from his harp, or reaped in the countless beds of self-offering women; however purely his soul could conjure the best of heaven, such moments were always shadowed with hell. He couldn't change. He could not accept that life is as it is or master his own wild heart.

There are cleaner memories. Ambrosius's last will named Arthur to succeed him on our throne. Few of the tribal princes supported him. More than one, including dear Marcus Conomori, tried to kill him, but Arthur outwitted them all to reach the place of the choosing, bloodied but a champion. I was there that day with Trystan, Bedwyr, and

Lancelot, when Arthur drew the imperial sword from the piled stones as all the folk knelt in homage. I was there when Cador submitted and gave our young king his daughter Guenevere in marriage; there when Arthur built his new seat of power on the banks of River Severn: Nova Camulodunum, which we always called Camelot. Rhian and I had a stone house and servant woman to ourselves within the walls, and it was good to come home of a night, stretch my legs to the fire, savor the contentment in Rhian and the sweet fruits of hard-won peace. Up Severn sailed the rich trade of the Middle Sea: Egypt, Antioch, Damascus, and the Afric shores. There even came letters from Rome offering to protect our shipping with their galleys (and perhaps a legion or two along our coasts). Ho-ho-*ho.* Arthur and Britain declined with thanks.

Ten years flowed away like the lilting of Trystan's harp. Rhian and I no longer thought in Irish or of going home at all. At least once a week all the *Combrogi* gathered in Arthur's hall, tables drawn in a circle, to feast while Trystan played and sang.

There were a number of harpers among us, music being just another word for a Celt, but none so gifted. Lord Pwyll ap Evan of the Dubhunni had more zeal than feel for the harp and envied Trystan's skill. Both were pagans but there the likeness ended. Pwyll envied alike Trystan's easy success with women, and small wonder. Where love was concerned, he was no sensitive soul—

"Sensitive?" Rhian hooted. "In the matter of women, he is no more than a goat."

—but to me and Trystan merely a trying bore who talked of little else but his conquests in those green fields. I believe Pwyll valued the oath-sword at his side far less than the one between his legs, and a pity because that was the death of the man.

Peace we had but always Cerdic as well, his swift keels prowling off our shores, darting in to raid, feeling for weakness in our defenses, especially on the Cornish coasts where Mark had neglected them. Arthur saw the need for reoccupying abandoned hillforts there and building new ones. At the next gathering of his council, he planned to argue or cajole them out of that suspicious, dark-minded prince.

A state visit by Mark and Yseult was ever a delicate matter for Arthur and Guenevere. Knowing Trystan's history with the woman, they always contrived to pack him off on royal business elsewhere when Yseult came to court. They had not set eyes on each other since parting in that Cornish meadow ten years gone, but this year Tryst's gods were with him—or against, if you will. Mark's ship was delayed, Trystan returned, they must be kept apart, and few in Camelot who didn't shake heads or smack their lips in gossiping speculation. And just who was it our clever king chose to attend Yseult while her husband sat in council?

"You?" The news flat outraged my Rhian. "That shameful woman on my husband's arm?"

"There's some would consider it an honor."

"Ha! Like Pwyll?"

"A little charity, love."

"Fich!"

"She'll be eased to speak her own tongue again."

"No doubt," Rhian grumbled. "At least Arthur chose a man who will cause him no trouble."

Speak of compliments with a sting. I was no wooing bard like Trystan, nor a Pwyll with his brain in his breeches, but no man wants to be thought entirely harmless. Now a lady-in-waiting to Guenevere, Rhian could voice no objections to the royal choice, though she need not have worried. When Yseult stepped off the ship on Mark's arm, she who was sung as the most dangerously wanton woman in Britain touched me far less with her glamour than an air she wore like a cloak, not so much of sadness as of someone faded. But she smiled with pleasure to hear the Irish greeting.

"Ban Rion, cead mille failte."

"Dia dhuit, Ghillie, agus go rabh maith agut."

Yseult could not have seen more than twenty-seven years, while Mark was well over fifty, a tall and fleshless man with sunken cheeks and hooded eyes that missed nothing. He was already on about the requested hillforts with Arthur, not seeing their necessity, only the expense to himself. . . .

As we rode or strolled about Camelot, I had time to take the measure of Yseult. No longer a girl, already inclining to flesh, and over all not so much sadness as a drab lack of happiness. Some of her luster shone in talking with me, nattering on of home and singing old Leinster songs. Beneath the coronet I came to know a very ordinary soul without Guenevere's learning or charm or even the tart liveliness of Rhian, and terribly alone in the life thrust on her. She rose to gaiety with an effort, only to sink again into that state neither happy nor unhappy, merely blank. Yseult reminded me of a dry, black candlewick when the flame's been snuffed. Rhian need lose no sleep, though curiosity nigh ate her up.

"And what does she talk about?" she plied as we put out the rush light and settled in bed.

"Of home mostly; how she would love to see a hurley game again."

"And of Trystan?"

"Not a word, nor am I the one to speak first." I slid my arm under Rhian's head as she nestled into my shoulder. "I must attend her early. Go to sleep."

To the frustration of Arthur and Guenevere, neither did Mark's wife speak of any state matters. I'd been told to remember anything of that nature that might pass her lips, but there I sifted dry soil. It appeared Mark confided nothing to Yseult, nor did she inquire, plainly uninterested. My escort duty began to wilt about the edges with polite tedium. Day by day the council dragged on, day by day Bedwyr, attending Arthur as his standard-bearer, gave me the snail's pace of its progress. Mark was being stubborn.

"Damned old man's blind, Gareth. The need for those forts's plain as blood on white linen, but no-o. The man won't see. If Arthur's to win him over, he'll need prayer and a miracle."

"Where's Tryst, then?"

Bedwyr's look well understood me. "Artos keeps him busy. And her?"

"She keeps me busy."

Bedwyr leered wickedly. "What would that mean now?"

"Ah—get stuffed, you horrible man."

On a day when I was showing Yseult through Guenevere's enclosed garden, she broke silence about her lover, and in a way that surprised and schooled me. Yseult sank down on a stone bench as if body and soul sagged alike. I asked if she'd been taken ill.

"No," she said after a pause. "How is he, Gareth?"

"Who, my lady?"

"You know. They say you are close to him. Where is he?"

"Oh. Well. The king has many duties for him this week."

Disappointment I sensed in her but relief as well. "That is best for him. He needs to be occupied always."

Yseult sat, silent, hands in the lap of her green kirtle or fidgeting with the gold pendant at her breast. "Once my husband told me he'd been lost or killed among the *Sassenach.*"

"Not a bit of it, *Ban Rion.* He was off among the heathen, true, playing his fine harp for their undeserving ears—and learning of their ways for Arthur's benefit."

She remained with downcast eyes while I studied that fabled face. Her beauty came from high coloring and pure evenness of feature, and yet not an interesting face but the living proof of Arthur's saying that there was nothing so dull in worlds or women as perfection. Such a thought would have been beyond me ten years ago. Had I changed or grown so much?

"Then you know Trystan well, my lord?"

"Too well some days, not enough on others. I was only *eachra*-man to a cattle lord before I went to Bard's Tor as a servant. Tryst is highborn and marvelous educated."

"High but sadly." Yseult shook her head. "Have you heard from him the tale of Lyonesse?"

"I never heard of it until now from you. What is it?"

"Lyonesse was the land just west of Cornwall near Land's End, a tiny kingdom. Trystan's father Melyod was king, and he married Ionwen, the sister of Mark."

She was speaking now of things Trystan never did in all those years, of his parents and beginning.

"Soon after they married, Ionwen found herself with child. She was filled with happiness. It is a joyous thing for some."

Only some? "Rhian and I have long prayed for that."

"And I will add my prayers," Yseult promised graciously. "Before Ionwen could give birth, Melyod was lured from his rath by a woman of the—the Good People, who cast a spell on him that dimmed in Melyod's mind the memory of his faithful wife. Some say no spell was needed, but you are from home and know their power."

I thought of that miserable starveling girl and her baby on *Cnoch-nan-ainneal.* Pride I saw in her but little power. I remembered Etain: If there was justice in heaven, let her by now have five noisy, nose-running children and no more figure than one of her da's cattle. "And what of the good queen, his wife?"

Heartbroken, Ionwen went in search of her husband, but the child's time overtook her, and she gave birth on the journey. The labor proved too much for her. She took ill and died, leaving her servants to carry her infant son to Mark at Castle Dore. Soon afterward a great storm came out of the sea with more fury than any man remembered. Some said, and Yseult believed, the malicious Faerie woman conjured it so that Melyod would have no home to return to and so never leave her. The demon-storm scooped up the sea as in a great tub and poured it like the Flood of the Bible over little Lyonesse, wiping it from all but memory.

"So it was, Gareth, that Trystan was robbed of all at his very birth, of father and mother, of home, unable even to walk the land that might have been his, where now only tumbled stones and timbers lie under fathoms of sea, and only fish swim through sunken forests."

Yseult raised her eyes to me. "What heart would not go out to such a man? Being his friend, can you not feel for what he has lost?"

"I can." And for what Trystan would ever seek.

"A terrible thing," she said softly, "to be so long without a hearth or heart to welcome him."

In a few plain words she had taught me the man and the *why* of him. Not this ordinary woman thrust into a life she never wished; not her at all but himself, his poet's heart creating Yseult as he would any song, trying to throw light into the pit of his loneliness. And natural woman that she was, Yseult opened her arms in pity on his pain and perhaps thought it love, as a mother would soothe a child, easing with all she had, her heart and body.

But at the same time, with a kind of soft shock, I felt she had been speaking of him as of an old sorrow long past. As of someone dead. Speaking out of a life weary beyond its years.

Yseult shivered and wrapped her arms about her. The sun had gone behind gathering cloud. From the look of the troubled sky, we would have rain today or tomorrow. "Will you go in, *Ban Rion*?"

"I will stay here. It is lovely." She gazed out over Guenevere's prized flowers which our queen let no hand but her own care for. "Lovely quiet," Yseult breathed. "But I will thank you to fetch a mantle from my women."

I did as she asked, though the women took a devilish long time fussing over which mantle would be fitting to go with their lady's green; too long as it chanced. When I trotted down the stairs, across the courtyard, and turned into the garden, Trystan had found her first. They stood locked in each other's arms, rocking back and forth with the force of their feeling, unable to kiss enough, hold tightly enough. I opened my mouth to speak—and shut it again. Jesus, where was Mark? Did he or any of his people see this? Or Arthur . . . ?

Arthur did. High above at a casement the king leaned over the sill, watching them silently. After a moment he moved away. I leaned back against the outer garden wall, warring with myself whether to intrude or not. Ah, what difference? The horse had already fled the barn. Then, as I hovered there, half hidden in the thick ivy that blanketed the wall, Trystan swung out the gate and away without spying me, shoulders back, head up and whistling gaily.

I waited until he was well out of sight, then went to fasten the mantle about Yseult. She had seated herself again and tried to conceal from me that she'd been weeping. She wanted to walk, keeping her face turned away, but she was scarce off the bench when one of her women caught us up with a message from Arthur himself. Would Mark's lady wait on him in the small audience chamber next day?

A private audience. The next day was to be a holiday for the council. Mark and most of the other princes would be off hunting. Possibly Arthur hoped to win her to his side in the matter of the hillforts and, not being a crude man, perhaps a few tactful words on Trystan. I was glad Arthur had seen. The matter was his to deal with, not mine who'd already stubbed my toes enough on the fate of others.

Rhian was still with the queen when Yseult gave me leave to go, clearly troubled as Trystan had been happy at my last sight of him. "My thanks, Lord Gareth, but I—I would go to chapel alone."

Rhian not home and still a few hours to supper. I thought to have Dilys hot me up a quick bath, but she was out the door and striding toward me with a basket of wash when I got there, a good-natured little woman of the

Demetae tribe west of Severn, not young but still sturdy. Dilys tended us well and without complaint about foreigners, which we hardly were anymore, and never nipped too deeply at my whisky.

"When you're after doing the wash, Dilys, I'll be wanting some hot water to bathe."

She halted by me. "Och, sir, you will not have time for that, I think. You've a visitor. Lord Trystan, and in very high spirits—oh, not from the jug," she added quickly, knowing the man. "Just careening and caroming off the walls with something he must tell you or burst."

"And what was that?"

"He would not say to me." Dilys shifted the basket to her other side, resting it on a wide hip. "Sorry about your bath, sir, but Lady Rhian will be at me if the wash is late."

"No mind; that can wait." I was thinking of Trystan, the mouse in my stomach wide awake and skittering about.

"I don't know what's taken him," Dilys said as she moved off. "The man hugged me like to squeeze the last breath from my bones."

Just then the door to my house flew open and Trystan waved me in. "Gareth, come! I've a blessing to share and a favor to ask."

The man's face was lit as with a thousand candles. He shut the door briskly and gripped me by the shoulders, damned near dancing me about. "God bless you, dear friend! I need your extra saddle."

"Why? You've a spare of your own."

"Worn and uncomfortable. Not good enough."

"We've saddlers. Have it repaired."

"Not enough time, man. We leave tomorrow. She's going with me."

I shrugged him off me. "So that's the way of it."

"Ten years, Gareth. Ten *years,* but the waiting and the wanting are done."

"You might as well know. I saw you in the garden."

Trystan barely heard me, spinning about like a giddy boy. "Can you believe it?"

"Arthur saw you too."

The man was all joy and past reckoning the price. "To hell with Arthur."

"You don't mean that, Tryst. You dare not. Not now with—"

"And to hell with Mark. I saw her first and loved her first."

"Oh, Jesus." I had to sit down.

"Don't Jesus me." Trystan stood over me, hands fiddling in the air as if some part of him could not be still now. "Ten years plodding after Arthur. You know, you were there. Eburacum, the Midlands, and all the rest. All the years when we barely got down off a horse to sleep. When we ate the horses' oats because we'd nothing else and no time to forage. And you know what I've borne beside. The leers and snickerings of men like Pwyll, the contempt of your Christian priests, the snubs from women holier than God because I loved another man's wife who was *my* wife first. Ten years without a word or a glimpse, but never out of my mind. Now she's twenty, now twenty-five. What is she doing this moment, what is she feeling? Is she thinking of me?"

"It was the making of you, Tryst, all to your good and Arthur's now. You know how he needs your uncle."

"My uncle," he spat. "When I think of—"

"You'll think of Arthur's need, boyo. That's all that matters now. Mark may have the soul of a snake, but this is all he needs to leave the council and go home insulted and cuckolded, and our king will have nothing from him."

An honest try but I'd not spilled much of the gust from his full sail. "I have earned her, Gareth. I can think of nothing now but her."

"Oh, Christ," I sighed, sick of the whole mad business. "Why me? Why do you burden me with this?"

"Who else?" He sat beside me, one arm flung about my shoulder. "Whose sins did I take on myself when you needed? Who has comforted me drunk or sober, night after night, ridden at my knee year after year? Our lives are joined. Will you give me the saddle?"

I couldn't look at him, couldn't tell him what I'd seen in Yseult, any of it. Whatever she told him in the garden, the woman's heart was long past him. "My saddle's in the stable. You know where. If I'm not there, how do I know who took it?"

Trystan was up and halfway out the door. "Thank you, friend."

"Arthur's been your friend, so he has, but be damned to you if you hold him and your oath so lightly!"

The door slammed and rattled in Trystan's heedless wake.

It rained and stopped, rained and stopped through the night, and morning came up sulking between wet and dry. When Dilys set our eggs and buttermilk before us, Rhian had already dressed to attend Guenevere, the prized ivory combs in her hair. The queen was always up at cockcrow, the same as Arthur, Mass heard and herself moving before anyone else, and she'd come to insist on my wife's early presence. Rhian never warmed to Guenevere but respected the queen's industry and mind sharp as the king's, if less smoothed with tolerance.

"But she's pleased with you, is she?"

"More needful than pleased," Rhian judged. "Morn to night she never stops, forever putting things down and forgetting where, and I'm the one who must remember."

With a cautious glance at Dilys by the fire, Rhian leaned across to me and spoke in Irish: the matter of Guenevere and Lancelot, while not yet open scandal, was no longer a secret. Just a matter of time until some tongue wagged . . .

I barely listened. If Lancelot was a worry to the king, Arthur faced one nearer and sooner.

"You do not have much to say this morning," Rhian prompted.

"Um? No, it is that I relieve Bedwyr as captain of the guard. With all these Dubhunni, Cornish, and others swaggering about, and all thinking themselves better than the rest, we've got to keep a sharp eye. And with the day so wet and warm, I'll take no joy in wearing mail."

Arthur's peace bound all councils at Camelot, but we never knew when some blood feud might flare up between men of different tribes with no love for each other. Saxons have it over us in this, a man's first loyalties not to blood but sworn lord. Trystan found them flinty but practical folk. That morning I could wish some of the quality had rubbed off on his reckless spirit.

I relieved Bedwyr in the courtyard, received the keys in charge with his report. The night had been mostly quiet. One of Mark's Cornish soldiers had run afoul of a Catuvellaun and invited him to a bit of exercise, but the guards broke them up before serious mayhem. I posted the new guard and then, about noon, already sweating under the mail shirt, I was shouldering my way through the men at arms milling about the courtyard when I saw Trystan hurrying my way, eager as yesterday by the swing of his stride, whistling one of his own bright songs.

"God bless, Tryst!"

"And you," he sang out gaily. "Can't stop now. Arthur's called for me, can't think why." But halt he did, stayed by another thought. "Have you seen her today?"

"I have not."

"Remember." Trystan searched my face. "As you love me, you know nothing."

"Don't do it, man. It is mad entire."

He only said again: "Nothing."

"Go along."

As he swung away, one hand beating out a lively rhythm on his sword hilt, I thought: *Some part of you's never grown up. You're still a selfish little boy.*

And what was I? Staying silent made me part of it. I was his friend; truly I owed him my life. I was also Arthur's comite with the safety of all Camelot in my hands alone this day and night. I could not let this happen. To hell with friendship. Arthur must be told.

As it chanced, there was no need. Scarce an hour later, I was alone in the gatehouse over a mug of soup and bread when someone rapped sharply at the door.

"Come."

The door opened slowly. Trystan stood there, sword belt in hand, glaring at me. If he'd gone whistling to Arthur, he came away without his insides by the stricken look of him. "Come in, Tryst."

He didn't move. "You told him."

"What? Not a bit of it. What happened?"

"She—She was there. Arthur knew everything. He made me swear never to see her again. Swear or leave his service. Arthur said that to me who loved him from the beginning."

He raised the sheathed sword, then hurled it at the stone wall. It hit and fell with a heavy thud. "I took off that filthy thing and laid it before him. Before the woman's eyes I made the choice, as if there was ever doubt."

"The man had eyes to see you in the garden and needed no word from me. You've no sense of caution. A flat wonder you've lived this long."

"Oh—" Something crumpled in Trystan; his voice broke with it. "She lied, Gareth. Promised to go with me, but she lied and said she didn't love me. She said such terrible things with Arthur there and hearing all. I wanted to die."

I got up and went to him. "You're all twisted in a knot now and not thinking clear. Go to the longhouse. Lie down for a bit of rest."

"Oh, there's panacea." Trystan shook off my arm with a hard laugh. "My life floating down Severn in pieces, and all you can suggest—" He stepped back from me, a hostile stranger. "You did curse me after all. I loved you as a brother. You and Arthur . . . demons, both of you."

"Jesus God, will you never wake? You can't have her. You can't bloody *have* her. I could have told you as much yesterday. I was with her."

His mouth twisted in a sneer. I had to turn away in disgust, preferring him dead drunk to self-pitying. When the man was like this, he could lash out at anything, anyone. "Coming up in the world, aren't you, when a stable man reads the mind of a queen."

"So I did, and I'll tell you this now. I was going to Arthur this next minute."

"Would you?"

"Only plain duty."

Trystan studied me with that cold, crooked smile. "Yes, you would. How honorable we've become. I raised you up out of my stable to live fat and content with your Rhian. I swallowed more than I knew with that stupid bread and wine, didn't I? And for what? A dirty little Irish dog."

His insults just ran off my back when I bled for the man and the ruin in his eyes, for the good of him the dark must always destroy. I picked up his sword and threw it to him. "I'll not hear more of this. Go get some rest."

Trystan paused with his hand on the door latch. "I ought to kill someone for this, and who better than you?"

"I am not a high-tempered man, Tryst, but remember your little dog has a blacksmith's arm."

As if he'd not heard me at all: "Or Arthur. I should have killed him years ago."

"Don't be foolish."

"Bitches," he breathed. "Bitches. Butchers' daughters, every one."

The door slammed shut in his wake.

With a sigh I went back to my cold soup, to dabble the spoon without appetite and then push it away. Why could the man not see where Yseult could, and she grown wise enough to know what could never be? Jesus, the waste of the man. There'd been women everywhere we rode who bowed down—hell, *lay* down happily for Trystan at the drop of a smile and a pillow. Surely one of them could have made him a life, made all the difference. What must he tear out of a woman that any in this world could possibly give?

Time to make another round of the guards. I shook out

the mail shirt, oiled yesterday but already wet-rusting again, and wrestled my arms into it.

"Hell. Hell, hell, *hell.*"

Our people call it the Sight; I call it my mouse. I have scouted many times for Arthur, even such quarry as Prydn, and never without knowing when I myself was being watched. The mouse has kept me alive by feeling things about to happen, as I did that night.

The rain settled into steady downpour after supper. Those Cornish or Dubhunni still out-of-doors turned up their cloak hoods and squelched away across the courtyard to their beds. Wrapped in my own cloak I paced my own horse about the inner walls and courtyard of Camelot, calling up to the sentries to show themselves, assuring myself each was in place and alert before I could return to the comfort of the gatehouse.

Must be late, close to midnight. The priests and monks had gone to chapel hours ago, a ghost line of black-robed shadows hurrying to answer the summons of the compline bell. No one about but me, the patient horse and the clop-clop of his hooves on the courtyard earth beating time against the rain.

"Captain of the guard!"

"Aye, who's there?"

"Gareth, it's me." The tall figure of Bedwyr came toward me out of the shadows to fetch up at my knee. "I've been seeking about to find you. All quiet?"

"Who else would be out on such a night?"

Bedwyr peered about the deserted courtyard. "Have you seen Trystan?"

"Not a hint since noon." But even as I said it, my mouse

froze still. *That* was the warning it whispered. "What's amiss?"

"He's been drinking. Hard and steady. If you see him, get the man to bed."

"I will and thanks."

"Give you good rest." Bedwyr chucked me on the knee and moved off. I turned the horse toward the timber longhouse at the western end of our walls. Since the council gathered, bachelor comites like Trystan had given up their quarters in the palace to visiting princes and moved to the longhouse grandly called a *dormitorium.* I'd be going that way to see if Trystan, cruelly hurt and angry as he was, had drunk himself to sleep.

Just then a door to the palace opened. Two figures staggered out, far in their cups and holding each other up. Not Trystan, there was luck, only Pwyll and one of the wives he brought from Caer Gloiu to keep out the cold of nights. Pwyll pulled her to him, so drunk he could barely find her mouth to devour. Finally he turned her loose, paddling her broad rump to send her off, and the woman wove unsteadily back into the palace. Wineskin raised high, Pwyll shouted raucous greetings to someone I couldn't see, inviting the poor, rain-sodden soul, whoever it be, to drink with him. He could fall on his face and drown in the rain for all I cared. I must see to Trystan.

The longhouse was dark but for one rush light near the door. I put a bit of candle to the flame and picked my way toward Trystan's stall. Men were snoring everywhere, in the stalls or sprawled on pallets laid over the plank floor. As I neared Trystan's sleeping place, far but clear, I heard a bellow of shock or pain. Two of the comites on floor pallets stirred, turned over and sat up, alert in a blink. "Who's there?" one barked at me, reaching for the sword by his head.

"Captain of the guard. Mac Diarmuid."

"Did you hear that? What in hell was it?"

I thrust the candle into Trystan's stall. His rumpled bed was empty. More rising sound from the other end of the compound now, men shouting, the sudden high scream of a woman. I hastened out of the longhouse and into the saddle, pushing the horse to a fast trot toward the swelling hubbub.

In front of the palace, just where Pwyll had stood, torchlights sputtered in the rain, throwing light on a nightmare. A sobbing woman crouched over someone who would never rise again, not only dead but hacked half in two. Farther away my guards ringed about Trystan, some with bows bent and ready to kill him. Trystan swayed on his feet, leaning on a sword from which rain was washing the last of something that gleamed darker in the torchlight. He gazed blank-eyed and grinning at the ring of guards as if they were far away on the moon.

"Trystan!"

Arthur strode into the guttering light to halt between two archers. "Drop your sword."

I eased the horse about the circle until I was behind Trystan, fearful that any moment the bows would loose. Trystan raised the sword and started for Arthur—not clumsily but with the cold intent that would have murdered Morlais, but this time I'd not be too late.

"Out of my way!" My spurs raking his flanks, the horse bounded forward through the archers as I cleared the stirrups, leaped feet first at my friend's back and battered him to the ground.

"Irons. Quick, fetch me some irons!"

* * *

Pwyll had been unarmed. Bald murder it was, and so Trystan was charged. Dishonored, guilty as Satan, Tryst would speak to no one but Arthur, nor offer any evidence in his own behalf. Something was broken in the man. I think he wanted to die, and surely the howling Dubhunni under Prince Kay would have no other sentence from Arthur. The trial, presided over by the king and queen, was so taut with hate that armed guards were needed to hold the crowd back in the great hall. Bedwyr and I placed Trystan close between us, not to restrain our pitiful friend from whom the life seemed already to have fled, but for his protection and to show the vengeful Dubhunni lords that he still had two friends to believe in him.

Three in fact. There he stood with the verdict handed down, the Dubhunni and even some Cornish straining forward to savor the sentence of death. For Trystan, beyond a few like Arthur, Bedwyr, and myself, was never respected or liked among the *Combrogi.* Smug mouth-Christians, mouth-holy one day out of the week, condemned him for Yseult, while the cruder lordlings resented his high-bred manner, his education, too many too often stung by his graceful mockery. They would watch him die but see him humbled first.

The bastards were fed only half their vengeance when Arthur broke Trystan's oath sword over an anvil and banished the man from his service and Britain forever. They screamed, surging forward against the guards' shields. Bedwyr drew his sword and faced them, threatening and terrible.

"If one of you tries. Just *one.*"

Prince Kay shook his head in dire warning at Arthur,

then turned his back on his brother, but our king had said. Before we led him away, Trystan embraced Bedwyr and myself, wetting our cheeks with his tears.

"Thank you, my brothers."

Then I saw again the fine Trystan who'd been my brother and friend: haggard, worn out with his own sorrow, but still remembering his graces. His smile held some of the old lighthearted charm. "It seems you're forever knocking me down for my own good."

"What can I say, man?"

"Say nothing. You tried to tell me. You tried to help. With Christians like you about, I may take up the Church after all. Farewell, Gareth mac Diarmuid whom I named myself."

Not for me to judge for I never knew the whole of it. Arthur strained many loyalties by sparing Trystan, but he got his Cornish defenses from Mark; so much good at least came out of that painful day. Arthur said little to me of the matter, and only long afterward over a cup of mead when I'd risen to become his lord-milite over the *Combrogi* and had earned his closer confidence. Trystan it was whom Pwyll hailed in that dark courtyard, Trystan who was already smoldering and waiting to flame. Pwyll expressed an unfortunate desire and intent concerning Yseult. Poor unlucky goat, true to his nature unto death.

Then and there I blessed the high king for his mercy. "To speak nothing of your courage when the Dubhunni bayed for his blood and even your own brother condemned him."

"Mercy was the price, Gareth," Arthur confessed. "Yseult's price. I desperately needed Mark's cooperation and her best efforts to secure it. She wanted Trystan spared; for that she promised to persuade her husband as a wife best can."

"Sir?"

"Lovingly."

I thought I understood at last, sure of it when Arthur added, "Beautiful woman, Mark's wife."

He paused, turning the cup in his hands, a man with a lost love and a lost time haunting the edges of his own life. "She can't read or write her name, Gareth, but all of a queen she is. She sent him away. What he wanted was gone, but he'll never know how much she still cared."

Arthur and Britain never saw Trystan again, but I did. The curse was not done with either of us.

IV

Isolt of the White Hands

rystan gone five years and our lot was still to patch and mend, patch and mend against stubborn Saxons, with never enough cloth in any year to cover our whole need. Though no warrior of our blood would speak the truth aloud, we knew, as animals feel death coming on them, that we could never win for good and all, only dispute each mile of ground and pray. Patch and mend while the land changed under us as we rode, the maps before our eyes, Saxons pouring over Britain and their Frankish cousins over the Rhine into Gaul.

Every spring we rode east to uproot the Saxon weeds sprung up in the last year. Our farmers cheered the long lines of us as we passed, and well they should. The *Combrogi* are the finest cavalry in the world—were the finest, for they're mostly a memory now, a tale to tell about the fire. Arthur is gone, and only a few old men like Bedwyr and myself to warm our memories with a cup before the hearth.

Five years had passed since my poor friend vanished from Britain into sea mist and silence, and myself within hailing distance of forty, Bedwyr long married to his Myfanwy and a father into the bargain, while Rhian and I remained childless. With the passing years we gave up hoping, and Rhian, the bitter lack fading like an old scar, knew the Sidhe woman had cursed her surely as myself. Yet we tried to count our blessings. We lived better than ever we'd expected to, and Rhian grew used to my being away from April to October. I was shortly to command the *Combrogi,* though like most of my men I could neither read nor write.

"Ah, what need?" as Rhian put it. None of the great Druids of Eire set one word of their deep mysteries in writing; to do so, as Rhian felt, lessened the power of their magic. "We've the good priests and our king and queen for that."

So we did. Arthur and Guenevere were fearsomely educated, stuffed with Latin and history, needing no clerks to read the dispatches that showered them daily from all parts of the country and abroad. To my mind they were wonders: up in the dark of the morning, snatching breakfast in the *scriptorium* that became the living heart of Britain, eating absently as they devoured the parchments and wax tablets before them.

On just such a day in spring, I was summoned to that small, cluttered chamber where the king and queen sat across a broad table, the remains of breakfast pushed aside, the usual documents piled before each of them, those to be read on the left, those disposed of to the right.

I knelt to them. "God bless our high king and queen."

A bit of cheese in one hand, parchment in the other, Arthur waved me to a chair. I will say this for my king: he was never impressed by his majesty, but wore it, you might say, like a garment that simply became him better than any other man. Guenevere? Ah, there was a difference. She was born of the Parisii and counted Boudicca of the Iceni and a god or two in her family tree, so I was not inclined to be as easy with her as I might with Arthur. Proud as Lucifer when young but, poor woman, she'd borne her troubles bravely enough, losing a newborn child with no more to come, and Lancelot years gone from court, though none ever spoke of that. She was still slender, but taken to using more paint than Rhian approved of and adding a touch of color to the auburn of her hair now and again. Arthur's hair was fading from sandy to white, but the tall, war-hardened body remained vital.

"We've a letter from Trystan." He held it up. "We thought you would want to hear."

My heart leaped up. "I do, my lord. Where is he?"

"He's traveled a bit, but now he's just across the Narrow Sea in British Armorica. A castle on the coast called Leon."

"Quite a remarkable letter," Guenevere added. "He writes that he's married."

"God grant the wife brings him happiness," I prayed.

"Amen," the queen sealed with a sigh. "He was no end of trouble, but we love him dearly. He sends the sort of news we need of Gaul. Listen."

We knew something of the situation in Gaul. For many years Britons from our east had been settling in Armorica after being driven from their lands by Saxons. Trystan's letter told more. In the same year he was banished, Clovis, the young king of the Franks, had defeated the Roman forces at Soissons, breaking their control in the north. Now Clovis was testing the waters in Armorica with raids among the Redones and Curiosolites. With a pride to do him credit,

Trystan vowed that Clovis might break Gauls or Romans but would never wrest one foot from Britons.

We here have been driven out once. Not one of us who did not look back through tears like bitter gall to our lost land or who will let ourselves be broken again. Though we yearn for and sing the songs of our home, like the great rocks piled by the sea upon Leon's shore, here we have come and here we stay.

"Ah, there's Tryst for you," I admired. "When the demons slept in the man, never such a bard for fine feelings or the music to make them shine."

"Driven out," Guenevere echoed. "Poor Tryst reproves us for sending him hence."

"To save his insane life," Arthur reminded her, returning to the letter. As Trystan wrote, Castle Leon had been held by Hoel, a Belgae chieftain gone to Armorica some thirty years past. Trystan married his daughter Isolt and, on Hoel's death, took command of the stronghold.

"Isolt," Arthur mused. "Spelled differently but quite a coincidence."

Guenevere said only, "Is it? I wonder."

Trystan reported his serious problem that of too few men, especially young ones. Armorica was thinly populated and only half the folk British, the rest of old Roman-Gaulish stock. There was no real Roman authority left, only castles here and there like Leon. An equal problem, he confessed, was his own lack of skill in training recruits—

—in those arts that made us Combrogi. *I am not patient nor have I Gareth's art to persevere with common men. If my lord*

Arthur could send me a lord-comite of his quality and experience, his friend and yours would be more than grateful.

The letter ended with Trystan's greeting and prayers for his only king and queen and the well wishes of Lady Isolt. While Arthur and Guenevere speculated on the news of Clovis and what he wrought in Gaul, my mind and heart were with my friend. *We yearn for and sing the songs of home.*

The plea burst out of me. "My lord, five years it's been. The man is older and surely wiser now, settled and married. Is it not possible to bring him home?"

"To what?" Arthur asked with a sad smile. "No, Gareth."

"High King, I beg you. Rhian and I pray for him every night."

"As we have prayed and Bedwyr begged," Guenevere said, "but few others."

"You know I loved him," Arthur spoke, "but we dare not recall him. The man is trouble anywhere. The Dubhunni are my own tribe; they are not a forgiving people. Kay himself accused me of favoritism. But that he's my brother, we might have had a revolt on our hands. For ourselves, we would bring him home tomorrow, but . . ."

The silence hung between them until Guenevere doused the hope with cold reality. "But we need Kay's Dubhunni more."

"Yes." Arthur gently closed the door on the matter. "Let it be."

Let the angels see I tried at least. I rose and bowed. "My thanks for sharing the news of him."

"Wait." Arthur stopped me with a knowing look at his

wife. "Of course, he did ask for someone of your quality in aid."

Guenevere took another dispatch from the unread pile. "Now where could such be found, Gareth?"

"Here!" I blurted. "If my lord could spare me."

"No more easily than I can spare Bedwyr." Then the dear man actually winked at me. "But for my genius of cavalry, I will suffer the inconvenience for . . . how long, do you think?"

A few months, the rest of spring and summer, no more.

Rhian now. For fifteen years and more the woman was used to seeing the back of me ride away in spring and the front of me home in September. Almost twenty years of marriage: you fuss and grumble at each other with no real irritation, the bulges of one fitting the hollows of the other. She nags (for your own good, mind) but knows to the instant how long Dilys should boil your eggs or leave your roast on the fire, while the half-thought out of one is finished by the other with a mere glance. Rhian and I had grown affectionately bored with each other. No, the truth of it was, we'd grown apart. I had traveled with Arthur, commanded men and dealt with princes who no longer awed Feargus's *eachra*-man, while rocks would change their nature before Rhian did. Surely I loved the dear woman, but began to look forward to summer campaigning, when my whole mind bent on scouting Saxons and not being caught. For months at a time I need not think of the years passing or the weary little mouse in my stomach who squeaked that somewhere I'd missed something—devil if I could put a name to it, but *something* that left me Lord Gareth, aye, but in a life gone flat as stale beer.

As for Rhian, this year's absence was no different from all the others. She packed my chests carefully, with a bolt of good linen for new if needed, oiled my mail, burnished my helmet. As on the black day I rode off after Etain ni Feargus, she carried my shield from our house through Camelot's sea gate in early morning, down the stone steps to the quay and the waiting ship. When all was stowed, Rhian rested her arms about my shoulders with a kiss sincere but habit-worn as the rest of our life together.

"You'll take Trystan my blessing, then?"

"I will."

"Lost as he's always been, tell him I pray he's found joy in his marriage."

The ship's master called from the stern: about to cast off.

Rhian asked, "Who is this Clovis Tryst writes of?"

"A boyo and a half, he says. King of the Franks at eighteen, no more than twenty-five now, and already swept Rome from northern Gaul as Dilys dust from the hearth. But that he's barbarian, Tryst likens him to Arthur."

"As if there were such an equal," Rhian humphed. "Nor need you deal with any heathens."

"I will not. I'm just to be teaching Tryst's men how not to fall off a horse."

So few men, Trystan wrote. So few good horses, nothing but bare courage against a young Frankish bear shrewd as he was crude and ambitious. Sure as seasons I'd be crossing his trail, but no need to fret Rhian with that.

From the ship again: "Lord Gareth, come!"

The vessel was already sliding slowly along the quay. I hugged Rhian one more time in parting—*"Slan agat, Acushla"*—and bounded aboard.

* * *

Our ship lay well out from Leon's harbor in the last moments of night before dawn.

When I came to know the tides, I saw why neither Clovis nor any other invader could storm Castle Leon from the sea. I'm told Caesar tried and tore the bottoms out of his galleys. At high tide only shallow draft keels can get up to shore; at any lower only small curraghs. There is a sizable island two to three miles off the headland and two wee islets to the north, Saddle and Little Hump, a light tower on each. The rocky base of Little Hump at high water can be walked about in a quarter hour. Just visible then is the long spine of rocks that connects it to Saddle. No channels are marked.

"Dangerous." I asked the Sicilian leaning over the rail by my side, "Why do they not mark a safe channel?"

The black-bearded sailor chuckled and spat over the side. "There is none—well, one, but it's never marked. Pilots have to learn. There on Saddle and the Hump? The lights are lit because you are expected. Anyone else can pile up on the rocks for all they care, these Britons."

A little more light now. I could just make out the high silhouette of Castle Leon on the headland.

"You Brit like them?" the Sicilian asked.

"I am not. I've lived there for years, but I am Irish."

My companion shrugged. "Been to both. Small difference."

I took no offense, marking the opinion as foreign ignorance. The light grew. Now I could clearly make out the square Roman castle, the broad stairs leading down to the water, and two tiny figures descending at a trot. "Is that our pilot coming?"

The sailor squinted. "Where away?"

"Just there, the landing stairs. Don't look straight on but a little to the side."

He tried and gave it up. "For a landsman, you must have the eyes of a hunting gull. I see nothing."

"They're in the boat now."

The Sicilian took my word for it. With brightening day, the nearing curragh was cried by our lookout and the order called for rowers to pull ahead dead slow. Tide was not yet full. Low in the water with cargo for southern ports, the ship's master would take no chances on these shoals. The sailor made up for his woeful ignorance by helping me bring up my chests and lowering them into the curragh when it hove alongside.

Full clear morning now. As the two pilots rowed me toward the landing stage, a familiar figure dashed out of the castle gate above, taking the stairs pell-mell two at a time, reckless as the first day I saw him plunging his horse down the cliff path below Castle Dore, waving wildly now and shouting joyous greetings I couldn't hear.

"I prayed Arthur would send none but you." Trystan crushed me to him for the tenth time. "How well you look, and how you are needed! I can't seem to teach these mules anything. Oh, welcome, Gareth! And Rhian, how does she?"

"She sends her best blessing. A new man you are! It is grand to look on you." My friend did indeed look worlds fitter, clear-eyed and somewhat older for the beard. He answered the question I would not ask.

"The sea air every day. I'm healthy to the point of tedium. My mornings no longer suffer from the night before. Well, not all that often. Look there." Trystan swept his arm up the stairs toward the castle. "Convenient of Rome to leave this to us."

His gesture drew my gaze upward to the open gate and the young woman emerging, a cloak draped over one arm. Before she could wrap it about her, the offshore breeze pushed the blue kirtle tight to her, outlining her slender body and legs. "That is your lady?"

"So she is. Isolt of the White Hands her father's people called her."

Above us, Isolt held out her arms in welcome. "Trystan! Bring our friend in."

Impossible, but in that moment I felt the arms of a strange woman were not strange at all and stretched out in welcome to me alone.

At first Isolt was no more than easy on my eyes, and little enough time I had for the looking with the task before me. Trystan's men gave scant promise as cavalry: about sixty in all, fewer young than I'd prefer and only half of them Brits, the rest of the Osismi Gauls with the usual mix left by Roman soldiers. The horses were more encouraging, geldings bred from imperial cavalry mounts, no more than fourteen hands high but swift, with steady, cold natures more reliable in battle than higher-strung breeds. Trystan had introduced the *Combrogi* stirrup but little in the way of new weapons, armor, or simple discipline. Beyond personal courage and dash that bound the men to him, he was a lackadaisical commander, but what can I say? The man was a poet, and such are more precious than soldiers. Must he be an Arthur as well?

Castle Leon's high position on the headland was a natural defense, made stronger in their day by Roman engineers with a bank and ditch outside the high, mortared walls. Before they came, there had been a fortified Osismi rath in what was now the lower courtyard. The circular rath remained, now quarters for Trystan's men, while its outer ditch could still be partly traced as a shallow depression in the earth. The square walls had six towers at corners and sides. Practical Romans that they were, a latrine house had been added down at the water's edge, washed clean by the daily tides and used more often than the one within the walls, which must be emptied frequently. There were two large stables, one serving in part as storeroom for grain and fodder, and a smithy. Trystan considered Leon impossible to take.

"Impregnable from the sea. On all other sides we can sit here and watch invaders grow old."

"I think not, Tryst." From where we stood at the top of the natural stone levels that formed a stairway to the lower courtyard, I peered beyond the south wall to the Roman bathhouse and the well used by the castle and villagers alike. "They could take you in a week. Two at most."

He cocked his head at me with amused surprise. "Oh? Could they? How?"

"I'm asking you: What bloody fool dug the well out there?"

Outside the south wall beyond the bank and ditch, sunk in softer ground and probably rebuilt from an older one for the convenience of the bathhouse. We could go without a wash, even store water against siege, but how much for how long? Cut off for weeks, every man, woman and animal within Castle Leon would be panting for water. When the Romans rebuilt the old hillfort, Armorica stood in no real danger of attack. Now, with Clovis eyeing this country like a hungry man his supper, Trystan surely did.

"Start them today, every man able to swing a pick. Dig there inside the south wall on the lowest ground."

Just there where Isolt was moving toward us like a second sunrise with her graceful, swaying gait. Why did I feel I'd known the sight of her all my life? For a moment I forgot what I'd been telling Trystan.

"You were saying, Gareth?"

"What? Oh. How often do your men feed their mounts?"

"Early morning, noon, and night."

"Too much at one time. Let it be four times with smaller measures, and always a little water first."

Trystan shook his head admiringly. "Genius indeed. Where would I be without you?"

"Lost, lad. Lost entire."

He laughed aloud, clapping me on the back and waving his wife to join us. "Isolt! Come, my love. Come and hear how Gareth will save us from the horrible Franks."

There's that you must know to understand what happened to me. I am a simple man, not made for shadows or sorrow. But for the curse that banished me forever from the Knuckles of God, I had lived nigh to forty years in that assuring simplicity. So long settled in my station and way of life that what, for a subtle and educated man like Trystan would be a thunderclap of revelation, took weeks to dawn on Gareth mac Diarmuid, nor could I deal with the light when it broke over me. Sure, if the sun took as long to come up over the world, there would be night half the year, but then I was busy, moving from morn to dark. There was the drilling of the men and horses, and always new report of the Franks prowling closer to the east of us. Pushing myself and the men each day, praying we'd have enough time to prepare before Clovis struck us in force.

Armorica had no high king and little left of Rome but a few aging decurions here and there. Just scattered strongholds like Leon, nothing of authority but the Church, which Clovis would never attack, married as he was to a Christian princess. Trystan reckoned the Frankish king's conversion more shrewd than pious.

"He's young but clever, Gareth. The murdering bastard has Rome to love him now. Such barbarians are making history by knowing when and which way to jump. And we, poor souls, are in the middle."

I didn't need to know how Clovis stood with God, only how he made war.

The summer days passed with the soft tread of an ambling girl, and sometimes, in the fresh sea wind blowing in over the harbor, I tended to forget the danger creeping toward us as refugees from the eastern tribes trickled into the villages beyond our walls. I was ever on the move, snapping at the men when they failed to keep their rath clean—

"If you live like pigs, you'll feel and act like pigs, and pig is not good enough for me. When I'm done, by God, you'll be proud, so you will, but right now it is a sorry lot you are. Sweep out this sty and scrub it down."

Inspecting the stables and armory for order and cleanliness equal to the rath; hastening the well diggers as they flailed away with picks and shovels at the rocky ground; hovering over the men feeding their horses until each knew to the jot how much grain to how much grass and when. Dinners taken with Trystan and Isolt on the raised dais in the hall while his men gobbled at the tables below us and the sun sank low over the sea beyond the open casement.

The lower floor of the castle was the hall. To call it the "great" hall would strain charity since twenty of my strides would take me end to end, including the kitchen area. The upper floor was one open space divided by tall curtains into three chambers. Trystan and Isolt slept in one, I in another, with a common room between.

In those first weeks when I closed my eyes to sleep, I still saw the castle walls, walking in memory what I'd paced through the day, hoping I'd overlooked no weakness beside the well. We had only two old onagers for catapulting heavy stones from the walls, and few archers.

Drifting toward sleep, my mind would betray me; not archers or engines I pictured on the walls, but Isolt. As the days wore on, her image intruded more and more. I gave that little note until, God forgive me, I realized how sharply aware of her I'd become and how seldom I thought of Rhian. Like a wet dog shaking water off its back, I would wrench my mind back to the problem at hand—only to look up and glimpse Isolt above, leaning from an open casement to wave, and I would need a moment to recall my errand.

She was much younger than Yseult though of the same coloring, white skin against blue-black hair, but deeper through the soul than Trystan's first folly, her face fascinating for the life in it. As I remembered her that day in Guenevere's garden, I thought of Yseult in stillness but Isolt always in motion. White Hands, the people called her. A man might wonder why, for they were neither pale nor delicate but strong and capable. It was in the excited way Isolt used them when she described something that caught her fancy, carving the shape of her thought in the air. Years ago, yet I can recall to this day the clear, dancing image of them. Nor had she Yseult's evenness of feature—never that, for the nose was too long, the mouth wide for a woman, her laugh a hearty *whoop!* when something tickled her quick humor. And a loving heart. You could see in the way her eyes were ever drawn to Trystan, how her hand trailed over his back as she sometimes passed behind his chair; you could hear in the very caress her voice shaped from his spoken name, that Isolt loved the man as life itself.

One hot, windless afternoon I was working in the stable, shirtless and sweating, inspecting the horses' mouths for bit sores, when I heard Isolt call me from the entrance. Embarrassed, I had on only a pair of army breeches to cover in modesty what was modest enough to begin with.

"Dear Gareth," she laughed as she swayed toward me, "what variety God gives to men." Her eyes swept up and down me, and I couldn't help hoping she liked a bit of what she saw.

"How's that?" I asked, wrestling my shirt on and feeling like a clod.

"Trystan has long legs that begin just below his waist. You have broad shoulders and a long body with short legs." Isolt giggled. "And bless me if they're not bandied."

"The arms come from pounding out horseshoes on an anvil." I was not accustomed to women so frankly discussing the form God saw fit to give me. "For my legs, they curve better about a horse this way."

"You look fine." She wrinkled her nose at me. "It all suits you somehow. Will you saddle me one of the mares? I must ride to the village to see if there are sick and needy."

Isolt touched my cheek as she said it, in a friendly way, but I felt that touch go deep through and down me where it had no business. *And I no business thinking so, but it is all of a woman you are.*

Sleep would not come that night for remembering the touch of her hand. How she looked in the stable doorway, the light behind her through the linen kirtle piercing me with the slender line of her legs and stirring in me what I'd never felt before. Rhian and I courted quickly and married young with scarce any hunger not soon or well fed, scarce time for the wedding before one or another task called, always the manner with common folk serving a lord. Yet . . . was this how it hurt to want and be denied? How Trystan suffered on that last foggy morning at Camelot, leaving his love forever?

I thrashed over on my side, taking my soul to task. *You are a fool and more for being no young one. Years married to a good woman while Isolt is married to your friend, and even if your pudding wits were nimble enough to reason that aside—*

Will you listen to him? Reason aside, says he, as if he had the right.

Devil it all. I heaved out of bed and stumped to the open casement to stare unseeing at the dark sea and stars above. A long time I leaned there—then heard a sound. Through two chambers and muffling curtains came a high, sharp cry—her cry, quickly smothered. I'd heard it before on such still nights; Trystan was making love to her. I slipped back into bed, pulling the covers tight over my ears, sick with the sound and what it did to me. Wrong, devilish wrong, the whole matter. Did I not want her to be happy with him? Was it that, without shaping the wordless thought in my heart, I'd begun to resent Trystan? I didn't know . . . I didn't know. As an army is blind without scouts, so is the man unable to understand his own soul, and here was mine suddenly speaking in tongues.

But was she full happy with him? When Isolt looked

after her husband sometimes, my eye or imagination fancied it saw unfed hunger and wondered what the woman could lack. Oh, were it mine to love her, she would know that every day and never want for one tender word. Isolt of the White Hands . . .

Why can I not sleep?

One night Trystan did not join us at the high table for supper. When I asked Isolt, she said he was above in the common room with his harp and drink. "He has his moods," she confessed softly while I gave enormous attention to my soup rather than deal with the nearness of her. "Inside himself he goes away. He . . . goes back, I think."

True. Searching like a starved hawk now, I could read it plain in the man, the way he stood sometimes on the north wall, staring at the sea and perhaps beyond the horizon to another place and time, when he now had twice the woman to love, and the thought would rise bitter in me: *I am not the only fool in Leon.*

I must move from the castle into the rath below, telling Trystan that round walls and thatching comforted me more than stone. I had to put distance between us, between me and the torturing fact of them together, the pain of having no right to pain. But how to put it without seeming awkward or, worse, letting her guess my reason?

Great, thundering Clovis himself opened the door for me. He'd taken one more stronghold from the Veneti on Armorica's southern coast. I decided to have a squint at this behemoth myself.

We were in the central common room of the castle's upper floor that early morning, Isolt and Trystan protesting against my urgency, but I knew my mind and prayed she would not.

"First he deserts us for that musty old rath," Isolt complained with tender injury. "Now he'd ride out with bare time to saddle a horse."

Trystan agreed. "You'd think he wants to be quit of us."

I tried not to notice Isolt between us before the long table. "Did you not say you had some maps?"

"Old Roman maps. Mostly they show what isn't there anymore."

"So they show the rivers and hills. Names I could not read anyway."

Trystan fetched them from the wall alcoves that contained his library, and I wished then I could read more than the shape of land. A touch of learning might ease the war in my heart—but then none of those wise poets and philosophers brought Trystan any peace. I suspect, like most men, they learned the way of fire only after passing through the flame, which helps little when you're burning.

Trystan pointed out this feature and that, reading the dead Latin names of camps long gone, bridges and rough tracks, the deserted army brothels. Armorica is a peninsula. As Trystan named the tribal areas east of us, Clovis's aim showed clear: sweeping south through the land of the Redones and Curiosolites, lately swinging west along the southern coast to subdue the Veneti fort at Vannes. Armorica was now completely cut off from the rest of Gaul.

"But we have time," he reckoned. "Everything Clovis takes he must hold. He'll be a year fighting his way this far west."

"But where is he now? Which way will he move?" Midsummer was close at hand. An ambitious young king like

Clovis would have more than enough good campaigning weather left him. "Where would my luck be most like to find him?"

Neither of us could guess. Isolt it was who supplied my answer. "I would say here." She slipped close to Tryst and slid an arm about him. "Here in the Carhaix region. While Clovis is bashing away at conquest, his army still has to eat. The Carhaix Valley is the most fertile in Armorica. It is only common sense."

She glanced quickly at her husband. "Well, everyone knows that."

Trystan brushed his lips across her cheek. "How clever you are."

"We must bear with my lord, Gareth. You know how little food interests him."

There was living truth. If Feargus were to award him the hero's portion, Trystan would merely pick at it and turn to his drink. I gave my attention to the shape of the mountains inland: Formed like a rider's spur, the two claws bent toward each other, almost encircling the Carhaix Valley. "You are wise, Lady. If it's that valuable, Clovis will want it for supplies."

I moved to the casement to watch the men strolling from the rath and stables to assemble in ranks. "I'm thinking a man like Clovis will not sit on the coast throwing stones at gulls. I'll use the time to find his strength, how armed, what kind of mounts, and I'd be knowing that *now*."

"But why must you go yourself?" Isolt protested, moving to me. "We have men."

I avoided her eyes lest she see the truth in mine. "I should have gone before this. Spying's a skilled business. I can't trust these lads yet to do it alone. I'll take two with me for the seasoning, and I will choose them today."

Outside, Trystan and I paused at the top of the flat stone levels leading down to the courtyard. In a bad mood for a start, I seethed silently at the lackadaisical way the company gathered, some of the married men who lived in the village just now ambling through the south gate as if they had all the time in the world. "God, but they are a shabby lot. They'll be squaring off smartly or I'll break their lazy backs, so I will."

"And what side of the bed did you rise on all this week? You've been biting heads off thirteen to the dozen."

"I get out of bed squared off, so I do, and time these fools learned the meaning of that."

Trystan studied me curiously. "Gareth, what is wrong?"

"*Nothing* is wrong."

"I've never seen you like this. All of a sudden the man I knew has gone behind a cloud."

"You wanted me to hammer these sorry mules into something like soldiers. I can't do that gently, and if I can't do it at all, we might as well just open the gates to Clovis when he comes."

I hadn't meant to betray my anger and willed myself to pull in the horns. "Be looking for the ship from Britain while I'm gone. The high king won't fail us if he can help at all."

At my behest, Trystan had written Arthur for new equipment we desperately needed: ring mail, heavier lances, and the longer cavalry swords of the *Combrogi.* I must teach these men the lessons we learned against the Saxons. As we strode down to stand before the assembled company, I knew these threescore were still pitiful long miles from ready, and cursed the sentiment that made me volunteer in a friend's need. Perhaps Arthur would order me home soon.

That would be shameful, leaving Trystan to fend for himself when I owed the man my life, endless trouble though he was. As I stood with him, glowering at the men and aware of Isolt watching from above, were there any kind of a ship, I would have left that day to be cured of the fever of her.

"Someday Lord Trystan is going to loose you on the Franks. Cavalry is an attack weapon, and attack you will. Come that day, I hope you'll have better weapons and armor. Pray God you'll be better men than I'm seeing today, because only He can help you if you're not."

They stirred uneasily; Trystan had never spoken to them so sharply. They were loyal to him, but he was too easy on them. Their slumped stance in ill-assorted armor, old Roman *segmentata* of iron strips over the shoulders and round the waist, some plain leather breastplates, here and there a billed cavalry helmet, ragged trousers gartered at the ankle under frayed tunics—whatever Arthur sent would be only half what these prideless men needed.

"Listen and hear me well. I have ridden with the finest, as well you know. Men like Bedwyr and Lancelot—aye, and Lord Trystan, who can tell you our history better than I. Ask of the Saxons who will speak of devil men on demon horses. We were seldom rested, always half hungry, but an idle day it was when we did not do the impossible. It is my task to make the lot of you into something like them."

Pacing back and forth before them, I stopped by Trystan, who was surprised as the rest at my open disgust. "My lord," I told him for all to hear, "to my shame I have to own there's the impossible and there is the *impossible*."

"What is this?" Trystan wondered under his breath. "They're good men." My naked doubt forced him to add, "Well, they're all I have but willing enough. Why do you insult them this way?"

"Because you haven't," I muttered back. "The only cure now is a stiff kick up the arse."

I faced them with the hopelessness of a man sent to fell a forest with a fruit knife. "You're a soft lot who have never fought, some of you a full stone overweight. I ask Lord Trystan now to cut your rations by a third."

Greeted by groans of protest, I barked even louder. "If you stay hungry, that's good. If you turn mean, that's better, for it's the clearer you will be thinking and the better fighting."

No one liked that at all, but I was not feeling kindly. "My lord, have I leave to choose out two of these ladies for the mission we spoke of? That is"—with a doubtful glance at the hopeless pack of them—"if any are fit for it?"

Trystan sighed and shifted his hands behind his back. His mien clearly said to me: *I don't know you at all anymore.* "As you wish, Lord Gareth."

I'd already culled the men in thought and made my choice. "Collen, Pindar. Step forward."

They shuffled out to stand before me, uncertain and reluctant: Where's the Whip going to lay his lash now?

"You pair were the last into line today. Do you think I did not see? You'd be here quick enough if the Franks were running up your backside, and soon enough they will be. You and I will be riding far, and God help you if you can't learn fast enough, for I don't fancy burying you along the way."

"Bury?" In a Cantish accent thick as bog peat, Collen

worried, "Sir, I hope you are not expecting us to be heroes. We have wives and children."

"Then glad I am you can do something right without serious injury. Heroes are not what I'm asking today. Now square off and follow me to the stable. *Lively,* damn it."

By late afternoon the three of us were resting, watering our horses and filling our water skins by the Roman bridge over River Elorn. Collen and Pindar kept glancing over their shoulders, expecting to see Franks behind every tree. Collen came of the Cantii, the first British tribe to be overrun by Saxons, a small, tight-knit man and no great burden to his horse. Gaulish Pindar was no larger, a mix of Osismi and every strain that had marched with the legions since Caesar. I'd bidden them travel light: no armor, only Roman short swords hung from a strap baldric, and small Sarmatian bows best for shooting from the saddle, and pray God they had no need.

I was satisfied with my choice of men. Both Collen and Pindar were settled and steady, not much younger than myself. If they were uneasy about meeting the enemy, that was worlds better on this journey than roaring, reckless-brave warriors like Cerball and Garbhan, who would surely shorten their lives and mine by hunting heads instead of information.

"But you'll not be sighting Franks this soon," I eased their minds as I tied the water bag to my saddle. "Perhaps not at all. Ai, Collen! What's so fascinating there? Have you never seen a bridge before?"

He stood with hands on his hips, gazing at the bridge across Elorn, built of thick timbers with breakwaters of three pilings each on the upstream side of each support. "I've heard every Roman *mulus* was an engineer as well. That is a fine piece of work."

"For sure, it's a wonder of design, and pity such must be destroyed."

Collen turned to me, unbelieving. "Destroyed, sir?"

Pindar protested as well. "The Osismi use this bridge all the time."

"So will the Franks if it's there. You'd not make their lives that easy, would you? Come now; it's time to learn."

On my folded blanket I'd laid out five objects: a pinecone, three stones of different size and color, and a horseshoe nail. "Pindar, make a square with any four, the fifth in the middle."

When he'd done so: "Now both of you study the shape and try to remember where each piece lies. Tell me when you think you know."

When they declared themselves ready, I bade them turn their backs and questioned them in turn. Where is the nail? The largest stone? The smallest. The cone? They did poorly the first time, little better the second when I arranged the objects at random.

"*See* each one, fix it tight in memory. You would not believe the stories some of the Brits tell of me, and the Saxons as well: Gareth can see a hundred miles and remember every tree and rock. Not magic it is but method, as I'm teaching you now. Try again."

And on and on with different arrangements, ten times over until Collen and Pindar began to *use* their eyes. "Warriors are one thing and a fine thing. It is a different and shrewder breed of man needed to get close, look and remember, and that is what he must do if his own force is not to move blind."

"And not get caught," Collen reflected with a healthy regard for his skin.

"If he's fool enough to get caught, it's all for nothing."

"But it is difficult," Pindar admitted, studying the new shape I'd laid out on the blanket. "I remember one shape that stays in mind, then all changes."

I winked at him. "You will have more fun with seven or eight to remember, and that we will do tomorrow."

When we rolled into our blankets to rest, I cautioned, "A fire is safe tonight, but none hereafter. Tomorrow you can be peeling your eye for Franks."

"I'm too hungry to sleep," Pindar said as his stomach rumbled its poverty. "One apple, one bite of meat, and a handful of oats in water. I've supped better."

"Two more days and you won't notice so much. Look for a she-goat or cow. If she's not been milked, borrow some. Or nick a vein for a little blood."

"Blood?" Collen sat up, unbelieving. "You'd have us drink blood?"

"To soak your oats in. Good that way. Many's the obliging cow's helped me so while I rode with Arthur. We learned that from the Picts."

"Make me sick it would."

Pindar's stomach protested again, very plaintive. "I might just savor it now."

I smiled up at the stars. *God's truth you would.* "I hope you lads value the education I'm giving you. Be savoring your sleep now."

Tired, they both fell asleep quickly, but not I. I lay by the dying fire, staring up at the stars, and silently said my prayers twice over. Even now she would be lying close to Trystan, perhaps with her arms and legs tangled wild about him in love, or nestled to his chest and still in the sweet, dreamless sleep to follow.

Stop it.

Christ, how could this happen to *me,* a plain, practical man of such cool humors that a woman beautiful as Yseult sparked nothing in my heart but pity for the sadness in her. How I'd hoped for the healing of time and distance, but Isolt still shone bright in the darkness behind my eyelids.

Bedwyr, that commonsense friend, would never have believed this of me. *I* would not. Would Trystan? Did he see it in my face, my mouth open in soft shock at first wounding sight of her above by the castle gate, her arms out and those arms two spears forged to pierce me? Fool I called him, yet folly and shame were now but feathers in the balance against the fever of her. *I will hide it, woman. I must hide it deep.*

From the south slope of the mountain, just above the highest pines, we could see for miles along the valley. I could, that is. Collen and Pindar saw only open heath, while I showed them how to cut the land into strips, one by one, for observation. The land showed them nothing at all, no tillage or any sign of use by men. I made out one lone animal grazing placidly in the far distance.

"Nothing," Collen admitted at length.

"Look again, man."

"There." Pindar pointed. "Movement."

"Where?"

"There, there."

"Franks?"

"Too far to tell."

"Only a goat," I told them. "Collen, don't say there's nothing until you know for sure."

"Can we take the goat?" Collen urged with only a mouthful of dried fish for breakfast. "We need meat."

If they wanted to break out into the open, and if the goat would be polite enough to stand still for them, and if they could eat the meat raw, because we'd be lighting no fires where smoke could be seen for miles.

We pushed on east, made a cold camp that night and the next. Pindar and Collen began to learn how far a man could go on a mouthful. We fed the last oats and apples to our horses. From here to home, the animals would have graze alone. But now we were sighting paths worn across the heath, later a stream meandering off to the south, ditched to provide water for sown fields. From our height we could see well past the fields to the tiny village beyond, perhaps two miles away. We'd also seen the smoke long before and knew there was trouble. Hay harvest was a month away. No one burned stubble in June.

"It's the village," Collen muttered.

Pindar wet his lips and for once, I think, forgot his hunger as something else squeezed his stomach. I've learned to feel danger long before it comes close enough to kill me. My mouse was up and skittering. "Look to each side of the village, back and forth."

Pindar tried. "Can't see for all the smoke."

"Wait."

Gradually the smoke thinned, but still we could make out no human forms. Pindar asked anxiously, "Do you think they killed them all, whoever did this?"

I didn't know. The villagers would be Veneti, not likely to raid their own, and the Redones and Curiosolites had already submitted to Clovis. Such villages had nothing of value to loot. No, this would be a terror raid meant to leave the invader's wound so others would hear of it and be afraid. A Saxon trick, but Franks were fruit of the same tree. "Look sharp now. Look for horsemen."

"The Veneti used to raid Leon for cattle and sheep," Pindar said in a voice turned flat and hard. "That was before Hoel came. Now it's their turn."

He might think that only justice, but he'd been a babe then, if born at all, and couldn't know how it felt to be helpless before great, murdering men on horses.

We could see the huts more clearly now and the horsemen milling about. As we watched, a knot of them left the others and started across the fields at a walk. I counted three of them leading three extra horses behind, most like to water them at the stream we'd passed. "Coming this way. We'll have a closer look after all."

Pindar worried: "Their horses could smell ours."

"Wind's wrong," Collen said. I gave them both silent approval: They were learning. Our geldings were quiet and steady; the approaching horses, at least the stallions, would ignore their scent, but best to be safe. "Pindar, tether the animals out of the wind."

He moved away to lead the horses to cover on our flank while Collen and I watched the ambling advance of the three riders and their string of mounts. Closer now: By the toss of his head and the way he answered the rein, the lead bay was a stallion, the rest geldings, but none of them under sixteen hands high—bays, chestnuts, and greys with thick bodies and legs and small, blunt heads. I'd never seen horses so large. They could easily carry a large man with arms and armor without tiring, but the *Combrogi* in me wondered how long would it take such Goliaths to reach full gallop in a charge.

Collen must have chewed over the same thought. "They have stirrups. Harder to knock a man out of the saddle, but I'm thinking our horses could dance circles about them."

Perhaps, but if one of them hit one of ours, fare thee well.

Two of the men carried spears like the Roman pilum, but longer, with an extended iron shank forward of the wooden shaft. When they were within fifty yards of the slope, they turned to our right.

"Heading for water, Collen."

Big men they were, like Saxons, dressed in brightly striped tunics over their trousers, axes with bell-shaped heads tucked into their belts. Their long hair was caught up in a fashion new to me: braids down the sides and a topknot tied to spray up from the crown like water from a fountain. Only one of them, the man on the bay stallion, wore any mail, a ring-shirt of the German fashion. The fine sword hung from his baldric and the polished amulet flashing at his neck told me he might be a chieftain.

Pindar returned, the mounts secured. By now the Franks were out of sight. My men waited for orders, but I was torn. We really needed one of those horses to take back so that I could learn their nature and what such an animal could do. For the same reason, I fancied one of those strange, flared axes and perhaps a spear. A few good men like Arthur or Bedwyr could dash in and be off without raising a sweat, but Collen and Pindar had never fought and weren't eager for the taste of battle now. There it was, then: too high a risk, too tempting to miss.

"Collen, boyo, how close must you be to kill a man sure with that bow?"

He touched the unstrung weapon. "I've never tried, sir. The closer the better."

Pindar blinked at me nervously. "Why?"

"Well, there's the question. We've seen the Franks and know where they are and their gentle nature. We could slip away home now—but I dearly need one of their horses. Listen now: you've not been in war, so this is not an order. I will leave deciding between you."

From the look of them, they knew what was coming, but neither would show his fear. Then Pindar rose and bent his bow to string it. Unstrung, the horn-strip bow curved like a letter C. Stringing bent the weapon back the other way, not as accurate as the long British bow but delivering a shaft with more power. "Well," he allowed with a glance at Collen, "there is no harm in a closer look."

Not to be shamed, Collen quickly strung his own weapon. "None at all before we go home."

"Good lads." But I couldn't guess how easily they could swallow another hard truth. "It is not that I'd have you fight them. If the matter comes to that, I just want you to kill them—not that the need will arise."

"Pray not," said Pindar, who I felt was not answering me but something unsettled inside him. "We will just look."

"Follow me and watch where you step. No noise, mind."

We worked our way along the wooded slope toward the stream below, crouching, stopping often to choose our next cover carefully before moving, gradually descending toward level ground and the stream. We could see the water now, sunlight flashing on the surface, and several of the great horses drinking. In a few moments others became visible as they grazed the near bank, one of them the big bay ridden by the chieftain. A magnificent animal, dark brown with a yellowish mane and tail.

The three Franks were not far below us now. "Listen."

My men did but heard nothing.

"The birds have hushed. They know we're here, and if those Franks had half of a scout's sense, they'd be knowing too."

Below and a little to our right, a man's sharp laugh barked out. Collen and Pindar were now glassy-eyed with nerves. But we needed a still clearer view. Twenty or thirty more yards we crept, slower now, until the three men were directly below us, one washing his feet in the stream, another stripped to the waist and splashing himself down. The chieftain lay on his back, arms behind his head. Clear shots for archers.

"Right, lads. Whatever we do, we do it now or go home."

Neither of them moved. "My lord," Collen told me in an earnest whisper, "I've never killed any but hogs for salting and chickens for the pot."

"Nor I." Pindar kept his eyes on the three men below, but now there was something beside fear in them as he glanced up at the smoke staining the sky overhead. His voice was tight as a hanged man's rope. "But it is not right, you know. Burn out a village, kill the people and just loll there waiting for God to admire the deed."

"No." With a smooth motion, Collen laid a shaft across his bow. "It is not. And Lord Gareth is needing a horse, God forgive us."

They were cold-frightened but committed as I'd been moments before killing Declan of the Sidhe, nor could I soothe their feelings afterward or say aught to help them sleep or forget. I gave the orders quickly. I would work back and down a piece, close as I could to the stallion but ready to snatch whichever animal came to hand if need be. "When I sing out *go,* shoot and keep shooting. Get closer as you do and, sweet Jesus, do not pause with second thoughts once you start."

Mouth dry and heeding the mouse, I crept down the hill. Most of the ground was silent-soft with pine needles, but a false step could snap a dry twig at the wrong time. In place now, frozen still, studying the ground between me and the big bay for anything to trip me up. Less than thirty yards to the horse, and Saint Padraic make it the swiftest thirty I ever ran.

Ready, rising, coiled. "GO!"

Leaping down the slope, I heard a bellow of pain as an arrow struck home, and then Collen screaming, half fear, half war cry. Running and praying: *Jesus, let them get all three.* My legs ate up the last of the slope and carried me out onto level ground. One blurred glance back at the Franks: All I could see was the big chieftain rising, drawing his sword as he started for me. No time. The stallion snorted and reared, but I'd got hold of his dangling reins and leaped his back without the stirrup. As I reined him about, the huge Frank raised his sword—then stumbled and went down with a grunt of pain, writhing with the arrow through his side.

Collen sprinted toward me, clawing another shaft from his quiver, hovering over the wounded Frank, wild-eyed and trembling. "W-We got the others. This I missed because he was moving."

"Are the others dead?"

"Or close to it." Collen looked back at Pindar moving from one still body to the other. "I think."

The hulking chieftain groaned and, incredibly, began to rise, fumbling at the shaft that pierced the fleshy part of his side from behind, the head protruding from bloodstained mail in front.

"Pindar, leave them. Fetch the horses quick!"

Hovering over the two slain Franks, Pindar stared at me like a man wakened from a bad dream, then broke into a lurching run toward the slope. I sat the bay, steadying him, the wounded man on his feet now between my sword and the bow visibly shaking in Collen's hands.

"Sir? Sir, I hope we don't have to—I mean, I don't think I can do it again."

Even in wound-shock the young Frank must have been made of iron. Without a sound he reached behind to snap the shaft. Glaring pure hate at us, he grasped the head, pulled it through, then dropped it at Collen's feet. He took a breath, then spoke what sounded like garbled Latin, stabbing a finger at each of us. "Veneti?"

"I know a bit of the holy language," Collen said. "He says the Veneti are conquered, finished, damn him." He slapped his own chest. "No. No Veneti. Canti. Briton!"

"Right he is," I snapped at the Frank. "Briton, you son of a bitch. From Castle Leon."

"Le-on," the Frank mouthed as if salting the name in memory. "Bri-ton."

He wilted back down on his rump again, helpless wounded, waiting to die, but with no fear I could see, and confident as Lucifer; the giant bastard even grinned coldly at me. "Christian?"

I saw Pindar hurrying back down the slope toward us, leading our horses. "I am Christian."

Another stream of guttural words out of him. Collen translated nervously. "He says he's Christian too."

"Aye, did we not see the high Mass he held in the village?"

The Frank growled out at us again; Collen cocked his head to catch it all.

"What's he on about, Collen? Our bad manners?"

"Oh my, sir. He says he's—Holy Mary, it's Clovis himself. I think he's saying we'll be sorry we learned his name."

We could be sorry tomorrow. As for this Frankish king, one foot in the Church and the other in the blood of the faithful, why I didn't send him to God then and there I'll never know for sure. One reason was his arrogance. To wound or even kill his flesh fell short of the anger in me then. To me, Clovis was Garbhan and Feargus, ui Chellaig and all the great horse lords who'd ridden over my kind since history began. I would dismiss him as undeserving of a warrior's death. An Irish insult and one to burn deep. *Ghillies* like Cerball and Garbhan, sent home by an enemy, their heads not worth the taking, would live with the stain of that all their lives, heedless-hurling themselves into fray after fray, praying for death in battle to wash honor clean in the songs of bards. As Pindar trotted up with our horses, I swept my arm toward the gutted village.

"You. Clovis. Go."

He just stared at me, and I knew I'd done far worse than kill him. Clovis struggled painfully to his feet and pointed at me.

"You. Little man."

From the way he hissed the words, it seemed he would

not forget me. Then he stumbled away after one of the horses along the stream bank.

"He's a hard one," Collen admired grudgingly. "Lord Gareth, I'm sorry. I could not kill him. I mean, him standing there close and staring straight into my eyes, I . . ."

Did I not know the rest too well? "No shame, man. A day came once when I could not either. You've done well enough. Now let's be putting some miles between us and his friends."

Across the heath, Clovis managed to fetch and mount one of the horses. The effort plainly cost him, but he forced himself erect in the saddle, wheeling the horse about to face the men who'd impossibly beaten and shamed a king. I don't know what took me, but I slapped my fist to my chest and flung the arm out straight to him in the old *alae* salute, and damned if young Clovis hadn't spirit enough left to return it. Given and returned in grim respect, but with the recognition of lines drawn and mortal enemies made.

Riding at my knee in our fast trot, the big Frank horse strung behind me, Pindar said, "When we dare stop, sir, we'd better forage. There's not but a few bits of dry fish left, not half a meal for one of us."

"You can have mine, Pindar," Collen offered in a voice white as his expression. "I've no appetite at all."

As I expected, Clovis's men followed us most of that day, but their horses were not that swift over open ground. We widened the distance hourly, pushing on until well into late summer dusk. Next morning there was no sign of Franks but, for us, no real safety until we crossed River Elorn. By then, leading horses done in as ourselves, we limped into an Osismi village and asked a wee bit of food and something for the horses. We were grateful the village was one of Trystan's. Food and fodder were no problem, but when I told their elder why the bridge must come down, he flat refused. His name was Rufius, he owned with a frayed and dusty pride, and he still wore the faded remains of a decurion's gown.

"Bridges and roads are my charge," he asserted in a mix of Latin and Gaulish Celt. "My father was decurion here before me, appointed by the provincial governor. Our bridge is on the trade route. It must be preserved."

And there, I was to understand, the matter ended. Neither Hoel nor Lord Trystan had *ever* sent such an insane order to Rufius, nor ever would. Didn't Arthur have his problems with officials of this dead Roman school? Every one the same: they had rules and one way and speed in doing things, and not even an emperor could budge these barnacles on the hull of government.

Secure from pursuit now, I had time to study Clovis's fine bay, always staying upwind of him when he grazed so he got used to my scent. He was cold-natured as a good battle horse must be, but stolid and used to a heavier seat than mine. When we tried a heat over a short course, our army horses left him far behind before he reached full gallop. But solid as a stone wall; a frontal charge from a line of such animals would rub our noses deep in our own mortality. Different tactics would be needed against them.

We came down the last rise onto the coast road that led past the village of Leon, the castle above standing high against a clear blue sky. The people streamed out to meet us, women and children. Collen and Pindar rode straight and stiff, tired though they were, as their wives broke out of the throng to run alongside. Collen's wife held up their youngest babe for him to kiss, and then we were walking the animals gratefully through the castle's open south gate.

Pindar wilted out of the saddle like a limp rag, Collen the same. They stood blinking in the sunlight as the other men in the courtyard broke off sword practice to gather about us.

"God be praised," Collen wheezed. "We did it and lived to tell."

"Not yet," I barked at him. "Give me the Frankish weapons. Walk those horses half an hour before water, grain and a good currying, mind, and stall this big fellow away from the mares. We are back now; time to square off again. The rest of you: Who's in charge of this May dance? Get on with it, get sweating. *Move,* ladies!"

"God pity us," someone muttered sourly as I stumped away toward the keep above. "The Whip is back."

Whip was it? And me feeling ten stone heavier with every step I climbed. I needed to pause at the top to breathe but denied myself in their sight. Clumping up the stairs to the common room, I heard casual chords drawn from a harp. Trystan sat on the casement sill, gazing out to sea. Isolt was not present, but her waiting woman Gwendolen wound wool yarn from a basket onto a spindle.

Trystan saluted me with a wave. "*Ave,* Eire the Terrible. I heard your gentle admonition to the men. Welcome home."

I set down the lance and ax. "Collen and Pindar did well. We found the Franks. Where's the Carhaix map?"

Trystan fetched it, hefting the ax with its curiously shaped head swept into the shape of a flower's bell. "I've seen these. I think they call them *franciscas.* Thrown or used hand-to-hand."

"And the lance is almost as heavy as the *Combrogi* carry. Is there anything come from Arthur?"

"Not yet. You say you saw the Franks?"

"We found Clovis."

"No! Himself?"

"Aye, we passed a word or two. I borrowed his horse." With the map, I showed him what happened and where. "Big men, biggest horses I ever saw. We'll have to—"

"Gareth! Home at last."

She stood in the doorway in her light summer kirtle, all blue and gold, and the sight of her, God help me, had not changed anything but only dug the wanting deeper into my soul. "Lady."

"Lord love us," Isolt laughed. "We're so glad you're back." She came and kissed my cheek with its week of stubble, scratching at it tenderly. "Bless me, Trystan, if our friend doesn't look frayed as an old rope. Gwendolen, up."

She spun gracefully away, bidding her woman order the bath house attendants to light fires for hot water. I had to drag my eyes from yearning after her, for there was no one in the room for me but her. I didn't hear Trystan the first time he spoke.

"Gareth? You must be tired. Collen and Pindar were not hurt?"

"No, never better," I shot back gruffly. "But they could use a wee bit of rest at home. Will you come to the stable? You should see that stallion."

I almost pulled him to the door without looking back, for I dared not let either of them see what was growing stronger in me, what I wanted and must deny.

In the middle of July when the Osismi cut their hay, a trading vessel dropped anchor off the Saddle. I prayed it came from Arthur, calling me home in need, but they were bound that way from the Middle Sea. We were surprised to hear they'd touched at the Veneti port of Vannes, which was now in Clovis's grabbing hands.

Trystan asked the squat sailor-messenger, "They gave you no trouble at all, took no tolls?"

They did not, only detained the ship long enough to deliver a written message from the Frankish king to Castle Leon. Impressed with the rare importance of his office, the sailor presented the parchment with a clumsy flourish and apologies for his haste. The shipmaster had bidden him deliver and return while the good wind held for Britain. He hurried down the quay stairs. Standing with me at the top, Trystan reflected, "I would say lack of foresight is not one of Clovis's failings. He means to have the entire coast, so he needs sea trade. Shrewd."

He broke the seal and scanned the writing quickly. "Fair Latin; he must have a priest or two in his train."

CLOVIS, most Christian king of the Franks—

Trystan winced at me. "Ye gods but new converts can be tiresome. Always flailing their crosses at you."

> *—to the lord of Castle Leon and the little thief of horses who serves him, greeting.*
>
> *I have beaten the Romans out of Soissons. I have bent to my will every tribe in the north from the Rhine to Ocean Sea. Now even the Veneti have laid down their arms.*

I knew that for a lie. "Not all of them, not by a long mile."

"Oh, he's far more vaunting. Listen."

CLOVIS, son of CHILDERIC, has never been defeated in battle nor ever suffered insult without tenfold redress. Let Castle Leon lock its gates. Let that little man who stole my fine horse, whose least drop of blood is nobler than his own, cower behind his woman, for Clovis will breach and sup within Leon's walls before the birds fly south.

Trystan rolled up the parchment. "Good of him to let us know."

And no honorable retreat to Britain for me. I couldn't leave now. Brave Trystan was, but no teacher of ill-armed men not ready for war. Without me, he would lose Leon to Clovis, and what then would happen to *her?* "Ah, the puffed-up manny just wants us to wait and quake in fear. Quick now, bring a wax tablet and stylus, Tryst, for you must write. You down there, sailor! Wait!"

I bounded down the stairs, bawling to the messenger who was just after setting his oars, and jumped into the curragh. "Where do you next put in? Castle Dore? Camelot?"

"We take on lead and tin at Dore," he confirmed, "and unload iron from Damascus at Camelot."

"You brought one royal message this day. Will you deliver another into King Arthur's own hand?"

His blunt face brightened. "I will."

As I thought, he relished the idea of being that important twice in the same month (for a consideration, please, himself being a poor man with children). Though he spoke the bastard dialect of sailors from Antioch to the Isles, here and there I caught a more familiar fall. "Would you be a man of Eire?"

"So I am. Of the ui Chellaig in Baile Atha Cliath. And yourself?"

"Of the ui Byrne and the Knuckles of God."

"I thought I heard Leinster in your mouth." The sailor's grin of recognition cooled a mite. "Ui Byrne."

"That's an old quarrel and none of ours now."

"True, I left young. Got sold away."

"Och, your poor mam and da."

"No tears for them." He spat eloquently over the side. "They did the selling. Where's this message? I've got to be gone."

Trystan jumped down the steps with tablet and stylus. For three gold *solidi* to one more wandering son of Eire, the message went to Arthur over Trystan's name and my mark: *Threatened with attack by Clovis before end of summer. Most urgently need all arms and equipments requested, including heavy lances.*

As the curragh dwindled with distance, Trystan and I tarried on the quay, wondering if the arms could already be coming, or if our message would reach Arthur before the Franks reached Leon.

"He shouldn't attack." Trystan hardly sounded convinced. "It isn't logical Clovis should try for Leon straight, not with hostile forces still behind him."

There was the modern, educated man for you. "It is a more ancient logic, Tryst. Clovis comes, as I do, from older ways in the world. In Eire shame on a king is shame on his tribe, perhaps its doom. The insult must be wiped clean, no matter the cost, else men may not follow him. The blunder's mine. I should have finished him."

"The blunder could be his," Trystan said, "and possibly

our advantage. If we can rally the other free castles behind us—"

"First you must send to Rufius to have Elorn bridge torn down. If they won't, we must bring it down ourselves."

Trystan gazed back up at the keep. "How we could use a few *Combrogi* now."

"Are there not two of us for a start?" Brave words spoken with far more feist than I felt.

"Gareth, how much time do we have? Really?"

When I scanned Trystan's face I read worry, and prayed he could not see what must be writ large in mine, for I saw not my friend then but a rival who claimed her, made love to her, and now demons of my own grew in me, putting the vile taste of jealousy in my mouth, and I hated what I was becoming.

Let me be gone. I'm not your savior. I didn't willingly ask to love her.

But the sin's as much in the thought as the act. Why could this sickness not have taken me when I was twenty, hale as a horse and no brighter? Then I might have suffered with the brief pain of the young and shrugged it off, but now? Jesus, were Britain not so far and Trystan not depending on me, I'd be in the water and swimming for home.

"How long, Gareth?"

"Clovis will need some healing, but if I were that shrewd young manny, I'd come just after the harvesting to count on good forage all the way. Six weeks."

Six weeks busy from first light till after the last. Tithing hay and storing supplies from every village and holding. Storing oil and stones for the onagers and to hurl upon men scaling our walls. Trystan sends orders to destroy Elorn bridge, but again stubborn old Rufius refuses. We must do it ourselves. Ten miles west of it on the same river is Castle Cornouaille, thirteen miles northeast Castle Morlaix. I ride to the first, Trystan to the other, showing the message, the maps and the danger. Elorn and its bridges are the key; surely they must see that. Banded together we could hit them from three sides on ground of our choosing. Alone, their castles only wait to be besieged at Clovis's pleasure.

The cautious lords listen and shake their heads; they have problems of their own. Besides, Clovis is coming for Leon, not them. They have no responsibility to Trystan for insults to the Franks. If Clovis comes against them, they will fend him off themselves, never fear. We ride back to Leon knowing the first precious week wasted in futility. When we meet over the maps in the common room, Trystan's mood is the blackest I've ever seen in the man sober. Isolt sits silently with fat, motherly Gwendolen, knowing more of her husband than any man can, while Trystan seethes like water stirring in its depths toward full boil. We try to pierce the mind of Clovis and what route he must take to get at us: How far and how long?

A sea landing anywhere on the rocky coast is dicey, at Leon itself insane. He must come overland. Our brooding over the map yielded at least one clear truth: Clovis had more than ninety hard miles to march, some of it over the southern claw of the mountains to reach River Elorn.

"Where he'll find no bridge," Trystan vowed. "That damned thing comes down tomorrow. We'll leave early, every man with an ax. If Rufius gives us trouble, he'll ache for it."

"He is an old man," Isolt reminded him mildly. "Serving Rome is all he ever knew, all he has to be proud of."

"Much I care," Trystan snapped. "I'm sick of this. And don't presume to tell me my business."

I put his temper down to strain. The man knew we were too few and that he could afford not a single mistake in judgment or preparation. "He must cross River Aulne first. He needs every bridge he can find. Tomorrow we'll disappoint him."

"I'll give the order."

Suddenly Trystan plunged his dagger deep into the table. "Name of all *gods!* Those stupid old men with their heads in the sand. Cornouaille, Morlaix—we could have met Clovis in the open, beaten or turned him back."

I'd had second thoughts on that. "Our men are not yet well skilled or armed for a cavalry engagement. Perhaps we're better served here where sixty of us are equal to two hundred of them."

"Don't be a fool. We could have done it." Trystan rounded on me. "We could have, but you—why in hell didn't you kill that rotten little man when you had the chance?"

Because I could not drive Collen to what I hadn't the stomach to do years before myself. "I don't know."

"You don't know; there's helpful," Trystan sneered. "As if we didn't do enough plain murder in the Midlands." He lunged away from the table, presenting the sorry sight of me to Isolt, who was shocked as myself at the anger fuming out of her husband. "Look at him: Arthur's genius of cavalry. He could have saved us all this. Now that Frankish pig wants all Leon in payment. I should have rutting well asked Arthur to send Bedwyr."

"You asked for Gareth," Isolt told him calmly. "You prayed to your gods for him." She rose and went to Trystan, arms open to soothe him. "We understand, all of us. This is a difficult time for—"

"Leave off, I say." Trystan turned away, denying her coldly. "Go away. Damn you, why must you always hang on me when I need to be alone?"

I saw the hurt in her eyes and couldn't look at either of them. Isolt faltered and turned away while I struggled past my own sudden anger to understand a man who was brave but never a leader. Fear of fear: not for himself but that he might make mistakes or prove unequal to what was coming. "The bridge will come down tomorrow," I assured him. "We have time enough for all if we waste none now. Come help me with this map."

The fury drained out of Trystan quick as it came. Without a word or glance for Isolt, no sign to make it right again, he bent over the map. "I want to know the moment he reaches Elorn. When will you send scouts?"

"My mouse will tell me."

"Mouse? What mouse, you ridiculous man?"

"I will know when." *But do not shame her so again. Do not make me think you unworthy of her, for I'm already wanting your place.*

We won no friends in Rufius's village when the bridge came down, but with forty-odd armed men behind us, they could do no more than glower and protest. The bridge was gone in a few hours, leaving only the breakwater pilings and main supports.

"When there is no more danger, we will help you rebuild," Trystan promised.

"There is no danger now," one villager spoke up. "I have used that bridge all my life trading with the Veneti. I'll lay five *solidi* the Franks never come."

"Cornouaille and Morlaix are laying more than that," I informed him. "They've refused to tear down their bridges.

One or the other, Clovis will go through them like locusts through wheat. Count your blessings, fellow."

Late July. Five weeks left at most. Trystan and I rode a circuit of his holdings, preparing the Osismi to gather in the castle when the order was given. They must bring all possible food supplies, their sheep and cattle. Nothing was to be left to sustain the enemy. Isolt herself, Gwendolen jouncing after on a mule, rode in our wake, calming frightened women and children, answering their fearful questions with resolution. Could they really come? Nothing like this has ever happened to Leon. Will we be truly safe in the castle?

The days passed. The growing strain on Trystan and myself began to tell on Isolt. She worked hard as we did in preparing, yet the more Trystan was forced to concentrate on defenses, the more he neglected her. She bore it well, but became more silent and downcast each day.

I drove the men and myself. My plan was to teach them *Combrogi* tactics, but first they and their mounts must learn to move as one mind and body. We drilled and drilled in simple formations: files wheeling into line, line to file, massed square into wedge, and myself bawling at them when square-to-wedge ended in milling confusion.

"Disgraceful! My old da danced nimbler the day he died. A-*gain,* ladies."

One evening in the bathhouse, as we were lying on our bellies, being oiled and strigiled by attendants, Trystan turned his face to me. "Isolt spoke to me this morning. Has she offended you somehow?"

"What? No, never."

"I shouldn't think so, but she seems to feel you go out of your way to avoid her."

"Not at all. Just busy with a hundred things to do and

remember, and only half of them come to mind when they should."

But did the woman know? Was she beginning to suspect or the needing her show in me? Those days I wished myself back among the Knuckles of God, and let the black Sidhe do their worst.

On a morning close to the Ides of August, we heard the bells ring from Great Island and the Saddle. A ship was sighted. Watching outside the sea gate, Trystan and I saw the trading keel crawling toward us over the horizon.

"Another love note from Clovis, you think?" Trystan wondered.

"No," I said hopefully, "they're out from Britain. Could it be from Arthur?"

Again I saw the change in Trystan, an eagerness that had nothing to do with Arthur or arms. Something in his face and eye, a naked yearning and an old hope worn smooth from rubbing against the heart of the man.

Low in the water with cargo, the keel rowed cautiously past Saddle toward Little Hump and lowered a curragh. "I'll send scouts out tomorrow," I reckoned, "but I'll be needing another look at the maps. Coming, then?"

Like life itself beckoning him, Trystan did not turn from the sight of the ship. "By and by. You know where the maps are."

The common room was empty. I spread the maps over the long table, mumbling aloud over my task. No more bridge at Elorn. Scouts must find a fording to the west or cross at Cornouaille. "Either way gives them flat country to the southeast . . . good view of any advancing troops . . . take a high position on the northern spur of the hills just *here,* yes."

"Trystan?"

Isolt stood with one hand on the drawn-back curtain

that closed off their bedchamber. "Oh. I thought I heard my husband."

"God bless you, lady." I started to leave, but she spoke again, coming forward.

"Why are you so short with me, Gareth? My name is Isolt." Then, as if voicing something she'd wanted to say for some time: "What has happened to you, you strange man? You never smile anymore."

I sat down on a wide bench, holding the map, needing that much distance between us. "Much to do and little time."

"But you barely speak to me anymore."

"I—There's a ship just anchored."

"Yes, I heard the bells."

"We hope it comes from Arthur."

"It *is* true," Isolt pressed, sure of herself. "You never look at me either. You and Trystan: I might have grown a beard for all the note either of you takes."

"Ah, that's foolish. It's a young man's calling to ride with these men and teach them. I get up in the morning, lying bravely that I'm twenty again, but by noon the truth weighs me down and I'm mightily tired."

Go away, woman. Be merciful and go away.

Isolt laced her hands in her lap. "Did you know he is drinking again? Oh, not much, but he never sleeps well, you know. I wake in the middle of the night and hear him playing his harp out here. Always the same song, the same notes over and over."

Many times I'd heard it, two notes rising, a pause, then a fall.

"He goes away in his heart," she regretted softly. "You are the only old friend left to him, and a dear one."

"Not true, Isolt. Bedwyr's not forgotten, nor Arthur nor Guenevere."

"But they will not call him home. He would die for that."

"He knows they cannot."

"I think that eats at him." Isolt sighed deeply and, as she brushed the heavy fall of hair back from her shoulders, I breathed in the scent of it, hearing her voice and the soft appeal it carried. "Gareth? This last year, I don't know what I've done or left undone, but I feel I have failed Trystan somehow. That he has never really been with me."

"Failed?" I had to turn to her then and let the sight of her burn into me. *How could such as you fail? How could you not be enough for any man?* "No, Isolt, you are a good wife. You are—"

In my earnestness, my arm naturally went round the woman in comfort, and I felt her gratitude at the touch. Isolt melted into my shoulder. In the next moment I'd be spilling over like blood from a wound, but God was kind. Trystan's voice trumpeted up from the sea gate. "Gareth! Can you hear me?"

I was off the bench like a spear from a catapult, head thrust out the casement to see the ship's curragh within hailing distance. "Aye, what is it?"

"They're from Camelot! Arms from Arthur! They're unloading on the Hump. Get every man and boat we've got."

"So I will before you can blink." I spun about to Isolt, thanking Providence I was saved for the time. "It's the help we prayed for. I've got to—"

But, as I made for the stairs, something compelled me to stop and grasp Isolt's hand. "You are the best wife that—you failed *no* one. You—"

I didn't trust myself to say more, just bounded down the

stairs two at a time. Arthur's aid come and the feel of her close to me, brief as it was, I *did* feel twenty just then.

We toiled all morning and into the afternoon, a busy line of curraghs like black water beetles, rowed by men like Collen and Pindar and sturdy young Milius. Trystan and I did not spare ourselves, sweating to load and unload, and whatever youth I'd fancied early turned to truth late as I threw the last new mail shirt on its pile in the armory and just dropped down, sweat-soaked, against the wall next to Trystan. For a few moments we stared silently at nothing.

"Early to bed this night," he vowed. "Let the men sleep an extra hour tomorrow."

"Gladly. I am not the man I was."

Trystan vented a wheezy laugh. "Who is?"

Our high king had sent all we asked for: heavy lances, mail, the longer cavalry swords of the *Combrogi,* mail-skirted helmets, the lot. The men would be better equipped now. If they could learn in time, the day might come when they drove the Franks from Armorica forever.

Arthur had also sent a wax tablet, written in his own broad hand, which Trystan read to me.

TRYSTAN, DEAR FRIEND: We hope these armaments suffice. We are unable to send any men at the present time. You have our prayers and love. In return we will need Gareth at Camelot immediately his mission to you is discharged/ ARTHUR

"Surely not before we teach Clovis good British manners," Trystan reasoned.

"Surely not." What else could I say?

"You'd miss the fun."

"Can't have that." I struggled up stiffly and clumped to the armory door. "My scouts are waiting for orders."

For the mission I'd chosen Collen again, and young Milius who had the same qualities as my first two: a small man with a good seat on a horse and quick to learn, if something of a boaster. They carried Trystan's request to Castle Cornouaille to let them pass should they require the bridge, and perhaps a night's lodging. Milius was eager to deck himself in all his new gear, loudly proclaiming himself a ready match for any Frank. I allowed them only cavalry swords but no mail to tire the horses. Collen was relieved to know they were not to get anywhere near so close this time. He knew exactly where to position the pair of them for the earliest sight of approaching Franks.

"We need to know where, line and speed of march, how many horse and foot. Likely they captured siege engines from the Romans. Count what you see, count again to be sure. Milius, stay close to Collen and do as he tells you, clear?"

The young man's eyes shone with the fire of excitement, possible glory, and nerves I remembered well from Eburacum long ago. "Sir, if they get close enough—"

Collen quashed that quick enough. "They won't."

"How do you know? You don't know everything."

Collen gathered his reins and bit noisily into an apple. "Because I've already got close, and I've a family."

"He's right, Milius," I said. "You'll look, you'll count and come back with what you learn. No fear, Fire Eater. Before summer is out you'll be seeing too many Franks too damned close. God bless."

I rode with them as far as the south gate, then walked my horse back to Trystan, who waited before his mounted and new-armed men still clumsy in the management of their heavy lances which swayed this way and that like saplings in a stiff breeze and rapped their drill mates on the helm or shoulder in any kind of close maneuver.

"Well," Trystan observed, "at least they *look* a bit like cavalry. By twos into line!"

We led them out the gate for the afternoon's drill, tired though all of us were. We knew our men too few and each sunset more sand run down the glass. The men wondered why all the horse drill when they'd be fighting within the walls. They would not appreciate my true sentiments. Because I'd spent my life fighting and pulling weeds sprung up in the cracks in an empire gone to seed. Because I wanted to be quit of this place and the sight of a woman like a knife in me. Because I didn't like what I was becoming, sick-jealous of my friend and wanting to bash someone, *anyone,* and for that Clovis would suit gloriously. We couldn't stop him forever any more than we could stop Saxons or time, but with God and luck we might make this last corner of Lesser Britain too costly for the most Christian king of the Franks.

Collen and Milius returned a week later. Clovis was moving in strength west through the Carhaix. The scouts lingered only long enough to number his force, then bolted for home.

"Five hundred," Collen was sure. "More with the onager and catapult crews."

"I divided us into them, Lord Gareth," Milius volunteered soberly. "Eight to one."

Collen nodded, uncinching his saddle. "Pray God I get eight small ones."

We had a few days at most. Time to herd Trystan's folk into Castle Leon, lock the gates, and wait.

V

"Thou Shalt Not Have Leon"

aking their best speed home, Collen and Milius had found only one ford, fairly deep, where they had to half swim their horses across. With heavy siege equipment and wagons, Clovis would need a bridge, and the nearest one, which meant the lord of Cornouaille, who refused to ally with us, must be left to his lot. Only later we learned that the castle closed tight against Clovis who, not being minded to tarry, simply stripped the near village of forage, burned a few huts, and passed on.

"Presumably to our obliteration," Trystan guessed. "A most single-minded man."

The force Clovis brought against us was no Carhaix village raid. By Collen's count two hundred horsemen, three hundred foot, some of them archers, five catapults, three onagers, and at least a dozen wagons. Progress would be slow since their point dare not range too far ahead of the slower engines and wagons, but by now Clovis could be no more than fifteen miles away.

"We have a day," Trystan estimated as we moved along the parapet. "Perhaps a little more."

More, I thought, watching the folk trudge toward us along the dusty crescent of the coast road. Why should Clovis push his men to arrive worn out, already confident of victory as a simple matter of time?

From the south wall where we stood, Trystan called down: "Open the gates!"

The first of the Leon folk neared the castle, more coming over the hills to the south: creaking carts, children skipping beside them with goads to urge on lumbering oxen, wagons full of penned geese and chickens, loads of firewood, sacks of hastily milled grain, hay, and household goods. In the heat of the day they poured into Castle Leon, one half-grown girl carrying the family's mangy orange cat. Franks might come and go, but rats were always with them.

Along the south and west walls, men piled stones by our two onagers or carried bundles of arrows to the corner towers. Even completely encircled, we would lose use only of the bathhouse and the waterside latrine.

Trystan wiped at the sweat on his cheeks and neck. "I'll miss the baths, though I'm sure the Franks will find them convenient."

"And the well."

We'd considered destroying that, but the well was vital to Leon's people, the only fresh water within a mile beside the new one within our walls.

"Recall the Midlands, Tryst?"

"As seldom as possible."

"No, but did not the Saxons have a shrewd way with wells?"

"Yes, very—" He broke off; I knew he'd taken my meaning. "Right. Did they not!"

The younger farmers, as soon as they came through the

gates, were sent back out with casks to draw and store as much fresh water as they could carry from the village well. No sense wasting. We would cask and ration water from the courtyard well for drinking and cooking, since what I had in mind would endanger our own well in time. As for the latrine, we had a lovely notion for disposing of its contents.

Now through the gates came the village priest, Father Antonius, on his mule, his wizened little sexton behind, driving a cart with the church's few treasures, the carved Chi-Rho, silver altar cups and embroidered cloth. Up and busy since dawn as the last hours ran out, Isolt quartered them in a place of honor, my old chamber next to the central solar. Village folk she crammed in where she could. Over a hundred of them, and none could be left in the open when stones and spears flew over the wall. By evening every sheltered space—armory, stables, hall, and rath—was packed with folk cheek by jowl with their sheep and cattle. As the hours passed, their fear grew. Men took to climbing to the parapets to stare anxiously off into the hills until Trystan forbade them. Nothing to see yet; rest while there's time.

He issued another order that evening in the crowded hall. His company would wear mail at all times until told otherwise. It was a helter-skelter supper, soldiers and villagers jammed together at the tables, along the wall in the kitchen area and outside, servers and cooks laboring back and forth with platters and pots of soup and frumenty. Within the hall, Trystan—ah, the man glittered that night, he *shone,* moving among the frightened people, harp in hand, putting fire back into hearts where fear had guttered its flame.

"Not within living memory has an enemy come against

the Osismi and not lived to regret it. Caesar tried and gave it up for a bad bargain. We Britons here—and do we not have our own memories and pride?—came to this land to make a life when Saxons spread like plague at home. Now their Frankish cousins come to try us. And why? Because of one young king's childish vanity. As Caesar learned to his cost, as Boudicca answered Nero, you and I will teach *our* lesson to his most Christian majesty, Clovis, and add to his Ten Commandments an eleventh he will write large in his gospel: Thou shalt *not* have Leon!"

The soldiers cheered him and thumped the tables. The villagers just shrugged as I and Rhian once did, listening to the boastful *ghillies* in Feargus's rath, and went on gobbling. I imagined they'd never eaten so well before and were mindful that they might not again after tomorrow. Trystan turned to wink at Isolt.

"What can you do with such a glory of a man but love him?" she glowed to me, and must I not agree just then despite my own turmoil? Trystan was a flower without the endurance of plain weed like me, bred to bloom splendidly for a moment. He set the harp in the crook of his left arm. "Now enough of barbarians. Who's for a song of home?"

"Here! A Belgae song!"

"No, Cantii!"

"Neither. I've in mind one from the Dubhunni." Trystan plucked a few notes from his instrument. "They once howled for my life, but they could always give beauty a voice."

He traced the first notes of "Bronwen in the Vale," then began to sing with a true Celt's voice, not deep but pure and effortless.

"Light the candles of evening and wait me, dear Bronwen.
Let your sweet song of sunset call me home to the vale,
Call me back to my lover, to where you are waiting,
To the banks of Wye water where once we were young,
Where we promised and plighted and married ere parting.
Far and long have I wandered, your face ere before me.
Light your candles, oh Bronwen, my wandering's done."

Oh, were you to mine the man that night, you'd find among the bitter dross rich gold washed down the twisting river of his life. He was taught by the wise men of Anglesey who remembered the way of the Druid, forbidden as it was first by Romans and then the Church. In the old days Trystan would have been one of them. For the rest, what can I tell you? Lives, like rivers, spilling clear from a pure source, can run foul through marsh before flowing home to the cleansing sea of God.

Next morning I had Milius leave off his mail and report to me in the stable, where I had his saddled horse waiting. Milius already had a bit of seasoning with Collen and surely guessed what was coming.

"It is time to be looking for Clovis. Patrol the coast road up into the hills for a mile or two. Return as soon as you sight them."

"I will, sir." With a bunch of straw, Milius impatiently swabbed at his boot soles. "Devil take it now. Damned stock in the courtyard. Can't step anywhere without—damn!"

He swung up into the saddle, and I tapped his scabbard. "You've a few fresh bannocks and some oats for the horse, Fire Eater. Try not to meet Frankish scouts, but if you must dance with them, leave a few for Lord Trystan."

Milius grinned sheepishly at the joke. "I did sound a great roaring ass at first."

So could any young man, but riding with Collen, Milius's first sight of armed Franks had carried him a long mile toward common sense. "Don't give it a thought, boyo. Wisdom's a virtue sure, but a man's got to make an ass of himself now and again just to stay human."

And you look now at the secret proof of that.

"Mark now, Milius. There was once a lord of Leinster, mind, who never did a wrong or foolish thing in seventy sober years. No conversation at all, they said. Dullest man in three clans; even the angels were bored with him. He always looked as if he'd missed something. God bless, Milius."

The courtyard and outbuildings were going ripe with the presence of cattle and sheep. In a few days Arthur himself would smell Leon when the wind was right. After supper in the too-crowded hall, I went to the kitchen with a request for the cooks. Gwendolen was there counting stores with one of the old cook-women and surprised to see me. What I asked surprised her even more as I shouldered between them and dropped my empty sacks on a table, too hot, tired, and short for manners.

"I need the scraps left from supper—bones, bread, broken meats, anything you'll not be saving for tomorrow."

Gwendolen did not understand. "Is my lord still hungry or taken to feeding stray dogs?"

"I am not." I started filling the sacks with what the cook set by for me, irritable and not of a mind to explain. "It's scraps I'm needing, scraps I'm asking, and if no one minds, I'd not have the entire castle knowing the matter. Give you good evening."

As I clumped out with my burden, I heard Gwendolen remark to the cook: "Lady says he used to be such a pleasant man."

The evening was yet light enough to see along the coast road for a mile and more. Nothing stirred, no sign of Milius. One of the onager men on the west wall labored at winding the skein, winching the great arm back while another waited with a heavy stone.

"Ai, lads? What are you about there?"

The young soldier heaved the stone onto the arm's spoon-shaped rest. "There, sir." He pointed out toward the road and the small white stakes planted at intervals along it, so placed as to be overlooked by anyone not aware of them. "Hundred, hundred and fifty paces, we can take the head off a sparrow. It's the longer shots giving us trouble."

I inspected the cocked arm. "What are you going for now?"

"Three hundred, sir."

"You'll be out early with a wagon gathering up stones. Can't afford to waste. Right, then: loose."

We should have looked before releasing the hook. With the dull thud of the arm, the three of us strained through dusk to mark the stone's flight toward the marker—and Christ, my heart dropped into my stomach, seeing the rider just turning out onto the road from behind a village hut. Milius it was, closing fast on just that point where the stone should come down. I screamed at him—

"Milius! Get off the road! Watch out!"

—but he was too far to hear, the stone a black gob of death descending on him like the hand of God, and the man who'd loosed it squeezed his eyes shut and turned away, sick with fear. "I can't look, I can't look. Please let it miss, *please—*"

The stone came down so close to Milius's horse that the animal shied sideways, rearing in terror. Milius fought to control it, then stopped still, staring at death come so close. He kicked the horse into a furious gallop.

I bawled down: "Open the gates. Scout coming in."

And returning to us with no Christian benevolence. Milius shot through the open gates, loudly cursing all but heaven as he reined about to glare up at the onager. "What are you doing? What in the name of rutting hell are you doing? I'm almost *killed*."

"You'd know if't was all the way. It's me, lad, Lord Gareth. My fault entire. We should have looked first."

He must have been shaking for I heard it clear in his voice. "Well, I do wish—well, if those two misbegot bastards up there aim as close tomorrow, I will forgive them."

"Where's Clovis, then?"

"Close. I rode out some two miles. Point of their column came in sight quarter hour past."

Clovis wouldn't try to array his forces in the dark. "Then we'll see him clear in first sunlight, won't we?"

"No later, sir." Milius dismounted, still shaken by his brush with death, jabbing an accusing finger up at the onager men. "Dying in battle is one thing, but you fools be *careful* with that thing."

The hook man threw him a friendly salute. "How could I dream of killing you, boy? You still owe me money."

"Secure the engine." I was already hurrying down the steps toward the south gate with my garbage sacks.

Not to be boasting now, but when Arthur broke Cerdic at Mount Badon—years later that was—the inspiration came to me to take the *Combrogi* behind the Saxons' rear and destroy their supply wagons. I like to consider the garbage of Leon if not genius, at least her handmaid. We frightened a year or two off Milius's life but shortened Clovis's siege as well. In battle a bowl of foresight is worth a bucket of heroism.

Early as I rose next morning, Trystan was on the south parapet before me, Isolt close beside him. Two sentries walked the walls, their outlines dark against the lightening sky. Trystan breathed deeply of the warm south wind. "We'll have another hot day. With this wind we'll hear them soon. Isolt, rouse the folk and see to the kitchens."

She'd already done so. "Cooks are setting out the porridge now."

Faint but clear on the wind I caught the distant rattle of drums, a ghostly quarrel of horns. "They're moving."

Trystan gathered Isolt close in his arms. "If you're afraid, it is all right."

She peered up into his face—into his soul, I think. "And you, husband?"

"Not now. It's when there is no music to make or aught to do with hands or mind that I—" Trystan kissed her lightly. "You know what I mean."

"It is then I worry about you. I don't know honestly if what I'm feeling is fear." Isolt gazed off toward the south. "But I wish we were past this and into next week. God keep you, Gareth."

"And you, Isolt."

She walked quickly along the parapet toward the keep and her duty. "She's never seen a battle," Trystan said.

I would not have guessed for the straightness of the woman's back. "It is the best of wives you have."

Eyes on the road, listening: "Yes."

We reckoned not to lay eye to Franks for at least an hour. I told the men to breakfast quickly, then rejoined Trystan on the parapet, calling up to the archers in the southwest tower to show themselves.

Collen leaned out over the crennel. "Sir?"

"Cry out when you spy them. Who's with you?"

Pindar appeared beside him. "Me, my lord."

"Enough shafts?"

The Frankish horns blared again, closer. Pindar glanced in their direction. "Enough."

"Heed the aiming markers. Don't waste. Wait for a clear target."

More light now. Our armed men began to file onto the parapets around us. The south and west walls would bear the brunt of the attack. The north and east parapets were manned by able-bodied village men wearing helmets and cast-off Roman armor to make our force seem larger. There was little danger of assault on their sides, being too steep inside the broad ditch, but they could warn if any attempt was made.

The dawn wind did little by way of cooling Leon; already Trystan and I sweated in our mail. Trystan's reflection had a hard edge. "I half thought Clovis would reconsider. Then I recalled a tale told of him after he took Soissons. One of his men stole a sacred chalice from a church. Clovis demanded he return it. The fellow offered him half the chalice and forthwith split it in two with his ax, allowing Clovis could return his half if he liked, which he did, but at the first opportunity he split the man's skull as neatly with his sword." Trystan broke off to chuckle at the thought. "Vindictiveness is a flaw in a man. Not that I haven't held grudges in my time."

"You can incline so," I admitted, "when you've had a drop in."

He rapped me on the arm affectionately. "My good Gareth: warm and bright as the sun at midday."

He gazed off along the coast road, searching for Clovis or perhaps an answer to the twisted riddle of his own life. "What a blessing to have a soul clear as noon."

"Oh, there's envy." I didn't trust myself to utter more. *I want to take your place with her. I want the right to hold and touch and keep her as you do, but far better. God help me, I don't want to hate you for just having her, but you have cast shadows in me where none were before. Envy is a mean sin and a deadly one, and I stink of it. If I live out this day, I'll be to the priest. Perhaps I should go now before the Franks come, and—*

No. I would confess to no one, my soul jealous even of that truth, for it was mine and new, this loving, with a curious, melting sweetness to the pain I could not yet forgo. Confession would pale that punishing pleasure.

Collen from the tower above: "There they come!"

Far to the west the first horsemen appeared on the road. Trystan wiped his brow and pulled the mail hood over his head. "I think the gods are with us."

"Which gods?"

"Yours, mine; I'm not particular today. A fine hot morning they've given us."

And in this growing light, no place for the darkness in me. "I'll fetch Milius."

At my call, the young soldier left his onager and trotted round the parapet to us. "Sir."

"Now's the time to be a hero, lad; to be a part of the victory."

Milius glanced nervously from me to the lengthening column pouring onto the coast road. "If it's all one to you, sir, I'm in no haste."

"Nothing for it. You shall be a hero today." Trystan clapped a hand on the youth's shoulder. "Necessary as the shaft to the arrow pile."

"As the very bow to that flight," I added. "And be noticed by a king more closely than grit in his eye."

Once more Milius looked to see the oncoming enemy and the huge man prancing his horse at their head. He licked his lips. "That king?"

"The very one. Lord Trystan desires you to nip out to the village well there and fetch us a bucketful."

So far, Milius hardly seemed inspired. Trystan encouraged him. "Lord Gareth vows no finer volunteer could be found."

"But I didn't—"

"You'll be in no danger," I assured him. "Do not refuse the hero's portion before I've carved the sheer beauty of it."

Beautiful it was, lovely, as we spread it before him, what Trystan would call the artlessness of true art. Milius walked out the gate with a large bucket and strolled in full view of Clovis to the village well. There he hauled up the bucket and filled his own, no hurry, all the time in creation to view the fascinating sight of the Frankish king's army, and there Milius stood, our men on the walls imploring him to for God's sake get back inside while he could.

Near and nearer the Franks came. When no more than a hundred paces separated Clovis from Milius, the boy waved a friendly greeting to the king and lugged his bucket back through our gate as Trystan whirled about to our onagers. "Loose!"

The stones flew from both engines. In the center of the enemy column, heads snapped up and ranks broke as men scattered in all directions to avoid the missiles. No one was hurt, but no harm in unsettling them a mite.

A lull then as the long Frankish snake deployed in readiness, hauling siege engines into place, horses led to the rear while several ranks of archers arranged themselves to the fore. We heard three notes from a horn, then two riders trotted toward us as Trystan climbed the parapet steps toward me, carrying a dipper of water.

"Stand easy," he assured the men. "Just a nuncio. Clovis would parley."

The Frankish nuncio was red-faced and glistening with sweat in the heat, but well chosen for his command of Gaulish Celt, his tone sharp, clear and ringing. He might have made a good singer in Eire. "Clovis, king of the Franks, would avoid bloodshed among the people of Leon."

Trystan climbed between the crennels and casually sat on one. "Would he indeed?"

"Where is the lord of Leon?"

Trystan took time to sip at the water before replying. "I am he. Prince Trystan ap Melyod. Give you good morning."

"From the king of the Franks, ruler of northern Gaul: Clovis has heard that Leon's lord is an unbaptized heathen beneath Christian mercy. Notwithstanding, on two conditions, he will spare all without stone or spear launched."

Again Trystan sipped water before answering. "We thank him for his consideration. We have heard of Clovis's conversion from Woden to Christ, and we have seen how he applied that gentle teaching in the Carhaix. What conditions?"

The nuncio began, "Clovis, king of the Franks—"

"We *know* who he is; to it."

"If you will surrender the castle and render up the little horse thief in chains, my king promises on his hope of heaven to spare every other life in Castle Leon."

Trystan grinned down at me from his perch. "Didn't I tell you? Single-minded. Gareth, get to the crews. There by the two-hundred-pace marker, they've set an onager and catapult too close to each other. Tell them to make ready to loose."

"*Prince* are we now? Dear, oh dear."

"Now and always and to hell with you. Loose on my command."

From my place with the onagers I watched Trystan, the very picture of a man reluctant to exert himself on a hot morning. He drank again, spat a mouthful over the wall, then bathed his face. "Frightfully hot day to do battle, but he offers a bad bargain. Whom he calls thief is King Arthur's captain and friend. The high king of Britain would charge me sorely for his loss. Even though Clovis is a pompous young ass who invades British soil, I also will be merciful—by nature if not his deity's grace—aye, and fair as well. He may have his horse back with my blessing. For the rest, Leon regrets."

From where I stood on the west wall, I could neither see the nuncio nor hear his answer, though it could not have been cordial. Before Trystan could call the command, one of the Frankish onagers lobbed a stone, followed by a few spears from their catapults, which shattered harmlessly against our south wall. The stone sailed high over us and thudded down in the courtyard, raising nothing but dust. Milius bounded up onto the wall, jeering: "Want to try again? You'll have to do better than that."

I yanked him down onto the parapet. "They will. Be quick now and fetch back that stone, for we'll be using all they send."

Trystan still lounged on the wall in full view of the enemy archers, calmly surveying the enemy efforts as he might a field of flowers or children at play. Distant boom and thud as more stones and spears flew at and over us. Our onager men concentrated on their targets, hauling both engines about to bear. They waited, ready to loose. I jogged around to Trystan. "All prepared. Now if you'd not be known as the late prince, will you get down from there and give the order?"

He hopped down. "They have the range?"

"For the last two days they've had it."

Trystan whirled about to the crews. "Loose!"

The two stones flew up, over and down, landing close enough between onager and catapult to scatter the Frankish crews scurrying to safety. In the southwest tower Pindar cried out: "Number one, adjust left, number two right."

"Ready."

"Loose!"

Once more the stones lofted, this time with deadly accuracy. One missile shattered the catapult, the other splintered the onager arm. Our men all along the wall raised a cheer, but I hadn't the time, snapping at the crews: "Load, for Christ's sake. Stand by for new targets—"

—as Pindar shouted down: "Take cover!"

A flurry of arrows whirred at us, and more stones flew over, landing in the courtyard again but closer this time.

They'd have the range soon enough. "Pindar, which engines were those?"

He thrust his arm out to the south. "There, sir."

"What's the near mark?"

"Hundred and fifty paces."

"Number one crew: Milius, there's your mark."

"I see it, sir. Bear a hand, lads."

As they grunted and sweated to haul the onager into new position, Trystan roared suddenly: "What fool left a door open down there? Get them *back*."

Even as he cried out and I saw the sheep pouring out of the armory, the stones were coming down in their midst, crushing one poor beast and scattering the rest. A curse ripped the air as one of the village farmers on the east wall leaped down the stairs three at a time toward the open courtyard to kneel by the killed sheep. Another flight of heavy spears already flew from the Frankish catapults; on the walls, all our fear was for the bereft farmer.

"Look up, man!"

"Get out of there!"

He would not, come spears or stones. "Damn, wouldn't you know it," he lamented to all of us. "Green-dyed ear: one of mine."

Men from the east and north walls were sent down to herd the sheep back into the armory. The farmer simply shouldered his dead beastie and lugged it up the steps toward the keep, still mourning his loss. "She was dear, she was. Gave the best wool and dropped fine lambs. Now we can only eat her before her time."

I fetched up next to Trystan on the south wall. "Their archers are aiming higher," he said. "This next flight will—*Down against the wall, all of you!*"

We flattened, hugging the wall. Few arrows overshot the parapet this time. Most came down on the walk, bounced or shattered. None of our men were hit, but now the Franks had our range. The next stones battered at the crennels directly over us. Trystan hissed in frustration, tearing the mail hood back from his sweaty head. "We've got to concentrate everything on their engines."

Ignoring the rain of arrows around them, our onager crews worked frantically, hauling the number one engine to the south wall, archers like Collen and Pindar finding the range of Clovis's crews to keep them too busy scurrying for cover to hurl stones or spears at us.

So it went all through morning and afternoon in the stifling heat, until the dull orange ball of the sun hung low over the sea and no more missiles flew. Only then did I become aware of the sweat-soaked tunic clammy under my mail, and sagged down heavily against the wall next to Trystan as he gulped water from a dipper and poured the rest over his head. All along the south and west parapets, the men, spent as much from heat as battle, slumped against the walls or lay sprawled at their positions.

Isolt appeared with the cooks, bringing pots of soup and loaves from the kitchen, and here came Milius dragging along the walk like a man twice his age. He wove on his feet over us, his few words an effort. "My lords, we—we've crippled one more catapult, damaged an onager. I think."

"Any of you hurt?" I plied him.

"No, just . . ."

Just what, Milius had not the energy to finish, though he need not. He'd never gone through a day long or terrible as this and couldn't imagine the same tomorrow. "They came too close sometimes, sir."

"Take heart," I said. "Pelted us all day and killed no more than one ill-fated ewe."

Trystan offered Milius a dipper of water, drawling, "You wouldn't think the conqueror of northern Gaul would take one silly horse so much to heart."

Milius tried to laugh but managed no more than a wheeze. He drank gratefully then plodded back to his onager to wait the cooks doling out rations. Some just stared at their food; others chewed slowly, vacant as cattle, too tired to taste anything. When Isolt reached us, I saw the fine sheen of perspiration on her upper lip and how the black-as-night hair hung loose in damp wisps here and there.

"Mutton stew, my lords, that went to God only today. Husband?" Those magnificent eyes swept up Trystan's form, devouring him as always in their silent feast. "Please say you have no hurt."

He barely glanced at her. "No, never better."

"You lie so still. I thought—"

"I don't manage the heat well."

Isolt knelt by him and pressed her lips to his bearded cheek. "I love you."

Though I hadn't eaten since early morning, like the men I found myself with no more relish for food than a stone. I put the bowl aside and rose to peer out at the Frankish positions.

"And you, Gareth?"

"Aye, lady?"

"Always turning away. Are you hurt?"

I kept my eyes on the four Franks approaching the village well, carrying buckets. "Tryst, come look."

He rose, grunting with fatigue to join me. "What now?"

"They're drawing water."

He smiled grimly. "Drink up, Clovis. As the Saxons say, may it well become you."

I turned back and caught Isolt leaning her head against folded arms on the wall, spent as the rest of us. Only a moment, then she straightened quickly, as if ashamed to be seen slack even for that little breath, and followed the cooks along the parapet. Trystan hardly seemed to notice.

What a waste to pine for a heart that returned only silence and denial when another breaks to answer you. I would have gone to her just now and held her, let her be weak for a little, only that the fine strength of the woman could take a fresh grip. You are a friend, but I wonder if you are worthy of her.

"I think they will attack tomorrow."

"Or next day," Trystan agreed. "They haven't the supply for a long siege, and we've left them nothing. Tell the men to stay in place and get as much rest as they can. They fought like veterans today."

Walking along the parapet past men already asleep against the wall or still as corpses on their blankets, the enduring truth of battle I learned at Eburacum came to mind. Young or old, they were veterans when the first stones flew over.

All of us slept on the walls that night. Before summer gloaming lightened to true day, we breakfasted in two hurried shifts and took up positions again, watching the Franks draw water from the village well. By my order, no archers loosed at them.

"An edifying sight." Trystan smiled, nudging my arm. "See there?"

Running forward through the foot soldiers forming ranks, several teams of three men each carried scaling ladders.

Collen sang out high in his tower. "Mind out all! Winding their engines."

They would attack soon, but we were ready. Two large tripods suspended over braziers of hot coals heated the oil to be poured down on men trying to climb the ladders. At other points stood three pungent tubs dragged from the latrine. By now their siege engines had been hauled farther back. The first missiles plummeted down on us, tearing chunks out of the parapet near me, while our own crews cursed and sweated to answer. They struck another catapult, easier to disable than the stout-beamed onagers.

Pindar shouted down: "Massing their archers."

Dozens of them striding forward, stopping as on a mark, bows lifted high and higher, loosing. The shafts swarmed up, hung a moment against the white sky before the deadly drop. Flattened against the wall, I *felt* the two shafts splinter inches from my leg—

"Jesus . . ."

—and heard the jolting cry as if someone had the wind knocked out of them hard. When I could look, Milius crouched over a downed man with an arrow protruding at a high angle from his back. But even now more arrows flew.

"Milius, you can't help him now. Get *down!*"

When the flight hit us with, thank God, no more wounded, Trystan leaped to his feet, roaring to all. "They'll be coming now. You on the west wall, come to the south. This is where they'll try. Ready the oil; you on the tubs, pour when the ladders strike the wall. This is no time to be dainty."

He leaned against the wall, grinning broadly as a boy deep in a prime prank. "The underside of valor, like the horse that kicked me at Eburacum. Heroes may resist a reign of terror but seldom a rain of shit."

Trystan spun about to glare at the massing Franks. "Come now, Clovis. Come *on*."

He'd not long to wait. With a deep roar the Franks rushed our south wall. Our men waited with long forked poles to repel the ladders.

"Now," I bellowed as the first of them thrust between the crennels. "The tubs. Give 'em the tubs and oil!"

I hadn't minded where I moved. Something scrabbled at the wall just by me, and I saw a helmeted head and a raised ax before thrusting the man away with my sword. He clutched at his throat and toppled backward; in another breath Milius heaved the ladder aside with his hook.

We held them off until they retired, burned or fouled, to form again. A hasty inspection then: Who's dead? Wounded? Minor hurts only; we'd lost not a man this time. Trystan strode along the parapet, wild energy rising off him like steam from a pot. "Collen, show yourself! Can you spy out the most Christian Clovis from up there?"

"Have I not been seeking him since there was light to see?"

"Your task is to find the man and, fine archer that you are, spare him the infirmity of age."

Once more they rushed the south wall, once more we drove them off, with hooks, boiling oil, and whatever came to hand. When the Franks again fell back, lull and silence descended over the battle, broken by an occasional *thum* as one of our archers found a target. We'd lost only one man this time, a fisherman scampering along the walk collecting fallen arrows when an onager stone crushed his head not two steps from Milius, who went white, dropped his pole and sank to his knees. I dove at him, hauling him to his feet.

"Get up. I need you—"

—as the top of the ladder banged against the wall to my front. Milius's eyes were glassy with shock. I slapped him hard and thrust the hook into his hands. "I said move! You've no time to faint today, lady."

His eyes came back into focus. He lunged at the ladder, hooked and thrust it away.

When the Franks withdrew, in the lull Milius lurched away to the west wall to kneel by the man arrow-shot earlier. One look told me it was a corpse he mourned. The others of his onager crew glistened with sweat, shaken but unhurt.

"Sir, this is my uncle Varinius," Milius said quietly. "He raised me, put me on my first horse. Permission to take him below?"

"Go on. The priest will be saying later what's needed."

I helped him lift the body, which he balanced on one husky shoulder and plodded away toward the steps, only to pause there. "Lord Gareth?"

"Get him below. They'll be coming again."

Milius glanced at his comrades by the onager. "Sir, there's that we would ask of you."

"Ask away, but quickly."

"My uncle here, this makes it personal. We know we are not *Combrogi* well as we know your temper can sometimes take your tongue, but would my lord mind not calling us ladies anymore? After this week, none of us deserves that."

No, there are things you can deny men only so long and so much, and who would know that better than one born low as myself? "That was to make you mad, boy, mad enough to do better than your best. But no, never again."

Milius clumped down the steps with his uncle's body.

Their next rush came at the south and west walls together. Trystan and I were everywhere, plugging gaps in our ranks, whirling in brief, savage dogfights when Franks managed to get over the walls. When we finally beat them off, all that day we dodged missiles and waited for them to come again. The narrow parapet became our parched, deadly world, older men silent, saving their energy, while the younger ones screamed insults at the enemy to drown out their own fear. Sea becalmed and no merciful breath of wind over us, we lived in the heat and stink of sweat, acrid oil, and latrine tubs—but we lived, we endured under the searing sun crawling so slowly overhead. Hours were measured by thirst and the water buckets carried up. So much time until Isolt appeared with her cooks to dole out rations, but between the heat and waiting for the next rush at the walls, none of us had much stomach for food.

Another night, dawn again. In my turn I bolted porridge and a bit of milk and plodded back up to the parapet. Trystan leaned against a crennel, observing the Franks as, one by one, they were prodded awake. Somewhere between night and morning he'd shaved off his beard. I rubbed at my own stubble and promised the same luxury when time allowed.

Watching the Franks straggle into line, Trystan said, "They're forming again."

But to his eye and mine, not with half yesterday's fight or as many of them.

"Which wall this time?" Trystan wondered grimly. "Or both?"

"Tryst, see there."

Behind and to the sides of the formation, a score or more men just sat listlessly, heads in their hands, while others had not moved from where they slept the night before. Still others simply left the ranks and walked away toward the wagons in the rear. Here and there commanders tried to restrain them; the men just shook them off. One brute of a boyo stopped walking, bent double and vomited on the ground.

I prayed: "Bless the heat, cruel as it is."

"Yes, I do believe it's begun."

"You men, all of you! Do you see out there? They're getting sick in bunches, they are. Water sickness. I filled the well with our garbage and let the sun do the rest. All you need do now is hold out while they weaken by the hour."

"We learned it from the Saxons," Trystan shouted out of a throat dry as mine. "When they saw Milius draw from the well and then me drinking, they thought it was from the same bucket. Pure poetry, no other word for it."

When the stones and spears flew again, none of our men needed warning. They dropped flat against the wall, waiting for the arrow storm to follow. Pindar suddenly exposed himself in the southwest tower. "Forming on the west; going to hit both sides again."

In his urgency he leaned far out to us. That is when it happened: The heavy catapult spear lanced through still air and pierced Pindar through. He jerked and would have pitched forward out off the platform, but Collen caught him. The man must have been dead before Collen laid him on the stones.

Trystan sprang up, shouting to the men on the north

and east walls to fill in on the west side. The farmers and fishermen didn't hear or perhaps didn't grasp his meaning. Trystan cupped his mouth to repeat the order, not realizing his back was unprotected. A mere two paces away I saw only the long blur of the catapult spear as it raked him a glancing blow on the side of his head and sailed over into the courtyard. Trystan reeled and dropped like a stone. When I knelt over him, the left side of his head was a red mess. *Jesus, he's dead. Slow or quick, he's dead.*

His breathing was shallow, but Trystan's eyes fluttered open and found me.

"He lives," I cried to the men. "Your lord lives. You there! Fetch me clean water and a cloth. The rest of you look sharp. They'll be coming. Any man who deserts his post, if the Franks don't kill him, God my witness I'll do it myself."

The blood poured from Tryst's wound as I swabbed away. I dared hope the wound was not that deep. At last the flow lessened, and I could see, stark amid the blood-matted black curls, the gash perhaps five inches long trenched along his scalp, but no softness that would mean a cracked skull. A hair closer would have spattered his brain over the parapet. His gods smiled on Trystan that day, if never again.

Then Milius's warning: "They come!"

I dragged poor Tryst close against the wall, drew my sword and waited for the muscular farmer from the north wall to stand ready with his pole hook. "I do not mind saying," he mumbled through his few teeth, "I'm woeful tired of this."

"So are the Franks." At least I prayed so, for we couldn't take much more.

Fewer of them tried to scale the walls this time. When they broke off and retired, the men raised a dry-throated cheer which should have gone to the village well for breeding poison among the Franks. Satan himself would love the dark beauty of it, for the water was not only drunk but in the food their cooks prepared, and mixed with the grain for animals. Nobler men like Lancelot, Gawain, or Peredur would doubtless despise such a trick, and did not Guenevere once in her royal rage call me a peasant dog? Dogs know where to bury the best bones.

Noon boiled overhead when Gwendolen and the cooks toiled out with water and food. We bolted quickly, always with one eye to the enemy, most of them now withdrawn behind their wagons.

"Lord Trystan still lives," Gwendolen told me gravely. "Lady has put a poultice and bandage, but he is in great pain."

If he dies, I will take her. I had no time to repent the shameful notion before Collen bawled down from his tower: "Lord Gareth, will you come and see?"

In his fatigue the man draped between two crennels and barely moved when I eased in beside him. "Sir, look there at the captains."

Far back among the wagons, men sat on the ground, heads in their hands, or lay stretched out, while commanders strode among them with angry gestures, trying to bully them onto their feet.

"They don't seem inspired, Collen. Have you ever suffered water sickness?"

"I have not."

"Pray God you never do. We'll be cleaning out that well and our own just to be safe."

"There, sir: Clovis."

Out of range but the man for sure. Even at a distance I could read fury and frustration in the burly young king. He hovered over a group of prostrate men, whirled his arm toward our walls, then kicked one man in the belly. The sufferer only curled up like a child and rolled over.

Collen chuckled dryly. "Whatever you dropped in the well, sir, you knit them up proper."

"A king like Clovis would call this dishonorable, and perhaps it is. Shall I be to Mass for it?"

"No," Collen denied with the stony conviction of his last three days in purgatory. "Never, my lord. It was you told Pindar and me not to fight them, just kill them. I was a fisherman before I married Eilwen, and then we farmed. I pulled the weeds and killed the vermin that took my crops, and turned all under for compost. Nothing went to waste; neither will the Franks. The dead they leave behind will manure our fields, but don't task yourself with dishonor. Not for them."

As the stifling day wore on, the scant movement among the Franks dwindled to none. A weird stillness fell over Leon, broken only by the screech of gulls and whisper of tide. I sent my cold thoughts out to the Goliath of Gaul. *What must you be thinking now while your undefeated warriors lie helpless, fouling themselves, unable to take Leon from a few farmers' sons? Will you come again or try to starve us out? No matter; I'll be here, Clovis.*

I will be here because herself holds me here and does not know, and perhaps as well I want just once to lead these good men against the murdering arrogance of you, slash the blade of their vengeance into you, see you break and run. I want that to sting all the plundering days of your life. God hear me. Amen.

By the look of them, little danger of another attack today. I sent the men to eat in the hall twenty at a time and planned to go with the last lot, but my legs had no ambition for all that way to walk, all those steps to climb. . . .

In my sleep I felt the hot wind on my face and smelled smoke, someone shaking me awake. My head ached dully where I'd fallen dead asleep against the wall. It was full dark, Milius standing over me, very grave.

"You should rise and look, sir. The bastards are burning the village."

I got up stiffly, hearing the rush and roar of flame, to see the ruins of Leon and, clear against the red glare, the slow moving line of men and wagons plodding away along the coast road. Milius narrowed his eyes past the fires to the faint lightening in the east. "We'll have the sun in an hour. Less."

I rubbed at my eyes. "Stay alert. This may be a trick to draw us out."

One small house collapsed in a shower of sparks, then another. All about me our men watched the silhouetted line of the enemy and, in the ruin of their village, the price of victory. A bard might compose a heroic poem for Leon, but these men watching the destruction of dwellings where their fathers and grandfathers had lived and died, knew only that they must begin all over again.

"Collen saw it first," Milius rasped tightly. "Saw them torch his own house. God amercy, but I'd weep were I not so tired."

Yes. In God's justice such men deserved their turn to strike Clovis where he lived.

"I must see to Lord Trystan. Come light, if there's no

sign of Franks, half the men can go below for some proper rest."

The dark hall smelled of every meal eaten there for the past week and the unwashed folk snoring on trestle tables or sprawled underfoot, mumbling in comfortless dreams. I groped my way over them to the kitchen to drink two full dippers of stale water, then tore a chunk out of the remains of a boiled chicken and just stood staring into the dark, vacant as a cow.

In his chamber above, old Father Antonius was just lifting his head from the pillow, sniffing sharply as a hound on fresh scent. "What is burning? I smell smoke."

"And not incense," I growled. "His bloody Christian majesty put Leon to the torch before leaving."

"Burning?" He heaved his thin frame out of bed and stumbled to a casement. "God, not my *church.*"

"No, he'd never dare that. You!" I booted the sexton with an ungentle foot. "Up with you. The people will be needing Mass and comfort this day if nothing else."

I clumped through the solar and parted the curtains to the bedchamber beyond, near tripping over the soft mound of Gwendolen on a pallet. She turned over and sat up, warning quiet with a finger to her lips. By the feeble light of one guttering candle, Trystan lay abed. Isolt sat beside him and must have been so for hours, her dark head now drooped on his chest. When he moaned weakly, she lifted the cloth she held to cool his face, half asleep herself.

"Poor child," Gwendolen pitied in a whisper. "Not off her feet or the clothes from her back for so long. Now this."

Isolt lifted her head heavily but hardly seemed to see us before sinking down again.

"How does he, Gwendolen?"

The old woman shook her head. "He wakes sometimes, but there's no understanding him. He will live or not as God wills. And you, my lord?"

I scarce had spit left to speak of that. "When he can hear you, tell him Clovis is gone. We've won."

Headed by Father Antonius and myself, the folk of Leon made a sad procession through the smoking remains of their village. A score of dead Franks had been left unburied; a dozen more, barely alive, were finished by the village men with no more regard than dressing chickens for the pot. Antonius gave unction to those who begged it before dying, but nothing else we could or were of a mind to grant them.

Collen volunteered to dog Clovis's retreat for a few miles at a careful distance. By his report, the tainted well continued to kill Franks. He passed a number of shallow graves left in the army's wake, and the swollen carcasses of horses and oxen, and abandoned siege engines.

"And no telling how many went to hell farther on," Collen finished with cold satisfaction, jerking his chin at the naked dead piled like logs at the edge of Leon's tilled fields. "Didn't I say? Manure."

From trading vessels out of Vannes, we later heard that Clovis had limped back to his base with no more than three hundred men, many of them on foot, and surely the truth of Trystan's eleventh commandment eating into memory: *Thou shalt not have Leon.* One might wonder if he'd learned the cost of vanity in a king.

Father Antonius said Mass for the forlorn lot of us in the courtyard, calling for volunteers from our company to help rebuild the homes lost to fire. I stood by him and surveyed my men, all of them glad to be out of iron for the time. Both wells needed thorough cleaning, for the taint in one, over any length of time, would creep into the other. We'd casked and stored as much clean water as possible, but I'd still taken a dangerous chance.

After Mass I gave the necessary orders and did not have to search for words by way of praise. "I promised never again to call you ladies. If ever I do, it is a black liar I'll be, for if you are not yet *Combrogi,* you are every inch soldiers. We will raise Leon again, and the day will come when you need not fight Clovis from your walls but carry the fight to him on the point of your lances and on the edge of your swords. What say the fighters of Castle Leon? Who's for bashing that manny good and proper?"

The men just stood there, too fought out to cheer, but young Milius spoke up with a hint of his old feist. "If you will lead us, sir, it's only good manners to return his visit, eh Collen?"

"We've already agreed." Collen spat on the ground. "We are all for that and soon."

In his bedchamber, Trystan lay clad only in his old *alae* breeches while Isolt bathed him with a cloth and Gwendolen wrapped his wound with fresh linen. He turned his head as I entered. "Is that Gareth?"

"Who else would it be?"

"My eyes," he fretted weakly. "Sometimes I see two of things."

Isolt laid her hand on his cheek. "You'll feel better for the bath. Is the pain gone?"

"Comes and goes."

"There." Gwendolen tied off the neat bandage. "Does my lord wish me to fetch more willowbark?"

"No, it does little good. Gareth, what is our condition?"

"Pitiful. We've made a start, but they'll all have to live within the walls yet."

"That's enough." Trystan pushed away Isolt's hand with the cloth.

"Stay, I'm nearly done."

"I said enough!" The petulant sting in his voice startled us but I laid it to his pain. "I feel stronger. Let me up."

"No, husband, you mustn't yet."

Under the new beard stubble that shadowed his jaw, Trystan's flesh had gone drab as mud. "I said I will rise. Don't hinder me."

He rose a bit at a time, setting first one leg and then the other on the stone floor. Isolt reached to help but he shrugged her off, managing to stand erect. "Gareth, are you here?"

I moved to his side. "Aye, what's the matter?"

Only a whisper but hoarse with confusion and fear. "I don't feel right. Dizzy."

Isolt and Gwendolen made to support him, but I waved them away: *Leave him be.* Trystan moved unsteadily to the casement to gaze, as so often before, long and longingly out to sea and beyond. He uttered a sound I could not make out, for it slurred as if his tongue stumbled in forming words. Trystan teetered and pitched sideways into my arms. I heard Isolt's smothered cry and, as I eased the man to the floor, I alone heard the bare anguished question.

"If I am dying, will she come?"

She did in the end, and your long dying was already begun.

Ships plying between Camelot and the Middle Sea brought more messages from Arthur: When would I return?

I sent replies that spanned the shameful stretch between evasion and flat lie. Trystan badly wounded and unable to command, therefore . . . and so on. Tryst's head wound healed but the headaches persisted. He drank more, and his temper became even more unstable. Oddest of all, the silver tongue able to dance over song and poetry all his life slurred often over the simplest words. One moment Trystan would be his old self, the next snapping at all around him, and Isolt felt most of his malice, as if he were blaming the woman not for his wound but his life. She bore it well, that and all else we put up with that September while the village was slowly restored, the hall and outbuildings still jammed with folk, and food needing to be rationed. Not an angel nor one to understand all, but strong Isolt was. She did what was needed for the women and children of Leon, and while I bit back so many feelings I dared not speak, there needed no Druid to see how unhappy she was, and why. The man to whom she joined her life now looked through her like a stranger.

Clovis would hang his mother before he'd harm a church. Ours being untouched (we wished they'd been as considerate of the bathhouse), the priest and sexton departed, leaving the upper floor of the hall to us, all others forbidden in the evenings. On such a night, the first blessed coolness wafting from the sea, Trystan and I, Isolt and Gwendolen, relished the privacy. Tryst seemed better that night, myself pouring the wine for all and for the first time in weeks letting myself be concerned with nothing.

Trystan tuned his harp, pinging softly at the strings, then tried the first notes of "Bronwen in the Vale," but his fingers faltered over the strain. He stuck out his tongue in comic dismay and tried again, slower this time. As he began the first line: "Light the candles . . ." he stammered on the *c*.

He stopped and began again. Isolt frowned in worry but said nothing. No comic face this time, only grim concentration. Trystan took a sip of wine, flexed his fingers and started in only to falter over the strings, his voice slurred and uncertain. Not terror in his eyes, not yet, only bewilderment. He bit his underlip and tried a different lay, the song of the Morrigu he'd composed for his contest with Morlais. How could I or anyone with an ear be forgetting that haunting three-note figure that ran through so much of his music like the dark river between life and death? How could *he* forget after so long?

Yet he did. The harp went silent. "Gareth?"

If the man had screamed I would have been less chilled. His voice was low and white with terror. "Wuh-Won't work. My fingers won't *work!*"

Isolt rose quickly and hurried to him. "You are only tired. Put it by and play for me tomorrow."

Trystan only shrugged her away. He tried the three-note figure again, then anything, harder and harder, his hand stiffened into a claw that ripped only discord from the harp. We could only watch and wince at the sight and painful sounds, helpless as Trystan tore and tore at the strings to find again some lost grace denied by his abandoning gods.

Father Antonius, the nearest Leon had to a physician, confessed only ignorance of Trystan's malady, though he'd seen such wounds before. "Sometimes they heal without harm, sometimes kill long after for no reason, but always they leave the mark of their passing. Lord Trystan is fortunate. We can only wait and pray."

As September passed, Trystan seemed to improve, often able to play and sing without the stammer or wrong notes like blots on his gifts, but the swift, sharp humor that could skewer and forgive the world in a phrase faded into silence, and the old amused curl of his lips froze into a mirthless scar on the humanity of the man. Trystan went away into a darkness where we could not follow. Nor could I answer Isolt's concern with any comfort of what I knew of the man who'd been a friend. All our years together, no matter how sunk in melancholy, Trystan could always fling it off, the best of him banishing the worst with a joke. That part of him I loved and love yet, a shining best but never strong nor hardy enough now to hold back the coming dark any more than day could stay the night.

In late September another ship bound for Britain touched at Leon, surely the last that year before the winds turned northerly and closed us in. My last chance to escape, but the company still needed me since Trystan dared not command with an infirmity that might cripple him before the men. Promising a novena to God, I lied shamelessly and sent to Arthur that I'd broken my leg in a fall from my horse. Arthur would surely find that hard to swallow; could I not hear the high king explode in frustration?

"Gareth can't fall off a horse. He doesn't know *how*."

So I pawned truth to another novena and added that water sickness laid me low as well. As the ship stood out from Little Hump, the weather darkened about Castle Leon within and without. Rain blew in from the sea, cleansing the air for a space, much needed since most of Leon still crowded for shelter into the hall and outbuildings, jammed close as peas in a pod and causing the usual problems.

There came a pleasant evening when the three of us and

Gwendolen gathered in the solar. Our mood was good for a change, Trystan quiet, sipping at willowbark tea. I was tired but content; the company's horse drill showed so much improvement that my plan to lead them against Clovis now seemed within reach. The scheme needed to grow, fine as it was, though this evening was not the time to put it before Trystan. He sat by his wife picking single notes or soft chords from his harp.

There was a general air of peace among us that night, Isolt and Gwendolen gossiping and making me laugh. Curtains hung over the casements bellied with sea wind, but the brazier of red embers threw cheerful warmth over the chamber. Tryst even smiled a little, if absently, at Isolt, but even to that little she opened as a flower to the sun, drawing us all into the doings of the day and saving the best for a sweet at the end. Well, then, Pindar's widow had buried her husband not far from their burned house, poor woman, but already she cast a purposeful eye among the unmarried men of Leon.

"Who can blame her?" Gwendolen allowed with charity. "Her with three to raise and not one half grown."

"But then Collen's wife—oh, Trystan, you remember her. The Canti girl with the wen on her neck?"

"Um." He only reached for the mug of tea, changed his mind and poured himself wine, wincing and rubbing at his left temple. I recognized the signs of pain settling in to pound at him.

As she spoke, Isolt's hands danced the story with sparkling mischief, and myself feasting on the gaiety in her, the first in many a day.

"Well, you know her by sight. Her name—oh, Gwendolen, what *is* that woman's name?"

"Eilwen, lady."

"Eilwen, the very one. Homely as a burnt bannock. They are among that fragrant horde who sleep below in the hall. Gwendolen, sweet, we *must* count the good plate and goblets after meals. Not that I mistrust our good folk, but the silver plate came from Britain with my mother, God rest her soul, and it is a temptation . . . where was I?"

I prompted, "Collen's wife?"

"Yes. Well, one day what does Eilwen see but her Collen passing the time and perhaps more, as she suspects, with Rhona, the wife of—oh, why do names escape me? Trystan, what is his name, the husband of Rhona?"

Eyes squeezed shut, Trystan finished his wine in two gulps. "I don't recall."

"The stabler," I said, hearing the strain in his voice. The mouse stirred warily in my stomach.

"Indeed, that very night Eilwen wakes to see Collen tiptoeing out of the hall and imagines he's off to the latrine—until, only moments later, who should rise and slip out ever so quietly but Rhona. Eilwen is not having any of *that,* so she follows to find—lo! Rhona, no less, pausing by Collen in the courtyard. Eilwen pounces on them—aha!—and the battle that followed, by the look of poor Collen and Rhona, must have made our Frankish troubles seem a quiet Sabbath."

Gwendolen chuckled deep in her double chins. "Now tell how it fell out."

"Poor Collen," I sympathized with a worried glance at Trystan, going grey with pain. "I did wonder why, after braving Franks without a scratch, he comes to drill with a black eye."

"And Rhona with a split lip," Isolt topped it. "Now does

it seem both of them were just bound for the latrine, so they swear, and it could be so, but there were words between Collen and the stabler, all a bit stiffish, mind, while Rhona and Eilwen are not speaking and will not, I warrant, until Brigid feast. Lord, I will be glad when they're finally cleared out and— Husband, what is it?"

Trystan lurched unsteadily out of the chair, swaying on his feet. On the instant, Isolt was up and reaching for him, but he turned on her with a look of loathing so naked the blind could read it. "You shallow, prattling fool, get *away*."

He slapped her then, so hard that Isolt jerked and reeled sideways to the floor. Gwendolen gasped while I could only stare at the impossible. Holding her cheek, Isolt threw one horrified look at Trystan and then me, shamed to the marrow that I'd seen, and fled through the curtains, Gwendolen close behind.

While I sat frozen and too shocked for words, Trystan pressed a hand to his head, croaking, "Sounds hurt me . . . the light stabs at my eyes. I know the signs by now. Tomorrow it will be my fingers again."

He took up his precious harp. The fingers of his right hand fell limply on the brass strings with a dull sound like a stake driven through a hope. Only then did he seem to remember my presence. Coldly: "I hope my lord Gareth has nothing to say, for I don't want to hear."

"No." For all his suffering, might God damn him forever. "Not a word, my lord. I could not trust myself."

I turned my back on him and left the chamber.

She forgave him, and that was more than I could do, but Trystan showed his remorse with a smile, a kiss, and perhaps a loving to boot. That was the wound under my own skull that would not heal, his loving her and Isolt still wanting him, paying any price for his smallest attention.

The weather turned colder and I with it until, were I turned inside out in the light, Arthur and even Rhian would not have known me. With a vicious will now I poisoned every good thought of the man with jealousy and hate with a dark strength to frighten me, making me small and mean, turning his every virtue to weakness beneath contempt. To my growing appetite for malice, his faults became delicious. I cherished the picture of him smashing Morlais's hand at Bard's Tor. I spat on the boy-man given his heedless way—Arthur and Britain be damned—when he believed Yseult his at last to vanish with. I detested the wounded self-pity that did not stick at murder when Yseult, making the decisions of a queen, denied and sent him away. The sodden animal who crouched in a circle of sputtering torches, sneering at Arthur in the moment before he would have killed him too.

The days went by, though the incident was never mentioned between us again, but the old bond of friends reeled with its death wound. I could not meet the eyes of a man I'd come to despise, nor those of my own soul. A dozen times I vowed to ride the mile to church and confess to Father Antonius what festered in me; a dozen times I denied even that healing. What use? Beside penance, the innocent old man would only murmur through the grate what I already knew. Adultery in the wish is a step on the path to the act. How often had I loved her so, imagined her lying close and naked, arms tight about me, my mouth taking hers, feeling it yield and open as the rest of her opened and drew me into her. To see that perfect woman grow with the child Rhian never gave me.

She was a fever in me, a hand of fire squeezing my heart.

I *hurt* with her, yet not so dishonest I didn't despise myself as much as Trystan. With time gone by now, I can forgive us all that year and say, "It was the way of things." I have fought for Arthur and for Guenevere while the last of Britain crumbled under us, saw her go into exile more magnificent in age than ever in youth, both of us grey and old then, past bitterness and able to say "the way of things" and know to the jot what we meant.

But that year in that foreign place, I would hate where I'd loved, love where I would in spite of all, and never in my too-long life, before or since, was I more *alive.*

The wells ran pure again, the homes rose, and more folk left the castle to take up their lives. Trystan still unfit to command, my days were taken up in training the company and improving my plan to deal Clovis a mortal wound. Once completed, I would present it to Trystan and lead the foray myself if need be. I'd become so much a part of Leon's life by now that not only his wife but his war I coveted.

The plan grew out of hard truth. No one castle could stand forever against Clovis, who could draw on the entire north for men and supplies. We must carry the fight to him, otherwise he would count his gains stronghold by stronghold while we counted only our dead. I hoped Trystan would be capable by then, but his drinking, black moods, and Isolt's deepening unhappiness gave me grave doubts.

One clear night long into the small hours, a chill wind blowing in from the sea under a full moon and stars, I gave up trying to sleep with all that warred in my head. Wrapped in my cloak, I climbed to the parapets to inspect the sentinels. Only two were needed now. I stopped by each with a friendly word. Night guard is lonely, and men appreciate a bit of company to while the time.

"Cold as it is," one soldier observed, "it is a relief to have a bit of space about me. Trying to sleep in the hall where we're so jammed together, even our dreams are crowded."

I bade them good night and walked along the north parapet. The full moon outlined Great Island, Saddle, and Little Hump, and turned the sea into a meadow of light where a man's fancy could pluck odd thoughts for flowers. . . .

Strange summer, strange fortune you've found, mac Diarmuid. By wind and sail Camelot is not that far, yet how much farther have you come? Have you grown? Are you wiser or merely changed?

Was that movement below? In the corner of my eye a dark figure stirred on the stairs leading down to the quay. "Who's there?"

The figure moved again but did not answer.

Curious: What benighted fool would be moon-gazing out in the cold wind at this hour? I descended to the small door in the sea gate. Someone had left it ajar.

"You on the stairs. Who's there, I say!"

"Only me, Gareth."

"Isolt?" I took the stairs two at a time down to her. She was seated there, her face moonlit pale against the dark cloak hood. "What do you here at this hour?"

Faint and muffled by sea wind, the bell rang from the church. "You hear? Sexton's ringing matins, and why's yourself sitting cold and alone as a gull on a rock?"

"Trystan sleeps poorly tonight. He might rest better alone."

"As if you've slept that much yourself."

That was not all of it tonight. Her voice was far from steady. "I wake thinking he calls out for me." Then a bitterness I'd never heard in her: "How much difference in a name cried out in sleep?"

Her cowled head fell forward on her knees. "Please stay by me, Gareth. Tell me what I can do."

I sat beside her, knowing full well what she meant but guarding my own feelings. Dangerous ground to be so close now when she was so open and needing. "Come in out of the cold for a start. We can't have you both taken ill."

"Does it matter?"

"None of that now. Don't be foolish."

"Foolish? Night after night he sighs or moans that name, and for a time I could lie to myself that it is me he calls."

Liar myself: "Of course it is."

"No." The sound of her squeezed tight with her pain. "You know him, you knew her. That night he struck me, that was the least of the blows. I can't go on like this, Gareth, there's not that strength left in me. I want to cry out, run and hide, but there's no place. You are his friend. You see what is happening to him. To us. For the love of God!"

Isolt's fists pounded her knees in frustration. "What *was* she, this Yseult? What spell did she weave over him? Was she so beautiful? Did she love him so much?"

"In the beginning perhaps. They hadn't much time together." What could I tell her, how unravel strands whose twisting began so long ago, and myself so close to the better woman now and not trusting myself to touch her? "I'm not sure."

Oh, there was a timid answer saying nothing. By Isolt's silence she expected more. I plunged on with the first notion to hand, lame as it was. "Well now, it's like food. Not many dishes tempt Trystan, as well we know, but if there was one that could—oysters. Fair craved 'em, he did, while the first in my mouth was the last. Well . . ."

I let the pale comparison trail off, Isolt deserving better from me. "Aye, I knew Yseult."

She was not to be put off. "And?"

"I've said: as the oysters. Truly, I respected her as queen, but Yseult, bless her belated virtue, was the dullest beautiful woman I've ever yawned through an hour with."

Isolt laughed tremulously and shifted closer to me. Before I could even think *no,* my arm slipped round her naturally as breathing, and I could feel her body shivering beneath the cloak.

"You feel so warm, Gareth."

Careful, man. "Och, who am I to judge a queen? I know men and horses. Tryst is a poet, and they are closer to gods than other men. He draws music out of the air, a gift of something fine where nothing was before. I think he drew Yseult as well out of need and dreams."

"Yes," Isolt murmured. "As God might have done dreaming the beauty of Man before his dream turned and wounded him. You are wiser than you know, Gareth."

She pressed closer to me. I spoke the truth and prayed she would not sense how much lay in it. "We love whom we love, girl. Sane, mad, or blind, there it is."

But my very caution betrayed me. As she turned to me, so close in the curve of my arm, by habit I pulled away. Whatever Isolt meant to say died on her parted lips, and in the moonlight I saw the knowing in her eyes.

"Yes, you did it again."

"Did what?"

"Every time I come near, you look away, move away,

for no good reason left a good chamber in the castle for a stall in the old rath. I thought at first you were that gruff kind of man who ignores women, or that I'd offended you."

Too dangerous now, more than I could risk. "Never that, lady."

"Then why will you not look at me now?"

"Come, you're cold. You must go in."

But Isolt stayed me, sure of herself. "Then, when I was lonely, I would remember a day in the solar, remember it as a starving man tortures himself the more with the memory of food."

"For God's sake, Isolt—"

"When I felt so lost, you took my hand and told me—I forget the words, but just that touch—I should have known."

"Isolt, believe me—"

"I would not have thought it possible."

"*Damn* it, girl—"

I dared not look at her, but she would be smiling, all the mystery solved, not in triumph but tenderness. "You need such a damn to deny me?"

"No." I hunched forward, shivering and miserable myself now. "I cannot deny anymore. I'm not that strong."

"You're the strongest man I ever knew."

"Will you listen to me?"

"And the gentlest."

"I'm none of those, just a poor fool, and whatever the fool wanted I know can never be."

We fell silent, understanding at last with the sea wind whining about us. As I rose to take her in, Isolt crushed herself to my chest with a smothered cry. "And what *I* will never ask, have no fear. But let me be selfish and greedy for just this moment and be held close a little, just to rest here on your soul."

I surrendered then, scared as she, holding her tight and close as so long I'd dreamed. "No, never selfish, never you. You are good and fine, and it is *sick* I am at how he treats you. If he ever strikes you again, I will—"

But I thrust her away with the last of my will. "May we go in now and forget this night ever happened? I'm an ignorant man married to a good woman forever, and I understand none of this."

"I know," Isolt murmured. "Trystan is my forever, and I am as lost in him as he in her, like one of those designs our people work in gold where you can't tell beginning from end. He and I and you whom I need now as much in my way—but yes, we must forget this."

Yet I would have stayed there with her through all seasons, all time, but she turned away toward the moon-bright sea. "No," she said, "it is too good in your arms, too easy, and you spoke too much truth. We love where we love. Oh, my blessed friend—"

Isolt turned again to me, and I heard her pleading tears before the moon struck them like jewels in her eyes. "Gareth, *help* me."

It happened then. I couldn't speak, frozen with the sharp, cruel memory. In that moment Isolt lifted her head toward the keep. "Light in the solar. He is awake."

But I could only stare at her, unable to speak while the sweet-terrible memory flooded through me. From high above came the sound of the harp struggling for one chord over and over as a stammerer will fight to utter one clear word. Again and again, gradually resolving to that shrieking, tortured sound I first heard at Bard's Tor.

"I must go to him," Isolt blurted in a worried rush, trailing the words behind her as she darted up the stairs. "He will be in pain."

I huddled in my cloak, letting the wind wear at my face, trying to deny the memory but unable, fear like deep cold in the marrow of my bones.

Could I have been so blind to what stared me in the face day after day or forgotten over so many years away from that world? Washed in moonlight, the bare soul of her appealing to me, I remembered the Sidhe woman's curse and the vision she showed a drunken fool in his terror.

Your heart will break for love that will never be answered, and from the day you truly know this, like to myself you will never draw one breath more in happiness . . . as you killed my Declan, see the spear that will pierce your heart.

Had it not all come to pass even as that vengeful creature prophesied? Could Christ or any merciful god help me? The poison was deep in me, *was* me now.

Oh, Rhian, even did you chain my hand and heart to yours, you could not spare me this.

Once more from the solar the harp struck up, stumbled and went silent. As I looked up, miserable, the light dimmed beyond the casement. She had taken him back to bed.

Frightened. Helpless, with no right to her, no strength to leave her. Whatever befell the three of us, locked together and lost as Lucifer, I would stay at her side, loving her and hating him, trampling honor no less than he did, to the last ugly moment when I must face Trystan, tell him, and let it go as it would.

For I would break the curse or let it shatter me.

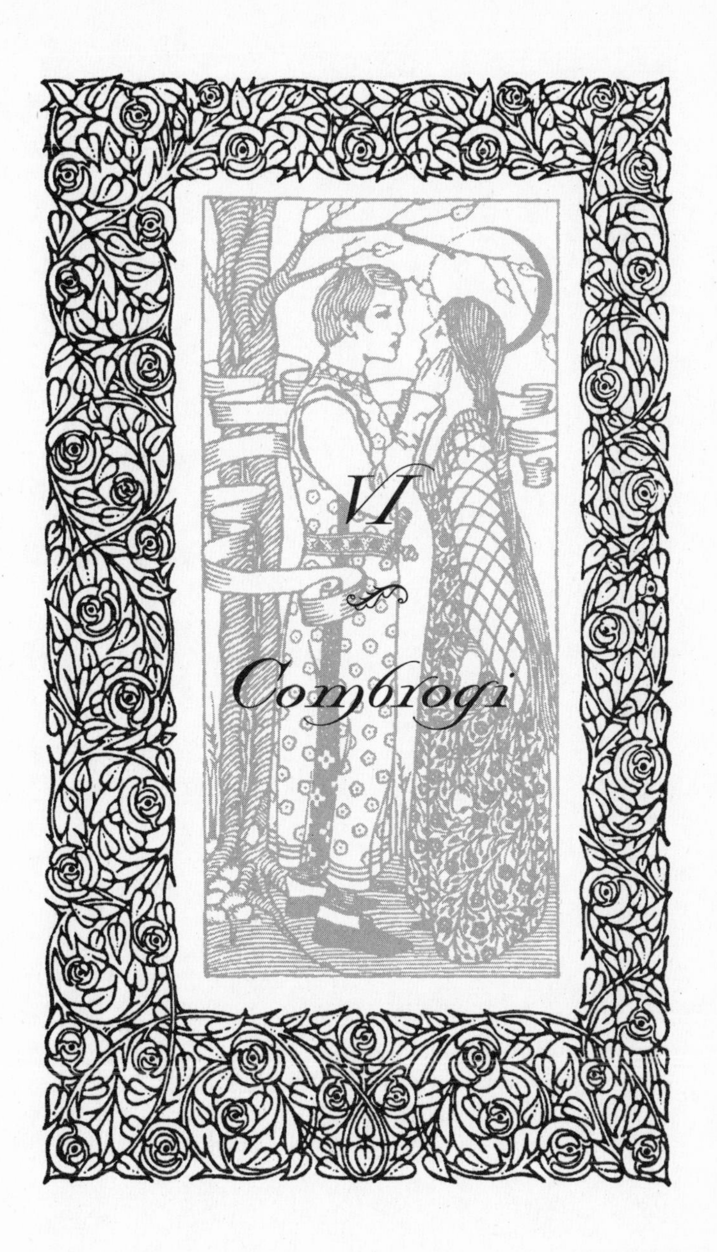

VI

Combrogi

n the wide meadow by Leon's church, Trystan and I watched our men assemble, smartly now, no milling about or wasted effort, forming quickly in two mounted ranks of thirty each, swords sharp, armor oiled, confidence high.

Trystan nodded in approval. "You've done it, Gareth. They are a command now."

And should they not hold their heads high? They'd defended Castle Leon against the strongest king west of the Rhine and put him to shame. But attacking Clovis in the open would be a far different and more difficult matter.

In the village, farmers were slaughtering hogs for the salting. Now and then the sharp October sea wind brought us the sound of their squealing. Badly wounded men sounded so, telling me I must train mine well that fewer of them need ever make such a sound. They were proper fired with the idea of hitting Clovis; now I must show them how.

Trystan seemed to be mending well enough, his moods neither dark nor light but more silent. Often I would catch him studying me or Isolt as if turning some thought in his mind, but gave it no weight with all I had to do. Neither Isolt nor I spoke of that night on the quay stairs. She knew my heart and I hers. She loved Trystan but as well honored my own, and I had at least that rag end of common sense to bank my fires, though they refused to die. There are times when a man can only bite on the leather and take the pain.

"Right, then." I mounted. "Let's take them to school."

While Trystan waited to one side of the formation, I walked my horse down the front rank. "Today you learn the Flower. Whenever you went at a man with your fists, if you were quick enough, you hit him with both, one-two. That's the Flower. The first rank charges, breaks the enemy line and passes on, and before they've time to wonder what fell on them, the second hits them. But the first rank, once through, must spread wide or the second will be running up their backs. Both ranks must wheel and reform quickly. Sharp now: watch Lord Trystan and myself."

Trystan and I trotted our mounts close together, then dashed away at a line of stakes planted fifty paces beyond. We shot through to each side of a single stake, then reined wide apart, halting and wheeling about so quickly that the horses went down low over their haunches.

"Can you hear? Did you see? Keep watching. Now we will charge in file, and you'll see the reason for the Flower."

Trystan spurred into a gallop, me flying close behind. As he plunged past the stakes he veered to the left, allowing me to pass close and plunge on, both of us reining short and charging back again through the stakes.

"Speed," I hammered at them. "Speed and control. Like swordplay, it is a series of *exact* movements done so often that you and the horse become one set of sinews to one purpose."

Two, three times I dashed across the meadow to a sudden stop, throwing my weight back, taking up all slack on the reins, pulling the horse up short on his haunches, then reining him right or left with my weight thrown to that side.

"Keep watching." I waved the stabler to me with the big bay that still wore Clovis's saddle. I took the stallion through Flower and quick wheel, Trystan on his gelding for comparison, but the difference was clear as black on white. Beside his mount—well, it was like giving mine the notion on a Sunday and him getting round to it Monday morning.

"And there's your advantage, speed," I concluded. "Don't waste any or you may never recover it. *Comp*-nee!"

They came to attention, lances high. I had both ranks count off. When each man knew his number and where his rank broke to right or left, I set them to a go at the stakes, in a slow trot at first.

"Better than I thought," Trystan judged. "But they've got to be perfect."

"They will have it. Half the battle is believing they can. They grew a deal of backbone fighting Clovis."

In late afternoon when the sexton rang vespers bell, we called a rest period, allowing those who wished Mass to attend. Trystan and I squatted over a smoothed patch of earth. Trystan looked off at the heavy stallion grazing apart from the geldings.

"Speed, yes, the only thing," he reflected. "But I would not want to stand head-on against such monsters."

He had gone to the heart of the weakness. "That would be good night, *Acushla*," I said. "Look here."

With my dagger I drew a line in the dirt and another approaching at an angle. "So we never allow that, never give them the chance for head-on. Always aslant, see? In and through and out, cut at them, then away. If we stay on the attack, we can keep them off balance."

"And foot troops?"

"The same. Strike them where they're not—in the rear, the flanks, like wolves circling a flock. Or use the Scythe."

Trystan looked doubtful. "Do you think they can? That's much to learn and drill in little time."

For that reason I'd begun with the more difficult Flower. The Scythe, two ranks attacking at once from opposite directions and flowing through each other, could be more quickly mastered.

My plan was to strike Clovis as soon as possible. If we could convince the lords of Cornouaille and Morlaix to support us, we could draw off the Frankish cavalry while they retook Vannes. We had already shown them Clovis could be stopped. A successful raid might give them the heart and determination to unite for good and all.

As always in such plans, without knowledge we were blind. We didn't know how large a garrison Clovis had in Vannes. "For sure he can't risk remaining himself so far from his seat of power. He may have gone north already," I hoped. "Our men have the will and the pride now. They've seen what happens when they just sit and wait. They *want* to do this."

"No more than I," Trystan said deliberately, drawing idle lines with his own dagger in the dust. "In a week or so I will be forty years old."

"So you will." And myself not far behind him, for all that meant.

Trystan winced slightly, touching the healed-over furrow in his scalp. "I've never seen myself growing old, yet here I'm more than half the road to it, and what have I accomplished? Not even children. Tantalus sups fuller than I while Clovis ramps and ruts his way to a dynasty."

This was a new mood in the man. Many times he had joked about the pointlessness of his life, clever jests with bitter lament at their heart, but never about aging. "You're not laid out yet, man. Is Leon and a fine wife so little?"

Trystan slashed through the designs in the earth. Again that searching glance at me, as if the man had a question he wouldn't speak but perhaps could find answered in my face. "Yes, my dear wife. Isolt was very young. As in the old Greek myths, she must have seen me like one of those gods come from the sea. She was loving, her father willing, and I was worn out with ships and roads and strangers. Isolt has great character and kindness. I was tired; I felt comfortable with her, but I never thought—"

He broke off and stood up, changing tack like a boat coming about in a stiff breeze. "Yes, I need to do this, Gareth. To deny Clovis this one place, show that fat Frank there is one bit of British Gaul he can't have ever. In my laughable life, that would be something."

The men were filing out of the church now, returning to their picketed horses. I rose to face Trystan, meaning what I said. "You do have your fine moments, my lord."

Again that questing look and the smile not easily read. "Apparently so do you—my lord. We'll need a spy in Vannes."

I'd considered several, but no matter where choice wavered, it always returned to Collen.

"No married men, Gareth. Collen has a family."

"He's a natural scout, takes to it like a babe to milk."

"With a Brit accent sure to be marked among Veneti."

"He's the son of a fisherman and knows the ways of boats."

"As does Milius. What of it?"

"Everything, Tryst. Jesus, man, whoever we send cannot prance into Vannes on an army horse. Speak of being noticed. Collen has a cool head and a bit of Latin from Father Antonius."

We couldn't agree. Trystan would not put the mission above Collen's marriage, which I knew was clouded over since that business of the stabler's wife. In the end we decided to send both and hailed them out of the ranks. They cantered their mounts toward us, erect in the saddle, lances no longer a burden to their hardened arms. Like the rest of our men, few as they numbered, Collen and Milius were snapped to and squared off smartly as any of us in the old Sixth *Alae.* Trystan greeted them warmly.

"Step down, lads. It is once again a time for heroes."

Dismounted and his lance tucked through his saddle straps, Milius stripped off his helmet and scratched dubiously at the black hair. "Sir, the last time I was a hero, I was sent out to the well with no more than a bucket and a silly smile between me and five hundred Franks. In all respect, my lords frighten me much more."

"No fear," Trystan assured him quickly. "Entirely voluntary this time."

"From first to last," said I.

Collen was more stoic in this, having his own reasons. "What's to do, my lords?"

When we disclosed the mission, Milius pursed his lips, doubtful, but Collen volunteered on the spot, maintaining there wasn't a word of truth about him and Rhona, not a hint of it, but Eilwen made his life so difficult since, that some time apart might soften her heart to trust again and give him some peace.

"Beside," he grinned wickedly at young Milius, "I've fished the waters about Vannes. They've several houses of Venus very friendly to fishermen, and Milius will profit from their attentions."

Day after day, on and on, we drilled the men in the Flower and Scythe, honing them toward the tight discipline of *Combrogi.* Each man always fell into the same place, the same comrades to either side, forming in ranks, files, or wedge at command so that they could never be caught out of attack formation. We didn't know the number of Clovis's cavalry. He'd lost men and horses withdrawing from Leon, but had he been reinforced? Outnumbered we would always be, but by how many? What formations and tactics did they employ? Giving us a clear picture of this fell to Collen and Milius.

Milius had no family left to concern him, while Eilwen, nose in the air, declared Collen might go where he wished; *she* cared not. As husbands have done through all time when wives will be angry, Collen called on his patience to weather the frost, embraced his children and prepared to go.

"At least she could kiss me goodbye."

"Don't press the woman," I counseled from years of Rhian. "When you're gone and the bed's too lonely and cold for her, let her be feeling guilty for that. As they say in my country: Let those who love us love us well. Those that hate us, let God twist their hearts to love, and if He can't, let Him twist their ankles so we'll know 'em by the limp."

Collen and Milius would go without weapons but with ample funds, much of the money in Roman coin salvaged from dead Franks. By horse they would travel to River Blavet running through the western Carhaix, where they would sell or trade the animals for a small fishing boat, make their way to the coast and east into the harbor of Vannes. They would fish often enough to smell of their calling, frequent the taverns, buy drinks for soldiers, number the garrison and, whenever possible, count and observe the cavalry while sounding out those Veneti ready to rise against their conquerors.

This accomplished, one of them would leave Vannes (hopefully without detection or injury) to bring us the intelligence, while the other, God and saints willing, would find the right men to open the city gates at the right time.

"This will be worth a ladder," Milius commented as they mounted to depart on a grey, cold morning. I had to dig in memory to recall the decoration, a medal stamped with a ladder given to Roman legionaries for being first into an enemy city.

"If we can find one, it's yours."

That same day, Isolt broke away from Trystan on the north parapet and hurried to me, wind whipping the heavy cloak about her. "Gareth, my husband will not see reason but insists the raid must come soon. In winter?"

"So it must."

"But why?" she wailed, tugging me by the hand back to Trystan. "My father never warred this late in the year for any reason. It's utterly mad."

"For that reason," Trystan said. "Gareth thought of it himself. Gareth?"

"So I did. The Franks won't expect it now."

"Insane."

Was it, Isolt? Who in all Brittany but Trystan and I would conceive such a reasoning? Who but Cerdic many years later would attack Badon in dead winter? And who but Arthur could have seen the possibility of the impossible and ridden east in time to stop him? Art and war alike need a hint of madness.

"Both of you *hear* me." Isolt stamped her foot. "You cannot do this with sixty men alone. What of Cornouaille and Morlaix? Have they agreed to join?"

"Well, that's the rest of it, lady."

Her coal-black brows shot high with doubt. "A large rest, Gareth. Very large. It is too great a risk. If both of you have done miracles, it is by the indulgence of God, mind, for neither of you is twenty anymore."

"That is why it will do Gareth good to leave this rock awhile for Cornouaille and Morlaix. He is looking tired lately. You must depart immediately, friend."

Though Trystan smiled, I heard no friendship in the words, saw none in his eye, only that questioning akin to suspicion. Still, the other lords must be argued to our side, and soon. Autumn wasted and we were committed, Trystan feverishly, and his reasons were not after all that strange to me, perhaps revealed in his own words.

In my laughable life that would be something.

A new manner seeped through Trystan's mien, a weariness like autumn and green fading out of the leaf. Being within a year of his age, I understood some part of it. Was this not my own drab color in Camelot before his letter came, restless and dissatisfied without so much as a finger to point or a word to name the cause? Women's bodies tell them plainly when youth is done, but what happens to us at the same age, no longer young but the memory of it fresh as yesterday? There is a sense of time and life slipped away too fast, too little left, and forever is not that far anymore.

A desperation whispers at your ear to turn back and find again something you can't name but lost sure as childhood.

Without words I knew that fevered light in Trystan's eye, what made him walk alone at night as I often did, spirit fumbling to find itself again, and why he pushed so hard for this campaign. It would be something.

A few days after Collen and Milius depart, I ride myself to Castle Cornouaille, not at all confident of success but, like the cat crouched at the mouse hole, ready to jump at any advantage. The men of Cornouaille are British Iceni; from the company, I chose sober Owain of the same tribe. Gwenallt of Morlaix, now, was a Trinovante, and so my other escort is Dunawd of the same folk. Both tribes were conquered or driven out by Saxons. Owain and Dunawd know broken pride, the loss of their homeland and the sting of defeat. These two ordinary men, standing in iron before those of their blood, are living proof that Clovis is not invincible, encouragement to join us, silent scorn for those who declined.

Cornouaille is a large fort, difficult but no more impossible to breach than Leon, were Clovis determined and not crippled by my trickery. In the hall, the warriors sit in a circle about the great firepit while, flanked by Owain and Dunawd, I stand before "Prince" Eurion.

No telling how genuine his title; his father may have been no more than a horse lord, but as Eurion settles himself in the high seat, studying me with hooded eyes under thick grey brows, I am reminded of Marcus Conomori. His thin mouth is masked behind two fingers as he listens: a suspicious man who keeps you at a distance. I argue the venture, making much of Owain's part in it, and from the cheers raised among the younger warriors, many of them are eager to join. They know whose man I am. *Arthur* and *Combrogi* are names to write large, to conjure with. These men cannot doubt what the world knows, and long for legends and heroes of their own. They will not be shown up by a peasant like Owain, Iceni or no, yet there he is before them, part of Leon's victory, part of the living deed.

Eurion commits nothing at first, only questions me. A winter raid is daring but fraught with risk. How many men would I ask and when? What of supply? He might field a hundred men, mounted and foot, but what guarantee of entry into Vannes?

I dare not compromise Milius and Collen, already at daily risk under enemy noses. I smile confidently. "Ah, my lord, that mouse is already in the cat's jaws."

Eurion measures me from behind his hand. "Will the Veneti rise in support?"

"Would not my lord leap to it himself if't were Cornouaille being freed by fellow Britons?"

"And what profit to Cornouaille for our part in this venture?"

Time to retreat behind my own hand, in a manner of speaking. "Better to ask what loss if my lord stays at home. Much of your land was sacked in Clovis's wake, and that merely in passing, mind. Denied our castle, he burned Leon to the ground. How when you and yours become the object of his ambition? Doubt it not, my lord: you will."

That strikes home among the warriors of Cornouaille. Many of them have lost property and lives to Clovis and now clamor for the chance to wreak vengeance, raising such a shout that Eurion promises his force *if* I can warrant the city gates will be open; otherwise he is not prepared or inclined to lay a long siege. Done. I can only pray that Collen will know where and wisely to spread the money he has for that purpose.

Another cold day's ride to Castle Morlaix and a different problem entire. Where Eurion is sharp and cautious, Lord Gwenallt is indolent and uninterested, a soft-rounded man in frayed tunic and toga with its senatorial stripe faded from many washings. He is Roman in all things, even reclining on a couch to dine, so please you, eating only with the right hand. Out of courtesy I and my men must do likewise, awkward as pigs dancing. In Arthur's early reign there were such lords with their heads in the sand who wanted the Romans to return, as if Rome could, with barbarians coming over their own walls and through the windows.

Gwenallt looks down at me from his chair of state and yawns to show he is neither swayed nor even impressed. Dunawd vents later the disgust he could not show before the lord.

"Dainty little tub. Ought to drown him in his scented finger bowl."

I must slog on, striving to enlist the hearts of his men as well. I tell them how Leon won out, not spinning so fine a tale as Trystan might, but raising a good deal of dust by way of interest. Gwenallt asks the same questions as Eurion and gets the same answers. I have not convinced him yet.

"Why?" he objects, elegantly peeling an apple with a silver-handled knife. "Why should Morlaix risk so much for a foreign tribe of no blood to us?"

I've honed that argument fine since Eurion. Because Britons united won under Arthur but met disaster when they would not. Can the men of Morlaix not see the ax about to fall on them? I *know* these Germans. Have I not fought their

Saxon cousins half my life? Arthur fights them still, year after year, but they keep coming. They will not give up. They can't because, like the Trinovantes here, they have been driven out by others as determined as themselves, and know they must win just to survive.

For my efforts I receive Gwenallt's halfhearted offer of (perhaps) some fifty men—which I trust as surely as the street urchin in Corstopitum pandering his scrawny mother whom he swore was virgin as Mary. There are those godless men who doubt Mary; certainly I doubt Gwenallt.

Rain fell all the next day. Starting early, we reached Leon near dark, wet through and out of sorts, but I was silently pleased with Owain and Dunawd for the care they gave their horses before thinking of themselves. We grained, watered, and rubbed them down before plodding to the armory to dry and oil our arms, finally to the rath and the comfort of its blazing firepit. I needed to be warm and in dry clothes before reporting to Trystan.

The men lounged about, some drinking mead, others just idle with the air of men used to discipline and suddenly without it. Trystan had not assembled them for the last two days, they told me, claiming the weather too ill for effective training. My mouse chittered misgiving; we'd never let bad weather stand us down before.

"Lord Gareth?"

Some of the men rose when Gwendolen called me from the entrance. Isolt's waiting woman came timidly to the firepit, unused to this place of men where her lady never entered. "My lord, my—that is, Lord Trystan asks for you in the solar."

From her naked worry I sensed Isolt rather than Trystan

had sent for me. "I'm just after drying off. Let me change and I'll come straight."

"Please hurry," she whispered. "Lady is afraid."

"Woman, what is it?"

Gwendolen's eyes flicked aside to the listening soldiers, telling me privacy was more fitting. I drew her into my own stall and pulled the curtain. Gwendolen seemed that embarrassed to enter with rough men about who might take any meaning from it. I was too tired to be gracious. She modestly averted her eyes while I pulled the dry tunic over my head.

"Now what's amiss?"

Her hands wrung and wrestled each other under her bosom. "Something's happened, I can't tell what. Lady will not say even to me, but the lord has been drinking these three days, pouring it down, and not wine but strong whisky. Lady is frightened, sir, and so am I. We've never seen him so black, no part of himself."

But I had. "Has he raised a hand to her? You know what I mean."

"No, he's done no such thing. Snarls at her, muttering something over and over in the holy language." Gwendolen struggled to remember. *"Mem . . . memento mori."*

"I have not the Latin."

"That much Lady has, little sense as it makes. 'Reminder of death,' she says. Oh, *do* hurry, sir."

"Go on." I slid the curtain back for her. "Say I'm half-way there."

Gwendolen hurried out of the rath, eyes lowered to avoid the stares of the men. I'd expected to report to Trystan promptly, but spent as I was and in no good humor myself, now I must deal with him black drunk. Please God, not this night. I would better welcome a broken leg.

Lady is frightened.

My mouse dancing up a proper storm, I belted a dagger about me for the meal I would take from the kitchen, and trudged up the steps to the keep. At the head of the stairs to the solar, my mouse stopped dancing and flat froze. Trystan sat at the long table with a jug and goblet before him, his sheathed sword and the Frankish ax near to hand. Beside him, Isolt raised her eyes to me—"Welcome, Gareth"—then dropped them to the sewing before her. I felt her fear like a cold hand.

"Behold." Trystan smirked, raising his goblet to me. "The bridegroom cometh."

From years with Tryst I knew he was less dangerous roaring at you than so deadly quiet. Whatever ate at the man, I'd give him no opening for quarrel, but asked Gwendolen to fetch me a cup. I sat down across from Trystan, helping myself to a warming drop. Whisky it was by charity alone, the raw stuff fermented by the villagers and no smoother than a Frank's manners.

Trystan did not move or look at me. "Not to your liking, Lord Gareth?"

"We've both had better and worse."

"What of Cornouaille?"

"Eurion promises his force of seventy-five horse. On condition the gates are opened at the right time."

"And Gwenallt?"

"Easier stealing horses in daylight. Fifty men, says he, but I'm thinking his pledge is faint as his heart. The same condition. Unless the gates are open and the Veneti rise to help when they go in, neither will risk it."

Trystan only drank and set his cup down. He seemed barely interested, miles away. "I see."

"All depends on Collen and Milius: what they learn, whom they can buy, how much the Veneti want Clovis off their backs."

I felt myself speaking to empty air and could *feel* the strain between Isolt and Trystan like pressure on my skin—he silent, her knuckles white about the sewing, plying the needle in nervous jabs, and mac Diarmuid himself raw as the bad whisky burning his throat.

"Jesus, what is it?" I demanded finally. "The humor's thick as fog in here."

Carefully, as if her one word might break eggs, Isolt murmured, "It seems my husband has something to say to you."

If so, Tryst would still not look straight at me. "This is my fortieth birthday, did you know? Seemed a meet time to sum my meager accomplishments, and what better company?"

"Are you on about that again? Thank God we've both lived so long when so many of Arthur's best never drew breath beyond thirty."

Trystan stirred at last, draining his cup and rising. "Shall I mourn them or they me? I could have done so much more."

He moved about the chamber, firepit to casement and back. A deceptive truth about Trystan: drink never made him weave or stumble, but I knew where to look for the danger signs. "Could have," he said. "Never such a man as Trystan for 'could have.' I could have honored my royal parents, save they left without farewell. I could have ruled

Lyonesse, save it's washed away. I might even have got on with Uncle Mark, but he—"

None of us needed this mourning, certainly not Isolt, suffering as she was. I said lightly, "Why don't you shut your gob? God's truth, but you're the bloody Fifth Horseman. War, disease, famine, death, and Trystan wailing his wasted life. There's much you can do yet when you leave off lament. Why have you let the men stand down with nothing to do? Not the weather; they know they may well be fighting in worse. We can't let them lose their edge."

"Peasant wisdom from our *eachra*-man."

I poured myself another drink. "You can be a galloping bore, Tryst, and you go down better if I have a drop too."

He ignored me as if I'd not spoken at all. "Did I tell you, wife, how he came to me pursued by a Faerie curse? I was young and happy then. I gave him a new life, even a new name and, in a rush of misplaced pity, took his sins and his curse on me in a quaff of wine."

"You have told me more than once." Isolt appeared to be tensed against the worst, like a child who sees the thrashing stick ready in a parent's hand.

"Lord forgive me for I knew not what I did. Odd to know a man so long and not know him at all." Trystan drifted to stand behind Isolt. "Don't you yearn for anything, Gareth? After all these months, not even Rhian? No, he wouldn't, would he, Isolt? Not now."

I could feel her pain like a pang; she might weep or scream any moment. "And what's that mean? I've made my report. What is it you'd say to me that can't wait until you've clean wits about you?"

Trystan's eyes lifted to mine, venomous over the cold-death smile. "When a man wakes on a moonlit night and looks from his casement toward the sea, who knows what he may glimpse that else might have been hidden?"

So that was it, and so like him drunk to come at it sidewise like an adder. "If I read you aright, what you saw was nothing."

"Nothing? I would not have dreamed you in the role of lover."

Isolt started to rise. "I have *told* you—"

He pushed her down with brutal force. I felt myself tense and coil. "Be still. We are in a pickle, aren't we?"

"My lord!" Even Gwendolen was moved to reprove him. "This is not worthy of you."

"It is not." I felt my own anger rising. He had hurt Isolt once, shamed her too often and not beyond it now. "Aye, we were there on the sea stairs. You slept poorly with your wound. She was worried about you, none but you."

I should have shut my own gob then and there but no longer wanted to. "Devil if you know what a good wife you have, and damned if you care. Why she loves you, why she tolerates the ruin you've made of yourself, is beyond my ken, you miserable man. I—I'm a temperate soul, Tryst, but let's leave this before I say that I'll be sorry for."

"And I." Again Isolt made to rise, and again Trystan shoved her down roughly, hissing: "You will be *still.*"

"Damn you, don't touch her!" I didn't care anymore, not now. "Do that again and I swear you'll bleed for it."

Trystan in this condition, any man could be that close to death, but I don't think he knew in that ugly, naked moment, Isolt silently beseeching my charity, how near he was himself. A red, savage thing glared out of me; I *wanted* to kill him. No need to spout my heart in words; she knew, but one more word out of him—

Only years of discipline saved me, wrapped a staying hand about the will to murder, taking death out of its reach. "I'll speak to you when you're fit to hear. For God's sake, man, remember who you are and what we purpose. The men and the task wait, and better sense it makes to kill Franks than one another."

That and no more. I turned to go but heard the scrape of the ax across the table and Isolt's horrified warning: "Gareth, guard!"

I dropped in a crouch as the heavy weapon flew over my head. Trystan was up, mouth twisted in a silent snarl as he snaked the sword from its scabbard. Sheer instinct took me. I knew that look, saw it at Bard's Tor and Camelot. The man would kill me, but my dagger was out, arm cocked and hurling with all my force behind it.

The blade went home in his right shoulder. His arm with the raised sword fell heavily. Trystan staggered and collapsed on a bench. In a trice Isolt was hovering over him, while Gwendolen, with a fine presence of mind, kicked the sword out of reach. Trystan stared at the blade sunk in his flesh. Clumsily he brushed Isolt's hands away, gripped the handle and went white as he drew it out.

With my blow, the rage washed out of me. I trembled there, stricken and miserable, sick in my stomach with what I'd done and more with what I'd been close to doing. Isolt threw me one glance that rioted with so many meanings: fear and relief, accusation and thanks, all in one.

"Isolt, I—"

"You couldn't help it," she muttered, tearing Trystan's tunic away from the wound. "Just go. We will tend him."

"You know I didn't want this."

"Please go, Gareth."

Trystan laughed weakly. "You always had a good arm. I should have killed you years ago."

There wasn't the strength left in me even for disgust. "And I once pleaded to Arthur for your life. No fear, my lord," I promised between my teeth, "I'll take the men to Vannes on the day we pricked."

Cold and wet on the walls of Castle Leon, but I stood long in the sea wind shaking with a passion that frightened me, made as much from caring and loss as rage. For a space I thought I must retch with it, but only dry, strangled sounds came from me. Let God bend his angels in aid over a simple man never made to hold such feelings any more than a cup can hold an ocean.

In defending myself I'd done for Trystan so far as Vannes was concerned. His sword arm would be useless for weeks, unreliable longer. In a manner of speaking, in saving my life I'd taken his, the one deed he desired to give himself meaning. I earnestly prayed he'd come to see that was all I took and worthless beside the wealth of her there for his reaching. Since the first day of planning, I think Trystan saw Vannes as a kind of ending, a wiping clean of all he'd botched in life, the last perfect line redeeming a flawed song.

While I trained the company to a fine edge and waited word from Collen, Trystan kept to his chamber. He'd left off drinking, not a drop. To keep his spirits up I passed every detail of the raid under his eye for approval, though it was some days before either of us could speak of the evil moment that might have left one of us dead. Trystan lay on his pillows, right arm in a sling, stabbing clumsily at his supper meat until I took the blade from him and cut it up.

"Thanks. Need I remark you have a deft way with a blade?"

"It's sorry I am for all, Tryst, but there wasn't much future in arguing with a drawn sword or an ax come within a hair of braining me."

Trystan speared, chewed, and swallowed a piece of pork, then laid the knife aside. "Gareth, it wasn't me. You must know that."

"It was you. Time you faced that and learned there's men who can drink and men who can't."

He nodded. A kind of fear haunted his eyes. "And those who must not dare."

"Remember that. You would have killed me."

"Would I?" As ever, his smile could mean honest affection or sudden death. "Not my lamest intent, you Irish serpent." Trystan's head fell back on the pillows. "I shouldn't miss the Fatal Natal for all the gold in your Eire, but it appears you must celebrate Christmas without me."

The Fatal Natal: Trystan's irony for the date of our attack. Christmas morning before dawn we would strike the Frank garrison. The devout among them might be at early prayers, but more would be sleeping off the excess of the eve, much of it provided by Collen and freely poured in the taverns. The more we murdered, the fewer left to fight. Churchmen might raise their eyes to heaven in horror at such a deed on that holiest of days, but it bothered neither pagan Tryst nor my baptized self one whit. The Midlands taught us that war with these people was one of extinction, Britain to be ours or theirs. Armorica, this last refuge of folk already beaten once, would be Celt or Frankish, no middle way between.

A few snow flurries sifted down, but the weather held

better than we hoped. I gave thanks to God, while the men took it for fair omen as they pampered the horses after riding all day and sharpened swords and lances. I began to worry in earnest: no final word yet from Collen. November gone, December wasting day by day, now the tenth, the twelfth, and where in hell *are* you, Collen? What word?

On the morning of the thirteenth, as Trystan, Isolt, and I shared hot herb tea with honey in the solar, the heavy footsteps of a tired man thumped up the stairs from the hall, and the grimiest ragamuffin in God's impoverished world stood before us.

"My lords," he panted. "Lady."

Gwendolen gasped, about to take a broom to the sight of him—

"And what might you be? If it's alms you're asking, the kitchen is below."

—before any of us recognized Milius: bearded, fish-fragrant and wrapped head to foot in the remains of garments a scarecrow would spurn in daylight. Worn to the bone with travel, Milius gulped down the warming tea Isolt offered him. From the remains of a sackcloth tunic he drew a wrapped packet of wooden shingles shaved clean and covered with scribbles and diagrams. "From Collen, my lord. The gates can be open. The town can be yours."

Though Gwendolen bluntly advised the reeking soldier to stand apart, Isolt had a softer heart and manners. "Come, Milius; have a bite and a bath."

If she'd offered him her virtue, she could not have kindled more eagerness in the man. "A bath? A *hot* bath?"

"And I myself will set them to heat the water while you breakfast."

But first his report. He had come through Castle Cornouaille. Eurion and his promised force were ready, though to Milius's way of thinking they were not what our lads would call squared off.

"And there's more." Milius gestured down toward the hall below from whence a sudden roar of men's voices thundered up to us. "Volunteers from Morlaix, my lords. Fifty of them. Met 'em on the road."

"Fifty is it?" I marveled gratefully. "And Lord Gwenallt with them?"

"No." Milius dismissed the truant lord with a shrug. "He thought the whole matter mad. Couldn't make up his mind, they said. So on they came anyway for a bit of exercise. But now they're here and hungry."

"And most welcome," I breathed with a song in my heart. God was clearly with us. "Gwendolen, love, tell the cooks to bloody well stuff them. Jesus, fifty! We can *do* it."

Informed by Collen's diagrams and Milius's good memory, Trystan and I went over and over the plan of attack. As we hoped, Clovis was gone, leaving a garrison of no more than two hundred horse and foot. Vannes was a small town and not walled until it became a port of call for trading ships. For some years when their merchants saw profit in Roman protection, there had been a small garrison, whose camp with its bank and ditch still stood near the town's west gate, now occupied by Clovis's men. The "fort" was scarcely larger than one of our old *alae* outposts on the Pictish border, its walls rickety as the buildings within.

"The bank's worn down," Milius declared, "and the walls no more than wicker and daub. Collen will try to have the fort gate open, but you could bash straight through. And Collen begs one change."

He needed at least ten good men to subdue the guards

on one gate, and ten he had recruited. That number he could direct personally; any more compounded the risk. Better to concentrate ten on the west gate and the fort rather than hope thirty could open two together at the right time. Trusting we would agree, Collen warranted that portal would swing wide when the church bells of Vannes rang the hour of prime on Christmas morning. Trystan and I agreed quickly. One gate was the surer thing. No dividing our force, but massed together to deliver them a crippling blow. With Cornouaille and Morlaix behind, we would sweep into the city and garrison. The surprised Franks able only to defend their lives, Collen would follow us into the fort with the Veneti, seize as many weapons as possible and take no prisoners. With luck Vannes could be secured in an hour.

"And without luck?" Trystan posed. "Give them any chance for pitched battle and you lose the advantage."

True, but no time to waste on misgivings. The Morlaix warriors, while strapping boyos, were hardly our match as disciplined cavalry, and those of Cornouaille were of untested mettle.

"So much can go awry." Trystan removed his arm from the sling and flexed it over the table. "Do you trust Eurion?"

"Not if the choice were mine, but it isn't."

In the grey early morning of eighteenth December, Father Antonius, before breakfast in the hall, said Mass and heard the swift-mumbled confessions of men with less on their souls than me but who would not face the unknown unshriven. Devil if I know why I didn't join them—Bless me, Father, for I covet my neighbor's wife—and let the good priest sort it out. A man's mind and soul are riddles within mysteries. If I'd grimed myself with wanting her, perhaps denial washed me a bit. Under Brehon law in my country there are ten degrees of marriage. As I moved through the last days of preparation, seeing little of Isolt but my heart open and listening for the beat of hers, I fancied we shared an eleventh degree, one of deep pity, compassion, and understanding. Later for confession, then, when I would be the last in a long line of penitents and hope the bored priest would doze through my sins.

With the men leading out their mounts to assemble below, I lingered at the top of the steps with Trystan. I must go quickly; from this morning every hour of daylight would be precious. The sea wind whipped and whined about us, and though I tried not to, my sight strayed again and again to the upper casements of the keep for one last sight of herself.

"Antonius said you neglected confession," Trystan remarked lightly. "So well at peace, then?"

"Or tainted with some of your damned educated doubt. I'm off to murder as many men as I can in their beds, and some of them Christian. I'm not sure what reckoning God will ask for that."

"When could we ever afford such scruples?" Trystan warned soberly. "You can't think of that." He gazed with open envy at the men below as they mounted. "I should be with them."

"Ah, none of that now. Count your treasures, man."

Time to go, but a sudden awkwardness took me. From his averted glance, Trystan must have felt the same. Best friends, bitter enemies, the bright image of her ever to stand between us now, yet we might be parting forever. "Be good to her, Trystan."

Still he would not look at me. I would make him. "Tryst, hear me."

"Aye, what?"

"When this is done I'm going home."

"In dead winter?"

"If I have to fly on an angel's back, I'm going home."

"Yes," he said at length. "That's best."

"Seems a lifetime."

"In a way so it has been. Who would have thought?"

From the courtyard below, Milius signaled me with his sword: formed and ready. But somehow I couldn't part from the man like this. "Trystan, look at me. Look into my face—and lay less sin to my soul than you think."

With both hands I pulled him around to face me. "I said *mark* me, you impossible man. Chance made me your servant, Arthur made me your equal, life made me your friend. Can we not part so?"

"As friends?" That slight, cool smile of his, faded now under a terrible weariness. "How we've strained the definition between us. I've hated you, Gareth."

"I've hated you, and no one hates better than friends."

"I recall in Sicily they have a saying: 'Good friends are like good food. To have any taste both must be hot.' "

"Lord Gareth?" Once more Milius signaled and called. The men were looking up to us now, waiting. Trystan lifted his good arm in farewell.

"Forget the curse," I urged, "for it never truly settled on you, as if it could. When I go, it will be mine still. You will never know how much." I gathered him roughly to me, squeezing my heart and his together that they might bond again. "Each of us has demons enough."

In parting I grinned into that self-ravaged face with the

old grace I hadn't spoken in years. "God bless you in the morning, Tryst."

Now I saw Isolt, wrapped in her cloak, descending the outer stairs from the keep, and cried to her with all my heart: "And bless all in the house! Happy Christmas, Tryst, you godless man!"

"Merry Yule, you little bog-jumper."

When I took my place at the head of the formation, I turned one last time to where Isolt stood by Trystan, one arm through his, the other lifted in farewell.

I tried that day to make an end, to close the matter fairly and regain a friend, but life is never neat as legends, and whatever gods or angels carve our destinies are clumsy at their trade. We were not finished, nothing closed, the song far from ended.

Pitch-dark of a cold Christmas morning and no Magi's guiding star above us, only the black end of a clouded night and, a mile beyond, the walls of Vannes. Few of the men needed to be roused. By my order each had drunk a good measure of water before rolling up in his blankets, so the need to relieve himself would wake him early.

We slipped about in the dark, no fires allowed, each man taking his horse from the picket line and saddling with little sound beyond the creak of leather. Our Morlaix volunteers were not used to such spartan conditions but, as we did, chewed a mouthful of dried apple and cheese and called it breakfast. With the eastern sky not yet beginning to pale, I gave the word to arm and assemble. The rustle and *chink* of mail and the occasional snorting of a horse were the only sounds as each man buckled his neighbor's mail at the back and fell into formation to stand at his horse's head, and here it was that Dunawd found me. His face, rounded by the mail hood, was only a pale blur before me, but the worry was all too clear in his voice. He'd retraced our route for a mile or so to find the lagging men of Cornouaille. "Had to go slowly in the dark, but there's not a sign of them."

"Thanks, Dunawd." I clapped him on the shoulder. "You know your place in ranks."

"We should have word from Owain, sir. We must."

"We will. Into ranks with you."

Not wise to show frustration or doubt before the men now, but I silently damned Eurion to hell and home again. He'd been trouble since he joined us at Cornouaille. Ready to ride, says he, but on *his* terms. He refused to travel without pack wagons, which meant extra fodder to carry. His warriors couldn't believe we carried so little food—just oats for the horses, dried apples, and a bit of cheese—or that we could cover so much distance in a day.

"My men can," I told Eurion. "They are *Combrogi.* My lord, you must keep up."

But that lovely man just looked down his princely nose at me and lumbered on with his heavy wagons. Naturally they fell behind. The first two days, Eurion's men caught us up well after dark, the third after midnight, the fourth and fifth not till morning. Now the hour to attack was at hand, we must move within minutes, and well over a third of our assault force likely still in their blankets. Damn all, we should never have counted on them. We'd even lost three or four of the Morlaix men whose horses were not up to our grueling pace, going lame or throwing shoes that should have been closely inspected before setting out. Jesus, I discovered during the march that some of them carried their finest clothes, expecting a proper banquet in Vannes. One brought a harp, if you please, to compose his own immortal song on the glorious defeat of the Franks.

At least one man in the Iceni column, I knew, would be up, ready, and, like me, boiling with righteous wrath. After the first day, I'd sent Owain to Eurion, as best he could to prod the prince to greater dispatch. Surely he'd bring some word; surely a man I trained would not leave me here with my thumb in my mouth. And where was Collen? What hour now? How long until prime?

Standing at my horse's head, my body not yet warming the armor under my cloak, I lived through a year of doubts as the minutes bled away. The men must be as uneasy with waiting. To keep them busy, I whispered back the order for each man to inspect his mount's shoes once more and the sack wrappings about each hoof to muffle our approach until the last moment. Now in the rear of our column I heard a murmur of subdued but expectant voices, then the ranks parted and the dim figure led his horse to me.

"Lord Gareth? It's me, Owain."

I let out my breath with relief. "Here."

Still too dark to see his face but the anger burned harsh in his voice. Owain was ready to spit nails. "Damn the man. Damn them all. I'll never call myself Iceni more."

"Easy, boyo. Where are they?"

"Oh, they're stirring, sir, and Prince Eurion will join you *when* they've built fires for a hot breakfast."

"Fires? Jesus, how far back are they?"

"Three miles." Owain couldn't keep still; disgust surged him back and forth before me. "They couldn't go any farther last night, poor little tykes. Not much chance the fires will be seen, but they should be here *now.* Eat in the saddle as we do, I told them. The prince just laughed at me and said

Cornouaille would give good account of itself. I swear I wanted to strangle him then and there."

"And I'd lend a hand. Well then—"

I broke off as the footsteps approached out of the dark. Two men by the sound, leading horses, coming from our forward picket positions. "Who's there?"

"Milius."

"And who else?"

"Collen, sir."

Thank God and holy Padraic: at least *something* went right this morning. "Come on."

The small, spare figure of Collen slipped up to us beside Milius, whom I sent to take his place in ranks. "Good on you, Collen. Condition?"

Between the cloak hood and overgrown beard, there was little of Collen to see in the darkness. He turned back toward the town below where only a few lights glimmered. As we watched, one more firefly glimmered and became a steady glow. "I'd say that's the sexton in Pig Lane church near the fort. He's up to breakfast and ring prime just after. Are all here, sir?"

Owain bit off the answer. "All but the Iceni."

"Christ, where—" Collen caught himself. "Sir, we must move now. I'll lead the way."

"And the gate?" Owain challenged bitterly. "What wager that won't be open either?"

"You would lose," Collen hissed fiercely. "There were two guards; now there's nine of mine waiting. We had to do it silent but could not do it neat. Don't ask how, Owain, and give me none of your mouth. Lord Gareth, there's something else."

More bad news? "What? We've not much time."

"Most of the Frank cavalry's gone from the fort. Rode out to the north yesterday morning, almost a hundred."

"Where are they, do you know?"

Not for sure, but the word was they'd gone to collect tribute from one of the villages north of Vannes. Scarce that many remained in the fort, and many of those drank deep and late in the taverns on the generosity of some fishermen, so it was said, who believed in charity and Christian brotherhood at Christmas.

"We must go now," Collen urged. "Prime is near, and it's a steep path down. The men must follow me in single file."

I gave the order to Owain to pass on: Follow me single file, each man holding the tail of the horse in front.

Pray God the sexton lingered over breakfast this morning. By my guess we had less than an hour to prime, if that. Soon enough my men would know how few we attacked with, and twice damn Eurion yet again to seven kinds of hell. The garrison worried me now far less than the Frankish cavalry, sudden new pieces loose on the chessboard, and who knew how close?

The west wall of Vannes rose dark against the night sky as we halted a hundred paces from the gates to reform by threes in a column. My word went back to the Morlaix men to stay behind Milius once inside the fort, above all to forget any notions of glory and follow orders. I was mounting myself when, from the church in Pig Lane, the bell pierced the cold dark, ringing the hour of prime like Judgment. We slipped forward toward the gates. When we were no more than ten paces from them—"Collen, you'll be blessed in heaven"—they parted like the Red Sea for Moses, and our hundred rustled into Vannes no louder than the morning wind.

Just beyond the gate a burly shape appeared at Collen's stirrup. I couldn't hear their few words, but Collen's head chopped up and down once. "Good," he said softly. "Same orders. Nothing changed."

The big Veneti faded away in darkness; Collen leaned toward me in the saddle. "Sir, one of us has surely lived a saintly life."

"Not I. What did he say?"

"That's Clitus. He took some of the Veneti to do for the guards on the fort gate. Said they found one and him dead drunk, snoring in his own vomit and the gate unbarred."

"Did he wake?"

"Not in this life, sir." Collen soothed a hand along his horse's neck. "Easy, now. Easy."

The gate unbarred; indeed one of us must have been living a stainless life. The nearest I could reason to such luck was the free drink Collen paid for in the taverns. The guard must have been stupid drunk when he took his post, and got tired of opening and closing the gate for men straggling in late. Feeling like death himself, he thought to hell with it or simply sank into drunken stupor, but not for me to stare down the throat of a gift horse as Collen led us up the narrow street toward the fort.

He vanished into the shadows by the fort wall. Against the slowly lightening sky I could see the timber tower to the west and the single figure of the Frank sentinel on the platform. Still quite dark; when the gates groaned open, I prayed he'd think us his own horsemen returning. When Collen reappeared I could already make out his bearded grin.

"Wide open, sir. You could drive the sins of the world through."

"Drop back to Clitus and your volunteers. You know what to do."

Collen wheeled his horse at a walk toward the rear of the column where his Veneti detail followed on foot. They would enter the armory, seize what weapons they could, and prevent any Franks from arming themselves. From his shingle drawings I had memorized the location of the two barracks and their distance from the gate. Now the rear half of our column swung out behind Milius, a deadly stream flowing toward the far barrack as I closed on the near one. As I did, the mouse suddenly leaped and turned head over paws in my stomach.

Jesus, what? Where? Not much time, the sky lightening more with every breath—

The tower sentinel. Drunk or sober, he couldn't be blind as well.

He was not. The helmeted man was rigid in his heavy fur mantle, gripping the rail, staring dead at me in the moment needed to know we were not Franks, not men in such long mail coats on horses so much smaller than theirs. He fumbled at something, raised it to his lips, and I saw the curved shape of the horn—

"Now, Milius! Go! *Go!*"

—that brayed its alarm through my shouted order. I had just time to see Milius's detachment dash forward and Collen's men break into a run toward the armory before my own men attacked. We jumped from the saddle, swords drawn, and I dashed for the barrack door that yielded to my shoulder. We charged into the dark beyond, hewing at anything we saw. Many of them must have been still drunk, others heavy sleepers. Most were not even moving under their blankets. It was quickly over. Amid the sounds of men dying before they properly woke, we heard the shrill screams of women. When I stumbled away from the house of slaughter, the men had collected four or five young women glassy-eyed with fear, clutching blankets about them. We might have known there'd be women, but the soldier who stood over the gibbering lot of them had no idea what to do with his charges until I came up.

"Tell them they won't be harmed. Send them home. Is this all of them?"

The soldier was not young, a fisherman before he joined Trystan's company. "No, my lord. There was two—I mean what with it being dark and us unable to see . . ."

I looked down at the dark stains on my own sword. "I know. Never mind. Just tell 'em happy Christmas and they can go home."

Milius jogged up to me, helmet askew and his sword glistening dark as mine in the growing light. "Done, sir. None left."

"Get to your horses before the smell does."

Wind blowing through the open barrack doors brought the scent of blood to our mounts. Well trained though they were, we could lose precious time calming them. Something made me glance up toward the guard tower: empty. There was one Frank survivor at least, and a man of very good sense. Safe but helpless in the tower, he could only skin down the supports, leap into the ditch, and make off beyond the town.

Collen strode up to me, swinging a *francisca.* "All armed, sir, every man, and not a Frank in sight. Do we wait for the Iceni?"

"Good question. How many Franks live outside the garrison? There must be some."

"Not many, sir. Stewards, servants, that sort."

"Can you find them?"

Collen hefted the ax. "Clitus can."

"You know what to do. Have Clitus and the rest spread the word among the men of Vannes to come here for arms." I bolted away toward the guard tower, overhanding my way up the ladder to the platform to peer westward toward the hills and the trail Eurion must take.

No movement. Nothing.

Eurion, you miserable, misbegotten—

Suddenly all the strength washed out of me. I put my head down on the hard railing, trembling as my body paid me back for the long night and the few savage minutes of slaughter, and I gave in to rage and despair before the habit of command stiffened my back again. The men had done well but needed orders, needed to know someone was in command and making sense out of a half-done task that could still fall into chaos. *Think. You're in command. They expect decisions. Make them.*

Sorry, I can't just now. Just let me rest a moment.

You may not have a moment, eachra-*man. Think.*

We could wait for Eurion; for that matter, we now had Vannes and could deny the Franks, who had neither the men nor equipment, to wrest it back from us. They'd have no choice but to leave.

Aye, leave, ride north—and how many villages would be looted and perhaps burned like Leon for supply on their thieving way home to Clovis?

They must be hit, must be broken. For this the men had sweated and trained half the year, good men honed sharp as their lances to this purpose. Under Arthur the *Combrogi* proved again and again: cavalry is useless in defense, all in attack. With our spirit and the advantage of surprise, the odds were with us.

I made the decision, perhaps not wholly my best, but the Franks were out there, Eurion no longer part of it, and while we hesitated we were blind.

I bawled down to the horsemen below. "Milius! Get me Milius!"

My nerves were strung tighter than I guessed; the sudden jangling of the bell from Pig Lane church startled me. Across the town to the north another bell took it up, shivering for miles on the cold morning air. If the Franks heard it, I hoped they took it for Christmas spirit. Beyond the fort households were waking in the early light, smoke rising from roof holes, doors opening and folk peering timidly into the streets.

"One of you down there: to the church. Shut up that shaggin' bell. Where's Milius?"

He was just rounding the other side of the near barrack, trotting his horse to the tower base. "Here, sir."

"Can you find Dunawd?"

"He took a moment to rest, sir. Didn't feel too well."

"Who does? What's the matter?"

"Same as most of us." I heard the pallid quaver in Milius's voice as if some of the wind had been punched out of him. "I never did a man with a sword before."

No use telling him to get used to what most men never really do. "Then you'll be wanting something clean to do. Take Dunawd, sick or well, and find me the Frank cavalry. They'll be somewhere north; Collen will point you right.

When you find them, wait for us. We'll be an hour or so behind you. And don't be seen."

Light enough now to see Milius was pale for sure, but he managed a dry grin with his salute. "Yes, my lord. A hero again."

"So you are, Lord Trystan's finest. Your ladder *and* a gold laurel of valor. And tell them at the north church to leave off that damned bell. They'll know they're free soon enough."

Trystan would rejoice. We'd hit the garrison so hard and fast that not a man among us took any wound worthy of the name. We grained and watered our horses from the fort's ample stores—

"Not too much, mind. We'll be riding."

—and found the larder so well provisioned that the Veneti must surely have been going without. The men found meat and cheese, buttermilk, tasty blood puddings, fresh loaves of bread, the lot. Rather than eat among the Frankish dead, the men stripped wood from the barracks and built fires in the open.

About half an hour, I judged, since the north church bell went blessedly silent, but still no sign of Eurion and the Iceni. Collen returned with about twenty-five able-bodied Veneti men to be armed, willing but wary, still not trusting their fate to rough-looking strangers in blood-spattered mail.

Owain was squatting by a fire, hands and mouth greasy with food. When I summoned, he rose, wiping his hands on his breeches. "First time I've been even half full or warm in a week, sir. Damned Franks must swill themselves like hogs."

"You see where it's got them."

"I don't know." Owain turned his lean face to the fire

and his comrades still munching like the locusts of Egypt. "I could eat that much again just for the pleasure."

"I want you to carry a message to Eurion."

With a reluctant sigh, Owain dragged the gauntlets from his sword belt. "Yes, my lord. But I'd rather ride with better men."

"I know, and so will Eurion by the very look of you. Tell the lovely prince that Vannes is taken. He is invited to occupy it as we are moving north to engage the Frankish horse."

"Invited." Owain's stubbled lips curled in a hard smile. "Aye, sir, that's good. If he's *quite* ready, of course."

"Don't say that. A man who was never a real prince needs all the dignity he can find. Off with you."

I'd given Milius an hour's start, but moving among my men as they sprawled by their fires, I knew they needed more rest, all they could snatch from moving time. They and the horses—lean men tough as boiled leather on mounts to match—had traveled a week, slept in the cold, and taken a town quick and quiet as a well-greased machine.

"I'd rather ride with better men."

We put this into them, Tryst, you and I. You need not search for something of honor. It is here.

They knew they must now search out and attack an equal number of the enemy on unknown ground, and it was this, I think, that left them sober and quiet about their fires. Some dozed, others just waited mute as their horses. They deserved the extra time. I allowed it until the church bell in Pig Lane rang the hour of terce—hesitant and almost subdued, as if the sexton, squelched by Collen, took pains not to disturb us.

I moved among my men, nudging the sleepers with a

foot. I could tell them later how proud they made me; time now to be the Whip again, but to rally them by the name they'd earned.

"On your feet! Up, *Combrogi!* See to your horses and arms. We're moving out."

"Moving?" The young Morlaix warrior who'd brought his silly harp along jumped up to confront me. "Then it is a fight we will see?"

"Did I not just say? Y'want me to *sing* it for you? Square off and see to your horse."

Weak sunlight struggled through cloud as we moved at a trot through the muddy streets toward the north gate. Many of the Veneti men and women were out now, lining our way to cheer and bless us as liberators. We passed a few bodies lying in ditches here and there, Franks by their dress and hair, and one dangling from a frayed rope in a hasty but well-deserved hanging.

Once beyond the town walls we stayed alert for any movement, especially the few patches of forest dotting the open ground where an ambush might catch us. The Romans had not bothered to build a proper road out of Vannes, only widened the single cart track and firmed it beneath with clay. We moved at the pace trained into the men for months: so long at a steady trot, then off the horses to walk them while we trudged on foot.

My mouse and I kept careful note of time by the feeble sun. An hour and a half out, by my reckoning, a horseman appeared on the track ahead, closing at a gallop: one of Milius's scouts coming back. I gave the order to dismount as the soldier churned up to us, vaulting out of the saddle.

"My lord," he panted, saluting. "From Milius."

"Good on you." Memory failed of his name but I recognized the long face and horsey yellow teeth protruding as if too large for his mouth. Dried blood sprinkled one cheek and the skirt of his mail coat. "There's blood. You're hurt?"

"No, I—" He swiped carelessly at his face. "From the barracks. You know, sir. When we went in."

"Yes. Column! Walk the horses ahead. I'll join you straight."

As the column plodded past, the scout knelt to scratch in the dirt with his dagger. "The shape of the land ahead. A wood about a mile round here." He traced a rough circle. "And a long hill range just east of it with woods for cover." The blade swept in a long, squashed oval with an X at the western end for Milius's position. "And a wide pass between them where the road goes on north."

"How wide?"

"A good mile, sir. Milius has a clear view of the flat land beyond, miles of it. Beyond that the hills rise steep."

"Franks?"

"Just their tracks," the soldier said. "Must be them, leading straight across the valley. Milius and Dunawd rode out far as they dared. No cover to hide a man out there. They saw smoke. Not much, just what you'd expect from a village in the morning. Wherever the Franks went, they've stayed the night."

If forced to abandon his position, Milius advised, he would rejoin our column. Otherwise he would remain in place, perhaps an hour ahead of us. He saw no reason to think the Franks would not return by the same route.

I rose and dusted my hands. "Right then, we'll catch him up."

"Look." The scout shaded his eyes, peering to the south. "Dust. Riders. They must come from Vannes."

Perhaps from Eurion, informing me he had arrived. *There's polite of you, Iceni.* But by the horses and mail, the two gallopers were of our company. Another moment and I recognized the leading rider's shield with its device of a flower and a harp: Trystan, and Owain with him. *What in hell are you doing, man? You're not that well, shouldn't be here at all. And what of Isolt with only farmers left to protect Leon?*

I sent the scout to join the company ahead. "Tell the men Lord Trystan is with us after all."

That would cheer them. Not the best or wisest commander, yet the better side of Trystan's nature always had their hearts. As for the dark in his soul, they'd never seen as much of that as Isolt and myself.

I couldn't call him a fool before Owain or demand his lunatic reasons for joining us when his shoulder could not be wholly healed, only wait and wonder in the middle of the road as they clattered to a halt before me, and the cold wind blowing over the three of us.

Trystan slid one leg over the saddle and dropped to the ground. "Gareth."

That was all, no smile or his usual gay greeting. The man's manner was grave as a funeral, Owain's no lighter. "My lord," I said, "you should not have come."

"That's the least of our worries," Trystan grated. "I couldn't stay in Vannes."

"Nor I." Owain looked ready to burst into flames.

"Then Eurion's arrived?"

"He has, sir." Owain dropped his eyes. "After all these months, all the work and sweat. The *shame* of them. Eurion, that—"

In a low and steady tone, Owain vented his opinion of the Iceni prince and his men in terms the lowest gutter would refuse and some I'd never heard, before reining himself in. "Pardon me, sir. Lord Trystan can tell you better."

Traveling with three relief horses, Trystan had no trouble following Eurion's trail with its deep wagon ruts and their casual pace. He'd caught them up this morning just after dawn as they were breaking camp.

"And in no great haste," Trystan commented with acid in the words. "You'd think they were just off to Mass. Then in fine column order, horns blaring, banners flying, Eurion *charges* into Vannes and takes possession of the fort and the town. In gilt ceremonial armor, no less, and with such pomp he might be Caesar accepting a triumph from his own senate."

"Owain must have told you. The Frank cavalry's loose and God knows where. We couldn't wait any longer. I sent to Eurion to occupy the town."

"He's occupying it to death!" Owain burst out. "Like a plague they are."

"What's this? What do you mean?"

"He's looting the town," Trystan said flatly. "Worse than Franks, snatching up everything not nailed down, even from the churches, men pulling women out of their houses." Trystan's head snapped back as he searched the heavens for something like sanity. "That wasn't what we intended, you know that. Our men know that. I protested to Eurion, I *begged* him. When I saw they couldn't be stopped, I rode out with Owain here. We wanted no part of it. We were sick, both of us."

"Sick's not the word." Owain's voice broke, his eyes bright with tears about to escape. "My lord, you—you should have seen. The people came out to welcome them. At first. Now they're cursing the lot of us."

I recalled sweet Eurion's first question to me: What profit to Cornouaille? Bastard. "What of Collen? Did you see him?"

Owain wasn't sure. "Some of the Veneti . . . there was fighting in the streets. I couldn't see much. We couldn't stop Eurion's men. We couldn't watch it."

Nor could I blame the man for the feeling or the wisdom to get out. "Join the company, Owain. And look you, not a word about this to the men. They don't need to know yet."

"No, sir. I'd take no pleasure in it." Owain picked up his horse's dangling reins and trudged away along the road.

"Tryst, there goes a good man who's had a long, bad day."

"And now to be ashamed of his own tribe." Trystan moved away, throwing the reins over his mount's back, but stood a moment just staring into the distance. "I knew I had to be here, but tell me: Which of us was inspired to enlist Eurion?"

"What matter? We've a battle afore and a stinking mess behind. Nothing to do but get on with it."

Still Trystan did not move. "And we were so keen to save all of Lesser Britain. How noble our motives were, remember? I felt clean then. At last I could do something right. Now I want to strip off my soul like a dirty shirt and scrub it for an hour."

"Not your fault nor mine."

"But we're part of it. I think, Gareth, that I've poured my last wine on a sacred tree. They are vicious children, the gods. They mock us to the end."

Nothing I could say. Eurion's savagery spread like grimy smoke over my own conscience. I saw how Trystan winced as he mounted, and hoped his arm wouldn't fail him against the Franks. For meet them we must now and destroy them entire. "Well, the black Iceni would only hinder us."

I mounted and ranged beside Trystan, who suddenly came back to life and flashed me the reckless smile I knew of old, cocky and arrogant, to hell with all the world but us and the thing to do.

"There is one consolation, Gareth. The Greeks had their Furies to drag them to hell or drive them mad. The Franks have us."

Maddening himself, but there was the man for you, elegant to the end. "Do they not!"

"Let us teach them a new meaning for misery."

Weak sun above told me it lacked not much of midday when Trystan, Milius and myself left the company behind to rest on the wooded ridge and made our way to a vantage point overlooking the cart track winding away across the valley to the north. Milius had chosen this position well. We would see the Franks for miles before they reached us. We had good ground for surprise and, please God, time to plan where and how.

"Well done, Milius," Trystan approved. "Couldn't be better."

Oh? My mouse was never a trusting creature, and sure I'd learned from Eurion how far a perfect plan could go awry. We had to expect the Franks in sight at any time, and Trystan's presence added a problem. We must be clear as to command.

"Milius, stay on watch. Lord Trystan and I need to have another look to the west."

Trystan following after, we jogged perhaps fifty paces through the trees to where the ridge dropped down to open ground, the cart track, and the small wood beyond. Not too steep here. Cavalry could remain hidden and then move out quickly. We considered the wisdom of a massed attack or a Scythe ambush from two sides. Trystan, estimating the distance to the other hill, thought it unwise.

"Too far. That element would have to run over a mile while the other was already engaged and outnumbered two to one."

No dispute there. I stripped back my mail coif and gave the matted hair a good scratch. "They'll most like be in column order. We'll have surprise, but it must be quick."

"I forget. What did Milius say about their attack style?"

"Only one that he saw, but they did it every time. One or two ranks charging forward, then sweeping in a straight line to the right. Which does seem impractical. Clumsy. Our wedge attack could punch clean through and split them wide. They must use others."

"Clumsy, yes," Trystan reflected. "But Tacitus, writing of one of the Rhine tribes, mentioned this rightward sweep as their habit. I believe it."

"The wonders of a fine education." I jerked a thumb at the valley to the north. "They could come now or hours from now. We have to decide what to do and which of us gives the word. They're your men, but you're not well enough to fight."

Trystan continued to study the ground west of us. "As you say, they're my company. Don't deny me this day, friend."

"So be it. You will command." *And mad you are to be here at all, mad to leave her, but we dare not let the men be confused or unsure.* "And I second, as it was in the beginning."

"Very gracious, thank you. No—wait." Trystan whirled

about to me, lit with his inspiration. "The other wood's too far, but what if—just suppose there's a dip or defile out there, anything within three hundred yards of the road? We could divide the men and use the Scythe. It would work then."

The Scythe, two ranks of horsemen slicing back and forth through an enemy from opposite directions, was a simpler maneuver than the Flower. To succeed here, the second "blade" of the Scythe had to be far enough out to escape notice from the road, yet close enough to attack in concert with the other, giving the enemy no chance to recover. Better to call it the Shears, but Arthur named it, and who was I to correct the high king?

Milius hadn't scouted in that direction, concentrating on the north. "I'll ride out myself with four men spread wide. If there's cover, we'll find it."

Trystan's chest swelled with a deep breath. "Is it not the old days come back, Gareth? *Dyw!* But I feel fifteen years younger."

And I wished he looked it, but under the windburn, Trystan's face was death-white.

Our time and choices were narrowing as I rode to the west with my detail. We scattered a hundred paces apart, searching the ground as we went. Fairly level with high, yellow grass and patches of scrub bush and gorse. Nothing to slow a charge once begun, and, Jesus, when we went there'd be no time for fumbling or second thoughts. Then a shrill whistle from the man off to my right. He pointed just ahead of him. He'd found the remains of an ancient ditch, mostly filled in by years and weather, not very long or deep.

"But it may just possibly serve," I reported to Trystan with a glance at the westering sun. "Shall we try?"

He gazed off to the north, then up at the sun. "Obliging of the Franks to give us time."

"And not much left I would say. Divide or stay together?"

"Less chance of confusion with the Scythe." Trystan slapped his gauntlets against his thigh. "Right then. Here is how we'll do it."

With something definite, something about to happen, fear and excitement mixed in the men to form and divide them quickly into the two "blades" of the Scythe, Trystan leading one and I the other. There would be only one simple change in the maneuver.

As my half hundred gathered about me, Owain and Milius among them, I knew the Franks were already on the move. Arthur often wondered and scoffed at this in me, but the mouse, up and dancing now, never lied.

"Ring me about and listen sharp. You all know the Scythe, done it until you and the horses dropped. Lord Trystan will attack from this slope. We're going out a bit, but there's a problem."

"Another one?" Owain inquired sourly. "We're to wait for dear Eurion again?"

Hard laughter splintered among the men until I shut them up. "I mean it now; there's little time. The Franks are in the saddle this moment or I don't know my calling."

"Not a hint of them yet, sir," Milius doubted.

"Trust me. Hark now, all of you. Our position is on the far side of the road—there, what's left of a ditch. Too shallow to stand without being seen from the road, so you and the horse must lie flat. Watch."

I took my gelding by the bridle, pulling his head around far back to the right. When he couldn't turn any farther, I gave him a shove with my shoulder. The obedient horse buckled his legs and went over. To manage this the horse must trust his rider, and every one of ours had been ridden, fed, curried, bedded down, and cared for by the same man since the beginning. Each mount knew the seat, rein, smell, and good intentions of his rider; there'd be little difficulty.

"Watch now." Crouched over the downed horse, lance in my right hand, I straddled him—"Up"—and let him scramble upright with me already astride. "That's the manner of it. Once in position out there, each man will try it that the wise horse will know what to expect and that you've not gone mad entire."

Milius cocked an ear northward as the wind brought us, ghostly faint, the sound of church bells from the village far across the valley.

"Nones already," one man grumbled, "and I'm starving."

"Listen to you," Milius jeered. "As if you didn't stuff yourself this morning."

"Eight hours ago that was."

"Think on the good of it." Milius shrugged. "Do you not avoid the sin of gluttony?"

"Combrogi!" I barked at them. "Column of threes after me. Snap *to* now."

Waiting.

Fifty men crowded into a narrow, shallow depression with their horses, reins wrapped about one fist, bits of bread or cheese hoarded from the morning in the other.

Well before vespers the short December day would begin to fade. What if I'd misjudged and the Franks lingered another night? If I was right, they'd want to raise Vannes before nightfall. From his height beyond the road, Trystan would see them far away and alert me. What's happening? Why don't you send some word? They must be close now.

Waiting.

Milius went to relieve himself beyond our hiding place. He returned shortly, hiking up his breeches. "Foot runner coming."

A moment later the messenger bounded down into the depression, cast about for me, then panted down the line to my place at the center. One of the young Morlaix men he was, with more than a drop of Roman blood by the olive look of him. "Lord Trystan's sighted the Franks. Three, four miles yet, column order."

"Coming how? Fast? Slow?"

"At a walk, sir. He cannot be sure yet, but he thinks there's packhorses as well."

Carrying "tribute" from the village. Good; that would be one more problem for them when we attacked. When I wet my mouth from a waterskin, the messenger eyed it greedily, licking dry lips.

"Here, drink."

"Ah, thanks. I'm dry as sand and not used to running afoot, but Lord Trystan wouldn't take a chance on a horse being sighted."

Not used to battle either, by the edgy manner of him now. "Glad to be here, lad?"

He drank thirstily and wiped his mouth. "I think so."

"Think as well on the tales you will carry home to Morlaix, and pity poor Lord Gwenallt when he grieves he did not come."

We had to place the handful from Morlaix carefully. Not trained in our maneuvers nor so tightly disciplined, they would form a second line for Trystan's element in the attack. "Good luck this day, *Mulus*."

There I was being friendly, and bless me if the lad didn't stiffen with offense. "*Mulus?* I am no common soldier," he would have me know. "My father was a lord among the Trinovantes, and I after him."

That's a difference today? I shook his hand warmly. "Do you say so? My father was a horse handler, and I after him. Tell Lord Trystan we're ready."

As he jogged away I rose and called the order along our line. "Ground your horses. They're coming."

Waiting again. Fifty men lying flat beside their horses, shield tight-buckled to the left arm, bridle in one fist, lance in the other. Time dragged or raced by, no measuring now. *They must be close. Have a look yourself.*

Soft nickering of Milius's horse, scrape of Owain's mail and scabbard as he shifted his cramped position. I soothed my own horse, whispering close to his ear. "Easy now, enjoy your lie-down. Quiet now, quiet as a thought. We'll go soon enough."

I bellied up the side of the depression, parting the yellow grass to see. Mary and Joseph! The Franks had broken into a trot, riders in the van nearing the point to place them squarely between me and Trystan. I squirmed back down, still seeing them in mind, judging their speed.

"Ready. Straddle."

A wave of muffled preparation rippled out from me along the defile as men crouched across their saddles. Milius shifted uncomfortably. "Here I just went and damned if I don't have to again."

In all my years of it, this moment never changed. "You

too? It's only your hot blood wanting a taste of theirs. And why should I suffer alone? *Mount!*"

"Up . . . up . . . up." The command whispered along the defile. I felt the power of my gelding as he gathered under me and surged up out of the ditch with the tide of us. I dipped my lance forward. "Hold your line! Charge!"

I wonder even now: What must the Franks have thought to see a deadly wall of horsemen spout from the dry ground like a miracle spring? Lances couched and coming at them like arrows, two hundred paces, one hundred. Confusion among them as they struggled frantically to cut loose packhorses and free lances from girth straps.

Seventy-five yards. They'd managed something of a line to meet us, the heavy horses rumbling forward when, with a great shout of challenge, Trystan's men poured out of the concealing woods and down the slope, taking bare seconds to straighten their line before the lances dipped and shot forward.

The Franks hesitated, and that was fatal, not knowing which line to face. In those dooming moments their lot was sealed. As they ranged into a ragged, wavering rank, some to us, others against Trystan, my line veered half left sharply after me. A breath later Trystan's did the same. We battered into them in two slashing slant attacks that sent many of them sprawling to the ground. No time to see now. We reined short, wheeled, and went for them again. My lance went home over one rider's shield as we battered through, trampling fallen men. My line held. Beautiful to see them rein and wheel like a single engine, then I was dashing forward with them once more, picking my target, seeing him set himself behind his shield.

The Frank was not new to this. His seat was firm. My

lance splintered against the shield, wrenched useless from my hand, and I saw him claw for the ax at his side before he and the horse went down before Owain's lance.

Again and again we hit them. No time to make out faces or friends. Many men were down, some of the Franks making a stand on foot as we sliced back and forth through them. Those enemy still mounted tried to close with us, screaming men swinging axes and swords, but we never let them stay us. Slash and run, slash and run, swift wolves tearing aslant at clumsy cattle, as Arthur would peel and tear at Cerdic's infantry in the year of Mount Badon when he broke the Saxon power for a generation to come.

Then of a sudden as I wheeled again with my line—not so many of us now—*Jesus, who's down?*—I saw Trystan, lance gone, whirling his sword high as he cried for one more charge, then battering through the slower enemy, his Morlaix men behind leaning from the saddle to hew at men on foot. I spurred forward and, as Trystan shot past me, saw the blood spread dark over the rent in his mail.

"Tryst, get away! Get out of it!"

But the mad joy glowed hot in his eyes even as the blood spattered his lips. He screamed high and terrible as the good horse went down on his haunches, wheeling obedient to Trystan's rein, and his line dashed forward yet again. The last I saw of him, Tryst was crouched forward in the saddle, sword whirling high in the light. I could only rally my own men and hurl us in once more while, overhead, the black ravens already circled, dirtying the Christmas sky.

We took no prisoners. As at the Leon they burned, we left none alive. Riderless horses stood or limped about, snorting at the smell of blood while the ravens settled on our fringes. We'd lost ten or fifteen men. Some I knew by name, others by faces, but all known. Later we tied them on any horses to hand for burial in Vannes, but still I couldn't find Trystan. Dunawd knelt by one of the Morlaix lads, wrapping linen torn from a dead Frank's tunic about a deep wound in his leg. Pale and drained with shock, the lad nodded to me, and he the one who'd jauntily brought his harp to play and sing of glory.

"Well now." I squatted beside him. "Come through with no more than a tickle, and what grand song will you sing of this day?"

He shook his head queasily. "I left the silly thing in the fort. I don't feel like singing anyway."

"Dunawd, where's Lord Trystan?"

He went on wrapping the bandage. "Over by the road, sir. Owain's with him. He's down."

"Is there any beside you can do for a surgeon?"

"He's past that, sir." Dunawd tied off the boy's bandage. "If my lord was of the Faith, he'd be needing a priest."

I saw him. Dying as he was, the man was fulfilled. He did something right and knew it then. I should go to him, and so I would in a little, but now I could only sit like a burned-out lump of coal and stare at nothing. Milius came up to tell me that the packhorses had been unloaded and picketed. "We thought you'd want that, sir, for surely we won't be riding tonight. Sir? Sir? Lord Gareth, are you hurt?"

I heard him from far away, and it was an effort to lift my head. "I am not. Pass the word to build fires. We rest here and move in the morning."

The mouse that had preserved me so long and never wrong, had learned sadder lessons as well, like the pallor of a fallen man who'd ridden his last. Owain had covered Trystan with a blanket and set a saddle under his head, now standing over him, leaning on his sword. He'd stripped off Trystan's helmet and mail coif. The matted curls, black as midnight when young, showed wisps of grey now. I ruffled them lightly.

"Going white. Vain as you are, you'll be dyeing your locks."

He managed a weak smile, showing teeth red-dulled with blood. "Dying indeed. You might have chosen a gentler term. Fetch me water, Owain—not in haste, mind. Lord Gareth and I must talk."

When we were alone, he asked: "The Franks?"

"Gone to Jesus, every one."

"The men—" Trystan coughed wetly, flecking his lips with fresh blood. I had to look away. "The men did well, didn't they? All of Lesser Britain will remember the men of Leon. No, don't." He stayed my hand when I tried to lift the blanket from his wound. "Nothing you haven't seen before. Depressing."

"You did what you vowed."

"And you without a scratch. Your god must love you."

"He ought for all the prayer I've thrown at Him this day."

Trystan's hand closed over mine. Cold it was. "Mark me. I'm not done. One thing more is owed me. I will not die here. I *will* myself not to die here. You must send me by boat to Leon."

His warmthless grip tightened in his urgency. "Until then I will not die. Do you understand?"

I thought I did. Trying to ride he would be dead in half a day. "Anything with a sail on it," I promised.

"Find a strong, swift craft. Bind the master by my orders. I will see Leon again, Gareth."

"You will that."

I believed because my poor friend believed. Between us and his boat lay Vannes and Eurion, but as Owain returned with the water, I just did not think that conquering prince would give us any grief. Like their horses, my men had the smell of blood in their nostrils and the taste in their mouths. Eurion had best step aside.

Trystan was racked with coughing again. I pulled the blanket closer about his throat as Christmas faded toward night and the wind whined cold about us.

In the morning we made litters of lances and blankets secured between two horses for Trystan and several others too hurt to ride. Before we moved I told the men of Eurion and Vannes—men who'd scoured the fort of Franks like scum from a pot and not stolen so much as a kiss from a girl before riding to finish the task here. They took the news in silence, but I could read their tight-lipped disgust and sense of betrayal and perhaps a shame like mine. We came for a good cause, we did our best, but like a blundering surgeon, killed the invalid along with his affliction.

However bad we felt, a few angels still looked over us. When we rode into Vannes, good Collen ran out the north gate to meet us. No glory seeker, he'd told his volunteers to hide when he saw nothing could be done against the ravages of Cornouaille. Sad to say, Eurion, waiting in Vannes's best house for us to report to *him,* if you please, felt cheated because the Franks had left little to take worth a prince's trouble. He was further insulted, his haughty messenger gave me to know, that no one had reported to him at all, and demanded half the tribute we brought back. We dared him to come for it and got on with burying our dead in Pig Lane churchyard. Seeing the dangerous look of us, Eurion did not press his point. Better trained, bitter sharp from killing a hundred men in a few savage minutes, a few more would not trouble us overmuch.

Most of the tribute taken from the Veneti village was in food and fodder, but some silver had been exacted. From this I bought the service of a sturdy coasting craft and its crew to carry Trystan and myself home. Making sure the boat was well fitted, I gave Collen charge of the *Combrogi* for their return overland. Poor Collen had lived for months in rags a scullion wouldn't use for dish clouts, and begged for new clothes before leaving.

"See Owain or Milius," I advised him. "There's ample of everything from the men we buried."

And so I embarked with Trystan. Through the long days our boat crawled westward past the ragged coast of Armorica, the crew rowing when the winds blew against us. The sea and I never natural friends, I nevertheless managed to keep my stomach civil as I tended Trystan under our leather tilt astern. He didn't bring up as much blood now, though he had the pallor of parchment. Fevered, he clutched my hand and whispered to me his last dream.

"Give me some more water. Mark, Gareth. She will come. She must."

"Ah, what are you on about? Will she not be waiting as she was the day I came, at the top of the sea stairs?"

But I misread his meaning. "No . . . no, listen. The boatmaster will sail on to Castle Dore and bring Yseult back. She will not fail me."

I thought the fever had him talking wild. I could say nothing, only cool his forehead and give him water when he thirsted and wonder if, after all these years, Yseult would leave her royal husband and chance a winter voyage for a ghost-lover no more than a memory now. And did he forget the choice she made years gone when she sent him away? No, he saw her with his eyes at twenty and never the marks time would leave on her as on himself. Trystan had the surety of a dream enduring as my own curse.

"If the boat returns with her, the master will show a white sail off Little Hump; if not, the sail will be black. But she will come, Gareth."

Would she, then? Even if she did, what of Isolt? What could so poison and blind the man that he forgot the thrice-loving woman frightened but brave as himself on the walls of Leon; who spent so much of herself in tending his wound that she dropped dead asleep over him? God, I felt sick with rage as himself with fever and death coming on, and I let my heart burn with it. *Die now, will you? Be generous once and leave them both be. Your friend I was and am, but I'm tired, worn out with you and cold with the shadow of you ever over me. As if you were all and the world turned only on your silly, selfish song of a life. Die, Tryst, and let us live, godless as I am with the wish.*

A foreign tongue his madness was to me, but I knew the depth of Isolt's love, as mine had matched it. The eyes that spoke out of a warm and knowing soul, the whole grace of her that wrote *woman* for the first time on my ignorant heart and taught its meaning.

I couldn't speak of this or share my own wound even as I washed the blood from Trystan's cracked lips. You cannot pull a barbed arrow from a man's guts without bringing half the man with the iron. So would it be tearing myself free of Isolt. Under the leather tilt that flapped dully overhead in the wind, I lay down by dying Trystan and, behind closed eyes, Isolt hurried from the sea gate to welcome me as I'd first seen her, arms open and a smile I had waited and sought and craved all my days, by Sidhe curse or my own need. But then Trystan's own blood poured over her lips—

I bolted up out of half sleep, thinking Trystan had called, needing me. "How is it with you?"

He blinked calmly up at me. "I'm well, Gareth. Go to sleep. I'll be here when you wake, and we will be home soon."

So certain he would not die, could not, waiting for her.

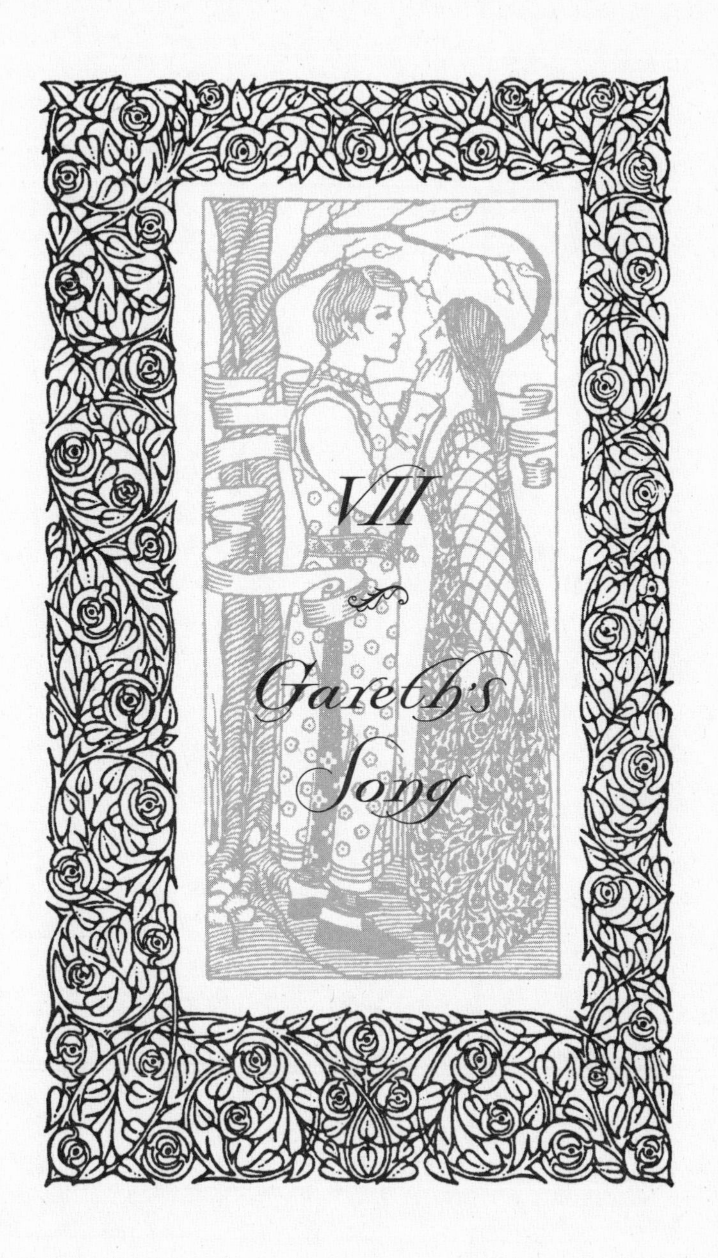

VII

Gareth's Song

n second January we rounded Great Isle in a choppy, whitecapped sea, gulls screeching and diving for scraps sailors tossed to them, and there on the headland loomed Castle Leon. I helped Trystan to the rail, where he yearned as long out to sea as at the square Roman walls.

"Not long," he whispered. "Soon."

We lay off Little Hump waiting for high tide, and the sailors hoisted our shields to the masthead that Isolt would know us. She was there before us, flying down the sea stairs, old Gwendolen bouncing in her wake, to stand searching the deck and finding only me. Isolt embraced me as I jumped ashore. "Gareth, thanks to God you're both home. And whole? No wound?"

"Ah, the great huge Franks thought me too little to bother with."

But with a gasp, she'd already thrust past me as two sailors lifted Trystan onto the quay. Kneeling by him, every line of her form wilted in love and pity. Trystan's lips moved; Isolt whispered in return, her hands, those marvelous picturing hands that carved her every mood, framing his thin, wasted cheeks.

Then her back straightened. "Bear him in."

Trystan was carried to his chamber, and I thought Death followed close after up the steps, that bad he looked. Isolt and Gwendolen made him comfortable in his own bed, and Father Antonius was summoned. Much as I wanted to be near the woman, I left them alone and stalked the parapet alone. The courtyard below was near deserted, all the villagers gone by now to the homes they'd raised again. I reckoned Collen and the company would be back no later than the next day. From the north wall I watched the sailors debark to rest the night before putting out again. That evening Trystan sent for me. There he lay, candles to either side as if already prepared for the keening over him. Death had followed him close since the battle, had sailed with us, and now as I sat beside my friend, the Leinsterman in me felt Death bending over my shoulder, reaching to take him, but Tryst would not allow that yet.

"The boatmaster," he breathed. "He must sail in the morning."

"So they purpose. How is it with you?"

"Tired," he breathed drowsily. "Father Antonius gave me something to help me sleep."

"A good old man he is."

"Yes, yes. He tempted me with the spiritual rewards of Faith that I might mend my life in time."

"You a Christian? You'd be years in confession alone."

"No fear. I found them wholly resistable. The boatmaster has my orders. With the wind or without it, he must sail in the morning."

I had to ask. "And your own wife? Have you told her or did it slip your busy mind?"

Trystan's fingers fidgeted over the covers. "No."

"Jesus, why not?"

"I couldn't. My courage doesn't reach so far."

"She's got to know. You can't just—"

"You love her, don't you?"

The question brought me up on a short rein. Trystan had not spoken of that since the night I wounded him, and now it was myself who could not look at the man. "Did I not say I was leaving soon?"

"You are an innocent, Gareth, not used to women or love at large. Save once, I've fallen in love at morning and out by noon. Go home to Rhian where things are simple."

I was desperate to be away from him then, away from her, wanting to run anywhere, leap clear out of my tangled life if I could. "What will Isolt feel if the queen does come? Damned if I don't feel like bashing you once more, sick as you are."

"Please, not again." Tryst winced with some of his old spirit. "You've been doing that since we met."

"You—" But my heart was too loaded full to speak of the miserable knot inside me. That night on the sea stairs, Isolt begged me to help her, but how could I, loving her and knowing for years the sickness in him with pity and anger and terrible understanding of what I was never made to bear, let alone heal. And now he'd tear open the same wound again. "You miserable bastard, you're wise not to take up the Mass. Heaven wouldn't have you."

"An innocent," he sighed again. Trystan turned his head on the pillow and closed his eyes. "I can sleep now. Tell the boatmaster he must sail in the morning."

Next morning watching from the north parapet as the boat dwindled, standing out for Britain, I knew I must tell

Isolt. The truth, mad as the man himself, would hurt less coming from me.

The priest came early to attend Trystan, and in the middle of the morning the returning *Combrogi* appeared on the coast road to the west, Collen riding at their head. Standing at the top of the courtyard steps, I heard Isolt's familiar light step behind me.

"God bless, lady."

"And you, dear Gareth." She slipped her arm lightly through mine. "There's been so much to do, mortaring medicines for Father Antonius, I've had little time to give you proper welcome."

"Did he rest well?"

"Well enough, I suppose. There doesn't seem—" Isolt broke off, peering away at the approaching column. Folk were running out from the village now, shouting and cheering to greet them and troop alongside. Clear enough to me Isolt wouldn't speak of what was surely coming for her husband. "Let me welcome the good men home with you."

"They'll be honored."

"The folk celebrated the new year properly on the thirty-first," she told me with a forced lightness, "but many of them in the old way, dressing in hides and horns, carrying torches and banging pots and pans to drive the old year out. Father Antonius was *livid.* He wonders how deep Christ really goes in them. Did you have such a custom in Eire?"

"They keep Samhain," I said. "The old calendar. Christ or no, the spirits are out that night and in no good mood. After sunset doors are barred and no one raises any noise to attract them."

"Very sensible." Within the folds of her cloak hood, Isolt's dark eyes squeezed shut. "He's dying, Gareth."

"I know."

Her arm tightened in mine. "The priest marvels that he still lives with such a wound. Can I tell you something? No, let me speak of it now. After all this time, after . . . everything, the sweetness and the madness in him. Since that night on the sea stairs, I have known your heart, Gareth. You must have wondered why I stay with him and love him beyond any vows. That horrible night when he struck me to the floor, and again when he tried to kill you."

"Wondered, girl? All that and more." And that night when my knife sank home, the wanting her and wanting him dead were one and the same passion. "If ever there was an angel so stained with hell."

"It was the angel I knew first," Isolt murmured tenderly. "Coming up the sea stairs, the wind blowing wild through his hair and the sun darting through it like light in dark waters. Men had asked for me before, but I didn't want them or Hoel thought them unworthy. But sitting in the hall night after night, listening to Trystan play the harp and tell of his travels, my father must have seen how I yearned toward him in everything I did or said, coaxing more time out of him, just a moment more before Father sent me to bed. Hoel must have known how we were drawn to each other and thought: Here is a prince, banished and landless, but a prince and a bard in one, and my child wants him."

The man was not drawn to anything but looking back as the fool's done all his life.

In the courtyard below, the porter trotted out of the stable to open the gates for Collen.

"Any man can love," Isolt said, "but not all can make a woman *feel* loved as Trystan did for me. That must be easy for such terribly needy men. I believed him. I lived in him.

While he could sing the song, the poet believed it too. When he cursed or struck me, he was only tearing at his own wounds. Now his poor hand can draw no more magic from the harp. And," she added with that cool practicality that still amazes me in all women at times, "his old dream grows older still in Cornwall, where I fervently pray the silly cow has grown fat."

"You should have seen him against the Franks. He was magnificent. In the whirl of battle, and a terrible wound already on him, he was the old Tryst to rival the sun for shining."

"Oh, yes!" Isolt's head snapped up angrily. "There's always that easy magnificence for men. But now his world narrows to a chamber and a last bed and no more sun than lights his casement. Narrows to me, Gareth. I have him at last because he is mine."

She'd a grand way with words, but the sound of her went through me cold as the sea wind at my back. The word *mine* struck my ear like iron on iron. She had him—dying but hers—and when I turned to Isolt I saw the naked truth of that possession. I should have guessed the mettle bred into this daughter of a Belgae chieftain. She might writhe but would not break beneath his last betrayal.

"There's that you should know." I kept my sight fixed on the approaching company. "The boat that brought us is bound for Castle Dore. He's sent for her."

Isolt's arm stiffened against mine. She pulled away and one hand came up clenched in a fist, then fell. "Not even his son to hold."

I took her by the shoulders, wanting to soften hurt any way I could. "You know Tryst. He's always cried for midnight at noon, then mourned the sunset. He's never happy with having, just the wanting. *Och,* girl, it's been years. She'll not come. The sail will be black."

"Black?"

That was the man for you, even in signals a poet to the end. "If the boat bears the queen, the sail will be white. If not, black."

But now with Collen riding before, the small spare frame of him lost in a cloak far too large, the company entered in good order through the south gate to draw up in four ranks facing us. As Collen flung us the sharp *alae* salute, Isolt raised her arm in graceful welcome. Guenevere she reminded me of then, and if by mad chance another queen did sail from Cornwall, she would find no less than a queen waiting.

Her welcoming arm still raised high to the men, Isolt said, "You need not fear however it falls. He has always been mine."

Early each day Father Antonius came with his medicines to keep at bay the mortification in Trystan's wound and lungs, also the scapular, wafers and wine in the event medicine could do no more and Trystan repented false gods. Day after day Trystan held on, waiting, as the priest laid fresh valerian poultice on his chest and administered bee balm tea. Each night Isolt brought him willowbark to fight the fever, chamomile to help him sleep. She herself slept on a pallet beside the bed, not to disturb what rest he could find. When he and I were alone, Trystan would have me search seaward from the casement.

"What do you see in the harbor?"

"Only fishermen."

"You've told Isolt?"

"I had to."

"That's well," he sighed. "She hasn't spoken of it."

"What need?" And I left, glad to be gone from the chamber that reeked of his sickness and selfishness. Nor did Isolt speak to me again of who might or might not come. As the days passed, Antonius marveled at Trystan's resistance both to death and his own spiritual urging. "It is God keeping him alive, not me."

Perhaps, but more surely the vision of a white sail.

For Isolt, her vigil over him went silent with resignation. Drawn inside herself she was, moving through days and duties as if something within her had resolved itself. I was glad to busy myself with the company, inspecting the men and mounts, seeing to what saddles wanted mending, hooves reshod or equipment replaced. Each night I begged God to take Trystan mercifully in his sleep. Each sunrise, though the cheeks Isolt shaved with such care were sunken, his eyes gleamed brighter with stubborn hope.

The priest spent so much time at the castle now that he'd taken to saying early Mass in the hall. On such a day after the sexton had cleared the long table of the altar cloth, I caught sight of Collen ahead of me, and, by God, the man actually danced down the courtyard steps in pure high spirits.

"God bless, Collen!"

He spun about, arms thrown out, grinning wide as the world. "And you, sir! It is a fine morning."

"Bitter cold and no sun? Where's the fine in that?"

"Would you believe it, my lord? I'm just glad to be alive."

"No dispute. And how goes it with Eilwen?"

"Oh now." A slow smile of utter contentment. "You

were wise, my lord. Ran to me along the road, weeping a river for my forgiveness. You'd think I'd been dead and resurrected. The woman's not hung on me so since the wedding. If there's not another babe come autumn, it will not be for want of trying."

Collen watched the men strolling to and from the rath, preparing for the day's work and drill. "About Daron, sir."

"Daron?"

"The Trinovante boy so fired to be a harper."

So that was his name. I'd seen him about since our return, especially at Mass, where he always prayed on his knees, outholying Father Antonius, but I'd been too busy to take more note than that.

"He wants to join us, my lord," Collen stated. "He'd a good horse and mail, so I gave him leave to come with us but that you and Lord Trystan had the deciding."

I heard Daron out in the rath, warming myself at the firepit while Collen was off drilling the company. A tall lad he was, just twenty as he owned, and of unusual coloring, a great mop of blond hair over dark, liquid brown eyes and a mouth most men would deem too soft and sensitive. Something, perhaps the strong nose, betrayed the Roman strain that had mixed with the Trinovantes since the time of Boudicca. Oh, but what a difference since he roared into Leon with the Morlaix volunteers. No swagger at all now and favoring his wounded leg a mite. His manner struck me as somewhere between hurt and bewilderment, as if he'd reached to stroke a dog's warm fur and touched the cold scales of a snake. When I offered him wine and we passed a word, the lad's plight became clearer. His world had turned upside down; two and two that should sum to four came to no more than three at Vannes.

"I was ashamed that Gwenallt would not come and do honor to our tribe. I went to find glory, but Vannes was . . ."

"Something less."

Daron looked down at his boots. They were finely made but old and hard worn. "I need to find what I've lost."

"Lost?"

The young man's head came up, beseeching. "Honor, sir."

And thought to find it here with men like Trystan and me, carrying our own sins like a hod of rocks? No, I didn't smile. You can't laugh at a boy still that pure and secretly shaming you a little. But Daron had deeper reasons and, with his third cup, poured them out for me.

"My father was Lord Rhystad. When he came from Britain we had little left but our pride, but all my life I heard how Arthur's *Combrogi* restored so much of it in the west. Men like Lancelot and Trystan and yourself. I learned the songs of you as I learned my harp. Such deeds, and you *did* them."

Devil if I know why, I suddenly felt very tired and more than a little old. "We did."

Clear to me that Daron's heart was Celt entire: Courage, poetry, and music were all of a piece to him, none separable from the rest. "That is why I brought the harp. Vannes was my first venturing, but how can I sing of that when I feel unclean?"

"It wasn't us, Daron, but we weren't there. We couldn't stop it."

That was no comfort to him. "Those people, the Veneti. No matter what we did for them, they stained us with the same curse. They spat at us when we rode out, and all I could do to hold my head up. Was it ever so with your high king?"

Arthur? How could he grasp the whole of Arthur, caught as the man was all his life between two wives and worlds? Or Lancelot who married Eleyne because he loved Guenevere and couldn't live with that, and so made a torment of honor and a bitter madwoman out of Eleyne in the end? Or Gawain's brother Agravaine, carved out of spite and spleen, a rabid cur who would die a dishonored rebel. That day I tried to answer Daron in the tongue of his ideals.

"First there was Britain's need, then honor in filling it. When you follow a king so well made by God that he understands—he *is* all men in one—you can't help feeling blessed."

Well intended but flowery. My own flaws bellowed for modesty. "Most of the time, that is. Others we could only offer up our good intentions from the muck heap and try to forget."

I couldn't hope Daron would grasp that whole, but he was a young one yet. Perhaps, like Peredur who was sickly all his life after the battle of Eburacum but lived to find the Grail at last, Daron would stay pure to the end.

"Come, we'll see if Lord Trystan will speak to you."

While Daron hovered outside in the solar, I drew back the curtain to Trystan's chamber to find him weaving on his feet at the seaward casement in his nightshirt with a knife wind blowing over him. "What in hell? Back to bed with you now. What are you doing there?"

"As the faithful say, my belief is my strength." He chuckled weakly as I half carried him back to bed and covered him. "But I spent it all getting there. She must come."

I secured the hide flap again and poked up the brazier

of coals by his bed, adding more from the scuttle and a vigorous puffing with the bellows. "There. And there you stay. If you're so bent on living, no need to help death along."

"You're an old woman. Complain, complain. How does the company?"

"Better than you, but there's a matter or two we need speak of. You'll be needing a good tesser since I'm leaving. Someone the men respect."

Trystan let his gaze drift again to the closed casement. We both knew I meant no second in command but a leader to fill the place he never could again.

"Collen," I volunteered. "The man's seasoned and tried. He's older, he has courage and the rare common sense to know when to show it and when not. No better in the company."

He assented with a listless nod. "As you think best."

"Well then, he and Milius deserve a ladder, being the first into the midst of the Franks and under their noses for weeks. Brave lads."

"A ladder?" Trystan smiled ruefully. "I haven't seen a legion decoration since Arthur and Bedwyr received the gold laurel from Ambrosius. Not much left of Rome itself," he reflected. "We must find some other way to honor them."

I told him Daron was asking his permission to join us. "One of the young Morlaix lords. He's waiting outside."

"I remember him. The harper."

"No longer, so it seems. He left the poor thing in Vannes. He's like to Peredur in the old days at Eburacum. Very serious, very dedicated, and sore distressed to find lords and battles can be less than noble. Black Eurion dirtied his principles."

Trystan agreed sadly. "A mortal case of ideals. A common ailment of youth and harder on a man than drink. Prop me up, Gareth, and give me my harp there."

I plumped the pillows behind him and tucked the harp in his left arm. "Is it in your mind to play the boy back to belief?"

"Like unicorns and dragons, bards are too rare to waste. Bring him in."

Daron slipped shyly through the curtains, approaching as if he were in the presence of the Grail. Trystan greeted him with a courtly wave of his hand. "Greetings, my lord. I remember you at Vannes. How does your leg?"

The boy was embarrassed to have so minor a thing mentioned. "It is nothing, my lord. I am honored you receive me."

"I have not done so yet," Trystan reminded him coolly. "Why do you wish to join us?"

"Why?" The young man flustered with pure adoration. Why would one wish to live? "Who does not know of Trystan? You are the best of us, one of the last warrior bards left to Britons. Were you not harper to Queen Guenevere herself?"

"In softer days. But why did you abandon your own harp?"

Daron hadn't lived long enough to find clear words for such feeling. "It is hard, but—"

"A true bard would renounce his gods first. Fortunately we've one on hand. Here." Trystan held out the harp easily as offering a bowl of nuts. "Take mine."

Pure amazement: "Oh no, I could not."

"Stop writhing with humility and take it. Please. You see, I no longer play." As he studied the boy closely, I saw the gleam of purpose in Trystan. "Just hold it, then, for I'm mightily tired."

Daron reluctantly accepted the instrument. His left arm curved naturally about its triangle, fingers straying over the brass strings.

"Your nails are far too short," Trystan remarked. "They must grow long and strong to do what you demand of them. And you will demand, I am certain."

Only hangdog silence.

"What *is* it, Daron? You look so pained. I can't tell if it's something on your soul or severe indigestion."

"You know what happened at Vannes."

"Too well. Your sentiments are not unique."

"Do you think I can sing what I feel now?"

Trystan sat up straighter with an effort. "Indeed? What do you feel now? Anger? Disgust?"

The boy choked out the question. "Don't you?"

"So do all of us," Trystan caught him up. "Then sing what you feel."

"That? I *can't*," Daron agonized. "So ugly."

Tryst's voice was a harsh whisper as he pointed to the harp. "Then give ugliness a sound. Damn you, it's the truth, isn't it? Beat out your anger on these strings, let them snarl your disgust, and be not afraid of what comes forth. *Listen to me.*"

Daron stood transfixed by the sudden power of the command. He saw a dying man, little flecks of blood bright on his lips.

"Betrayal? Dishonor, disillusionment? Before Vannes they were only words to you, but you will not waste them now. I will accept you into our company only with that harp on which you will practice as I did every day, you hear me?

Do not be impressed by resounding lays of heroism or the poetic lament of some lord languishing for lost love like a castrated bull. Any minstrel cadging a meal and a night's lodging can do as much. Do you think art is all sweetness? Will you dine day in and out on honey alone?"

Trystan faltered and sagged back. "Gareth, hold me up."

"No, you must lie down."

"Hold me up!" Sudden coughing racked him. After a moment his eyes opened again and fixed the stunned boy with what he must somehow stamp into him.

"Promise me," he rasped. "Promise me now that you will try never to draw from these strings any sound less than truth. It will take courage; the world is more comfortable with lies and half-truths and pays better for them. But dare, man, *dare.* Look past the obvious and the battles into the hearts of those who listen to you, and don't be amazed to find, when you've howled and clawed out truth, a beauty of your own beyond. Men like us are blessed or cursed to *see,* Daron, and give truth a sound. Warriors serve kings, but even the greatest like Arthur are only a moment. When you dare truth, you serve the ages. Promise me."

Daron could only bow his head over the harp, awed and frightened as Moses receiving the tablets and the heavy Word, barely understanding what he bound himself to. "My lord, you have my oath."

"So I do." Trystan let me lay him back down. "Good then. Welcome, Lord Daron, to the *Combrogi* of Castle Leon."

Daron bowed his head in near holy respect. "Sir, if I may?"

"Be off now." I waved him to go. "He needs his rest."

Trystan opened his eyes. "What is it, Daron?"

"If I found any honor at Vannes, it was in following you in that charge."

Along with his deep faults, Tryst always had the charm of graciousness when most needed. "And I in finding such as you to lead. Work hard to become a fine *combrogus.*"

"Thanks, my lord. And I pray daily that you will recover to lead us again."

"Oh. This." Trystan brushed a hand over his bandages. "There is a bright side to all misfortune, Daron. This is certain to cure me of my vices. Go now."

After the boy backed out, bowing still, Trystan was so quiet I thought exhausted sleep had claimed him for all the strength he'd spent, but as I started to leave myself—

"Gareth?"

"Aye, what? You fair killed yourself putting the bard back into him."

"Some things are worth the dying. Look from the casement once more?"

"You're just after looking yourself."

"Please."

Dutifully I pushed the flap up again. A few curraghs bobbed between us and Little Hump, but the horizon stretched away unbroken. "Nothing."

"Then I'll sleep awhile." As I reached to pull the curtain aside, he spoke again. "How long it's been."

"Will you for Christ's sake give yourself some rest?"

"How long it's been since someone looked at me and saw honor. I'd almost forgotten the word."

Impossible man, impossible in this world as the dragons and unicorns he joked about, but in his words to Daron, I'd never heard in twenty years, played, spoken, or sung, any sound out of him so deeply and passionately meant.

"There are times, Tryst. There are times. Good rest to you."

Worth the dying? I hope so, for he gave his last strength to Daron. Next day the weather cleared and brilliant sunshine washed over Leon and the sea while Trystan sank fast. Our priest said all his Masses in the hall now, hoping to the last that Trystan accept the Church while time remained, and Isolt left her husband's side only when she must to snatch a hasty meal which I doubt she tasted before hastening back to hover over him. Old Gwendolen bore as much burden as her mistress, plodding from the bedside to the kitchen, the hall, or wherever she was sent, and from her I heard hourly of the approaching end.

"He won't live out the night," she predicted, hoarse with strain and weariness. "Father Antonius is sure of that and fears my lord's teetering on the brink of hell. He does not say as much but urges and offers salvation like good food a sick child will not swallow."

The good old man might save his breath. Trystan always suspected deathbed religion as false or at best a want of conviction. I knew Tryst would face his coming night with the same reckless courage that led his last charge, and be judged, I prayed, by a merciful God who read the soul and not the name.

Before puffing up the stairs to the keep again, Gwendolen added, "My lady would have the men come to say their farewells."

"I will see it done."

I let Collen pass the word I hated to give, and soon the long line of men began to trudge up the stairs. I held off myself; though I'd prayed for his painless death, I shrank from the reality. We Irish are not a logical race. In the matter of life and death, our old ways are barely covered by the new. When death claims a friend or a love, there's a black and bewildered anger toward the thieving thing that steals our own and gives no reason, no answer. So we drink and weep, drink more and break each others' heads, and then make love, and what is more loving of life than that? For my friend and the large piece of my life gone with him, I would weep and drink alone.

The sun dipped lower over the sea, the tide going out, as I paced the north parapet alone.

"Gareth?"

Isolt turned the corner of the walk and came toward me—slowly, for the woman was weary. She wore a man's large cloak double-wrapped across her chest and thrown over the left shoulder against the sharp sea wind. She leaned over the wall beside me and dropped her dark head on her arms.

I asked, "Is he gone, then?"

"No. The men come one by one to kneel by him. He was good to them and they love him, but all of them over and over—I had to get out just for a little."

Isolt fell silent as I stared out to sea, not knowing what I or anyone could say to her now. Then she raised up. "Yes, it will be today. Soon."

More silence between us.

"Collen tells me he is to be made an officer."

"Yes." I was glad to speak of anything but what must come. "Trystan approved it."

"His father was no more than a fisherman."

"Saxons would not cavil that, Arthur did not, nor should you, girl. The old ways are going. To make Collen a lord is no more of a raising up than Arthur did for me or Bedwyr. Perhaps I can remember some of the ceremony, but it must be formal for the men to see."

"If I asked, Gareth . . ."

"What?"

"Would you stay?"

Had I not stayed too long already for her, for him, for the men and God alone knew what else, and part of me would linger yet only to be near her. "I sent Arthur a black lie in order to remain, but how long does a broken leg need to mend? You know I can't."

She moved closer, slipping her arm through mine while we looked out to sea. "Trust Collen," I urged. "Trust them all. They're fine men and the best in Lesser Britain. God have mercy on Eurion if he tries against them."

"You made them so. Oh dear." Isolt laughed suddenly. "How I remember the day you roared 'Ladies!' at the shocked lot of them."

I narrowed my eyes on the horizon. Far out where the flat, unbroken line of sky met the darker sea a moment before, something else rose. Still too far, no more than a tiny bump, but . . . a sail? "Isolt, look there."

"Where?"

"There, do you see? Just breaking the horizon."

"I can see nothing."

But I could, clearer every moment. "A ship."

"Only fishermen."

"So far out this time of year? She's from Britain."

The sail grew larger, took on shape with the driving wind, finally color. "It is a white sail, Isolt."

Thanks, misgiving—my own feelings churned so that I barely caught the new note in her voice as the wind snatched and whirled it away. "They don't put in here in winter."

But the vessel bore steadily for the Saddle and Little Hump where no light burned, night coming and the tide going out. Already some of the higher rock islets were breaking surface in the shallow harbor.

Now Isolt could plainly see the white sail in the last orange glare of the setting sun. "So it is that she comes after all."

"I must get out to Little Hump with anyone who knows the channel, and light the beacon. It'll be dark that soon. Isolt, I don't know if it's her, but if it is—Jesus, he's got to know."

Her eyes on me were deep black pools where I could read nothing, only a closed door. Her lips moved; I could barely hear her for the singing wind. "Even now he does this."

"What can we do? He won't last the night. We cannot deny him. We will not."

For the good in the man, for the courage of him at Vannes, and most of all for what he gave young Daron at the end, this last mercy must be rendered, and I could give you no clearer reasons than that as I scanned the rocks and shore below for beached curraghs, anything able to float. Isolt had not moved.

"Girl, go tell him. Now."

I dashed along the parapet, bounding down the steps to the gates, down the sea stairs, shouting for men and a boat.

The sun touched the sea before I found a fair-sized fishing boat and the owners, two sturdy villagers mending their nets. We carried the craft out into the receding shallows, and I took a vigorous turn on the oar myself. No mistake;

the white-sailed craft with its leather tilt astern was the one we'd hired at Vannes. Pulling toward Little Hump I blessed its crew for their loyalty as well as the small figure standing in the stern. For the Isolt I could no more help loving than breathing, I prayed, *Bear this only a little longer, be strong, and merciful God help us all.*

Late sun faded to dusk. We rowed carefully around and through the treacherous rocks that lined the Hump. With time precious, I scrambled out of the boat and up over the boulders toward the fire basket kept ready with tinder, flint, and dry wood but lighted only when ships were expected and welcome. As the ship neared in the growing dark, I struck furiously at flint and steel, but the sparks flared only to die. Again and again I slashed one across the other until one tiny spark grew to flame in the tinder as I nursed it. The boatmaster had seen these shoals only once before and not at dangerous ebb tide. As the fire rose up I frantically waved them to heave to, breathing easier to see them collapse the sail and throw out the anchor.

I clambered down the rocks to the waiting curragh, and we rowed for the craft and Yseult waiting.

The fishermen rowed us steadily through the dark toward the lights of Castle Leon, Yseult between myself and Brannin, the Leinster woman who'd served her since she left Eire so many years before.

For Tryst's poor sake I was glad Yseult had come, nor dared I ask how or even if she'd justified it to Mark. No matter now; as we neared the quay I sensed all of us hurled toward an ending like a cataract none could hold back.

Out of the boat, hurrying up the sea stairs, a woman on each arm—"Open the gates"—into the hall, leading Yseult up the last steps, through the solar to thrust aside the curtain. "Tryst! See who has come."

For one sick moment I thought we might be too late. No one in the chamber moved, Antonius silent by the near side of the bed, Isolt to the far, Gwendolen in the corner, and over the still sight of them the candles dancing shadows on the wall.

Father Antonius threw one look of bewilderment at the queen, then to Isolt. "But we thought—we were told—"

I led Yseult to the bed, where she passed Isolt with a bare nod before kneeling by Trystan. He saw her. As his own dark came down, his eyes widened with a last joy, then clouded with a terrible understanding.

"Black." He labored for the words. "You told me a black sail. Gareth, she said . . ."

His head fell back on the pillow. Yseult bowed her head over the hand prisoned tenderly between hers, and with a prayer fervent as any since birth, I hoped I'd mistaken his meaning. No. When I looked to Isolt, the truth was there in her face. Love and possession barren as our victory at Vannes, but as complete.

He has always been mine.

Jesus, I might have known. Why didn't I come myself to tell him? How could Isolt do this? I loved the woman, wanted her, thought I knew her, but before I damned her, something of wisdom stilled the blame. How much pain had he dealt her? For all that, she took this much as her due. I'd loved Trystan when I hated him, often wished him dead, even in the mad moment, as hell measures time, when I tried to kill him. Rhian, Rhian, what innocents we were. It has a savage heart, this loving, and takes no prisoners.

". . . said black, Gareth."

"The fault is mine, Tryst. At the distance I mistook. Forgive me."

Try as I did to take the sin on myself, as ages past he'd done for me in a bit of bread and wine, Isolt it was who paid, for she must watch her husband draw another woman close even as he died.

"You have not changed, you could not. You are still lovely."

"My dear, it is only that it is night," Yseult murmured. "And the candles are kind to me."

More than kind: extravagant, leaving the man's dimming sight more than enough to remember and adore, but to mine the queen's bowed head betrayed a double chin, and the kirtle beneath her thrown-back cloak bulged with the flesh of her past thirty and coming too soon to middle age.

Suddenly the very candles seemed to burn brighter with the clear sound of Trystan's old, light laughter. "Well," he sighed, "haven't I made an unholy mess of it all?"

"Don't shame yourself," Yseult reproved gently. "You found riches. You married someone who loves you. Part of me you were, and we had what we had while we could."

"You sent me away."

"It was not easy. I had to be a queen that day."

"Forgive me?"

An odd thing then that's stayed in memory all these years. Trystan's gaze was fixed, but before Father Antonius bent to close the eyes, I couldn't tell, in the dim light, of which love he'd begged the grace.

Antonius took the dead hand from Yseult's and crossed the arms on the blanket. "He is gone. I did for him what healing could. I only grieve for what my faith could not."

Yseult kissed the stilled lips and rose, speaking for the

first time to Isolt. "Lady, if we cannot share warm friendship, let us at least understand each other and all we've done this day."

Isolt dropped in a deep curtsey. "Your Highness is wise and welcome. Gwendolen, prepare the chamber beyond the solar for the queen."

She was older now, Yseult, and as an older Arthur once reflected, some things did not matter so much anymore. Her smile for Isolt was wry but not unkind. "I might doubt the welcome but will not strain it. Thank you. The ship will bear me home tomorrow."

She touched Isolt's cheek lightly. "It is you who are beautiful. So young. And he and I were so long ago. These things pass, Isolt. They pass. Come, Brannin."

Isolt poured fresh water into a basin by the bed. "Father Antonius, you did all you could and more. Lord Gareth and I will prepare my husband. Go and pray for him."

We were alone with the body. Isolt brought fresh linen cloths, oils, and a strigil. "Help me off with his nightshirt."

"No. Wait." I faced her across the death of him. "Why?"

She hiked up the shirt over Trystan's slender legs. "Do you hate me for that?"

"Him dying there, was one truth so hard?"

"In a way harder than your gallant lie."

"But I never thought—I should have come myself."

"Gareth." Isolt stopped me, controlled but fierce. "You are a lovely man, but do not ask of me now. Mine he was and mine he died. Help me."

We slipped the shirt over Trystan's head, freed his arms, and I cut the bandage from the great, mortified wound in his chest. "There's nothing yet to do that can't be done without me after this. I'll be sailing with Queen Yseult."

She handed me a wet cloth. "You do blame me."

"No. I don't know. Only that I can't remain here."

"He needed you when you came. I need you now more than ever."

A lord for Leon or a husband for the woman of her? "You know why I cannot."

She caressed the cloth over the remains of her love. "I beg you, Gareth."

I plied my cloth over his legs and loins. Trystan had left the world with fewer scars than most *Combrogi;* pray Collen and the rest would be as fortunate. "You once said you knew my heart, woman. Know it now. If I stayed, if I threw the rest of my life into the sea for you alone—Rhian, Arthur, Britain, all I might be, and me standing before you naked as Trystan now—could you answer the love that's grown unbearable in me since first sight of you?"

Her hand paused; draft from the casement shuddered the candles' light over her face as she turned to me. "Oh, Gareth, I should have." She spread the oil over Trystan's skin. "Unbearable? Day by day you made it bearable for me. If ever I loved a man at first sight and with all my soul, it should have been you."

As it was with me and as the Sidhe woman foretold. How much did I cast away with the killing spear that pierced the life of her son?

"But it was him, and when he hurt me, my love went dark and cruel to hurt him back. I will remember you every day, and when I marry again—you heard her: This will pass, and you've given me the faith to believe that—when I have a child to ask me the meaning of *gentle* or *human,* I will answer 'Gareth.' "

She went on spreading the oil, but even as she spoke to

me, those capable hands loved his body for the last time. I leaned over my friend's face upturned at last in peace. Though he would not be buried in consecrated ground, Antonius would stretch his holy office to breaking for my friend. And why not, for mercy's sake? Good and half good men have died by the millions before Jesus came, some easily, more in pain and bewilderment, while monsters die rich in their beds with a smile on their lips. Wherever Trystan's soul rose or fell, to heaven or to hell, the one would hear better music for his hand on the harp, the other be gentler.

I bent to kiss his brow. "*Slan leat,* Tryst. And may the road be kind to you."

My strigil followed after Isolt's hands, and we were silent under the sea wind lost as myself and keening all we know or can know, a suspicion of God, the certainty of death, and the ruthless need for love.

To Arthur (and Rhian) I lied enough to need a thousand novenas and went on with my life that would never again walk wholly in the sun but ever in Isolt's shadow. What Arthur guessed or heard, he never spoke, nor did I as we armed and rode to Badon, Camlann, and the only future left us.

Old ways fade now. The Faerie are fewer and fewer in Britain, still feared but rarely seen in Eire. Rhian believes to the end and makes a warding sign with her wrinkled hands at mention of the Good People, but I know there is no good or evil magic strong as what thrives or festers in ourselves. And I will always ponder how much of the curse was Sidhe vengeance, how much my own wanting.

I followed the high king until his death and Guenevere after him for all that was left of Britain. After the queen was lost to us, I led the rest of our *Combrogi* for Arthur's nephew Emrys against Constantine of Cornwall, while Saxons moved ever westward and watched us tear ourselves apart. By then Rhian and I were old, ague stiffening my hands on the reins, and I knew I would not ride much longer.

For years I could feel no proper ending to my time in Leon, only something torn down the middle, but in the last year before Emrys and Constantine ravaged the poor remains of Britain between them, there came a kind of closing, a last verse to my secret song. At Cair Legis we heard of an Osismi bard come from Lesser Britain singing new tales of old heroes and ladies. Emrys quickly sent for the boyo to perform at his "palace," the remnant of Legis's old Roman forum, crack-floored and crumbling.

Rhian and I found him a disappointment, no true bard in the old sense, only a minstrel with small talent and tricks of the harp Trystan would have spurned out of hand. He was applauded for sure, young and brash as he was, with just enough wit to think he had more. I was yawning behind my hand until he announced his last song.

"This true tale was taught me by him who composed it," he vouched. "No other than Lord Daron he was, and no man put finer hand to harp since Trystan himself, of whose death this story tells, and here is the way of it."

Rhian asked me, "Did you know this Daron?"

"I did. He was only a boy then."

No yawning now. I sat up straight as a lance, exulting. Good *on* you, Daron, to make Tryst remembered so.

Our minstrel sang of a prince who married a princess of Armorica but was fated to love a queen. On suffering his death wound at the battle of Vannes, he sent for his true love across the sea and clung to life, never doubting she would come to him.

"Will you listen to the liar?" Rhian frowned. "Since when was Trystan's wife a princess?"

My own lip curled with the gilded falsehood. "She was not."

But the minstrel had only begun to profane. I listened with dismay as the tale plodded on to its tearful end. In the very moment that Yseult hurried to kneel by Trystan's bed, he embraced her and breathed his last, and she, her heart broken with mortal grief, expired beside him, whereupon the noble Princess Isolt, even she of the White Hands, had the two bodies borne to requiem Mass and buried close together. I remembered the "black" sail; Isolt was not that saintly forgiving.

Jesus, you'd think the minstrel's feeble gift had called down angels. The younger folk who remembered Trystan only through his songs, and Yseult not at all, shouted and cheered for him to sing it again—aye and again after that while men grew somber and silent, women wept, and I went sick with a different death.

Daron, Daron, why did you betray his gift and your own? If the man was part devil, it was the angel of him put the harp in your hand and took your promise to sing truth alone.

Corrupt as it was, the tale troubled me so that I sought out the fellow afterward as he guzzled and stuffed himself with Emrys's hospitality. Why, I asked him, why did he shame truth with such a sticky sweet lie?

"I was there, boyo. Queen Yseult left Trystan's deathbed in sadness but excellent health to live many years as a queen and later—as she does to this day—a nun at Avebury. Do you tell me Lord Daron composed it so?"

"No, my lord, he did not," the minstrel boasted through a mouthful. "To be plain, he could not; he had not the invention. In the way of poets, Daron was strange and most contrary. Often he tuned his strings to bring forth a peculiar and unpleasant sound close to discord. His ending to the tale pleased no one who heard it, sailing the queen ho-hum back to Cornwall. I ask you, my lord: Is that how one ends a tale to break the heart? They expected her to die with him. They truly believe now she did, wouldn't have it any other way, should not *be* any other way. Daron's ending was so flat."

"But he would not change it?"

"Not that Trinovante, not ever. Don't you think my version the more satisfying?"

"I do not, you wee giftless manny." I might have been angry with the young pup but for the redeeming thought of Daron. Tryst's own harp passed sacred into his hand, he kept the promise after all. "You ought to be trussed up in your harp strings and boiled in your own honey."

He gaped at me, injured to the soul. "Please, my lord. I mean *really*. My art is welcome everywhere, while Daron, had he not been a soldier in Leon's service, would have starved."

I should not have crushed him so. In time he might grow to real gift, but was yet all young vanity, defending his song by its popularity. "Did these lords and good ladies not demand I sing it thrice? Did you not hear them? They *adored* it."

So they did and so, I suppose, they always will. The shining, shallow lie against the deep, sad truth that no harper could draw from wit or strings, but even in darkness and agony Trystan tried and Daron after him. Did the boy find at last the honor he thought he'd lost or, with men like Collen and Milius, did he learn to spell it differently?

There's always that hope. I never heard from Isolt again, but Leon has never been taken. Of nights when the wind blows over the water, and the gulls *scree* over the beach at dawn, I lie half awake and remember a face too full of life to be beautiful, a heart too strong to be defeated, and both sing in me. Rhian stirs beside me, turns and nestles into my shoulder for warmth through the last of night, and if the bottom dropped out of my heart long since, she need never know. Sleep, *Acushla.*